X

07 JUN 2022
28 JUN 2022

A Valley Secret

ANNA JACOBS

A Valley Secret

Backshaw Moss Saga Book Two

HODDER &
STOUGHTON

First published in Great Britain in 2021 by Hodder & Stoughton
An Hachette UK company

1

Copyright © Anna Jacobs 2021

The right of Anna Jacobs to be identified as the Author of the
Work has been asserted by her in accordance
with the Copyright, Designs and Patents Act 1988.

A CIP catalogue record for this title is available from the British Library

Hardback ISBN 978 1 529 35352 5
eBook ISBN 978 1 529 35353 2

Typeset in Plantin Light by Palimpsest Book Production Ltd, Falkirk, Stirlingshire

Printed and bound in Great Britain by Clays Ltd, Elcograf S.p.A.

Hodder & Stoughton policy is to use papers that are natural, renewable
and recyclable products and made from wood grown in sustainable forests.
The logging and manufacturing processes are expected to conform to
the environmental regulations of the country of origin.

Hodder & Stoughton Ltd
Carmelite House
Embankment
London EC4Y 0DZ

www.hodder.co.uk

Dear readers,

Welcome to the second book in my new series set in Backshaw Moss. It follows on from *A Valley Dream*.

This will be the last series set in Ellindale, my imaginary Pennine valley. There is one more book to come in 2022, but as this second book goes to press, I haven't started writing the third one yet (*A Valley Wedding*).

This time *A Valley Secret* gives us Maisie's story. She inherits the second house in the trio at the end of Daisy Street and once again the house is full of surprises. These were solid houses built to last, but when they were built they didn't usually have bathrooms and certainly not electricity.

This story is set in 1936 and we're getting closer to my own birth date. I was born at the beginning of World War 2. My goodness, the world was so different then!

I've added a couple of my family photos again because you seem to like them, dear readers! The boy is my father aged about 10 in 1930, approximately.

Since I shared a photo of my maternal great-grandfather (who fathered 12 children!) in another book, I've also added photos of my paternal great-grandparents (who only had four children). These would most likely have been taken towards the end of the 19th century. They were the most 'posh' of my ancestors. He's a dignified looking fellow, isn't he?

By the way, I knew the grandfather we lived with during the war till I was nearly 5 by his surname, i.e. Grandpa

Wild. We didn't address older adults informally, however close we were to them.

I grew up among a crowd of relatives born in the 19th century and I knew people born from the 1870s onwards. It's no wonder I enjoy delving into history, is it? I have a long view of the years, thanks to their tales and my own experiences. And now we're in the twenty-first century, 150 years later.

How quickly a lifetime passes! I can remember walking home after dark towards the end of World War 2, aged 4. I was holding my mother's hand because there was a blackout and no street lights were allowed. When a dog which seemed huge to me appeared suddenly from one side and jumped up at me, my screams echoed down the dark, moonlit street. I can still hear them! It took me years to get over being nervous of dogs that I didn't 'know'.

I shall end as always by hoping you enjoy this new story. I thoroughly enjoyed writing it – well, I am totally addicted to storytelling.

Anna

A Valley Secret

I

Lancashire 1928–1936

One evening when her mother had had more to drink than usual at the pub where she worked, Maisie Bassett tried yet again to find out about her father. 'All I know is his name. I'm nearly eighteen now. Surely you can tell me more?'

After a pause Ida said softly, as if talking to herself, 'He weren't called Bassett, so you don't know anything. I just picked that name off a label on a box of liquorice allsorts when I found I was expecting. I bought a wedding ring and came to have my baby in Rochdale.' She gave a wry smile. 'Oh, I made such a sad, grieving young widow!'

She dashed away a quick tear at that memory.

'What was my father really called, then?'

'Mmm? Oh, Lawson. Simeon Lawson.'

'What happened to him?'

But her mother had fallen asleep. In the morning, when Maisie brought this up with her, Ida gaped at her daughter. 'I never said he was called that. 'Cos he wasn't.'

Her daughter could usually tell when she was lying, so was fairly sure that had been her real father's name.

She tried several times over the following years to get more information about this Simeon Lawson, but Ida always denied everything and never spoke of Maisie's father again.

'It's in the past an' that's where it should be left. Never let a bad patch pull you down. Get on with living, I allus say. I've had to, haven't I, or I'd have gone mad?'

Her mother had indeed got on with living, the girl thought enviously. Ida enjoyed her job and lived comfortably on her wages because customers gave her generous tips. What's more, the landlady at the pub knew a good worker when she found one, so passed on leftover food as a bonus. It was a good thing she did, because Ida hated cooking and meals were mostly bread and jam or dripping, and sometimes fish and chips from the shop round the corner.

Then, four years later, Maisie lost all chance of finding out more about her father because her mother died suddenly at the age of forty-seven, coming down with a heavy cold which rapidly turned into pneumonia. Even though a neighbour drove her and Maisie to hospital, she continued to struggle for breath and the doctors couldn't save her.

Ida begged her daughter to give her a decent funeral and a marked grave, gasping it out a couple of words at a time, but died before she could explain how to pay for it.

Maisie had stood staring down at her mother's body, feeling upset. How could she afford even the cheapest funeral when there was hardly anything left in the housekeeping jar on the mantelpiece? Her mother had never saved a penny that she knew of, had not only spent the money she earned but had even taken most of her daughter's wages from the shop at first, till Maisie protested.

Hearing about the lack of money for Ida Potter's funeral, the customers at the pub had a whip round and the landlady topped it up to provide enough for the cheapest funeral and a grave in the poorer part of the cemetery.

★

The day after the funeral Maisie began clearing out their small flat ready to move into lodgings, which would be cheaper. She picked up her mother's sewing box and studied it, wondering whether it was worth keeping.

Ida had always referred to it as 'my grannie's box'. It was scuffed and scratched and had hardly ever been used for its original purpose because her mother had loathed sewing and hadn't mended clothes unless she was desperate. Yet for some reason, that box had gone with them on every one of the many house moves they'd made.

Maisie had been forbidden even to touch it as a child, on pain of a good smacking, and once she'd learned to sew properly at school, her mother had bought her a sewing box of her own. From then on, she'd had to do her own mending and alterations. Since she liked to look nice, she'd persevered and even asked her needlework teacher's help a couple of times after school.

She easily came top of most classes, but her mother only shrugged and never offered a word of praise. 'What good does all that reading and writing do anyone?'

Ah, what did that old pain matter now? Maisie picked up the box which was her only family inheritance. She'd hardly ever touched it before. It was bigger than hers and wouldn't look bad if she polished it up. Yes, she'd tidy out the mess inside and use this one from now on.

She sold her mother's clothes to the second-hand dealer at the market because she was taller than Ida and built more sturdily. Every penny would help. She also sold most of the furniture because she'd be living in one cheaper room from now on.

After emptying the box, she began gently sponging the faded red brocade lining in an attempt to freshen it up. Something rustled underneath it so she tried to find out what was causing it, surprised to discover an opening hidden under a fold of material at one corner. She poked her fingers inside and felt some papers pushed right up under the decorative trim at the top.

What had her mother been hiding? She wriggled the bundle out bit by bit and squeaked in shock as she found herself holding some neatly folded banknotes. Ida must have been saving for years on the sly.

Maisie marvelled as she counted the notes slowly and carefully. There were fifty-six pound notes hidden in the lining. It seemed a fortune to her.

And she'd nearly thrown the box away! *Oh, Mum! How could you be such a fool? Anyone could have stolen this.*

She felt around in the box again to make sure she hadn't missed anything and as she did, something else rustled further along. She had to wriggle it about to get it out without tearing it. It was her birth certificate and it said 'father unknown', showing anyone who cared to study it that she was illegitimate.

She was tempted to burn it, but didn't. For good or ill, it was all she had to show about where she came from, and it did have the names of her mother's parents: Frank and Primrose Fletcher.

Was that all? She felt around behind the lining and found one more thing. A letter from Simeon Lawson. It said he was going to London where he'd been promised a job. He would come back for Ida once he had enough money saved.

The letter had little smudges on it, as if her mother had cried over it. Maisie sat staring at it in shock. It was the first time she'd had proof of what her mother had told her once, and once only: her father really was this Simeon Lawson.

But he'd never come back, had he? What had happened to him in London?

She had a little weep for her mother, left on her own with

a baby to bring up. Like Ida had done, she too had to move on now. She slipped the two papers and the money back inside the lining and dried her eyes.

You could weep as much as you wanted, but it didn't bring back a loved one who'd died.

The next day, terrified of someone stealing it, she took the money to the bank and asked to open a savings account.

To her dismay the teller counted the notes, then looked her up and down scornfully. 'Where did someone like you get such a large amount of money? I think we'd better ask the manager about this. And don't try to run away.' He signalled to the doorman and sent the office lad running to fetch the manager.

Mr Stavener also looked at her suspiciously and demanded to know how she'd got that much money, so Maisie asked if she could speak to him privately.

After a moment's hesitation he took her into his office. 'Well, Miss Bassett?'

'My mother died a few days ago. She'd hidden this in her sewing box, under the lining. Fifty-six pounds. Just imagine, all that money left lying around. She must have been saving for years.'

Her companion shuddered visibly.

She put on a scared voice. 'I don't like to keep so much money in the house, Mr Stavener, so I thought I'd put it in the bank. It'll be safe here, won't it?'

He nodded, looking at her differently now, then answered in an almost fatherly tone. 'This is the safest place of all, young lady, and the money will earn you interest as well, which means just over a pound will be added every year you keep that much money with us.'

She knew perfectly well what interest meant, but tried to look amazed.

'I don't like to speak ill of the dead, Miss Bassett, but you seem to have more sense than your mother, a lot more.'

She let out a sigh, relieved that he'd believed her tale. 'I've been saving some of my wages in the Post Office Savings Bank for a while now, but perhaps I should add that money to this in my new account? What do you think? I have nearly twelve pounds saved. Look.' She took the bank book out of her shopping bag and showed him.

As she'd expected that made him look at her with even more respect.

She went back to work the next day and drew most of her money out of the post office account during her lunch break. When she took that into the bank, Mr Stavener noticed her through the glass panel in his office and came out to fuss over her and say once more how wise she was to be so careful.

Once again she lowered her voice to a whisper. 'I'm ever so grateful for your advice, sir. You, um, won't tell anyone else about this money, will you? I don't want men pestering me to marry them because they want to get their hands on my savings.'

'You can always rely on the bank's discretion about customers' accounts. I think you're very wise to keep your savings secret. Don't hesitate to ask my advice about money. It's my job to help our customers and you seem to have no one else to turn to.'

From then on she continued to add to her savings, and got tears in her eyes the first time she was paid interest on her account. How wonderful to see her money increase.

She began to feel a real hope of one day being able to buy a small cottage, something which had been her dream for years. She and her mother had never even rented a whole house, just rooms. From what she'd read in the newspapers, no bank would allow a single woman, even an older one, to take out a mortgage, so she'd have to save the whole amount.

Was that possible? It had to be. When she grew too old to work she'd need somewhere to live where she didn't pay rent.

She sometimes marvelled at how different she was from her flighty mother, who'd craved fun and the attention of men. All Maisie longed for was security and a quiet life.

Once her daughter had turned twenty, Ida had spoken more frankly about how she spent her spare time. She said she enjoyed being bedded by a fine, strong fellow, and Maisie should try it. There was no feeling as good as doing it. As long as you were careful – and she'd even explained how to be careful, to her daughter's huge embarrassment.

Her mother's suggestion had horrified her, still did. The love of bed play had clearly been Ida's weakness and explained how she'd fallen pregnant without being married.

Maisie wasn't going down that path. She didn't trust men at all, especially not the younger ones.

The trouble was, after Ida's death, some men seemed to be expecting Maisie to be as immoral as her mother. This showed no signs of stopping, in spite of her leading a blameless life and attending church regularly, so in the end she decided to move away from Rochdale and hopefully leave the taint of her mother's reputation behind.

Perhaps she should change her name while she was at it so that no one would be able to connect her to Ida. Could you do this by some legal method or did you just change it? She'd have to find out.

She decided to look around for jobs elsewhere, but first told the manager of the shop where she worked why she needed to move. Mr Vaughan went to the same church and was a kind man.

He listened carefully and nodded, 'You're right to protect yourself. I too have heard rumours, which I knew to be false. I'll keep my ears open for jobs.'

A few weeks later he told her about a job in a town called Rivenshaw in a valley on the edge of the Pennines, and both he and Mr Stavener gave her glowing references when she applied for the position.

Maisie didn't care where she went, she just wanted to start a new life and save her money. The job was in a big grocery store, which was the sort of work she'd been doing already. There would be no chance of promotion wherever she worked because only men got promoted to manager.

She knew some of her mother's family still lived in Rivenshaw, but she didn't intend to contact any of them. From what her mother had said, they sounded to be a feckless lot, which was another reason for changing her name.

With Mr Stavener's help, she arranged to transfer all her money from the local bank to a branch in Rivenshaw, and when she explained to him that she wanted to change her name because of her mother's reputation and asked him how to do it legally, he helped her with that as well.

She chose the name Lawson this time. Why not? Her mother had been telling the truth about who her father was, so she was entitled to it. Well, sort of entitled, given that the two of them hadn't actually been married.

She didn't let anyone she worked with know where she was going, and hired a man with a van to take her and her possessions there, giving him only her new surname.

Her new manager in Rivenshaw recommended seeking lodgings with a Mrs Tucker, so Maisie wrote and arranged that, again needing to give references.

It was a good choice. There were other women there, the place was immaculately clean, and the food was good. It was cheaper than trying to get a room of her own, and there was company in the evenings when she wanted it.

That was as good a life as she could expect.

★

Maisie settled in easily, attending her new church regularly, even though this minister's sermons were rather boring. But for a young woman on her own, church was the best place to meet people and make friends, as well as establishing that you were respectable.

She enjoyed living in Rivenshaw, which was a small town, at the lower end of a Pennine valley, so she could go for walks on fine weekends with some of the other lodgers, or catch the midday bus to the tiny village of Ellindale and buy a glass of ginger beer at the small shop there, then walk the few miles down the hill back to Rivenshaw.

The trouble was, for all her precautions, men still wouldn't leave her alone. At least this time they kept trying to court her honourably, telling her she was beautiful and looking at her in a stupid, soppy way.

She was at her wits' end how to stop this, dressed as plainly as she could, scraping her hair back into an old-fashioned low bun. But however hard she tried not to draw attention to herself in any way, men still pestered her.

She became almost a hermit, not going out much apart from work, church or outings with the other lodgers. For entertainment she borrowed books from the library. That was free, and anyway, she loved reading, not just stories but books which told you about the wider world.

Perhaps if she saved hard, one day her dream really would come true: a cottage with a small garden where she could grow flowers and vegetables, feed the birds, and sit peacefully in the garden on fine days.

2

January 1936

In London Albert Neven stared at his chief clerk in dismay. 'She's not there?'

'No, sir. Ida Fletcher hasn't lived in Littleborough for over twenty years. She simply vanished one night and was never seen again. Corden's questioned relatives, neighbours, friends, but no one seems to have any idea where she went. He says he's exhausted every avenue and can do no more.'

'He's been very slow at finding out even that. Thank him for his services and pay him off. I'm going to hire another detective, one who displays more initiative. How about that Biff Higgins fellow who's already worked in Rivenshaw? From what Sergeant Deemer told me last year when we were dealing with Miss Porter's inheritance, he sounds to have a sharp mind.'

His chief clerk looked at his employer in surprise. 'Where self-preservation was concerned, yes, but *we* wouldn't normally employ a man like Higgins.'

'That's the whole point. The woman we're seeking is from a poor background, so he may have a better idea of where to look for her.'

'I'm afraid Higgins has left the company and set up on his own as a private detective. Why, only yesterday, Corden was laughing at the effrontery of such a person doing that. Higgins will only be dealing with small cases from now on, not working for important lawyers like you.'

'Penscombe, you're a snob. I wish to meet the man as soon as it can be arranged. If I don't like the looks of him, we won't hire him. We need to find this Ida Fletcher somehow.'

'But sir—'

'I made a solemn promise to Miss Chapman when she was dying that her wishes would be carried out, so please contact Higgins at once!' When he emphasised this by thumping his clenched fist down on his desk, a rare display of anger, the clerk hurried out.

Miss Chapman had been adamant that the three run-down houses she owned in Backshaw Moss, on the edge of the Lancashire moors, should be passed on to some of her poorer relatives in such a way that they had to work hard to make something of their inheritance.

Daisy Street might lie at the edge of the worst slum in the valley, but the houses were larger than average and soundly built. The first bequest had been the middle house, Number 23 Daisy Street, which had been dealt with in a satisfactory manner, but the second bequest, Number 21, was proving much more difficult as they had been unable to find the designated heir.

Corden's investigations had ended in the small town of Littleborough, also in Lancashire. Surely someone there must know where this Ida Fletcher had moved to? A person couldn't just vanish! Well, not unless they'd been murdered . . .

There were provisions in the will for choosing alternative heirs should one of those designated be dead, he'd made sure of that when he drew it up. But Miss Chapman had been emphatic that she much preferred the houses to go to the three persons she'd chosen.

Pulse quickening in excitement, Biff Higgins stood by the window with his back to the room, rereading the short note brought to him by a fresh-faced young clerk, and hoping his excitement didn't show. It said that Mr Albert Neven wished to discuss a job in a town called Rivenshaw, in Lancashire.

It didn't matter what the job was because he knew if he did well for such a highly respected lawyer, it could be the making of him and his fledgling business as a private investigator.

He'd do whatever it was even though he'd been to Rivenshaw before and had vowed never to go back there again.

Since setting up his own business in his home territory of London, he had barely earned enough to keep the wolf from the door as yet. He'd left his former employers because he'd grown worried about their increasing willingness to accept any job, legal or not, as long as it paid well – and then they'd send out the investigators they employed to take all the risks.

He wasn't going to break the law for anyone, employer or not, not only because he didn't want to risk prison, but because he believed in honesty and the rule of law.

He tried to speak calmly. 'As it happens, I am free at the moment.'

'Mr Neven would like to see you as soon as possible, then, to discuss this job. He gave me the money to get a taxi back.'

Biff tugged out his battered pocket watch. 'Will he still be in his office?'

'Yes, Mr Higgins.'

'Then I'll go to see him straight away. No need for a taxi. You can ride back with me in my car.'

'Very kind of you, sir.'

Oh, how Biff relished being addressed as 'Mr Higgins' or 'sir', not 'Higgins' or 'Biff lad'! It was a small thing, but highly satisfying.

Albert Neven studied the private investigator, pleased with what he saw. He liked a chap who looked you straight in the eyes.

The best word to describe the detective was nondescript. Higgins seemed neither young nor old, was of medium height, and presented a neat but easily forgotten appearance. You'd not give him a second glance if you passed him in the street, which must be a good thing for his type of work.

He explained the situation in detail, and Biff frowned. 'I have to be frank with you, sir. My appearance isn't likely to attract attention, as you say, but my southern accent stands out in the north as different. I wonder though . . . Hmm, perhaps I could adopt a slight Irish accent, like my grand-father's? That might do it.'

'Would it matter that much?'

'I think so, yes. I've already found that a southern accent makes it harder to stay unnoticed in the north. The way people speak in Rivenshaw is very different from here in London, and they stare at those who speak differently. However I did notice a few people there speaking with an Irish accent, and they weren't stared at. I wish to be honest with you about that sort of detail. It can matter.'

He changed his accent before adding, 'Sure and I'd be happy to take on your job, sorrh.'

Mr Neven laughed. 'You're good at the Irish accent and I appreciate both your honesty and your attention to detail. You're hired. Penscombe will arrange for you to receive the same payment and expenses as Corden, with a bonus if you succeed in finding this Ida Fletcher.'

'I'll do my very best, I promise you, sir.' A bonus, eh? He could certainly use the money.

'When can you start? The sooner the better, as far as I'm concerned.'

'I can drive north overnight and start my search there tomorrow,' Biff said at once. Thank goodness he'd invested nearly half his savings in a car. Seventy pounds had bought him a second-hand Austin 7, with a sound motor but slightly shabby body. It was a common vehicle, as unremarkable as he always tried to make himself.

'It would be excellent to start so quickly. But won't you need to fill the car up with fuel on such a long journey? These modern petrol stations are very useful, far better than carrying a spare can and adding more petrol ourselves as we did in the early days of motoring, but these new places usually close in the early evening.'

'I always carry an old-fashioned can of petrol in the boot as well, just in case. To drive so far, I'll carry more than one can.'

Mr Neven gestured towards the rather sour-faced older man. 'Penscombe will give you the details of the job and some money to cover your initial expenses.'

The clerk led the way to a small office at the rear of the building, where he went through the exact provisions of the will and what had been discovered so far about this Ida Fletcher.

When he'd finished he looked at Biff and said in a grudging tone, 'Well, at least you ask sensible questions, Mr Higgins.'

'My work can often depend on obtaining the correct information, Mr Penscombe.'

'Mine too.'

As Biff drove back to his lodgings he was unable to stop smiling. It'd be a difficult job, no doubt about that. Well, he'd not have got it if it had been straightforward, would he?

One thing that gave him hope of success was that he knew something about Corden. People in their line of work said that the man was thorough but past the stage of being hungry for work, as well as far too set in his ways and slow to act.

Biff, on the other hand, was definitely hungry for money, as well as fiercely determined to succeed in his new business. He would try anything legal to find this woman.

3

After a long drive north, Biff arrived in Rivenshaw early the following morning and stopped the car in the square outside the railway station. He got out and stretched his tired body, staring round the big open space at the centre of the town and smiling wryly at being back again.

After using the public convenience he strolled in the direction he thought he'd seen a baker's shop last time. To his relief the delicious smell of newly baked bread reminded him which street to turn into.

The shop was already open, with a row of fresh loaves sitting in solitary splendour on the glass shelf in the middle of the window. A customer wearing a headscarf pulled low to cover her curlers hurried out of the door carrying two loaves wrapped in tissue paper.

Biff's mouth watered in anticipation as he went inside, pleased to see two small tables to one side. 'I'm wanting to sit down and have something to eat. Will it be possible to have a pot of tea with it?'

The woman behind the counter indicated the tables. 'I'll come and take your order in two ticks, sir.' She finished putting some rolls into a glass-fronted display cabinet under the counter, then came across to him.

He ordered a 'bacon butty' and a mug of tea, trying out his Irish accent for the first time. To his delight, it had caused no reaction from the woman. He didn't want to be recognised from his last time there as the man who'd helped a villain.

His employer had sent him, and he hadn't liked the man he'd been assigned to or approved of his morals. That was one of the reasons he'd set up his own business. He didn't want to help folk break the law, however much they paid him.

After he'd satisfied his hunger on the gigantic bacon sandwich that was plonked on the table in front of him on a big plate, and drained the huge mug of tea that the woman had refilled without him asking, he paid and strolled back to the square.

He couldn't help smiling as he left the shop. Speaking like that had reminded him of his childhood. He'd once mocked how his Irish granddad spoke and got a clout round the ears from his mother for doing it.

He was glad to see other small vehicles now parked near his car, presumably by people travelling by train. Good. That made his car unlikely to stand out, so he left it where it was. From here he could walk the few streets to the police station, and he'd be less likely to be noticed if he turned up there on foot.

He was relieved to find Deemer already there. On his last visit he'd found the old sergeant shrewd and capable, in charge of maintaining law and order in the whole valley, not just the town of Rivenshaw at the lower end, but the villages of Birch End and Ellindale further up.

Deemer frowned at him from behind the counter. 'I remember your face.' Then the frown lightened and he snapped his fingers. 'Biff Higgins.'

He tried the Irish accent again. 'Yes, Sergeant. And I remembered you, too, which is why I'm here today. I've set up my own detective agency in London, and an important job has brought me back to Rivenshaw. I thought I'd start my enquiries by explaining to you what I'm doing and asking whether you have any advice or information to offer.'

'And your client is?'

'Mr Albert Neven, the London lawyer.'

The frown vanished completely. 'I've spoken to him on the telephone but haven't met him in person. Very sensible of you to come and see me. Let's go into my office. I'll get the constable to make us a pot of tea.'

Biff could usually fit in another cup of tea, but was glad he'd visited the public convenience again on the way here when faced with another large mug.

The sergeant was studying him with a frown. 'I don't remember you being Irish.'

'My granddad was. My London accent made people round here stare at me last time I was in town. They seem used to the Irish, though. What do you think? Do I sound genuine? Will my idea work?'

'Definitely. Good idea, that. We have quite a few Irish in the town. Now, let me think what to tell you to bring you up to date. First, do you remember Thomas Beaton, the chap you were doing a job for last time?'

Biff nodded.

'He died the day you left.'

'Did someone kill him? I'd have liked to wring his neck, he was such a nasty sod, trying to steal his cousin Bella's inheritance, but I was sent up north to work for him and had no choice. It was do what he wanted or lose my job, as I told you then.'

'He had a seizure. Good thing you left town before that happened. It means no one is likely to connect you with the trouble he caused.'

'I couldn't get away fast enough, didn't want to be involved in breaking the law.' He gave the sergeant a very firm stare. 'I don't work that way.'

That got him another approving nod.

'There's one person you should avoid, a builder called Higgerson. You shouldn't have any trouble remembering a name so like yours, eh? He's been keeping quiet for a while, after narrowly avoiding some serious trouble, but he's starting to poke his head out of the trenches again, as we used to say in the Great War. If you encounter him, don't trust him an inch.'

'Thanks for the warning, Sergeant. Higgerson, eh?' Of course he remembered the name. The man was an out-and-out villain, well hated in the valley, but had got away with his nasty tricks so far.

'He might call himself a builder, but that's only part of how he earns his money. He also owns quite a few of the poorer properties in this town and even more slum properties in a hamlet up the hill called Backshaw Moss, just near Birch End. You'd think he'd keep them in better condition being a builder, but he doesn't spend a penny on maintenance if he can help it. Some of them are real fire traps.'

Biff could only hope that he'd changed his appearance enough so that no one would recognise him. He was dressed much more smartly this time.

Between mouthfuls of tea he explained the details known so far about his job hunting for the lost heir, then waited patiently as he watched Deemer think about what he'd said.

'Well, you did right to come to me. That other detective chappie should have done that too, if only out of courtesy.' Another pause then, 'Actually, I think I may be able to help you a little.'

'You know what happened to the woman?'

'No, but I can give you one or two pointers on tracking her down. I know my valley, and I know the Fletchers.'

Biff waited.

'Ida quarrelled with her family. First about walking out with Simeon Lawson whom they didn't approve of, then, when he went off to London, about her being in the family way without being wed. It's no use talking to them now because they disowned her. She worked as a live-in maid in Littleborough till the baby showed.'

'That's where Corden lost the trail.'

'Well, I happen to know an old lady who lives there and who generally keeps abreast of the local gossip. She was a friend of my mother and they kept in touch till my ma died. Nearly ninety she must be now, but still in full possession of her faculties. I'll give you the last address I had for her, but if she's moved, people nearby will know where she went because she's well liked – and well-connected too.' After another pause to drain his mug of tea, Deemer nodded thoughtfully. 'Yes, if anyone can help you find what happened to Ida Fletcher, it's Granny Gormley.'

'There's no mention of a Mrs Gormley in Corden's notes.'

The old sergeant grinned. 'I heard about him, but when he didn't come to ask my advice, I didn't seek him out to volunteer any information. He upset a few folk by looking down his nose at them.'

Biff smiled. 'He looked down his nose at me too, Sergeant, and bad-mouthed me to folk in London. But I know your reputation from my last visit, and I would really value any help you can offer.'

You shouldn't look down on anyone until they proved themselves unworthy of respect, in Biff's opinion. From what he'd seen of the world, most folk did the best they could with what life dished out, and some unlucky folk had a very hard time of it.

'I'll do that, but I'd be grateful, Mr Higgins, if you'd let me know anything else you find out as soon as you can after finding it. Even the smallest detail about what happened to Ida or anyone close to her could be useful one day. I'm a magpie when it comes to collecting information about my valley, and I sometimes find that one fact connects me to others. It's often like putting together a jigsaw puzzle.'

'Agreed, Sergeant. Aren't I a bit of a magpie meself?' He put on his Irish lilt again strongly in the last remark and the sergeant grinned.

'Have you found lodgings yet, Mr Higgins? You won't want to stay in the same place as last time, not with that accent.'

'No, Sergeant. I need to look for somewhere respectable but quiet, where they don't mind the Irish. I don't want a place full of people who might gossip about my comings and goings.'

'My cousin takes in an occasional lodger, not because she's desperate for money, though a bit extra always comes in useful, but because she's a widow and gets lonely. She has only one spare bedroom, so it'd just be you staying there. I sometimes send a person I trust to her. She won't mind you being Irish if I recommend you to her.'

'I'd be extremely grateful if you'd help me in that way.'

Deemer nodded, then scribbled on two pieces of paper and held them out. 'One address is for Granny Gormley with a note about you, the other's for my cousin Lorna, ditto.'

Biff put them carefully in his inner jacket pocket, smiling as he left the police station. He'd been right to consult the wily old sergeant.

Since it was still only mid-morning, Biff took Sergeant Deemer's advice and drove over to Littleborough, where he found Granny Gormley as easily as the sergeant had said. The first neighbour he asked told him that the old woman was now living with her widowed daughter only one street away.

Mrs Gormley listened to his explanation that he'd been sent to ask her help by Sergeant Deemer. She then inspected the piece of paper with the sergeant's scribbled message on it, after which she inspected Biff even more carefully.

Eventually she gave a little nod. 'Well, you look me straight in the eyes, you obviously keep yourself clean, and if Gilbert

Deemer vouches for you, you can't be a bad 'un. Come inside and if you'll put the kettle on for me, we'll share a cup of tea and you can ask your questions. Only half fill the kettle, mind. We don't want to waste the gas money heating extra water.'

He followed orders and produced a pot of tea, amused at her peremptory commands and careful ways. She'd have been offended if he'd turned down her offer of a drink, but he was already full of tea. Fortunately, he managed only to part-fill his cup without her noticing.

She sighed happily as she took her first mouthful. 'You make a good brew of tea, lad, an' you've got good manners, but you're not really Irish, are you?'

He didn't attempt to deny it. As the sergeant had said, she had all her wits about her, more wits than most folk started off with, he reckoned. He'd noticed before that intelligence and interest in the world around them seemed to shine in a person's eyes, and hers were absolutely sparkling with it.

'No, I'm not Irish. Very clever of you to notice.' He explained why he was pretending to be, and she nodded.

'You'll pass as Irish with most folk. It's not a bad attempt at the accent. Now, tell me exactly what you're doing in Littleborough.'

'I'm a private detective and I've been asked to look for a lost person. Ida Fletcher, she's called. Well, Fletcher was her maiden name. I don't know whether she got married or not.'

'Hmm. There was another chap asking after her round here a week or two ago, my grandson told me. Folk didn't like him, he was such a toffee-nosed snob, and Gilbert Deemer didn't send *him* to ask my help, so he didn't get very far with his search.'

'He didn't speak to the sergeant and ask his advice, that's why.'

'More fool him. No one knows more about our valley than Gilbert Deemer. Why does the lawyer want to find Ida?'

'She's got an inheritance waiting for her.'

'She has? Who from?'

'A Miss Sarah Jane Chapman, who is a distant relative.'

'I used to see her around the town. Eeh, years ago that'd be. Nice lady she was, allus dressed neatly, allus polite to everyone, rich or poor. She'd be Abigail Chapman's daughter, and Abigail was a Fletcher afore she got wed. Didn't often make old bones, that branch of the family. Go on. What has Ida inherited?'

'I don't know exactly. A little cottage, I think, but I wasn't given the details.'

'Lucky devil.'

'Well, she'll be lucky if I can find her. She disappeared suddenly from Littleborough years ago, it seems. The sergeant thought you might have heard something about where she went.'

It'd have looked unprofessional to cross his fingers for luck, but he did it mentally as he waited for a response. This could be so important. He desperately needed another lead to move on from what Corden had found.

'I did hear it whispered that Ida went to live in Rochdale. It's not far away from here but the sort of folk she associated with don't travel around much, they're more interested in going to pubs and swilling down beer, so she might as well have gone to London. I'll remember the name of the street if you give me a minute, because she wrote to thank me for helping her leave without anyone knowing where she went.'

'That'd be a big help.'

'She'll likely have moved on again, though. She never stayed long in one place, Ida didn't, always looking for the moon, she was – or rather, looking for the man in the moon.' She cackled with laughter at her own witticism, then suddenly said, 'Bassett, her new name was, and she lived at the top end of Toad Lane. Silly name for a street, isn't it?'

When she said she didn't know anything else, he chatted for a few more minutes to be polite, thanked her, and left.

Biff would have liked to drive over to Rochdale immediately and continue his search, but he was tiring rapidly after a sleepless night so instead he went back to Rivenshaw to find Deemer's cousin Lorna and see if she could put him up.

When she showed him the room, he was delighted with its cleanliness and took it immediately.

'Would you mind if I had a nap for a couple of hours? I drove here overnight and have been busy all day so far, but I must admit I'm worn out.'

'I don't mind as long as you take your shoes off and don't make a mess of my bedcovers. Do you want your tea providing?'

'If it's not too much trouble, I'd be most grateful for an evening meal.'

'It'll be an extra two and sixpence.'

'Fine by me.'

He asked her to wake him up when tea was ready, and later enjoyed a hearty stew followed by rice pudding and stewed plums. He enjoyed her company too. A sensible woman of around his own age, he'd guess, who read the newspapers and kept an eye on the wider world. His late wife had been a similar sort of person. He still missed her.

After chatting for a while, he went back to bed. He was getting a bit old for staying up all night, but he'd found out some useful information today, tired or not.

He hoped things would go smoothly tomorrow. If he could earn that bonus he'd be able to rent a proper office and get a telephone installed.

4

At the beginning of her third year in Rivenshaw, Maisie was introduced to a man called Jeff Conway at church. He'd been working away from the valley and had just returned. Her heart sank as she saw *that look* in his eyes.

Unfortunately he proved to be far more persistent than her other would-be suitors. He kept inviting her out, however firmly she refused, and he simply wouldn't take no for an answer.

He waylaid her nearly every day to pester her to give in to his demand to go out walking with him. She felt increasingly nervous and didn't know what to do. He was a burly man and obviously used to getting his own way.

When he joined her in the street one evening as she walked home from work, she told him bluntly to leave her alone, speaking before he'd even opened his mouth.

'It's a free country. Why shouldn't I enjoy the company of the prettiest girl in town?'

'Because I don't want to go out with you and I never shall.' Something about his lumpy face and heavy body made her shudder.

'Ah, you're just playing hard to get, like all the good girls do. An' if it's marriage you want, I might be tempted by a pretty girl like you. I wouldn't mind a son or two.'

'I'm not a *girl*, I'm a woman grown, and I have no desire whatsoever to get married.'

He ignored that comment. 'Anyway, I've bought tickets for

you and me to go to the church social together next Saturday.'
He grabbed her arm to prevent her running away from him,
something she had done on a previous occasion.

'Let go of me.' She tried to jerk away, and he laughed as
he dragged her closer. Unfortunately there was no one around
to call to for help, and he was holding her arm so tightly it
hurt. 'I said no and I meant no! I've refused you several times
already: I am *not* going out with you, not now and not ever.'

'And I'm not taking no for an answer. Not now and not
ever,' he mimicked. 'I've already told people we're going to
the social together and I'll make damned sure we do. Whatever
it takes.'

'Well, you can just un-buy the tickets and tell everyone
you've changed your mind because I won't do it. To be blunt,
you have a bad reputation.' When he laughed at that, she
added, 'I happen to know you forced yourself on a girl I work
with a few weeks ago because I found her crying in the lav.
I despise men who do that, and I'm not risking you trying it
on with me.'

He gaped at her in shock at such blunt talk, then flushed
slightly and muttered, 'I didn't have to force her. She wanted
it.'

'You did force her. It's only by good luck you didn't get
Jane into trouble or you might have had to marry her. She
was afraid to tell her parents or complain about your attack,
because she's the one who'd get a bad reputation if it was
known about. I wouldn't be afraid to tell people, I promise
you. I'd go straight to the police if you tried to force yourself
on me in that way. And I'd complain to your boss as well.'

She saw him flinch at that and pressed the point. 'Mr
Higgerson goes to our church. He'd probably sack you if you
got a bad reputation for attacking women. Now go away and
leave me alone from now on.'

Instead he took hold of her shoulders and shook her slightly.

'I'm *not* letting it drop and we *are* going to the social together, Maisie Lawson, I'll make sure of that if I have to drag you there.'

He paused but she still shook her head and glared at him.

'Aw, come on, you might at least give me a chance.'

'No is what I said, and no is what I meant. I don't even like you.' She felt his grip slacken slightly and took him by surprise, wrenching her arm away from him and running off down the street. To her relief he didn't follow her.

At work she was now in full charge of the cheese and bacon counter and was skilled at using and cleaning the bacon slicer. It wasn't a very challenging job and she could handle it with ease. She'd learned how to handle the manager, too, and do things how he liked. She took a pride in keeping everything immaculate.

She was paid five shillings extra each week for doing the work and looking after the equipment. She had only got that because she'd threatened to leave if she wasn't paid for the extra work like the man who did it before her had been. She knew there had been far less wastage since she'd taken over, so was saving them well over five shillings a week.

'I'll agree this time, but you'll not get paid more than that, whatever you say or do, Miss Lawson,' the manager warned her. 'And if you say one word about your wage increase to anyone else, I'll sack you on the spot.'

'Yes, Mr Midgely. I won't say a word.'

It was no use being ambitious for anything better, like training to become a manager. They simply didn't let women do that. She'd heard the men she worked with laugh openly at the mere thought, saying that younger females would only marry, and older ones were past it – and anyway, women weren't as clever as men. Well, she wasn't ever going to marry, and she reckoned she had as good a brain as any man she'd ever met. Better than most. But she still had little to no chance of finding a better job.

Jeff Conway's attentions were starting to seriously worry her. Why wouldn't he leave her alone? Since they both went to the same church, she tried to speak to the minister about him and ask for help, but to her dismay he suggested she give Jeff a chance and see how they went. After all, that young man would make some lucky woman a fine husband because he would always bring in enough money to put bread on the table.

Even Mr Higgerson thought well of him apparently, and he didn't praise many of the men who worked for him. But Jeff was as strong as an ox and nearly always had a job laying bricks or doing other work for Higgerson's, the town's biggest builder, even in bad times.

She didn't agree about Jeff making a fine husband. Everyone knew he could be violent when he became angry. Well, they could see it for themselves. He must regularly get into fights, judging by the bruises he sometimes sported.

And he might bring home good wages, but that didn't mean he'd share them with his family. She'd heard he was a heavy drinker. You heard a lot of things in a shop.

What's more, she felt quite sure he'd beat any woman who was stupid enough to become his wife. Everyone pretended that sort of thing didn't happen, that the bruised women had fallen or bumped into something, and even the women who'd been hurt pretended the same thing. But folk knew the truth about such occurrences.

Two days later Maisie walked to the library after work to change her books. She loved spending a quiet half hour in the big hushed space, choosing new books and sometimes reading the newspapers. It was her favourite place to go – and it didn't cost a penny.

She saw old Mr Johnson who lived in her street reading a newspaper at one of the big tables at the back and timed her own return home for when he left.

'Can I walk home with you, please, Mr Johnson?'

'Of course.' He looked at her shrewdly. 'That chap Conway been annoying you again, lass? I can't help noticing.'

'Yes. He's outside now, waiting at the end of the street.'

'I shall enjoy your company. It's a poor lookout when a decent lass can't walk the streets in safety, it is that! I wish I were young and strong again. I'd trounce that rogue for you good and proper, by heck I would.'

He waved his walking stick threateningly as he spoke and had to grab the nearest chair back to steady himself. He was such a dear.

Five days later, Maisie went to change her library books in time for the weekend. The librarian didn't believe she could read so quickly, given that she borrowed four books each visit, and he looked at her suspiciously as usual, but she didn't care what he thought.

There was no one to walk home with this time, but when she looked down the street before setting off back, she saw no sign of Jeff Conway, so hurried off, walking as briskly as she could.

As she turned the corner at the end of the street, someone grabbed her and dragged her into the alley between the rows of houses. She tried to scream for help but by now her attacker had got his hand over her mouth.

'You'll not refuse me again,' a voice said hoarsely in her ear. 'And if I have to marry you because of this, I shan't be upset to wed the prettiest unwed woman in town. I'm ready to settle down.'

Jeff Conway!

She struggled desperately, but he had a piece of cloth ready and stuffed it into her mouth, then tied her hands behind her back. As he grabbed her skirt, he tore part of it out of the waistband in his eagerness. She felt tears start to run down her cheeks and vowed that whatever he did to her and whatever the consequences, she'd not marry him.

'You won't weep when I've taught you how to enjoy it,' he muttered as he unbuttoned his trousers and started to climb on top of her. 'I'm doing you a favour, really.'

Then he suddenly yelled in shock and the weight of his body vanished. She was able to roll sideways, hoping to run away, but it was hard to get to her feet with her hands tied.

She watched as a man she didn't immediately recognise punched her attacker in the face. When Jeff tried to fight back, her rescuer hit him even harder and knocked him to the ground.

He bumped his head against the wall as he fell and seemed to have been sent dizzy for a few moments, thank goodness, because he just lay there groaning instead of fighting back.

The gag was removed from her mouth and the man pulled her to her feet, cutting the rope from her wrists with a penknife. 'Better get away while we can. I doubt I can fight him off when I haven't taken him by surprise. Can you hold your skirt in place?'

'Yes.'

'Come on!' He seized her free hand and pulled her out into the street before letting go. She ran willingly beside him, clutching the top of her skirt. She had no fear of this man because he had a kind expression, and anyway, he'd come to her rescue, hadn't he?

When he stopped next to a van, he asked, 'Will you trust me enough to drive away with me, lass? You'll never escape him on foot. I'll take you to my mother's and she'll help you mend your clothes. That brute's torn the skirt so badly that if you go anywhere looking like that, people will think the worst.'

She shot him another quick glance. He looked vaguely familiar, as if she'd seen him in the street, but she still didn't remember where. But for some reason she trusted him absolutely, so she nodded and got quickly into the van, sitting shuddering in the passenger seat while he started the engine and drove off.

5

Gabriel drove towards the road up the hill, but his companion exclaimed suddenly, 'Wait!'

He braked at once. 'What's wrong?'

'I want to report this to the police. Would you bear witness to what happened?'

'Yes, of course I would. If you're sure you don't mind it being known about.'

'I'm sure I want Jeff Conway stopped, so everyone will need to know what he's like, won't they? If I don't do something drastic, he'll only try to take me by surprise another time. He's been pestering me for weeks, even though I've kept telling him I'm not interested. No one's ever known me go out with a lad, so the sergeant only has to ask around to find out I'm not encouraging that sort of attention and the trouble it can bring.'

It was out before he could stop himself. 'Don't you like men? You're pretty enough to attract any unmarried man you want.'

She could feel herself flushing at the admiration in his eyes, because he was a good-looking man, a little older than her, probably married. The nice ones usually were. 'What I want is a peaceful life, and I don't want to act in the same careless way as my mother about men.'

Oh, heavens! She'd betrayed what her mother was like, though normally she didn't speak about Ida. To her relief he didn't comment on that, or on her blush.

When they stopped outside it, they could see that the police station was closed, but her rescuer said, 'I'll ring the emergency bell. Sergeant Deemer lives in the house behind the station and he'll come to see what's wrong. You'd better stay in the van till he gets here.'

He did this and she waited, sliding down a bit in her seat, wishing she could become invisible.

When the door opened, she got out of the van and Sergeant Deemer gaped at the sight of her. 'Eh, whatever's happened to you, lass? Come inside quick.'

They both followed him and watched as he checked that the blinds were pulled right down and locked the door again before switching the lights on. He gestured to one of the chairs. 'You're looking pale, lass. Sit down and take your time telling me what's happened to you.'

'How about I tell you what I saw and did, and that'll give the young lady a chance to recover?' her rescuer asked.

'All right, but give me your name first, if you don't mind, miss.' The sergeant took out a notebook. 'I know you already, lad.'

'But the young lady doesn't. I've seen her in the street, but we haven't met properly. I'm Gabriel Harte, miss, and I live in Birch End with my mother and one of my brothers.'

Her voice came out soft and wobbly, because the violence of the attack had suddenly upset her. 'I'm Maisie Lawson.'

'You must be Ida Fletcher's daughter,' the sergeant exclaimed suddenly. 'You're the spitting image of what she looked like when she was young.'

'Yes. I am Ida's daughter. But I hope I'm not like my mother in any other way than looks, which is why I moved here. She married again, so was called Potter even after he left her. We lived in Rochdale until she died.'

Her voice was bitter now and she stared at him, waiting

for him to comment on her mother's immorality which he must know about. To her relief, he didn't.

She sat quietly as Gabriel explained what he'd seen and how he'd saved her.

By the time her rescuer had finished his tale, the sergeant was looking extremely angry, but that didn't stop him scribbling down notes in what looked like shorthand.

'That's about it,' Gabriel finished. 'I'm taking Miss Lawson to my mother, so that she can help her do something about her skirt before she goes out in public again. But Miss Lawson wanted to see you first to lay a formal complaint.'

'You were right to trust Gabriel, lass, and right to come to me, too.'

She didn't know why she'd trusted Mr Harte when she'd never met him properly before, only he had such a kind, honest face, and was good-looking in a quiet way.

'I wish more people would complain about that Conway chap because he's rough with lasses – worse than rough from what I hear. You're not the first he's attacked, but you're the first to complain.' The sergeant shook his head in disgust.

'He's horrible, looks at me in such a leering, nasty way, it's embarrassing. Even in church! He's been pestering me to go out with him for weeks and I told him I never will. As if I'm that stupid! Other men look at me sometimes, but they don't stare at – you know, my figure. And they don't *attack* me like he did today.' She continued to blush.

'Well, you're a good judge of character, Miss Lawson. I had to warn Conway to leave another lass alone a few months ago after her father came to see me about it. He's a bad 'un and getting worse. I've heard about happenings, but people won't complain so I can't do much about him.'

'Well, I'm here to complain now and I shan't change my mind.'

'Good for you, lass. Conway went away to work in the south a couple of years ago and I wish he'd stayed away. I reckon he got in trouble again and had to move on. And it's only a matter of time before he does something that'll put him in real trouble with the law here, whatever he tells folk about wanting to settle down.'

'I was told at church that his employer thought well of him.'

'That's because Higgerson's cast in the same mould and thinks women are fair game, sadly. I've got my eye on him as well. But it's even harder to catch a rich man out.'

She was surprised. 'But he goes to our church.'

'Only because it's expected of someone in his position to attend, but I bet he only goes every now and then, and I'd be surprised if he ever listens to what the minister preaches about. Now, never mind Higgerson, tell me in your own time exactly what's been happening with Conway, not just today, but since he first started making a nuisance of himself.'

She went through everything she could think of, letting the sergeant stop her to answer further questions about some details.

'Do you think we could persuade this lass you know to make a belated complaint about him forcing her? Two complaints at once would make sure Conway got put behind bars for a while.'

'No. She's terrified of anyone finding out.'

He sighed. 'I can understand that. Sadly some folk are quick to jump to the wrong conclusions and they usually blame the women for encouraging such attentions. Unfortunately, getting away with it only encourages men like that to go on and attack other women. You won't back out if I take this complaint to the magistrate, will you?'

'No. Definitely not. But I'll probably lose my job if word of it gets about.'

'Nay, why should they sack you because someone attacked you?' Gabriel asked in surprise.

'The reason you said: Conway will tell everyone I encouraged him, and they'll believe him and think I'm immoral.'

Gabriel turned to the sergeant. 'I'll be happy to tell the magistrate what I saw. Miss Lawson was definitely trying to fight him off, not encourage him. Well, you can see for yourself how her skirt got ripped as she struggled, Sergeant.'

'Good lad. As for your employers, I can have a word with them if it's needed, Miss Lawson.'

She shrugged. 'Mr Midgely doesn't really like women. He'd just wait and find a reason to get rid of me later because of the gossip. I'll probably have to move to another town, but at least that'll get me away from Conway. Perhaps I should move anyway.'

'Do you want to leave all your friends and family?' Gabriel asked involuntarily.

'I don't have any family now my mother's dead, or close friends, come to that. Most women my age are married, you see, and busy looking after their homes and families. Anyway, I like a quiet life on my own. I get enough of people in the shop where I work.'

Gabriel felt sorry for her. He didn't believe she *liked* a completely quiet life; she was too intelligent. He'd guess she was just trying to stay out of trouble. But since she was one of the most beautiful women he'd ever seen, that'd be hard.

He exchanged disgusted glances with the sergeant, but there was nothing else they could do about the situation at the shop. 'Shall I take you to my mother now, Miss Lawson?'

'If you're sure she won't mind.'

'I'm absolutely certain she'll be delighted to help you in any way she can. She's got a kind heart.'

The sergeant walked with them to the door. 'I'll discuss

your case with the magistrate, Miss Lawson, but he's old and might want to let Conway off with a warning. Eh, I was so angry about this, I nearly forgot to ask where you live.'

'I lodge with Mrs Tucker and have done for years.'

'You'll be easy to find, then. I'll do all I can to bring Conway to account. If not, I may be able to encourage him to leave because I know a few things about his past,' Deemer assured her.

'Thank you.'

As she turned to leave, Gabriel suddenly pushed her back inside and blocked the doorway. 'Hold on a minute and don't move. There's someone coming along the street.'

He turned round, leaning on one half-raised arm as if chatting to someone inside. She stood motionless, close to him and just about face to face. She was quite tall for a woman, but he was tall enough to hide her from a casual passer-by. Again, she thought what a lovely, kind smile he had. When their eyes met, he smiled at her as they waited for the person to pass by, and she smiled back at him involuntarily.

Once the street was clear, Maisie quickly got into the van, holding her skirt in place as she ran across the street, and trying not to let anyone see her face.

The sergeant came across the road and patted the van, saying loudly, 'I heard you'd bought yourself a vehicle, Gabriel. Is it a good runner?'

'Yes. I got a good bargain.'

The sergeant went back to stand in the doorway and wave them farewell, calling, 'Nice to see you again, Gabriel lad.'

She could guess why he'd come outside to pretend an interest in the van: to make sure that if anyone was watching from a nearby house they wouldn't think she and Mr Harte had gone to the police station for the wrong reasons.

★

Deemer decided to deal with this straight away. He left his constable in charge and went to see the magistrate, finding that the new man had come early, because the old one wasn't well. That pleased him. He'd met Dennison Peters before and had a great deal of respect for him. He was hard on violent crimes like Conway's.

'Do you know where Mr Peters is staying?' he asked the housekeeper who'd answered the door.

'With his sister.'

'I know where Miss Peters lives.'

The new magistrate was horrified at what had happened. 'You're sure she's a decent lass?'

'Definitely decent. *She* isn't the problem; it's Conway. He isn't going to change his ways. I wonder if we could frighten him into leaving Rivenshaw again.'

'What do you mean?'

Since he'd known Mr Peters for a long time, Deemer dared suggest, 'He worked down south for a while. If you could call him in to deliver a warning and hint you know something else about his behaviour, I'll tell him we'll put him straight in jail if it happens again, maybe he'll leave the district of his own accord and not come back this time.'

Peters thought this over for a moment or two, then nodded. 'We can try. Can you bring him before me informally?'

'Certainly. I'll go and find him now.'

Deemer went round to a pub he knew where Conway was often to be found, and struck it lucky. He went across to him and said in a low voice, 'You're wanted by our new magistrate. Now. You can come quietly or I'll handcuff you and take you to see him by force.'

Conway stared at him in shock, then shrugged. 'I don't know what this is about. I've done nothing wrong. I don't mind going to see him.'

'We both know what you tried to do earlier this evening.'

Conway looked at him warily. 'Don't know what you mean.'

'The lass has come forward to lay a complaint, and for once there's a witness, who is also prepared to testify.'

That shut Conway up for the time it took to walk the few streets to Miss Peters' house. They were shown into the dining room, and Peters treated Conway icily, giving him a warning that he was to appear before him in two days' time for a formal hearing. He was not to go near the young lady he'd attacked ever again or he would be put straight in jail.

Peters leaned forward when he had finished his formal speech and said, 'I agree with the good sergeant. Men like you who attack innocent women should be locked away. I'm going to get the sergeant to ask around and see if we can find other women you've treated badly so that they too can complain.'

Conway looked from one grim-faced man to the other and muttered, 'Yes, sir.' Once he'd been shown out of the house, he walked away quickly.

'I bet he leaves town,' Peters said.

'I certainly *hope* he leaves town. I have enough trouble to handle without the likes of him adding more.'

6

Gabriel drove her up the hill to Birch End, a village Maisie didn't know well, because she tended to keep herself to herself at weekends. She'd not even tried to go out walking up the valley lately, let alone get as far as the moors, because of Conway. She was too nervous of being out of sight of other people when she was on her own.

If she went for a walk on a Sunday it was usually to a local park, and she slipped out of the back door of her lodgings to get there, so that no one at the front of the house would see her leave. At the park she kept to the paths where there were families.

She'd ventured further afield when they lived in Rochdale and her mother had been alive, but here she had no close friends of her own age to go out with, no relatives to invite her to tea.

A quiet life could be very . . . quiet.

Maisie could have got married more than once. She couldn't help realising that. Only, she hadn't met any man who'd made her wonder even a little about changing her life. They weren't – well, interesting enough, didn't read or think about the world. She'd have been bored to tears living with them.

She'd have liked to have a family, of course she would, but she was terrified of anyone she married finding out about her mother's immorality and the fact that she herself was bastard born.

When they got to Gabriel's home, it proved to be at the rear of a large house where his mother was the housekeeper.

Maisie was extremely nervous as he took her inside, but to her relief, Gwynneth Harte proved to be just as kind as her son. She too had dark hair, though of course hers was frosted with grey at the temples now. But she was still quite pretty for her age.

She lent Maisie a dressing gown and mended her skirt because the younger woman was still in shock from her ordeal and was having difficulty holding a needle steady.

'What am I going to do?' Maisie whispered to her kind new friend. 'That Jeff Conway won't stop following me, I know he won't.'

'Maybe he will if the sergeant has a word with him.'

'Sergeant Deemer said he would try to get him to leave town, but I doubt he'll manage it, and Jeff would just get more sneaky about how he came after me.'

Her hostess looked at her thoughtfully and a short time later she got up to make them both a cup of cocoa, then called out to her son to give her a hand with the mugs.

When he came into the kitchen area, which had a movable screen between it and the sitting room, she tugged at his arm to stop him going straight back, and said in a low voice, 'That girl is going to need protecting from now on.'

'I'll pass the word to the lads to keep their eyes open for Conway.'

'That won't be good enough. You wouldn't – no, I shouldn't ask you.'

'Out with it, Mam. What are you dreaming up now?'

She kept hold of his arm as she spoke to prevent him turning away. 'You're thirty-two and haven't found yourself a wife. People wonder about that. It'd do your reputation good if you pretended to be courting Maisie for a few months. Conway should have found himself someone else to badger by then, and you can pretend to break up with her – if you want to.' She was hoping he wouldn't break up with Maisie by then, because she had really taken a liking to the lass and would enjoy having a daughter-in-law like her.

'What? She won't want to pretend something like that! She's told everyone she doesn't want to get married.'

Gwynneth shrugged. 'She's terrified of him now, and with reason, so I reckon she might be grateful for your help if you explain exactly what you're offering. She can always say no, after all.'

He frowned at her. 'It'd look strange, me getting engaged to someone I hardly know.'

'It already looks strange you *not* getting yourself a young woman, Gabriel Harte – as I've told you and told you. I thought you'd clicked with Bella Porter, but no, when you said you were just good friends, you really meant it. By the time they reach your age, most men are married and have kids.' She dabbed at her eyes. 'I'm starting to think I'm never going to have grandchildren.'

'Jericho's got wed. He'll give you several, I'm sure.'

'I was expecting a house full of them, and big family gatherings by the time you lads were this age. Little kids can be such f-fun.'

The hitch in her voice showed how upset she was, and that upset him too. 'Times have been hard. I didn't want to marry and bring a family into the world, then see them go hungry because there weren't any jobs.'

'Well, you've got a permanent job now with Roy Tyler the builder, so that's no longer an excuse.'

'I can't just magic a wife and grandchildren out of thin air for you, though, can I?'

'You could work on that if you liked Maisie enough to stay with her. I think she's a lovely person – and lonely.'

'Mam, leave it be. I'll find my own girl if and when I want one.'

'But that's the whole point, you haven't even tried. I can see the sadness in Maisie's eyes. She's deep down lonely, that's what she is, with no family at all. And now she's got that brute pestering her. He'd frighten any lass, that one would. He's like a – a big hairy gorilla! Only, a gorilla would be nicer than him.'

Her son stared at her in obvious dismay, but she didn't let that stop her saying her piece.

'Besides, you heard what she said: if her employer found out about Conway pestering her, she'd be blamed for egging him on and she'd likely lose her job.'

'Do you really think they'd sack her?'

'Oh, yes. Men in positions of authority are always ready to blame the woman, and if one who is so pretty stays unwed, they think there's something wrong with her. And that manager of hers is a horrible man. He's all over the richer customers, and treats his staff like idiot children or worse.'

'I still can't do what you suggest. I hardly know Maisie. What would it be like, getting engaged to a stranger?'

Gwynneth shrugged. 'I didn't say get engaged, I said pretend to be courting her. That's what courting's for, getting to know someone better before you decide whether to get wed or not. By the time you've been for walks or to the cinema or dances, you know what the other one's like. Anyway, I'll say no more. It's up to you. It was just a thought, a way of helping her and, I'll admit, giving you a nudge. Will you at least drive her back to her lodgings when I've finished mending her clothes?'

'Of course I will. And see her to the door.'

They went back to join Maisie, but Gabriel hardly said a word and left the chatting to the two women. His mother hadn't been exaggerating: the two women did seem to be getting on like a house on fire, and he was enjoying listening to their lively conversation.

★

Gwynneth was watching her son more carefully than he realised. She thought he was attracted to Maisie, she really did.
He certainly kept looking at their visitor and smiling at the
things the lass was saying. She hoped she hadn't put him off
with her suggestion. She shouldn't blurt things out like that.

He was a friendly sort of fellow, her middle son, and had
made friends with one or two women over the years, like Bella
Porter, who'd inherited a house on Daisy Street, but that was
all it had been, just friendship. He kept his deepest thoughts
to himself, had done all through these hard years since the
Great War ended. Eh, seventeen years that was now. Time
passed so quickly.

And now she was fifty-six, with her hair turning grey, and
had nearly died last year. She'd be too old to play games with
her grandchildren soon, if she ever got any, that was.

When Gabriel had driven Maisie home, Gwynneth sat down
and had a little cry about it all.

Her younger son Lucas came home and caught her
weeping. When he asked why, she told him, knowing that
he'd tell Gabriel. Maybe that would nudge him a bit more.

She didn't let herself go on weeping though. Women her
age did feel a bit down sometimes. She'd get over it.

Besides, her sons would go their own sweet way whatever
she said or did. They were all three over thirty now. Eh, how
quickly the years had passed. Before you knew it, you were
old and wondering how long you'd got left.

Early on the Wednesday morning, his second day in the north,
Biff set off from Rivenshaw, heading for Rochdale and the
address Granny Gormley had found for him.

He found the house easily enough and the landlady
remembered Ida, even after so many years.

'Beautiful woman, she was, you couldn't forget her. But
her surname wasn't Fletcher when she was with me, Mr

Higgins; it was Bassett, *Mrs Bassett*. Poor lass, to lose her husband so young. She was so upset, missed him so much. Pretty little daughter she had, too.'

Daughter? No one had mentioned a child – though the daughter would be a young woman by now if his calculations were correct. Corden certainly hadn't mentioned a daughter. Ha! Biff had definitely got more information than he had. That would stand in his favour.

'Really well-behaved, the little 'un was, even as a baby. Now, what was she called? Oh yes, Maisie. Short for Margaret, I suppose. It usually is. But I never heard her called anything else but Maisie.'

He scribbled both names down hastily.

'The child was far better behaved than her mother, if you ask me. I used to look after her sometimes for Ida. Never a bit of trouble and pretty as a picture. It was years ago now, but I've never forgotten them because I had to ask Ida to leave in the end, even though I knew I'd miss little Maisie, which I did.'

She shook her head disapprovingly. 'I run respectable rooms and once she'd recovered from her grief about losing her husband, Ida started bringing men home. It's not as if she was courting or anything. I might have turned a blind eye to that. We're all human, after all. She just liked spending time with a fellow, if you know what I mean.'

'Ah. Like that, was she, eh?' It'd probably mean she couldn't inherit because the heirs had to have good morals, Mr Neven had said. But Biff would leave that sort of decision up to the lawyer.

'Yes. Not fair on the child because Ida used to leave her on her own, she was too young for it to be safe. Then, as Maisie grew older, Ida would send her to sit outside on the front steps when she brought a fellow home, if the weather was fine. Shocking, I thought that when everyone knew why she was out there.'

'Do you know where Ida went next?'

'Yes, as it happens. She moved in with a chap in Shaw, just a few miles up the road from here. Potter, he was called. She stayed with him for a few years, claiming they'd got married, and they were all lovey-dovey at first, I will admit. All I can say is, if they had got wed, no one knows where they did it. It definitely wasn't in Rochdale.'

He hoped he'd looked suitably shocked. 'Dear me. Go on, please.'

'Well, I'm not one to listen to gossip, but everyone knew they'd started having rows, they both had such loud voices. Then he up and left one night. Never came back, never sent word where he'd gone. She was really upset, you've got to give her that, an' she went on calling herself Mrs Potter. She moved back to Rochdale and didn't live with any other chaps, but she was seen with more than one, so even broad-minded women wouldn't have anything to do with her. She wasn't considered respectable, though that didn't stop her getting a job as a barmaid in one of the better pubs.'

The landlady gave him the address and directions to get to Shaw, and he drove off again. This wasn't looking good. If Ida Potter, or whatever she was calling herself now, was still behaving immorally at going on for fifty, Mr Neven definitely wouldn't allow her to inherit. That had been one of Miss Chapman's firm conditions, Mr Penscombe had told Biff as well.

He moved on three times in Shaw, then Rochdale during the next few hours, feeling more worried about what he'd found out about Ida with each visit to new lodgings. Then the trail went cold at the fourth place because the former landlady had moved away and the person now running the place had never met Ida, nor had any of her current lodgers, none of whom had been there long enough.

It was getting late by then so Biff drove back to Rivenshaw, worrying that he hadn't been able to pick up even a hint about what had happened to Ida next – and he wasn't even sure what she was calling herself now.

Should he go and see Granny Gormley again tomorrow? Yes, why not? She might be able to guess where Ida was most likely to have gone, even if she didn't know for sure.

Granny looked at him when he turned up again. 'No luck?'

'You were right about her being at that address years ago but she's moved on a few times since, and now I'm stuck again. I wonder if I can pick your brain once more, Mrs Gormley? And I'd like to offer you a little present for your trouble.'

He held out a bar of chocolate and she smiled as she took it from him.

'All right, lad. Not too big a bribe, but it's softened my heart. Come in and put the kettle on.'

Over another pot of tea he explained exactly what he'd found out and looked at her hopefully.

'Well, there is one thing I can tell you for sure: I remembered after you'd gone that Ida worked as a barmaid sometimes. You might ask around the pubs near the town centre of Rochdale, not the posh ones and not the rough boozers either, but the lively ones that are just about respectable.'

'What about the daughter? She'd be over twenty by now, so she'd be working too. Or married, even. Trouble is, I don't know what surname she's using.'

'She started off as a Bassett, as her mother claimed to be Mrs Bassett when she arrived here, but everyone knew Ida had been a Fletcher before her supposed first marriage.' She looked thoughtful. 'It wouldn't hurt to try the cemetery as well if you don't come up with anything.'

'Ida would still be alive, surely?'

'Fletchers aren't usually long-lived. Just keep that idea in reserve. If all else fails it'd be worth a go.'

'Hmm. I'll remember it. And I really appreciate your help and suggestions.'

She grinned, that urchin's grin on a wrinkled face that made him remember his own lively little grandma.

'An' me and my daughter will really appreciate the chocolate tonight, Mr Higgins.'

He smiled as he drove away. Mrs Gormley had more life in her than most people half her age.

He liked old people, especially those who weren't afraid to offer an opinion or two about the modern world. He only had one or two older relatives left now and none as lively as the lady he'd just visited. But not as few relatives as this Ida Fletcher sounded to have had.

It'd be a pity if he found her and raised her hopes, then she couldn't inherit because of being immoral. He was getting quite worried about that possibility.

7

It took most of the following day to find the pub where Ida had worked for several years and to his relief, the landlady remembered her clearly.

She looked at Biff sadly when he asked where he could find Ida now.

'Eh, love, didn't you know? She's dead. Died two years ago – or would it be three? She got pneumonia and was gone like that.' She snapped her fingers.

'Oh dear.'

'We were all upset because she was a right good barmaid and got on well with our customers. We had a whip round to pay for a funeral because her daughter couldn't afford one. Well, Ida liked to live in comfort, didn't she, and Maisie was upset that they didn't have enough saved for her to afford a decent funeral and burial plot.'

It seemed obvious what his next step ought to be. 'Do you know where the daughter is now?'

'No, love. Sorry. She left town a few weeks afterwards. You could ask her old boss. He's still the manager at Redman's grocery store on Yorkshire Street.'

'I'll do that.'

But Biff rang up Mr Neven first to make sure he'd be doing the right thing trying to find the daughter, reversing the charges as he'd been told.

He wasn't in luck. Mr Neven was in court and would be

there again the following morning, so couldn't be reached till the next afternoon.

'Could I speak to Mr Penscombe instead, do you think?'

'I'll see if he's free.'

'Tell him it's an emergency. I'm sure he'll speak to me.'

Biff waited and sure enough, he was put through to Mr Penscombe. After he'd explained the situation there was silence, then the clerk said, 'I think you should definitely try to find the daughter. But could you please telephone tomorrow morning just in case there's anything to bear in mind legally? Mr Neven will be free around ten o'clock.'

'I'll do that.'

Biff decided to go and see Maisie Bassett's former boss. Surely he'd have some idea of where she'd gone? Another employer usually wanted references before they gave anyone a job, after all.

When Gabriel drove Maisie back to her lodgings from his mother's house, she was looking as neat and tidy as ever, but she glanced round nervously when he stopped, hesitating to get out of the van.

'Conway wouldn't attack you round here, even if you were on your own. Too many people.'

'No. I suppose you're right. I'm beginning to wonder if I'll ever feel safe again. I can't thank you enough for saving me today, Mr Harte.'

'My privilege. If you need help again, get in touch with me or Sergeant Deemer, or even both of us. Don't hesitate.'

'Yes. But maybe I should simply move to another town, somewhere in the south even, and get permanently free of him. I'm seriously thinking of doing it.'

Gabriel didn't like the thought of her going away. His mother was right about one thing: he *was* attracted to Maisie.

He watched her get out of the van and run to the front door, but she fumbled with her door key and dropped it, looking panicked as she scrabbled on the edge of the footpath for it. Eh, he didn't like to see anyone so afraid. His heart went out to her.

He thumped the steering wheel in frustration. Dammit, his mother was right! Poor Maisie needed protecting all the time till Conway gave up pursuing her, and why would he, when she didn't have a chap to look after her safety?

Why hadn't she got married? She was a beautiful woman and you'd think men would be queuing up to court her, decent men, not bullies like Conway. She seemed determined not to marry at all. Would she ever change her mind about that?

He was a fine one to talk. He hadn't tried to find a wife, he had to admit, not after seeing friends struggling to survive through all the lean years since the Great War. His mother had needed looking after because their father had died young. She was the best mother ever, but he hadn't realised how despairing she felt about not having grandchildren. She'd hidden that well.

Life was a series of choices and you often found it hard to work out which was the best path to take at a turning point. He'd felt so sure that he shouldn't marry and bring children into the world only to see them go hungry till times got better. Only, now his mum had started him thinking about it, he realised how much he'd like to have children before it was too late. But only with a woman he could love and enjoy living with, particularly one who would get on well with his family.

An image of Maisie came into his mind and he tried in vain to dismiss it. She'd got on so well with his mother. She was such a lovely looking woman.

But just because a woman was beautiful outside didn't

mean she was beautiful inside, or that she'd make a good wife and mother.

It didn't mean she wouldn't, either.

Oh, what did he know? His mother had got to him, that's what. She did that now and then when she wanted one of her sons to do something, planted a seed in their mind that grew whether they wanted it to or not.

And would it be bad to pretend to be courting Maisie? He smiled ruefully. No, it wouldn't. When she'd relaxed with his mother, she'd been lively in what she said, a person as interested in the world as he was.

Biff wasn't able to see Mr Vaughan at the shop until the following morning. When he explained that he was trying to find Maisie Bassett, the manager grew stiff and suspicious.

'Why do you need to find her?'

Biff handed him one of his business cards. 'Because I'm a private investigator and a London lawyer called Mr Neven has hired me to do it. It looks as if she might have come into an inheritance, or at least she might have if she's of good moral standing.'

Mr Vaughan jerked back in his seat. 'I do not employ people of bad moral standing in this shop, Mr Higgins. Miss Bassett was always properly behaved and a hard worker to boot.'

'I'm glad to hear that. Can you please tell me where she's gone?'

'I'm not sure I should do that. She said she didn't want information about her present whereabouts passing on to anyone, whoever they claimed to be.'

'But what about her inheritance?'

'Hmm. I think you should contact Mr Stavener, who used to be the manager at her bank and is now retired. He kept a fatherly eye on her after her mother died, and he'll have time to look into your claim properly. I'm a busy man.'

He led the way inside, wrote down the bank manager's address, then handed it to the detective. 'This street is just off Halifax Road on the left, about half a mile out of town.' Then he folded his arms across his chest. Clearly he didn't intend to give any further information.

So once again, Biff had to drive across the town. The street wasn't easy to find and he had to stop and ask directions twice before he found the retired bank manager's house in a shady cul-de-sac. The maid who answered it kept him waiting on the doorstep while she took his card in to her master.

Eventually he was shown into a small parlour at the rear of the house where a portly, bald-headed gentleman gestured to him to sit down.

After explaining the situation all over again, Biff waited.

'Can you prove what you say, Mr Higgins?'

He thought for a moment. 'You could phone the lawyer's rooms in London.'

'I'll do that. One can't be too careful where young ladies' safety is concerned. I'd be obliged if you'd wait in the hall.'

Biff stood up. 'If Mr Neven isn't there, the chief clerk is Mr Penscombe and he's been handling the everyday business of this case, so he knows me too.'

He was kept waiting for nearly a quarter of an hour by the time a connection had been made by the operator and Mr Stavener had spoken to someone.

This time the bank manager came in person to find him and show him into the small parlour again. 'I'm sorry to have kept you waiting, Mr Higgins. Mr Penscombe speaks very highly of you and has confirmed why you're searching for the young lady in question. She's changed her name to Lawson, by the way, because of her mother's reputation.'

'But she herself is respectable?'

'Of course she is. I've never had any reason to doubt that, and her former employer always spoke very highly of her, too.'

'Good. Could you let me have her address, please? If you have it, that is.'

Once again Biff watched someone scribble on a piece of paper.

'Please don't give this to anyone else. She kindly sends me a Christmas card every year so I've heard from her recently at this address.'

As Biff left the former bank manager's house, he looked at the paper again and chuckled. All roads led him to Rivenshaw, it seemed. How ironic that she must have been there all the time he was driving around to nearby towns searching for her in vain.

He was humming as he drove back and couldn't stop beaming at the world. He'd done it, found the young lady. Put that in your pipe and smoke it, Corden.

That bonus was looking more and more likely.

But it was too late to do anything today. It was almost dark, and strangers knocking on their door at night could make people nervous and uncooperative.

The evening seemed to go on for ever, though, despite him having brought a book to read.

The following morning Biff waited impatiently till nine o'clock, then went to the address Mr Stavener had given him, only to find that the landlady didn't want to give him any information.

He looked at Mrs Tucker pleadingly. 'If she's left here, could you please give me her new address? It's very important that I see her.'

She studied him for a moment or two and he must have

passed some sort of test in her mind because she asked, 'Why are you looking for her, Mr Higgins? You're not from round here, judging by your accent.'

So he explained yet again and showed her his business card.

She chewed the corner of her mouth as she thought about it. 'Well, you could try her place of work if it's that important.'

When he had the information, he thanked her and drove into the town centre, parking the car in the square as usual and strolling along to the biggest grocery store in Rivenshaw, which looked as if it served mainly the better class of person.

He paused by the door, studying the three women behind the various counters, and it seemed to him that the youngest lady fitted the description he'd been given. She was standing behind the counter with the bacon slicer on it at the far end. Half of the counter had a big marble slab with a partial side of bacon, some cooked meats and sausages set out on it under a glass cover.

'May I help you, sir?'

He turned to find a man wearing a pristine white apron standing next to him. 'I'm looking for Miss Maisie Lawson. I have some important news for her.'

'I'm afraid our staff aren't allowed to deal with personal business during working hours.'

'Perhaps she could take an early dinner break, then.' Biff once again pulled out a business card. 'I've been sent by a London lawyer to find her.'

The man, who was presumably the manager, looked suspiciously at the card, then at Biff. 'May I ask why it's so important? Has she done something wrong?'

'Of course she hasn't. I have some good news for her, that's all. If you're in any doubt about me, I'm sure Sergeant Deemer will vouch for me.'

The man's suspicious expression abated a little. 'Ah. Well,

I'll just check with our good sergeant, if you don't mind. One has to be careful with strangers who approach young women. If the sergeant vouches for you, I'll make an exception and let her take an early dinner break at eleven o'clock.'

He came back five minutes later and nodded. 'Sergeant Deemer has indeed vouched for your bona fides, so if you'd come back at eleven, she'll come out early.'

You'd think the young woman was guarding the Crown Jewels instead of a slab of bacon, Biff thought as he went back outside. Some of these shop managers acted like petty dictators towards their staff. They'd feel very at home in Germany these days with that Hitler chap, who seemed to be causing a stir over there, and not in a good way.

Biff had been horrified about what he'd read in the newspapers about recent events in Germany. He did a lot of reading because there was inevitably a good deal of hanging around in his job. No one looked twice at someone reading a newspaper, and you could keep your face mostly hidden behind its pages if you were careful.

He passed the time by going for a walk, coming back just before eleven.

A lady went into the shop and a young male shop assistant fussed over her as if she were a cousin of the queen. It took all sorts! Biff wouldn't like to do a job where he had to fuss over people like that.

He glanced at his watch.

8

When Mr Midgely told her he wished to speak to her in private and beckoned to young Larry to take over her counter, Maisie's heart began to thump in her chest. Had the manager heard about the attack on her? Surely not? She kept her expression calm as she followed him into his office.

He didn't offer her a seat but took one himself. His idea of good manners didn't accord with hers, she thought, not for the first time.

'There is a man to see you and he's waiting outside. I said you could take an early dinner break to speak to him. He said he knew Sergeant Deemer and when I phoned the police station to check that, it proved correct, so you will be safe speaking to him.'

'Thank you.'

'He's come all the way from London to speak to you. It must be important or I'd not have upset the rotas.'

'Very considerate of you, sir.'

'Make sure you're back on time.'

He nodded dismissal and she slipped into the tiny women's cloakroom to take off her apron, wash her hands rapidly, and put on her coat over her white overall. She hurried out of the side door, anxious not to waste a minute more of the half hour allowed for the midday meal.

The man waiting at the front of the shop looked respectable and, when he saw her, he immediately tipped his hat to her as she approached him, which showed he had better manners than Mr Midgely.

'Miss Maisie Lawson?'

'Yes.'

'My name is Higgins. I've come from London to find you with some news from a lawyer there.'

Someone going into the shop nearly bumped into him and said, 'Excuse me!' in an annoyed voice.

He moved sideways. 'Look, can we go somewhere quiet to talk? I could buy us a pot of tea if there's a café nearby. Only it's starting to spit with rain, so we can't very well stay out here in the street.'

'There's a café round the corner but it isn't cheap.'

'That doesn't matter.'

When they were ordering he asked if she'd like a cake as well, but she was too anxious to bother about food. 'Just tell me what you're here for. I don't even know anyone in London.'

He explained about coming to find her mother because she was one of the beneficiaries named in a will to inherit a cottage from some distant relatives.

Maisie felt her mouth fall open in astonishment, but though she managed to stop herself gaping like a fool, it was a few moments before she managed to speak, and only in a voice croaky with shock. 'I didn't think my mother had any relatives in London. Who would that be?'

'A Miss Jane Chapman and a Mr James Beaton, distant relatives. The lady lived here in Rivenshaw, but her nephew lived in London, hence the lawyer who is carrying out their combined wishes coming from there.'

'I never heard Mum speak of any people with those surnames.'

'I gather she was one of several distant relatives to whom they left bequests.'

'That seems so strange. Are you sure you have the right person in Mum?'

The tea arrived and they had to stop talking while the waitress was at their table.

When the woman had gone, he said, 'She was definitely the right person.'

'What a pity you're too late. She died a couple of years ago.'

'Yes, so I found out. I'm not promising anything yet, but it may be that the inheritance will now pass to you instead.'

She stared at him, finding this even harder to believe. 'A cottage! I can't believe it.' She didn't dare. It sounded too good to be true.

'Everything has been carefully checked, and your mother was definitely the beneficiary, and you are her only child.'

'Yes, I am. She didn't have anything to do with the rest of her family, though. The only thing my mother told me about them was that they'd always struggled to make a living and that she managed better without them. So how could one of them have a cottage to leave me?'

She took a gulp of tea, waiting for him to do the same.

'No one knew about your existence when I was sent to find your mother, so I need to ask the lawyer concerned whether the inheritance will indeed come to you, Miss Lawson. It seems likely. I wonder if you'd give me your address? I think it would be better to contact you outside working hours from now on. Your manager seems to be very, um, nosey.'

'Yes, he is. And so bossy, it's a wonder he doesn't tell you when to breathe in and out. That'd be better than coming to the shop to see me, but only a little. The trouble is, my land-lady won't let any men inside the house, and all the cafés are closed in the evenings. It's dark by teatime anyway at this time of year.'

'I shall need to have a way of speaking to you.'

'Well, if you come to the front door, Mrs Tucker will fetch me to speak to you. We'll just have to walk up and down the street, rain or no rain. It's well lit, at least.'

He looked at her thoughtfully. 'It's difficult being a single woman and not having your own home, or even a family nearby, isn't it?'

'Very. Especially if you're young. You have to stay extremely respectable if you want to keep your job, whatever that takes.'

After they'd both taken another mouthful of tea, she frowned. 'I hope you didn't tell Mr Midgely I might have inherited a cottage?'

'Oh, no. I had to tell him I'd been sent by a London lawyer because I could see he'd not have let you speak to me unless I gave him a very good reason. I was also able to give Sergeant Deemer as a reference.'

'It's a good thing you didn't tell him any details. He'd have a fit if I owned a cottage and probably find an excuse to sack me on the spot. He doesn't believe in women owning property, and he'd be furious at an employee owning more than he does. I know for a fact that his own house is rented. Well, it's a small town.'

'What a strange, old-fashioned attitude! Women have always owned property, the ones whose families can afford it, anyway.'

'I know. But I've read in the women's magazines about some of the problems they can still face legally. It's less than ten years since all women got the vote, after all.'

'I should think so, too.'

'Yes. But when you go out to work, single women still get paid only about half as much as men, even if they're doing the same work, so they can't usually afford even to rent a whole house. I certainly can't.'

He blinked. She seemed a very intelligent young woman, not a man hater like some of the harridans he'd met years ago when women were still agitating for the vote. Those women had made him nervous as a young man, the way they went round breaking windows, going on marches that upset the traffic, and causing disturbances at meetings.

She glanced at the café's wall clock. 'I don't want to sound rude, but if there's anything else to tell me, you'll need to do it quickly. I daren't be late back.'

'There's nothing at the moment, except that in case you're worried I'm not telling you the truth about this, I'll tell you the same thing as I told your manager: go and see Sergeant Deemer if you want to check on me.'

'Mr Midgely has already told me he'd phoned the police station about you. You must be all right if the sergeant vouches for you. He's very well thought of in the valley and I'd take his word about anything.'

She drained her cup then glanced at the wall clock again. 'We'd better start back.'

Biff walked back with her to the shop and was surprised when a van passing by screeched to a halt and stopped, then a young man jumped out. He came to join them, looking at Biff suspiciously.

'Are you all right, Maisie?'

'I'm fine, Gabriel. I'll tell you about it after work if you have the time.'

'I'll always make the time for you. Don't walk back to your lodgings on your own. Wait for me outside the shop after you finish.'

'All right. I'll see you later, Mr Higgins.'

Biff watched her pause to scowl at the front of the shop and sigh before walking round the side of the building. He wasn't surprised. The manager was a petty tyrant. He must be very unpleasant to work for.

When she'd disappeared, Biff eyed the young man. 'You

seem to feel a responsibility for the young lady. Is she a close friend of yours?'

'She's a—' he hesitated, then finished with, 'good friend of my family.'

'And your name is?'

'Gabriel Harte. If that's any concern of yours, Mr Higgins?'

'It may become my concern. I'll leave it to Miss Lawson to tell you of my business with her, though, if she wishes you to know the details. And it is only business.'

Biff raised his hat and walked away. He hadn't missed the protective way in which this Harte fellow had come to stand next to Miss Lawson, or the way she'd greeted him with a warm smile. What was going on between them? He hoped for her sake that it was something above board and respectable.

He'd have to mention Harte to Mr Neven. He didn't want to leave out any piece of information which might be important. Details could be so crucial in his business.

The following morning Deemer happened to be walking past Conway's lodging house and saw a sign saying 'Room vacant'. Hoping this meant what he suspected, he called in and found that Conway had run off after breakfast that morning, owing a week's rent.

Deemer saw a scruffy-looking man was eavesdropping, and spoke more loudly, 'I'll arrest Conway if he comes back to this town. That's two crimes he's committed.'

He walked off smiling. Maybe this time he'd be lucky and get rid of one problem at least. The fellow had probably only attended church because it gave him a chance to meet young women.

Mind you, he might have been attracted to Miss Lawson in his own bullying way, because she was a good-looking woman. But that didn't give him the right to rape her.

She'd be better off if she found herself a husband. It was surprising that she hadn't married by now. Gabriel Harte would make her an excellent husband. He hadn't married previously because of the need to look after his widowed mother and the difficulty of finding a steady job during the hard times in Lancashire, but times were getting better, and Gwynneth Harte was now working as a housekeeper. There was nothing to stop her son finding a wife

To add to the day's difficulties for Maisie, Sergeant Deemer turned up at the shop just before four o'clock. After he'd gone into the manager's office, she was once again summoned to join them there.

Mr Midgely looked at her sourly as she went in. 'It seems the magistrate wishes to see you, but I'm assured it's not because you're in trouble but because you're a witness to a crime.'

She swallowed hard, not sure what this meant except that she was already in the manager's black books for the earlier interruption to the day's work, and he hadn't been happy when she didn't tell him what Mr Higgins wanted. He'd consider two interruptions in one working day quite outrageous, she was sure.

Sergeant Deemer stepped in, 'It's about the, um, disturbance that you witnessed yesterday evening, Miss Lawson. The magistrate wishes to interview you. I might say that Mr Peters is extremely pleased that you're willing to give evidence and he'll be equally pleased with you, Mr Midgely, for allowing Miss Lawson time off work to see him. Very public spirited of you.'

The manager's glare lessened to a frown. 'Well, it's in all our interests to maintain law and order in the town, but see that you come back straight away, Miss Lawson. It is highly inconvenient to have staff not available for their duties.'

The sergeant winked at her. 'That's why Mr Peters sent me to fetch her today, Mr Midgely. He thought it'd be less busy than tomorrow.'

'That was thoughtful of him.'

Midgely waved one hand dismissively at Maisie and she hurried to get her coat and hat for the second time that day, walking outside through the front door, for once, because the sergeant was waiting for her and simply led the way.

Deemer gave her one of his kind looks. 'I came in my car, but it'll be better if you smile while we're outside together, so that nosey folk will know you aren't in any trouble.'

She smiled, hoping it looked genuine, but feeling the stiffness of her face.

As she got into the car, Deemer said genially, 'Officious little idiot, isn't he, your manager?' then pulled out into the street.

That brought a genuine smile to her face. 'Yes. Thank you for trying to make it easier for me at work, but he'll be huffy with me for days because I had to see the detective from London earlier today.'

'Higgins?'

'Yes. I gather Mr Midgely rang you about that as well. Two interruptions in one day – why, that might signal the end of the world.'

The more Deemer saw of her, the more he liked her, including her sense of humour. 'Well, let him be huffy. It's important that we bring Conway to book.'

'Have you spoken to him about his attack on me, Sergeant?'

'I can't find the man and there's a vacancy at his lodgings. He works for Higgerson, who says he's doing a job out of town for a day or two. Which is probably a lie, but I'll be waiting if Conway reappears. Oh, yes.' Deemer didn't think he would ever come back, though.

He drew up and they went inside the town hall to see the magistrate.

Mr Peters was a gentleman in his middle years and had an elderly female secretary sitting behind him with her notepad. He was very polite, phrasing his questions delicately, clearly somewhat embarrassed by having to ask them.

At one stage, his secretary leaned forward to whisper something and he added another question.

When the interview was over, Deemer drove Maisie back to the shop and came to the side door with her, saying very loudly, 'Thank you for your help, Miss Lawson. Much appreciated. And please thank your manager for me again.'

She nodded and hurried inside, shedding her coat quickly and putting on her apron, then washing her hands.

Her manager came across to her. 'Everything sorted out now?'

'I hope so, Mr Midgely. The sergeant asked me to thank you again for your cooperation.'

'Hmm. Well, see that you clear up properly before you go. Young Larry isn't as meticulous as you are.'

His scowl, this time aimed across the big space, made her guess that the shop lad had borne the brunt of his annoyance. Which took some of the heat off her.

But the interview had brought back memories of the attack and upset her all over again.

She'd had nightmares about it and was grateful that Gabriel was keeping an eye on her after work. What a lovely person he was!

9

Gabriel went back to work after seeing Maisie but couldn't get the stranger she'd been with out of his mind. Not exactly a gentleman but not a poor man, either. And with a slight Irish accent, which seemed strange for a man coming from London. What had he wanted with Maisie?

His mother was right. Their new friend might well need protecting for a while. It was a good job he'd arranged to drive her home from work. It would give him an opportunity to suggest they pretend to be courting without anyone being able to overhear their discussion.

Surely Maisie would agree to that? Once their relationship got known, it should deter Conway and help keep her safer generally.

The afternoon seemed to pass slowly, but at last Gabriel finished the job he was working on and rushed away in his van. He was still thrilled every time he used it to get somewhere in a hurry, thrilled that he'd managed to save up and buy it, even. He'd happily worked long hours on it to improve its run-down exterior, but thankfully the engine had been in good condition.

Maisie was waiting for him outside the shop, which was now closed. There were only a few other people around in the street and she was looking anxious, standing at the back of the doorway. Her face brightened when he drew up nearby, but she still glanced round nervously as she left the doorway to get into the vehicle.

'Conway has made me afraid to be outside on my own,' she confessed. 'I know it's cowardly, but he's so *big*.'

'He's a brute.'

As Gabriel drove away from the shop he asked, 'Would you mind if we stop somewhere and talk for a few minutes? I have a suggestion which may help you.'

'I wouldn't mind at all. It's very kind of you to think of me. And your mother is kind too. Um, I have something to tell you as well.'

Eh, he'd nearly blurted out that it would always be his pleasure to help her. Where had that thought come from? He was glad he found a place to stop under a street lamp in front of a blank wall shortly afterwards. There was no one around, not likely to be at this time of day, either.

When he'd switched off the motor, she said, 'You go first.'

He took a deep breath and started hesitantly. 'This is my mother's suggestion, actually. She, um, thinks we should pretend to be walking out together.'

Maisie's voice was rather sharp. 'That sounds as if you don't really want to do what your mother suggested, and if so, I'm sure I don't want to trouble you.'

'No, no! That's not how I meant it to come out.' He sighed and looked down at his hands, which were gripping the steering wheel tightly as he tried to find the right way to say it. 'The truth is, the minute I start talking seriously to a lass about that sort of thing, I get all tongue-tied and what I want to say comes out wrong.'

'Oh?'

'I can see I've upset you now and I didn't mean to. Sorry. I'm not reluctant to help you in that way, Maisie, not at all. Truly!'

She turned to stare at him. 'Just say it simply, then, but say what *you* want, not your mother.'

'Well, it is her suggestion and I did turn the idea down at

first because it took me by surprise. I like to think things through before taking any big steps.'

'So do I.'

'Only, when I saw you looking so upset and nervous, I *wanted* to protect you. And what I think now is . . . well, we should tell people we're walking out together, partly to keep you safe, but also because I *like* being with you.'

That surprised her but she just murmured 'Hmm' and waited for him to continue.

'It came to me – if you don't mind, that is – we should give it a try for real? Walking out. Courting, I mean. If I haven't said something to put you off being with me.'

He dragged a grubby handkerchief out of his pocket and dropped the pencil stub that came out with it. After fumbling on the van floor, he shoved it back in his pocket and wiped his forehead, looking flushed and embarrassed. 'I really am sorry it came out sounding grudging. I didn't mean it like that at all.'

When he turned an even deeper shade of pink as he said that, visible even in the feeble light of the street lamp, Maisie couldn't help smiling at him. 'Could it be that you're shy with women, Gabriel Harte?'

'When it comes to courting and such, yes. I can be friends with them when that's all it is, all it's going to be. I don't get nervous at all then. Silly, isn't it? And there's also the fact that, well, I'm a bit old for you, actually. I'm thirty-two. I hope you don't mind that. Only, I've not been in a position to court anyone for the past few years because times have been hard and I didn't have a steady job.'

'And now you are – in a position to court someone, I mean?'

'I think so. Just about. I've got a job and I've even managed to buy this van. Oh no! Did that come out sounding wrong again? The van isn't as important as you would be if we were getting to know one another, of course it isn't.'

She smiled, realising how flustered he was again, and patted his hand. 'Well, let me put you out of your misery, Gabriel. I'd welcome the protection I'd get if it was thought that you and I were walking out together.'

She hesitated, and now it was her turn to feel embarrassed, but she was determined to be honest about this because their getting together would be meaningless if they couldn't tell the truth to one another. 'I'd also welcome the chance to see how we get on for real. But only if we're both honest about how we feel and if either of us have any doubts, later on, about building our lives together, we should agree to speak out.'

He looked at her thoughtfully, gave her hand a quick little pat in return, and nodded agreement.

He was smiling now, she thought, a real smile, a lovely smile. But she had to make one thing plain. 'There's something you don't know about my family – I'd have to tell you about my mother if we did decide to think about marrying. I'd like you to remember that in case you hear anything about her.'

'Can't you tell me about her now?'

'No. I don't like to talk about her, so I'll only do it if you need to know.' She could feel her cheeks getting warmer and hoped the street light wasn't bright enough to betray her blushes – though they'd given away his red face to her, hadn't they?

What a pair of idiots they were!

There was silence, then he said simply, 'All right. So we're officially courting from now on.'

'Yes. But there's another reason why I'd particularly welcome your protection and this is something you do need to know about straight away. Mr Higgins said my mother had inherited a cottage and, as she's dead, it might come to me instead.'

He stared in shock. 'Good heavens.'

'If that happened, if I did inherit a cottage, it'd not only be Conway but other men who would pester me to try to get their hands on it. *You* said we should try courting for real and see if we suited *before* you knew about the possible inheritance, which shows you don't have any ulterior motive, and that's very important to me.'

He started fiddling around with the steering wheel. 'But now I do know, you might think that's *why* I stay with you.'

She chuckled and could see that this surprised him. 'I don't think you're a good enough liar, Gabriel.'

He let out a huff of laughter and looked her straight in the eyes for once. 'No. I'm not, never have been. All right, then. We've agreed to try spending time together. Let's get you back to your lodgings, then I'll go home and tell my mother. She'll be pleased.'

'I'd better tell my landlady as well or she'll wonder what I'm doing, letting you bring me home in your van. She's keeps a suspicious eye on her lodgers and I haven't been seeing any other young men, and I've kept insisting I didn't want to get married, so it'll come as a shock.'

She paused then added, 'It's surprised me, I must admit.'

'You're not the only one.'

'Anyway, I'll tell my landlady that your mother approves. She must do if it was her suggestion. I think your mother is a lovely person.'

'She likes you. That's important to me. I'd never m-marry a woman she didn't like.'

The word 'marry' made them both catch their breath and they drove the rest of the way without a word. When he stopped they sat for a few moments in silence, then they smiled at one another rather shyly.

She started to open the van door, and he said, 'Let me.' He got out and hurried round to her side, opening the door and giving her a mock flourish with one hand.

As she got out, he took her by surprise, holding her hand to steady her on the uneven pavement and then kissing her on the cheek. She didn't pull away. Not only would this action let anyone watching guess their relationship, but to her surprise, she'd liked the feel of his hand in hers and his warm lips on her cheek.

Two women passing by nudged one another and slowed down to stare at them, but she didn't care if the whole of Rivenshaw knew now.

Though why such a chaste kiss on the cheek should have made her pulse race, Maisie didn't understand. Meeting Gabriel Harte had changed her, and quickly too.

'Just a minute.' He pulled a crumpled piece of paper out of his pocket and rested it on the van's roof to scribble on it. 'If you need me and it's important or something's frightening you, you can phone the top number during working hours and the bottom number at other times. Whoever answers will let me know and I'll come to you straight away.'

He held it out towards her and added, 'Once I've told them about us, my family will help you too. In any way you need. Us Hartes always stick together.'

'That's lovely to know. Thank you.'

She watched him drive away before she went inside. It must be wonderful to have a family to turn to. If she married Gabriel, they'd be her family too.

Oh, she was getting ahead of herself. They hadn't even had a go at walking out together yet.

Only when she stopped to chat to the landlady did she realise she was still clutching the paper, and she shoved it hastily in her pocket.

Their conversation went well. But it was hard to keep smiling when she received hearty congratulations on courting a Harte.

'It's early days yet to talk about courting,' she protested

involuntarily. 'We're just, you know, spending time together to find out if we suit. Walking out.'

'Oh, you will suit. What's more, a man who looks after his mother will look after his wife too. You grab that young man and keep a tight hold of him. He was worth waiting for.'

Maisie didn't need the hall mirror to tell her she was bright red again.

Maisie had hardly got up to her bedroom than Mrs Tucker's maid puffed up the stairs to fetch her.

'Sergeant Deemer has called to see you, miss. He's in the little room, waiting.'

'Oh. I wonder what he wants.' Maisie ran lightly down the stairs and into the room where Mrs Tucker allowed her guests to talk privately to visitors.

Sergeant Deemer stood up and smiled at her. 'It's all right, lass. It's good news. Conway must definitely have left town because I just heard that Higgerson has hired someone else to do his job.'

She stared at him. 'You're sure of that, Sergeant?'

'Very sure.'

Tears came into her eyes. 'Thank goodness! Oh, thank goodness.'

She escorted him to the front door, feeling as if a burden had been lifted from her shoulders.

But what would Gabriel say? Would he not want to see her now she wasn't in danger?

Gabriel parked the van in its usual place on the street outside his home, then sat for a moment or two gathering his courage. Lucas would probably be back from work by now, so he'd be able to tell his brother and mother his news at the same time.

He wasn't unhappy about asking Maisie to let him court

her for real, on the contrary. It'd surprise his family and friends though, he knew.

Best to get the fussing over and done with. He got out, locked the van doors carefully, then went round the back of the house to their part of the building.

He was greeted by a delicious smell of lamb hotpot but didn't comment on that, just stood looking across at his mother. He could never lie to her or even bend the truth slightly.

She paused and stared back at him, eyes narrowing. It always amazed him how quickly she could pick up her sons' moods. He heard his brother using the bathroom to wash off the day's dirt. He should wait to tell her till Lucas joined them.

He couldn't wait.

'I did it,' he blurted out as she raised one eyebrow questioningly.

'What did you do, love?'

'Asked Maisie Lawson to walk out with me.'

She dropped the spoon she was stirring the food with and, as it bounced across the floor, scattering a trail of gravy drops, she flung her arms round him and swung him round a couple of times. 'Oh, Gabriel lad,' a kiss was plonked on his nose, then another on his chin, 'I'm so happy for you.'

'It's to look after her and—' He fell silent, then muttered, 'Well, we like one another so we said we'd see how things went for real. Aw, come on, Mam. There's no need to cry.'

Lucas came into the room, face a rosy pink from washing, and stopped dead. 'What's wrong?'

'Nothing at all. It's good news. Our Gabriel is walking out – with a lass.'

'Well, he'd hardly walk out with a dog, would he?' He stared at his brother. 'She must be rather special.'

'She is.' That was one of the few things he was certain of.

'And she's beautiful too, but nice with it. I really like her.' Gwynneth wiped her eyes with her apron, bent to pick up the spoon, and gave it a good rinse under the tap. 'Your turn to find a lass next, Lucas.'

'No, Mam.' His voice was very firm. 'Don't get your hopes up about me.'

'If our Gabriel can find someone, you can too.'

'I was going to tell you tonight. I've heard of a scholarship for working chaps like me and I'm going to apply for it.'

'Scholarship to where? You're far too old to go back to school.'

'Not too old for the Workers Educational Association tutors to help me prepare for this scholarship. Turns out the tutors in Rivenshaw have had their eyes on me for a while. There's a special programme for fellows from poorer families like me and for women too, come to that. It's run by Leeds University. I've been doing the WEA courses by correspondence for a while as you know, and the tutors, um, well, they think I stand a chance of getting into the university to study there.'

He broke off as both of them stared at him as if he'd grown horns.

'Imagine me studying at university, Mam. There'd be so much to learn about there. It's my idea of heaven.'

'But university is for rich people.'

'Or for those who get the financial support of a special scholarship.'

She let out her favourite exclamation of shock, 'Well, I'll go to the foot of our stairs!' This second surprise had made her drop her spoon again, this time into the food, and she suddenly noticed and fished it out again with a fork, then wiped the handle. By that time she'd got past the desire to cry. She'd rather Lucas got married, but the sight of the sheer joy in her youngest son's eyes kept her from saying that.

Instead she grabbed him and pulled him towards her to smack a big kiss on each of his cheeks. 'Eh, Lucas lad, I'm that proud of you for even trying, whatever comes of it. But wouldn't you, well, feel strange at a university? It'll be full of posh people. And what will you do without your wages? How could you live?'

'To answer your first question, I suppose I would feel strange there but I wouldn't let that stop me. And for your second question, they give you enough money to live on, or at least, they do if you're very careful. I'd scrimp and scrape for the rest of my life to feed my brain and get a more interesting job, you know I would.'

'Eh, you allus were the odd one out, even at school. And the way you are with sums, adding things up in your head before anyone else can blink, is amazing.'

'I reckon if I get this scholarship, I'll seem even odder to folk round here. But not a word to anyone, Mam. It's not settled yet. I have to prove myself worthy of it. I just wanted to give you time to get used to the idea.'

Gabriel joined in. 'I'm sure you'll get this scholarship. You always were good at book learning, and arithmetic especially.'

'They call it mathematics at the university.'

'Mathematics then.' He clapped his brother on the back and the two of them grinned at one another.

They were all thoughtful as they ate their tea.

There was a lot to think about, a lot of changes coming to their small family. Could things really be going so well? They all knew how quickly life could change.

10

The following day, which was a Saturday and half-closing day, Biff phoned Mr Neven at the time arranged, using one of the cubicles in the main post office again. He was put straight through to the lawyer. After he'd explained the situation there was silence, so he waited for the other man to think about what he'd said.

'You're sure this young woman really is the daughter of Ida Fletcher?'

'Oh, yes, absolutely certain. Not only does she claim to be and can give details about her mother's life, but Sergeant Deemer says she's the spitting image of Ida Fletcher at the same age. She's quite a beauty, but she dresses modestly and doesn't encourage attention.'

'I suppose I'll have to come up to Rivenshaw, see her for myself, check with Sergeant Deemer, and then go through the formalities. Would it matter if I waited a week to do that? Is there anything pressing at your end?'

'I'm afraid there is a problem, sir. There's a fellow who's been pestering her to go out with him, but she's been refusing, and I can see why. He's a brute. A couple of days ago he grabbed her off the street and tried to have his way with her in an alley. Fortunately, a passer-by called Gabriel Harte rescued her. And he's a man in good standing in the community.'

'Good heavens! Was the attacker arrested? Is there going to be a court case?'

'I'm afraid he's run away and can't be found.'

'You're quite sure she didn't – you know, lead this man on?'

'She definitely didn't. Harte saw her trying to fight him off and punched him.'

'Where is she living?'

'In lodgings in a respectable area.'

'Not good for her to be walking home alone after dark if this man continues to be a nuisance,' Mr Neven said slowly.

'No. But if she inherits the house, how would she be any safer, living there alone?'

'I don't know. I've never been inside it. The first bequest we dealt with was the house next door, which had been used as a lodging house, but no one's been inside the other two places for years apparently. It was stipulated in the will that they be locked up and left, though the exteriors were to be kept weatherproof.'

More silence, but Mr Neven was paying for the phone call, so Biff was happy to hold on for as long as necessary.

'You've seen the houses, Higgins. They're bigger than average, I gather.'

'Yes. Detached residences with three floors, sir.'

'Hmm. I simply can't leave my current client in the lurch to come up there myself, not for a while. Look, can you stay in the north for a few more days? All expenses paid, of course. You could keep an eye on the young woman for me.'

'Happy to do that, sir. It's an interesting situation and well, I'm only human, wouldn't mind seeing what's inside the house myself.'

Another silence, then Mr Neven said, 'I can't even be certain I'll be free next week. Look, do you think you could find a lawyer in Rivenshaw or nearby who could act on my behalf in this matter, give it the necessary legal approval? We'd need a person who would handle the young woman's affairs with discretion.'

'I'm fairly certain I can do that. I'll ask Sergeant Deemer who would be suitable. He seems to know everyone in the area. Um, how do we get into the house? Does someone have the keys?'

'I do. I'll send them to you overnight by special post. Oh no, it's Saturday. There won't be a post to get to you till Monday. We'll have to wait. I'll also send you a copy of the will to give to the lawyer we hire. He can check Miss Lawson's credentials and tell her about her inheritance, though you should be present as well when he does that. Then he can liaise with me about legal matters if necessary. Just a minute.'

There was the sound of a voice nearby and he said, 'Good heavens, Penscombe, is it time for me to leave already? I'm afraid I have to go now Mr Higgins. My clerk will sort out the practicalities with you. Hold on. I'll pass you over to him.'

The elderly clerk came on the phone.

Later, when the call finished, Biff beamed at the world as he walked out from the post office into the street. This would mean another week and a bit's work at the very least, and with living expenses thrown in. He'd be able to put a few pounds away if he was careful.

He whistled cheerfully as he drove across town to the police station to ask Deemer for help in finding a lawyer. He'd have liked to walk and stretch his legs, but he might need the car to go and see someone quickly. Speed was definitely of the essence here, for Miss Lawson's sake.

But the house alone wasn't going to guarantee her safety. He'd have to think about that.

The constable on duty told Biff that Sergeant Deemer had just nipped across the yard to have a word with his wife, his home being behind the police station.

'Shall I come back later or wait?'

'Oh, you should wait, sir. He'll only be a couple of minutes.

He'll want to see you, I'm sure. He didn't tell me the details, but he said you were here to undertake an intriguing job.'

Well, it was nice to know that the sergeant also thought this was an interesting case. He saw Deemer come in the back way shortly afterwards.

'Come into my office, lad.' The sergeant didn't wait for an answer, but led the way, gesturing to a chair. 'Now, what can I do for you today?'

Biff explained that Mr Neven needed a lawyer to work on his behalf in Rivenshaw and asked if the sergeant could recommend someone. He was rewarded by a quick nod.

'That's easy. Henry Lloyd has just taken on a new partner, a younger chap. He must be all right or Henry wouldn't even consider working with him. The new partner won't have a lot of clients yet, so will be free to help you, I'm sure.'

'Might I ask what *you* think of this new man?'

'I've only spoken to him a couple of times but he seems sharp-witted and looks you straight in the eye. He's called Angus McLean – Scottish, obviously. Shall I ring through to their rooms and see if he's free to talk to you now?'

'Please do.'

After a short conversation, Deemer put the phone down. 'He's free straight away. If you drive me across town to their rooms, I'll introduce you, then leave you to it and stroll back. I like to get out on the streets regularly. You can't keep an eye on what's going on by sitting in an office, or even by peering out of a car window. Not that a car isn't useful sometimes in our job.' He paused, head on one side. 'You'll keep me up to date with what happens?'

'Of course I will. And if you think of anything else that might help what I'm doing, don't hesitate to tell me.'

Angus McLean was short, ginger-haired, and scrawny, looking to be full of suppressed energy. Biff instantly took a liking to him and was pleased at how quickly he grasped the situation.

The sergeant lingered to listen as they chatted.

'What's the young lady like?' Mr McLean asked.

'She works in a shop, seems intelligent, and is a decent lass as far as I can make out.'

'And the house she might have inherited? What's that like?'

'No one knows what it's like inside, but it's bigger than average. It's on Daisy Street, which lies between Birch End and Backshaw Moss.'

'Ah. I've heard Backshaw Moss mentioned, but haven't been there yet. It's a bit of a slum, isn't it? What do you think of Daisy Street, Sergeant?'

'The far part of it from the house in question is where the real slums start. I like to keep a close eye on that area. But the end of the street where the houses are is near to Birch End and isn't too bad. That part is currently being improved. The council got a grant, so some houses were condemned and knocked down and they're building new ones in their place, with proper modern drainage and amenities.'

Angus looked thoughtful. 'My senior partner is on the local council and I gather they're keen to get the whole of Backshaw Moss cleaned up. But there's apparently a group of men on the council who are against improvements. If I remember correctly, there's a builder chappie called Higgerson who owns slum properties there and is slowing the improvements down because his rents might go down. Am I right about the situation, Sergeant?'

'You are indeed, sir. The lady who died, a Miss Jane Chapman, owned three houses and left them to distant relatives. One has been handed over, but there are two still to be dealt with.' The sergeant looked at his pocket watch. 'Have to get on now. Why don't you let Mr Higgins drive you up to Backshaw Moss, then you can see for yourself?'

As his companions both nodded, he got to his feet. 'I'll show myself out.'

Angus turned an enquiring gaze on to Biff. 'You sure you have time?'

'Yes, and actually, I reckon I'd better take a look at those houses and the area nearby before we take Miss Lawson there. I'm a stranger to most of Backshaw Moss myself. All I know is how to get there and the house number.'

'I'd be grateful if you'd take me there. I'm definitely going to buy myself a car. Not much public transport round here, is there? Henry says I should see a chap called Todd Selby about that. He's apparently on the council too. How far away is this place? I've arranged to see Selby and a car he thinks might suit me at four o'clock.'

'It's only a couple of miles up the hill. We'll be back long before four, I'm sure. We can't get inside the house till Monday anyway. The keys have to be sent up from London, together with a copy of the will for you. I can drop that off at your rooms on Monday morning after it arrives.'

'Good idea.'

As they walked out to the car, he added, 'Will you be free on Monday afternoon, Mr McLean? I feel we should both accompany Miss Lawson up to the house after you've told her more about her inheritance. It wouldn't feel right to go inside without her.

'I'll catch her coming out of work this lunchtime and ask her if our arrangements suit. I've also got some good news for her.' He explained quickly about the Conway problem and the man leaving town suddenly.

It only took them a few minutes to drive up the hill and through Birch End to Daisy Street.

The two men got out of the car and stood looking at the three houses, which were identical in structure, with a central door and a window on either side of it, three windows on the floor above, and three smaller dormer windows in the roof, presumably for the attics. All the houses seemed to share a narrow front garden, which was in a mess in front of the two unoccupied houses but bore signs of having been recently cleared up in front of Number 23, the central house.

Across on the other side of the street was a building site, with bricklayers working on the walls of a new row of terraced houses, and a mess of earth and rubble spilling over on to the road in front of the space.

By unspoken agreement the two men stood looking round. Further along from the three houses were several smaller houses in miscellaneous styles, one or two of them looking quite old. Some of these were shabby, but they were all reasonably well maintained with no signs of leaks or broken windows.

There was a crossroad beyond them and beyond it Daisy Street was much narrower, angled slightly off towards the right. The first houses on that part looked to be in urgent need of maintenance. A couple of them had windows with a pane boarded up, and one was missing tiles from the roof.

Two ragged women were standing chatting near the first shabby house and a small child was playing with a ball, bouncing it against the nearby front door till one woman yelled at the little boy to 'stop making that racket or I'll clout yer lugs'.

'Clout yer lugs?' Angus queried.

'Box your ears, I think, from what I heard on my last visit.'

'I'm having trouble with the local dialect.'

'You don't have a strong Scottish accent.'

'No. My parents moved to London when I was twelve. You've only got a slight Irish accent.'

'For similar reasons.'

Angus jerked his head towards the far end of Daisy Street.

'I can see why Henry wants to improve this part of the valley if Backshaw Moss continues in that sort of condition.'

'I was told it gets worse in the side streets,' Biff said. 'Clover Lane is the worst, if I remember correctly, but I doubt if this area has seen any clover or daisies for decades. I didn't stay there long, didn't feel comfortable walking about on my own. I'd don some shabby clothes if I had to go there again to make myself less of a target for being mugged.'

'That bad? I'll take care not to go there, then.'

'Yes, that bad. But there seems to be an unwritten law not to bring unruly behaviour into Birch End.'

They strolled along the fronts of the three houses. There were narrow passages between the high walls enclosing the backyards of each house. These passages were paved with big flagstones. The two men chose to walk round the outside of the group, not go along any of the passages.

'Do we know who has inherited Number Twenty-five?' Angus asked.

'I don't. Mr Neven probably does but hasn't even hinted.'

'Well, the two outer houses certainly look to have been adequately maintained on the outside even if they've not been occupied. Miss Lawson shouldn't have to spend anything on Number Twenty-one.'

Even so, Biff couldn't see how she could afford to live there, unless she took in lodgers, but he didn't say that. He tried the gate of 21, but it was locked, so pulled himself up by the arms to peer over into its yard. 'Nothing to see.'

'I hope she has enough money to sort out the inside. If no one's been inside the last two houses for years, I should think they'll both be in a mess.'

'I doubt she has any money at all of her own.'

'I don't envy her the job of opening up the house, then.'

'If it's too much, I suppose she can always sell it.' Biff frowned. 'Unless there's a clause about that in the will.'

'We'll find that out on Monday.'

Biff intended to have a quick read of the will when it arrived before he passed it on to McLean. 'Funny sort of will, wasn't it?'

'But kind of the old lady to leave the houses to poorer relatives in need, don't you think?'

'I suppose so. The lady who inherited Number Twenty-three had a hard time of it because a rich relative was determined to take it off her. He didn't need the money, just wanted to keep her as an unpaid servant.'

'I hope this lady doesn't have grasping relatives to contend with.' McLean stopped again. 'The sides of the house don't show any signs of leaks or other weather damage, fortunately.'

'I don't know what she'll do, but if someone gave me a run-down house, I'd be happy to work my fingers to the bone to set it to rights again and have a home for the rest of my life.'

'I'd be the same.' Angus grinned. 'Even lawyers aren't necessarily born rich, you know. My family struggled to support me through university. What she really needs to look after it is a husband.'

'I agree. Well, there are heavy curtains drawn shut at all the windows so we won't be able to see inside till Monday. We might as well go back. I'll bring the will across to your rooms when it arrives in time for you to go through it. Miss Lawson will be at work now but fortunately Saturdays are half-closing and the local council is rather strict about enforcing that.'

'After I've looked at the will on Monday we'll all go and inspect the inside of the house with Miss Lawson, if she can get time off work. Will you be all right to drive us up there?'

'Of course.'

The two men returned to Rivenshaw and Biff dropped off the lawyer before strolling round the town again.

★

Early that afternoon he drove across town to wait for Maisie when the shop closed for its half day. He wasn't surprised when Gabriel drove up and joined him as he waited.

'How are things going?'

Biff shrugged. 'All right.'

He didn't volunteer any information and the shop assistants started coming out just then, so the two men turned to greet Maisie.

She looked anxiously from one to the other. 'Is everything all right?'

'Everything's fine.' Biff waited till the others had left and the three of them were alone. 'It looks as if you really are the heir, Miss Lawson. Can you come with me to visit Mr McLean, who is a lawyer, on Monday afternoon? He's going to arrange with your manager for you to take that afternoon off.'

'He'll have to be very persuasive. Mr Midgely has been very sharp about me having time off twice in a day, even though strictly speaking once wasn't time off but an early dinner break.'

'I'm sure he will be. Mr McLean will explain to you about Miss Chapman's will and then we'll take you to see your inheritance.'

'Can I bring Gabriel with me?' She flushed as she added, 'He and I are walking out together, so he'll be involved in all this.'

'Is this recent?'

'We've known one another for a while,' Gabriel said tactfully, 'but only just decided to take things further.'

She joined in. 'We didn't tell people till we were sure, then he told his mother yesterday.'

'Which made it official.' He smiled at her.

Biff smiled too. Anyone could see they were fond of one another. 'Congratulations. I've spoken to Sergeant Deemer and he has said how closely you resemble your mother, Miss Lawson. Do you have a birth certificate?'

She hesitated, then nodded. 'Only there isn't a father's name on it.' She threw one quick glance at her young man. 'My father had gone off to a job in London before she knew she was expecting, you see. That was one of the things I wasn't looking forward to telling you.'

Gabriel put one arm round her shoulders. 'I've already said, it doesn't matter to me what your mother did, Maisie.'

'It'll matter to other people if it gets known that I don't have a full birth certificate.'

'Do you know anything about your father?' Biff asked.

'I know his name, and there's a letter from him in with the birth certificate. I don't think he ever knew about my existence. He asked her to wait for him when he went to London, but he never came back, so she had me on her own. I think from the loving letter that he'd have married her if he'd found out she was expecting. I don't know what happened to him. Her parents threw her out when they found out, which is why I don't want anything to do with any of her family who may still be living in Rivenshaw.'

Biff cleared his throat to get their attention. 'That won't make any difference legally, as long as *you* aren't an immoral person. The lawyer will need to see your birth certificate, though. Do you have anything else from your mother's family?'

'Just an old sewing box. I think it must be very old. I looked in some books about furniture in the library and saw a photo of one like it dating from the 1860s.'

'It wouldn't hurt to bring that along as well. The keys should arrive from London on Monday morning and with them a copy of the will. Can you come to Mr McLean's office about one o'clock that afternoon and bring everything with you?'

'You're sure Mr Midgely will let me do that?'

'Yes. Sergeant Deemer will speak to Midgely to put pressure on. People in this town listen to him.'

'I'll drive you,' Gabriel offered.

'Thank you. I was going to ask you if you could come to see the lawyer with me, given that we're—' She hesitated.

'Courting,' he said firmly.

'Yes. I'd better get back to my lodgings now. Those of us who finish work at one o'clock have a sandwich lunch, and I don't want to miss out.'

Biff watched her drive off with Gabriel. He felt sorry for her mother. It was women who bore the shame of a child born out of wedlock and the men who'd been equally involved in creating that child often got away with it. He had an aunt who'd been caught out like that. Even though her man had married her, the baby had been born only four months after their wedding and she was looked down on afterwards. They'd emigrated to Canada in the end and not been heard of again.

Eh, you never knew where life would take you next. He hoped things would turn out all right for Maisie and her fellow. They both seemed decent types, and what a good-looking pair they made.

In the car Gabriel said abruptly, 'I don't care two hoots whether your mother was married or not.'

'If it gets known, some people won't speak to me.'

'There's no reason for people to find out.'

'If you and I get married I'll have to produce my birth certificate, and then people will see the words "father unknown". I don't want to do that to you, or your kind mother. I'd be really grateful, though, if you'd continue to pretend we're courting for a while.' She hesitated briefly then added, 'Sadly the more I think about what would be involved in us

marrying, the more I think I shouldn't impose on your kindness after it's settled whether I inherit the house or not.'

'I don't agree.'

She forced a smile as she gave him another opportunity to
stop seeing her. 'Sergeant Deemer says Conway has left town,
so I'll be all right if you – if you're having second thoughts
about us. I'll have somewhere to live rent free. I might take
in a lodger if the cottage I inherit is big enough.'

'I knew about Conway and I'm not having second thoughts
about us. Are you?'

'No. I like being with you.'

'Good. I feel the same.'

They stared at one another and both smiled at the same
time.

He took her hand. 'Let's carry on getting to know one
another, then. Don't make any rash decisions now or later
without talking to me about it. Promise me.'

She felt breathless and happy inside. She'd resigned herself
years ago to never getting married. She could come to terms
with that again if she had to.

But the idea of being part of a family was so – tempting.
And she really liked Gabriel Harte.

11

When Maisie left her lodgings on the Sunday morning to wait for Gabriel, who was going to escort her to church, she felt excited.

When she got into the van, Gabriel said, 'How about we go for a walk across the tops instead? It's cold but fine and the walking will keep us warm.'

'I'll have to change my shoes.'

'I can wait.'

He drove right up the hill to the village of Ellindale which lay on the edge of the moors, then left the van there.

It turned out to be one of the happiest days of her whole life. They started off walking along briskly in silence, but then began to chat. Soon they were eagerly exchanging views on anything and everything, since they both loved reading books and newspapers.

When they came back to the village they were hungry so Gabriel went to the back door of the little general store in Ellindale and persuaded its owner to sell them something to eat, even though it wasn't officially open.

They sat in the van munching apples, cheese and cream crackers, and drinking ginger beer made at the little factory in the village itself.

By the time Gabriel dropped Maisie at her lodgings they were far more comfortable with one another, and she was so tired that she slept like a log.

★

In the morning she put on her best clothes to go to work and waited for Mr Midgely to tell her she could have the afternoon off. She was sure he'd be in a bad mood about it and he was.

'It seems your lawyer needs to see you urgently,' he said sharply. 'Don't you think I should know what this is about?'

'I'm not sure myself. But if he needs to see me I hope to find out.'

'Well, I'll have to dock your pay.'

The manager was so sharp and huffy, she was relieved when time came to leave.

Gabriel was waiting for her outside and her heart lifted at the mere sight of him. She felt she knew him better after their long walk and chat, knew and liked him even more than she had before.

He kissed her cheek in greeting and she hoped Midgely was watching them.

Gabriel took her back to her lodgings first to collect the things she'd inherited from her mother, as Biff had suggested. She put the documents inside the sewing box and wrapped it in an old towel. It might not look very nice, but it was nobody else's business what she was carrying.

At the lawyer's rooms, Biff was sitting in the waiting area and gave them a cheerful smile, but she couldn't match it. She was nervous about seeing the lawyer.

'The parcel with the keys and a copy of the will arrived safely this morning,' he told them.

'Good.' As she looked round the nicely furnished waiting room, she wondered what this lawyer would think of her birth certificate and the old box as proof of who she was? Surely they'd be enough?

It was a relief when Mr McLean came out to greet them. He had such a lovely smile her worry immediately lessened.

After he'd ushered them into his office, he asked, 'Are those your family items?'

She nodded and watched as he took the bundle from Gabriel, set it down on his desk, and looked through the papers she'd brought.

'Why did you change your name?'

'So that I could make a new start. The bank manager's letter was in support of my reasons for that.'

'Ah yes. Good sort of witness to have, a bank manager.'

He unwrapped the box and his expression softened. 'This brings back happy memories. My grandma had one just like it and I loved to play with it as a child.'

She patted it fondly. 'I don't keep anything inside it except some of my mother's papers now. After she died, I found some money tucked inside the lining but I put that in the bank.'

When she showed him the gap, he nodded and asked, 'Does it have a secret drawer, too, like my grandma's did?'

She looked at him in surprise. 'Secret drawer? I've never noticed one.'

'May I?'

She watched as he studied the side panels, running his hands over them. She'd taken these to be simply decorations at each side of the box, but when he pressed both of the carved flowers in the back corners at the same time, there was a soft click.

'Aha!' He looked at her triumphantly.

As he pulled his fingers away she could see that the bottom panel on the right had opened slightly to reveal a shallow drawer.

She gasped and bent forward. How could she have missed that?

'Did you not know about this?' he asked.

'No. But my mother would never let me fiddle around with it and bought me my own sewing box.'

Why hadn't her mother said anything later, though, as

Maisie grew up? Probably because no one expected to die at the age of forty-seven, least of all an optimist like Ida.

Everyone watched in fascination as Mr McLean pulled the drawer fully open to reveal the papers it contained.

'Let's look at them.' He picked up the top envelope and studied the post office date stamp. 'This was sent twenty-five years ago, and it's addressed to Miss I. Fletcher.'

'My mother.'

He slipped the letter out of it and studied the signature. 'It's from a Simeon Lawson.'

'My father, well I think he is.'

'Perhaps you'd like to read it to us?'

She took the letter from him, her breath catching in her throat, and it was a moment or two before she could begin to read.

My dearest Ida,

I've found a good job now and I'm sure we'll build a better life here in London, away from both our families.

I've even found a nice room as well, but it won't be vacant for another two weeks, so I'll be coming to pick you up then and bring you back to London. Then we can start our married life together properly.

I've kept our marriage certificate safe, so no one in your family can destroy it, as they threatened.

Maisie gasped and stared round. 'Marriage certificate! Mam never said she'd married my father. She only told me his name once, and that was by mistake. But I've never forgotten how gentle her voice sounded and how sad she looked. I could tell how much she'd loved him. She wouldn't share anything else about him, though, said you just had to carry on.'

She continued reading aloud slowly.

I miss you dreadfully, my lovely lass, and hate having to pretend that we're not man and wife. Your parents were wrong to try to stop us getting married, just because they didn't get on with my family. If I'd had a proper job and somewhere for you to live, I'd have brought you with me straight away, as you begged.

I'll send the details of when I'm coming to pick you up in my next letter after I've booked my train ticket.

Your loving husband,
Simeon

No one spoke until she looked up, brushing tears from her eyes with one fingertip.

Mr McLean took the letter from her and put it back into the envelope. 'I'll give it back to you eventually, but for the moment, it's important evidence.'

He took the next paper out of the drawer, a much smaller one that looked like a cutting from a newspaper. 'I can't tell which newspaper this came from, Maisie. It says— Oh, no!'

When he held it out she saw that it was a death notice for a Simeon Lawson, dated only a week after the letter.

Tears came into her eyes. She'd found a father only to lose him almost immediately. How must her poor mother have felt?

It made her feel so sad that it was a moment before it sank in what this meant for her. She wasn't bastard born. All her life she'd tried to hide the shame of that, and suddenly it felt as if a weight had been lifted from her shoulders.

When she glanced at Gabriel, he beamed at her as if he understood what she was thinking, looking as if he'd just received some good news too. Was it possible he might really want to marry her? Did she dare believe in something as wonderful as that?

But how could she prove, after all these years, that her

parents had been married when she didn't have the marriage certificate? If her father had been in lodgings, the landlord would probably have kept his possessions after he died. The marriage certificate would be long lost, which would explain the lack of a father's name on her birth certificate.

She realised the lawyer was speaking to her again and tried to pay attention.

'You've had a shock, Miss Lawson. Please take a minute or two to pull yourself together. We don't need to carry on till you're ready.'

She reached out to clutch Gabriel's hand, feeling as if the foundations of her world had been shaken. But all three men were waiting for her, so after a minute or two she forced herself to let go of the warm hand and sat up straighter, not wanting to seem a weak person. 'I'm in control of my emotions now. Please continue.'

Mr McLean nodded in her direction. 'Good. Just let us know if you feel at all faint.'

'Thank you, but I'm not the fainting sort.'

He gave her an approving glance. 'Do you have your birth certificate?'

'I only have one that says "father unknown".' She took it out of the main part of the sewing box and gave it to him. 'It's wrong, isn't it? Why do you think my mother put that?'

'Probably had to because she didn't have her marriage certificate to prove anything different.' He studied the birth certificate she'd given him. 'May I keep this for a day or two as well?'

'Yes, of course.'

'If necessary, you know, we can get a copy of their marriage certificate.'

'I don't know where they were married, even.'

Biff intervened. 'I can find that out for you.'

The lawyer took over again. 'Fortunately, Miss Chapman

left an addendum to her will which makes it clear that if the person named in any of the bequests is dead, the house is to pass to *the eldest surviving child*. It says nothing about whether that child had to be legitimate or not, so with your birth certificate and the letter from your father, plus the sergeant's statement about how closely you resemble your mother, I see no difficulty in confirming that you're the person who should receive the legacy.'

She could only nod.

'I'll check with Mr Neven as to whether we need to obtain a copy of the marriage certificate, but I'm sure he'll agree with me that there's no need. I'll take an official declaration from the sergeant about the resemblance, just to be safe.'

She sagged in relief. 'Thank you.'

'The ceremony must have happened in the vicinity of Rivenshaw. Your mother was over twenty-one at the date on this letter?' He looked at Maisie, who nodded.

'Good. So she was legally able to marry without her parents' permission. There is one other piece of information for whoever inherits Number Twenty-one: the contents of the house are included in the inheritance and the heir is advised to go through them very carefully indeed before throwing anything away.'

She was surprised that her kind relative had thought it necessary to say this. She'd never in her whole life been able to afford to throw anything away as long as it had any use, even a worn-out garment that was only fit to use as a mopping rag. And if she had no use for an item herself, someone else usually did. She'd given garments she considered worn out to people begging on the street corners and seen them gratefully accepted.

Oh dear! She was keeping them waiting again. 'Of course I'll check everything in the house carefully, Mr McLean. It's what I would have done anyway.'

He glanced towards the window. 'I think we should now go and see the house you've inherited before it gets dark, because even if the house has an electricity connection, it won't be working till you've signed up for it again.'

'My employer worked on the modernisations to Number Twenty-three,' Gabriel said. 'It didn't have electricity or inside plumbing, so I doubt Number Twenty-one will have.'

'We should waste no time going there, then, while it's still light. You can leave your box and papers here, Miss Lawson. They'll be perfectly safe.'

'What's the address of my cottage, Mr McLean?'

'Sorry. Didn't I tell you? It's on Daisy Street, Number Twenty-one.'

'Whereabouts in Backshaw Moss is that?'

'In the better part, almost in Birch End. Though it's not what I'd call a cottage; it's a house.'

Whatever it was, it would seem like a palace to her. She'd only ever lived in rented rooms.

'Right then. Mr Higgins has kindly agreed to drive us all there.'

She was installed in the front passenger seat but it was hard to sit still as she was driven up the hill, she was so excited. She was praying it'd be a pretty house, a place where she could settle in and never have to move again. Even becoming a lodger at Mrs Tucker's had been good because she'd been able to stay in the same place for a few years.

She watched out of the window as they turned off the main road and went through Birch End. When the car stopped next to three large detached dwellings, however, she looked at the lawyer in puzzlement.

Before she could ask why they were stopping, Gabriel got out and opened the car door for her.

'That's your house, Number Twenty-one.' The lawyer pointed to the third house from the end of the street, a big detached residence.

She was speechless, staring from the house to Mr McLean, then back again. He was holding a key out to her, but she was so shocked she couldn't move to take it.

He put the key into her hand. 'It seems appropriate that you should be the one to unlock the door, Miss Lawson. Before you do that, however, I'd better warn you that no one has been inside the house for several years, even though the outside has been carefully maintained. I have no idea what it's like inside, or indeed whether it's furnished or not, because as you can see, there are heavy curtains at all the windows.'

Her breath caught in her throat and even though she knew she was keeping the others waiting, she didn't move till she'd studied the exterior once more. How could she possibly own a house as big as this?

Only after Gabriel had given her a gentle poke in the side did she begin to move slowly along the short paved path to the front door.

What would they find inside?

12

Gareth Higgerson scowled at his wife. 'I think I'll take a turn round the garden for a while. I do not wish to be disturbed. It will be nice to have a bit of peace while I get some winter sunshine on my face.'

Did he think she wasn't aware of why he was going out? Probably. He was arrogant enough to believe everyone else in his household was stupid. When the back door closed behind him, Lallie ran up to the spare bedroom, certain he was up to something.

She peered cautiously round the edge of the curtain. Sure enough, that horrible, sly fellow who worked for her husband was standing just inside the garden near the back gate, hidden from the rear alley and from everyone in the house except her.

The servants knew better than to go outside when the master was taking the air, but she didn't think any of them realised that Lallie had found a way to see who he chatted to out there, let alone that she could sometimes tell what they were saying by reading the movements of their lips.

Her mother had been better at that than her, because her grandfather had been deaf. She'd taught Lallie to do it, not only for fun, but so that the two of them could communicate without anyone overhearing. She and her mother had both been forced to marry unkind men and had needed to protect themselves in any way they could.

Lallie had taught her own sons to lip-read for similar

reasons. She smeared away a tear at the thought of her boys. Her elder son, Felix, had been twenty when he'd run away after a violent quarrel caused by his refusal to ill-treat those who worked for his father, and an equally firm refusal to cheat anyone he dealt with to increase the final profits.

Before he left, he'd told her that his father's slum properties were not only immoral but dangerous because of overcrowding and poor maintenance. Lallie agreed, but she had never dared even hint at her feelings about how her husband made his money.

Meanwhile her younger son, Kit, had only a few months to go before he finished his schooling at a fancy boarding school chosen by Gareth so that his sons could meet useful people from good northern families. As if good families would ever acknowledge Gareth socially. None of the ones she'd grown up knowing had so much as called on her after her marriage.

It hadn't occurred to Gareth that his sons would also meet different moral views of the world at the boarding school, thank goodness.

After Kit finished his schooling he'd be facing the same dilemma as his brother: whether to work for his father or not. Gareth had already told Kit that he must take his older brother's place and work in the family business, and then he'd inherit everything one far-away day. But she'd seen her son's face become expressionless as he said, 'Yes, father.' She'd been able to tell how reluctant his nod had been, even if her husband couldn't.

She didn't think Kit would agree to work like that, either, but he was a clever lad and knew he could do nothing about his future life yet. She could only hope his brother had kept in touch with him and would help him after he left school.

She closed her eyes for a moment to push way the pain of not having seen Felix for two years, then returned to watching the two men in the garden. She managed to pick up some parts of what they were saying, but wished she could see her husband's face better. This meeting was taking place because Gareth was planning to cheat someone else by paying a lot less than a property was worth, it seemed.

While she watched, she rubbed the sore bruise on her upper arm absent-mindedly. Gareth hadn't hit her for a while, but he'd suddenly started doing it again. She made sure she yelled as loudly as she could whenever he did it, so that the maids could overhear, but she had no way of protecting herself from his blows, and he just laughed at her screams as if enjoying them.

The servants were on her side and occasionally managed to help her in small ways, but most of the time they were even more helpless against Gareth than she was. They had seen maids who dared to leave their employment against his wishes regret it and end up begging on the streets unless they'd managed to find a job away from the valley.

She prayed every night that her husband would drop dead, and if that was morally wrong, she didn't care. He was a wicked man and the world would be a better place without him.

Higgerson listened intently to the man standing near the garden gate, cap in hand. Dobbs had found out who had inherited 21 Daisy Street, and Higgerson was growing angrier by the minute about it. He'd had his eyes on those houses for a while because they were perfectly suited to his purpose. He'd lost the middle one to a woman who had suddenly turned up in the valley claiming to be the heir and tricked people into supporting her.

He'd not managed to get rid of Bella once and for all as she deserved, the upstart bitch. Not yet. But one day he would, and then he'd take over Number 23.

And now another woman had inherited 21, damn her.

On top of the frustration about that, there had been some unhelpful changes to the town council in the last elections which had taken away his majority support on it and made it more difficult to carry out certain plans.

Well, those who went against him would find they'd been foolish. He was making plans for the future of his business and for dealing with the interfering sergeant. He had a few friends in useful positions in the county and was going to call in a favour or two when the time was right.

The trouble was, you could only call in a business favour once, so it didn't pay to use it wastefully.

Deemer was getting on in years and should be easier to get rid of now. A little accident that left him too incapacitated to work wouldn't be easy to arrange, but it'd be Gareth's preferred option, because he'd enjoy seeing the old man help-less. He had nearly succeeded in getting rid of Deemer a while back, but someone had helped the sergeant escape from his trap.

His thoughts returned to the three houses on Daisy Street and he sighed. They'd be perfect for turning into multiple rooms for letting and would bring in a fortune if their interiors were changed to create superior rooms at the rear of each ground floor to accommodate the better class of whores.

His brothel in Backshaw Moss had proved to be his most lucrative investment over the years, closely followed by his houses in Primrose Lane, where he'd managed to cram whole families into single rooms, and make an extra room in the cellars by a little judicious digging out of more space beneath the houses.

He kept the roofs waterproof, of course, but hadn't wasted his money on other repairs, let alone fancy modern services like electricity and more than a cold water tap inside each house. Why, even his own house didn't have electricity up in the servants' attics.

He scowled at the thought of how the council had recently obtained a special grant and wasted it on knocking down the row of houses at the end of Daisy Street, two of which had been bringing him steady money for years. The compensation money he'd received for the compulsory purchase of the houses had been pitiful.

The council had even run the sewage line and electricity poles into that end of the street now. Talk about coddling the poor. No wonder the rates were so high for house owners in the valley.

Backshaw Moss was *his* territory, he'd bought into it over the years. Even the council didn't know how many houses he owned under other names.

Dobbs cleared his throat to get his attention. 'They're saying this young woman who inherited the house is Ida Fletcher's daughter. The one who was going to marry Simeon Lawson till we stepped in.'

Gareth came as near to smiling as he ever did. 'We put paid to that and rid the valley of a troublemaker at the same time, didn't we?'

'We certainly did, sir.'

'Lawson shouldn't have crossed me.'

'You have some clever ideas for making money or getting rid of troublemakers, Mr Higgerson. I admire that, I really do. Never seen anyone think up ideas like you do. She never come back to Rivenshaw, did she?'

'She wouldn't have dared. She knew I'd get rid of her if she did. But that's old history and if the daughter has inherited, then Ida must be dead. What I need now is to see what exactly that damned will says about who is to inherit the third house.

And I need some way to speak to the heir to Number Twenty-one. I'd prefer to buy her house legally, even though it'll cost me more.'

'She goes to your church.'

'Does she? She must be ugly or I'd have noticed her.'

'Sits near the back, quiet sort of woman, keeps her head down. Not your sort at all, sir. I could bring her across to have a word with you after the service. People often stay behind for a chat, and it's nice and quiet among the graves at the rear.'

'Point her out to me in church and bring her to speak to me. It's about time I attended again anyway.'

Dobbs grimaced.

'And you keep going to church regularly. That means every single week. If you think I don't know you've missed a couple of Sundays, you're losing your grip. I pay you to keep an eye on these so-called respectable folk, and you'll just have to put up with being bored by the services.'

'Yes, Mr Higgerson. Sorry about that. I've been a bit under the weather.'

'Ignore it. We all have our bad days, but we don't let them interfere with what needs doing.' At the moment Gareth was finding the thought of turning sixty very annoying. He'd expected to have retired from active work by now and be living at the seaside. But he wanted to live there in style, not in an ordinary house like he had here. And for that he needed those houses on Daisy Street and the ongoing income they'd give him.

'That's all for now.' Higgerson waved one hand dismissively.

By the time Gareth came in from the garden, Lallie was downstairs again, and was bent over some embroidery in her little sitting room.

He gave her one of his wolfish smiles, which instantly told her that he was plotting something.

'I think I'll attend church with you next Sunday, my dear.'

She managed to hide her disappointment. He didn't often attend church and she enjoyed being away from the house and him, chatting to friends without worrying about whether he was eavesdropping.

But she didn't dare say anything except, 'Yes, Gareth.'

The front-door lock was stiff and it took Maisie a couple of tries to turn the big old-fashioned key. When she heard a click suddenly, Gabriel had to remind her to turn the doorknob as well. Oh dear, she was losing her wits with the surprise of being left such a big house. They would think her an utter fool.

She was rather worried about what they might find inside if the place had been shut up for so long. Taking a deep breath, she pushed the door wide open.

The three men held back, letting her go in first.

She didn't go far because it was so dim inside and hard to see clearly with the only light coming from behind her. She sneezed suddenly and no wonder! You could see the dust floating in the air after being disturbed by the door opening. It was lying thickly on the floor and the furniture. She wouldn't like to sit on that hall chair till the layer of dust had been removed.

There were doors leading off the hall, but though they were open, not much light came from beyond them. She could make out the faint outline of a window at the far side of the nearest room, which was the front of the house. The heavy curtains they'd seen from outside were closed, though.

A musty smell made her wrinkle her nose; but as her eyes gradually grew more accustomed to the dimness, she realised that the hall was larger than she'd expected, larger than any of the rooms she'd ever lived in. Wooden panelling covered all the walls to just above her head height, but it was dull, needing a good polish, and the parquet floor was so dusty she couldn't make out its condition.

'Do you want me to go round and open the curtains downstairs, Miss Lawson?' Mr Higgins asked.

'I think I'd rather do that myself as we come to each room, if you don't mind. It'll be a help if you close them after we leave the rooms, though, to keep people from staring in.'

'Happy to help in any way.' He stepped back.

She took a quick glance sideways. Gabriel had stayed closer to her than the others. He was staring round as if shocked rigid by what he could see. Well, the house was so *big*. Why would someone have left it to her mother?

She tried to think what to do first. 'We should leave the front door wide open while we go round, to let some fresh air in as well as light, don't you think?'

There was a murmur of agreement from the three men.

She walked forward to the nearest doorway. It must have been the sitting room, judging by the sofa she could see inside. When she pushed the door fully open, however, she stopped in surprise at how much furniture was crammed into the room. Far too much, even for a huge room like this, with some pieces piled on top of others. She moved forward slowly and carefully, nudging a low stool out of the way with one foot, edging to and fro to avoid various pieces of furniture that seemed simply to have been dumped there.

She was aware that her companions were still standing in the doorway, but felt the most important thing was to draw back the curtains and see the room properly before it filled with people. It took a couple of tugs to get one of the heavy curtains moving, but as its brass rings jerked along the rail, dust showered from it and she jumped back, sneezing several times. She pulled her handkerchief out of her pocket but it wasn't big enough to tie across her nose and mouth.

'Here. Use mine.' Gabriel came into the room and thrust

it into her hand, giving her a searching glance and whispering, 'You all right?'

'Yes, thanks.' She raised her voice again. 'Stand back, everyone, or you'll get covered in dust, too.' She made a triangle of the large handkerchief and tied it round her nose and mouth, knocking her beret crooked. Impatient to continue, she pulled it off and stuffed it into her coat pocket anyhow before turning again to tug the curtains apart in a series of small, dust-showering jerks. What her hair now looked like she dreaded to think.

Beneath the heavy velvet curtains were cotton lace curtains covering the whole window and they looked filthy. She left them in place because they let in enough light to see the room, but still prevented passers-by from peeping in.

She was awestruck at how fine the furniture was. You could tell, somehow, from its elegant, balanced shapes and curves. But why was there so much of it? You could hardly thread your way across the room, there were so many smaller tables and chairs between the sofas and armchairs. Several bookcases stood sentinel round the walls, and there was a large glass-fronted cabinet full of ornaments to her left.

You'd never be able to sit comfortably in here till you'd removed three-quarters of the furniture.

'Do come in and look round, gentlemen,' she called, 'but be careful you don't trip over anything.'

They moved forward slowly and carefully.

'I've never seen anything like it,' Mr McLean said, and Mr Higgins murmured agreement.

Gabriel had stayed near her. Strange how his mere presence made her feel more courageous.

Mr Higgins stopped suddenly 'Good heavens! That's a piano over against the back wall. It's got things piled all over the top.'

Maisie couldn't resist going across to it, moving some books from the lid of the keyboard and lifting it. She pressed a few notes at random, intending to pick out the tune of 'Cherry Ripe' as she had learned to do at a friend's house. She'd always wanted to learn to play the piano properly.

Unfortunately the noises that came out weren't very musical and Gabriel chuckled. 'There's a good piano tuner in Rivenshaw.'

Mr Higgins took out his watch. 'If you don't mind me saying so, I think we should only look quickly into the rest of the rooms, Miss Lawson, because we don't have time to look at them all in detail before it grows dark, given that the house has three floors.'

'I suppose you're right. Do you know how the house is laid out, Mr McLean?'

'I'm afraid I have no idea. The hall isn't quite like the one at Number Twenty-three.'

'We'll have to find out as we go, then.' Once again they waited for her to lead the way and she felt like an explorer in the wilderness. She wondered if she'd ever feel at home in such a large house.

The room across the hall and the one behind it were just as full of furniture as the sitting room had been, and there were also tea chests at whose contents they could only guess.

'There's more than enough stuff here to furnish a dozen smaller houses,' she muttered. 'Surely even rich people don't normally live like this?'

She saw Gabriel and Mr Higgins look at the lawyer, who probably came from the richest family background of any of them.

'No one I know or have ever visited has anything like this much furniture in their homes,' he said. 'It must have been put here for some reason, but it baffles me what. It's actually more like a furniture shop than a dwelling.'

'The kitchen should be at the back of the house,' Mr Higgins said. 'It usually is. How about trying that door over there, to the rear of the hall?'

She opened it to further darkness because it led into a narrow corridor with no windows. 'I'm a bit nervous of walking blindly forward,' she admitted.

'Shall I go first?' Mr Higgins asked. 'I'm told I have good night vision.'

'Please do.'

The first door he opened revealed a big cupboard full of glasses, dishes and vases. One shelf held what looked like a matching set of fine china crockery.

The second door opened on another cupboard, but the third took them into the kitchen, which was large and very old-fashioned. Since it had ill-fitting blinds on the windows they could see roughly what it was like even before Mr Higgins raised one of them.

There was a coal-fired kitchen range and old-fashioned gas wall lights. She sighed with relief as she saw a gas cooker underneath piles of saucepans partly covered by a couple of dusty, greyish tea towels.

When they went beyond the kitchen into a scullery, they found a huge brownstone sink with low sides and one tap at the back corner. Did the kitchen range heat the water, then? She'd have to get a gas geyser if she came to live here.

She couldn't help thinking 'if' every time she thought of doing that, because it continued to feel so unreal.

Gabriel reached out to turn on the tap and it made some groaning noises before spurting out brown water intermittently till he switched it off. 'The plumbing and gas will need attention. Goodness knows how many things won't be working properly after being left for so long.'

Maisie opened some of the cupboard doors, gasping at the sight of piles of everyday crockery and dishes of all sorts in the upper cupboards. There were smaller cooking and baking utensils in the lower ones, and larger saucepans and frying pans hanging from a ceiling rack. 'How many people lived here to need so much equipment?'

'You couldn't fit enough people in the house to need this much,' Mr McLean said. 'And since there are several different patterns of crockery, I'd guess some came from elsewhere.'

Why? she wondered, but didn't say it aloud.

'Shall we go upstairs now?' Gabriel prompted. 'We won't have daylight for much longer.'

'Yes.' By now she was so shocked by what they'd found that she didn't care what the others thought, but grabbed Gabriel's hand openly for reassurance as they walked up the stairs together. The other men followed a few steps behind them. Everyone was silent. Were they as surprised as she was by what they'd found?

It was the same story in the five bedrooms on the first floor. Two or three beds in each room, chests of drawers galore, and when Maisie opened a couple of the drawers they proved to be full of what looked like very old-fashioned men's undergarments. Ugh. How ugly!

The wardrobes had both women's and men's clothes hanging in them, and again, some were extremely old-fashioned. Two bedrooms contained children's clothes, and a dusty teddy bear sat in forlorn state on one chest of drawers.

It looked so like the drawings in one of her favourite children's books, *Winnie-the-Pooh*, that she couldn't help picking it up.

She saw Mr McLean smiling at that, but it was a nice smile not a sneering one.

'It looks like the teddy bear in my niece's favourite book,' he said.

'*Winnie-the-Pooh*.'

'That's the one. If I've read it to her once, I've read it fifty times.'

She smiled. 'I've read it more than once as well. But for myself. I was sixteen when I saw the book in the library and I borrowed it because I loved the illustrations. My mother said I was stupid to read a children's book.'

'Then I'm stupid too. Have you read the sequel, *The House at Pooh Corner*?'

'Yes.' She had a sudden thought. Once she'd settled down, she might even be able to buy copies of the books for herself. There was a bookshop in Rivenshaw that she hadn't let herself visit in case she was tempted to spend her money. She looked at the display in its window sometimes, though. Perhaps she wouldn't have to watch every penny she spent from now on.

She shook the bear to get rid of some of the dust and took it with her when they left the bedroom.

'None of it makes sense,' Gabriel muttered. 'Why is there so much furniture?'

'Who knows?'

'Was your relative, um, in her dotage?' Mr McLean asked.

'I have no idea. I've never met her – or any other Chapmans, either.'

He looked surprised.

'There must be something in the house to explain it,' Mr Higgins said. 'Though I doubt we'll find it today.'

Gabriel tugged her hand. 'Come on. We've just time to check the attics.'

Half the attic consisted of a large space full of boxes and other clutter. Along one side were three very small bedrooms and these were the only rooms in the house not crammed with furniture. They were bare, except for each having an iron bed frame and a rolled-up flock mattress so dusty that they'd need a good beating out in the open air before they could be used.

'Servants' rooms probably,' Mr Higgins said.

Well, the owner can't have cared about the comfort of her servants, then, she thought, but didn't like to criticise the person who'd left all this to her mother and her.

She turned back to go down the narrow stairs. She felt as if her head was bursting with images of rooms full of furniture and was almost glad it was getting dark so that the visit would have to end. She needed time to think about all she'd seen today.

She cuddled the teddy bear even closer. It had such a nice little face. It was almost as if she'd found a friend – or the toy bear she'd always wanted and her mother had refused to spend money on.

'We'd better go downstairs again, don't you think?' Mr McLean gestured to her to lead the way, so she did.

At the bottom she took Gabriel's hand again. It felt so comforting.

13

Darkness was falling fast as they left the house. Maisie took the key out of her pocket and locked the front door behind them but when she held it out to the lawyer, he smiled. 'It's yours now.'

She was glad to sit quietly in the car and be driven away. She stuffed the toy bear into her handbag out of sight, sure the men would think her stupid to keep it.

More than anything else, having the large old-fashioned key weighing down her bag made her feel as if she really did own the house. That thought made her breath catch in her throat.

When they stopped the lawyer said abruptly, 'Can you come to my rooms tomorrow, Miss Lawson and we'll discuss what to do next? Unless you have some special need to see me sooner, in which case I'm completely at your service at any hour of the day or night.' He took out a business card and scribbled on the back of it. 'This is my home address, just in case.'

'I shall have to go to work again tomorrow. I can't keep taking time off.'

'But surely you don't intend to continue working at that shop?'

That thought made her stare. 'I haven't got so far in thinking it all out. What would I live on without a wage?'

He smiled. 'You have plenty of objects to sell, and you need to clear some space in the house. Actually, if some of that furniture is of as good a quality as I think, it wouldn't matter if you didn't earn any money for a year or two, if not longer. You'd only need to sell a few pieces to live comfortably.'

Oh, what a lovely thought, not going back to that boring job and no longer having to kowtow to Mr Midgely. The idea of freedom from his peremptory orders and ridiculous fussing over customers as if they were gods come down among fools lodged in her mind and filled her with happy hope. After all, she had her savings to fall back on as well. She'd not told any of these people how much that was, not even Gabriel.

Then she sighed. How could she live in that big house on her own? She'd be far too nervous and it wouldn't be respectable anyway. Besides, it'd need clearing out before anyone could live there. She'd have to think about it, work out what was the best way to deal with her inheritance.

She realised Mr McLean was waiting for her answer. 'Sorry. I hadn't thought about giving up work, so you took me by surprise.'

'Do you enjoy working there? The manager seems very . . . well, officious.'

'He's a tyrant.' She turned to look at Gabriel, needing his approval, somehow. 'I can give up work, can't I?'

'Of course you can. In fact, you *should*.'

'It will only be fair to go into the shop tomorrow morning and let Mr Midgely know I'm leaving. I'm supposed to give a week's notice.' Oh, how wonderful it would be to see his face when she told him about her inheritance!

When she got out of the car, the lawyer came to stand beside her and say earnestly, 'You don't need to rush into anything, Miss Lawson. It might be best to ask for a few days off work and not tell them any details until later. There will be a lot of paperwork to deal with, as well as checking out everything in the house. No reasonable boss would refuse you, given the circumstances.'

'Mr Midgely isn't at all reasonable.'

'Hmm. I must admit I didn't find him easy to deal with.'

One thing was certain: she wouldn't be able to concentrate on slicing bacon and fawning over customers if she still felt this confused about the future, and she was always aware of how dangerous the equipment could be if used carelessly. One of the shop lads had cut his finger very badly. Mr Midgely had been more annoyed that they had to cut off some of the blood-stained bacon and throw it away than the fact that the lad had lost a fingertip. Only he hadn't thrown it away, had he. He'd wrapped it up and put it in his drawer. He'd prob-ably fed it to his cat.

She couldn't pretend nothing had happened. They'd soon find out about her inheritance, she was sure. Someone would have seen her going into the house or leaving it, and wondered what she was doing there.

In the end she said, 'It's a lot to take in. Would it be all right for me to go back tomorrow and look at the house properly, Mr McLean?'

'I can't see any reason why not, but I'd advise you not to go there on your own.'

'No, I wouldn't like to do that.'

He glanced quickly at his wristwatch and frowned. 'If there's nothing else you need tonight, perhaps you'd like to pick up your box from my office and then I must go home for tea.'

She'd watched enviously as he checked the time. More and more men were wearing strap watches now, and older men had stopped calling them 'ladies' bracelet watches' in scornful tones. Some people had taken to calling them 'wristwatches', whether it was women or men wearing them.

No wonder they had become popular. They were so much easier than taking out an old-fashioned pocket watch and opening it to look at the time, then putting it away again. Or opening a fob watch pinned to your bodice and looking at it upside down, as ladies coming to the shop sometimes did. Mr McLean was too young to have served in the war and at first it had been mostly former officers who wore the modern watches, her mother had said.

Perhaps she would be able to afford a cheap wristwatch now. It'd be so useful. Her only way of telling the time in her room at Mrs Tucker's was a battered old alarm clock with an annoyingly loud tick. It had belonged to her mother and sat by her bed at Mrs Tucker's. No, she mustn't even think of such extravagant purchases until she was sure where she stood financially.

She went inside the lawyer's rooms and he took her box out of a cupboard. Gabriel was about to pick it up and carry it out for her when she had an idea. And yes, the teddy bear fitted perfectly inside it. She couldn't resist patting it before she closed the lid and caught both men smiling at that. But once again, they were kind smiles.

'It's a nice bear,' Mr McLean said. 'My sister had one, but I never liked its face, or the hump in its back. Your bear looks to be smiling and it hasn't got a hump.'

It seemed to her that even the bear was smiling.

After watching the lawyer go back inside his office, Maisie turned to Gabriel. Would you be able to get time off work tomorrow and come with me to the house?'

'Probably.'

But Mr Higgins was looking thoughtful. 'May I come with you as well, Miss Lawson? I'm being paid by Mr Neven to keep an eye on you.'

Gabriel gave a quick nod. 'I think that's a good idea, Maisie.'

'So do I. We'd be happy to have your company and help, Mr Higgins.'

'Good. Do you want me to drive you back to your lodgings now, Miss Lawson?'

'Yes, please.'

Gabriel intervened. 'Mum says to invite you to tea, Maisie, and I've got my van. I can take you home again after our meal. Why don't you join us as well, Mr Higgins? You'll be all on your own this evening, otherwise.'

He looked surprised. 'I couldn't impose.'

Gabriel smiled. 'It's not imposing. We're only going to buy fish and chips from the chippie in Birch End. It's cheaper on Mondays because they use up the fish from the weekend before it goes off.'

'I'd love to come to tea.' Biff hesitated, then turned back to Maisie. 'Actually, Mr Neven has asked me to stay on in Rivenshaw for a week because he's rather worried about your safety. I prefer to do that openly, with your consent. Only, I can't help noticing how nervous you are at times, so maybe it won't upset you to have me around as well?'

She couldn't help shuddering. 'Upset me? I'd be grateful to have you around still. You're right. Since I was attacked, I feel nervous whenever I go out.'

'I can probably take time off work tomorrow, but not for the whole week,' Gabriel said. 'And I'll have to go in and ask for tomorrow off. It'd only be fair. So it'd be good to know Maisie will be safe with you, Mr Higgins, in case Mr Tyler can't do without me.'

She smiled at them, thinking how lucky she was to have two protectors. 'Thank you. Um, in that case, had we perhaps better say that Mr Higgins is a distant cousin of mine? Otherwise people will wonder why I'm spending so much time with him during the coming week when I'm supposed to be walking out with you.'

Gabriel nodded approvingly. 'Clever thinking.'

'Then if I'm a relative, you'd better start calling me Biff.' He gave her a wry smile. 'It sounds more friendly, anyway.'

'Biff it is, then. And I'm Maisie.'

Anna Jacobs

Gabriel smiled at them both. 'That's settled, then. Now, let's drop off the sewing box at your lodgings quickly before I take you to my home. I'm famished.'

'So am I.' She and Biff said it at the same time and chuckled, which relaxed the tension still further.

'You can follow us there, Mr Higgins – I mean, Biff.'

In case they got separated Gabriel explained how to get to his mother's house, then he and Maisie called in at her lodgings and told the landlady she'd be going to his mother's for tea.

After that they enjoyed a few quiet moments on the way back up to Birch End, sharing their amazement at the discoveries made that day, especially the fact that Maisie's mother and father had been secretly married.

'What I can't understand is why this Miss Chapman crammed all that furniture into the house,' Maisie admitted. 'What on earth am I supposed to do with it all?'

Gabriel stopped the car. 'What Mr McLean said: sell it.'

Biff drew up behind them just then, so she didn't pursue that point. It was the obvious solution, after all. Only, what did she know about the value of antique furniture? Nothing, that's what. She'd hardly ever had even a comfortable armchair to sit on till she took up lodgings with Mrs Tucker.

But she didn't like to take such a drastic step as selling things until she had some idea what her kind relative wanted doing with it all. There must be some reason for leaving it there. It was so frustrating.

It was just as Gabriel had told them, the meal cost very little except for the cups of tea provided by Mrs Harte, since they all paid for their own fish and chips. A couple of older neighbours had joined them, casually invited as they all queued at the chip shop. Mrs Harte was such a friendly person.

It was fun to eat the food out of the newspaper it was wrapped in and to chat with such kind people.

Maisie blushed a few times at the sly teasing about her and Gabriel getting together. If she ever got her future settled and had a bit of money to spare, she'd be kind to lonely people too.

'You've done all right there, lass,' one old lady said to her when Gabriel was speaking to someone else. 'Nice lad, Gabriel. His younger brother's a nice lad too. Eh, he's a real bookworm that Lucas is. Good thing the library is free, or he'd need a fortune to buy all them books he reads.'

The only ones who didn't tease them were Mrs Harte and Lucas, but they made her feel welcome, and what more could you want? Mrs Harte rolled her eyes at something one neighbour said and told her to stop teasing the poor lass or she'd never come again.

'Eh, I didn't mean to upset you,' the woman said at once. 'It's just that anyone can see how well you two suit one another, and it's about time Gabriel started walking out with someone, yes, and got wed too, or poor Gwynneth will never have any grandchildren to play with.'

Which made Maisie blush all over again.

Biff too fitted in well. He seemed to have the ability to get on with all sorts of people, and everyone accepted that he was some sort of cousin, one woman even saying she could see the family resemblance.

Maisie was sorry when the evening ended and she had to go back to the quiet of her little room at Mrs Tucker's.

When she was alone, Maisie took the teddy bear out of the box and sat him next to her bed for company.

Mr McLean was right. The bear did seem to be smiling at her.

'What's your name?' she asked it. 'How about Walter? No, that's too solemn.'

Then she remembered a young heroine in one of her childhood books who had called her teddy Archibald.

'What do you think of that for a name?'

She liked the sound of it, so made him nod his head, then laughed softly. 'Archibald Bear it is, then.'

When she picked him up, she couldn't resist giving him a cuddle, then she stilled and looked down at him. 'Is it my imagination or did I hear something rustle?'

She touched his nice little felt jacket and yes, something did rustle. A little shiver ran down her spine. Last time that had happened, she'd found over fifty pounds in the lining of the sewing box.

What would she find this time? Something good, she hoped.

She turned him over and took off his jacket. Yes, there was definitely paper hidden in the lining.

It didn't take her long to find the rough stitches in a thread that didn't quite match the rest. They'd been set carelessly in place to hold the lining shut at the back of the waistcoat. She got out her own sewing scissors and snipped the stitches carefully, finding a slip of folded paper inside the jacket lining.

She pulled it out, smoothed it carefully, and read the words on it aloud.

Dear descendant,

There's a book to look for next. Can you guess which one it is? This teddy bear is a clue.

If you're right, you'll find a nice surprise waiting for you in it.

Jane Chapman

She'd seen that signature on the will and this one was in the same handwriting. It definitely belonged to the kind relative who had left her the house.

'What have you hidden, Cousin Jane?' she wondered aloud, calling her benefactress 'cousin' because she didn't know their exact relationship, only that it was quite distant.

It was easy to guess which book she was likely to find the surprise in. She'd been attracted to the bear as soon as she saw it because it looked very similar to the illustrations in *Winnie-the-Pooh*. When she was younger, she'd dreamed of reading stories like that to her own children, before life taught her that dreams didn't often come true.

Well, maybe she could start dreaming again.

There were a lot of books in her house. *Her house!* Mr Milne's delightful story might be among them? Wouldn't it be lovely to own her own copy of it? And what surprise might it contain?

She yawned suddenly. Time to go to bed. It had been an eventful day.

But before she did, she slipped the piece of paper back into the bear's little coat and used a small safety pin to hold the opening shut. She'd show it to Gabriel and Biff when they got to the house tomorrow, but not to anyone else.

She'd look silly carrying a teddy bear around, so she got out the large bag she used for shopping. Yes, Archibald the bear fitted into it very nicely and she could cover him up with an extra scarf.

She'd expected to take a while to get to sleep after all the excitement, but it seemed as if her bear was keeping guard over her.

'Sleep well, Archibald.'

She could have sworn he'd nodded to her. Oh, she was being silly. Well, why not? She was enjoying being silly, after having had to be so sensible for the past few years.

14

Her husband was in a foul mood at breakfast and Lallie wished he didn't insist she sit with him every day to pour his tea and make sure everything was done properly.

She kept her head down as she buttered his toast and poured him a second cup of tea, but it didn't stop him venting his annoyance.

'Dobbs came round yesterday evening after you'd gone to bed. It seems a young woman who's been serving in the grocery store has inherited Number Twenty-one.'

'Goodness. Is she related to Miss Chapman?'

'Must be. What does a shop assistant want with a house like that?' He thumped his clenched fist down on the table suddenly, making her jump and spill her tea.

He ate his toast in big snapping bites, then grunted. 'Another piece.'

By the time she'd buttered it and passed it to him, he had gone from anger to a thoughtful expression.

'On the other hand, maybe it's a good thing. She won't know the value of the place. I may be able to get her to sell cheaply.'

'They could be pretty houses.'

He laughed. 'They could be lucrative houses, which is much more important.'

'Yes, Gareth.'

He went to work soon afterwards.

She sat on for a while, as she usually did, eating her own

breakfast now and feeling sorry for the poor young woman, whoever she was. Gareth never dealt fairly with anyone, if he could help it.

Maisie woke early and snuggled down in bed for a few minutes longer, marvelling at how her life was about to change.

She still didn't say anything about inheriting the house as she ate breakfast with the other lodgers, didn't tell them she wasn't going to work today, either. But someone must have seen her with Gabriel, because her fellow lodgers started teasing her about having 'picked up a clue' – such a silly phrase for meeting a nice young man.

Then someone exclaimed, 'Oh, look at the time! We're going to be late for work!' and they scattered, all except Maisie.

Mrs Tucker came in to clear the table and looked at her in surprise. 'Not going to work today, dear?'

'No. I'm probably going to stop working at Midgely's. I can't tell you why yet, but I will soon.'

'It's for a good reason, I hope?'

'Yes. A very good reason.'

'That's all right, then. And I'm glad you've found a young man, Maisie. I knew you would, for all you kept saying you weren't ever getting married. I've seen it happen time and time again to those who protest the loudest that they're never going to marry.'

Maisie couldn't take offence because it was kindly meant so she murmured, 'It's early days yet.'

To her relief Gabriel drew up outside in his van just then and she had to rush upstairs to get her outdoor things and join him.

Biff was waiting nearby in the little car, so she waved to him as she got into the van.

★

'Everything all right?' Gabriel asked. 'Your face is rather red.'

'The other lodgers were teasing me about you, you know, us going out together. Do you – um, mind that it's somehow got known?'

'No, of course not. I expected that. It's hard to keep anything secret in this valley.'

'Did Mr Tyler mind you taking the day off?'

'No. As it happens he had no urgent need of me today. But I saw Mrs Tyler give him a nod after I asked, so I reckon it was really her who said yes.'

He set off. They didn't talk much but it was a very comfortable silence.

Biff followed them, but most of the traffic was coming down the hill towards Rivenshaw, people going to work, and the little bus bringing folk down from the village of Ellindale at the very top of the valley.

When they got to Daisy Street she said, 'It's exciting, isn't it? The house, I mean.'

'It certainly is. I wonder what we'll find there today.'

As they got out of the van, a chill breeze was blowing but at the same time a wintry sun was brightening the world.

'The house looks happy to see us,' Maisie said as Biff locked his car and came along the footpath to join them.

'You're right, it does,' Gabriel said in surprise. He wasn't usually given to flights of fancy but even though they were dirty, the windows seemed to be managing to send a twinkling smile back at the world.

He suddenly snapped his fingers. 'Eh, I nearly forgot to tell you. Mam said she'd come round with some sandwiches for us at lunchtime and would beg a peep inside the house. Is that all right, Maisie?'

'It's very all right. I really like your mother.'

Biff said softly, 'So do I. She's a kind lady, your mam is, having us all round to eat at your place last night, as well as some of the neighbours, and treating me as if I really were part of the family.'

'Do you have a family?'

'Not many of our branch of the Higgins left now. My wife and I didn't have any children and she's been dead a year or two now.'

'Well, come and join our family then. Mam likes people – the good ones, anyway. She seems able to spot a bad 'un a mile away though, and I really trust her judgement.' He saw Maisie shiver and said, 'Let's get you inside, love.' But he wasn't sure it was the cold weather that was making her shiver, or worrying about the future.

'Shall we leave the front door open to air the place out a bit?' Maisie asked as they stood in the hall.

Both men said, 'No!' at the same time, and so firmly that she stared at them in surprise.

'You must never leave the doors unlocked when you come here,' Gabriel told her. 'We were lucky no one came in and pinched something yesterday. From what I've heard, Higgerson is going to be furious that you've inherited the house and I bet he tries to buy it off you.'

'Why would he do that?' Biff asked.

He and Maisie both looked at Gabriel for an answer.

'To cram people in and turn it into a lucrative slum. Don't forget we all lived in one of his slum houses while Mam was recovering from her operation. He won't hesitate to send someone to threaten you if he sets his mind on buying it. Everyone knows what he's like, how he decides on some house and makes it uncomfortable for anyone else to be the owner, then buys it dirt cheap. I've seen it happen a time or two.'

Biff turned to look out of the front door, pressing himself against the wall and trying not to be seen. 'Hmm. That chap who was standing on the corner has now walked along to the other side of the road from this house. I'd guess he was watching for whoever came here.'

'So soon after I found out I'd inherited it?' Maisie asked.

Gabriel nodded. 'Higgerson doesn't waste time when he wants something, and everyone knows he pays money for information.'

'The chap's stopped again at the corner and is still watching,' Biff said.

'Oh, dear. I'll definitely keep the doors locked then.' Maisie felt as if some of the brightness had vanished from the day.

Gabriel closed the door and slid the bolts, after which the hall seemed very dim.

She walked across to peep into the sitting room. 'We left the curtains open last night. It looks such a jumbled mess in the daylight. Let's have a proper look at the other rooms this time.'

They all moved across to the dining room and this time took their time at looking round. It was also crammed with oddments of furniture, and there were two large mahogany dining tables in the centre, both with dust-covered packages piled up on them.

Maisie couldn't believe she was the owner of so many things. 'It's going to take a long time to go through everything in the house.'

'I think you should definitely stop working at the shop and concentrate on doing that,' Biff said. 'Sell a few items every now and then to give you money to live off – and make it into a home, room by room.'

Gabriel nodded. 'That's what I was going to suggest.'

'I hope I'm not annoying you by expressing my views,' Biff said hastily.

'Of course not. All ideas will be gratefully considered,' Maisie said. 'Who would I sell the unwanted things to? It must be someone I can trust to give me a fair price.'

'Sell them to Charlie Willcox,' Gabriel said at once. 'He'll not cheat you, or anyone else, come to that.'

'I've heard of him. He owns some pawnshops, doesn't he?'

'And a few other shops. He sells top quality second-hand furniture at the back of his new furniture store, so he'd know the value of yours. And the pawnshops might give you money for the cheaper items. In fact, you should ask his advice and invite him round to see what there is. He's famous for being first with the news, so I bet he'd absolutely love to be one of the first to see inside this house.' He smiled suddenly. 'That'd really annoy Higgerson. The two of them do not get on, both in business and on the Town Council.'

'I recognise the name but I can't remember what he looks like. Well, men don't usually do the grocery shopping, do they? I think I heard someone in the shop saying they thought he'd be the next mayor.'

'They're probably right. He's well liked by decent folk, rich and poor. And he's totally honest, which is one of the reasons he doesn't get on with Higgerson.' He grinned. 'The only thing Mr Willcox is bad at is driving cars. His is dented from where he's hit gateposts.'

'How will I know what to sell to him and what not to sell?' she wondered aloud.

'There's no right and wrong,' Biff said. 'I reckon you need to get rid of more than half the stuff in the house for starters. Keep the things you like most for yourself.'

She looked round. 'I can't even see myself living here, let alone choosing the right furniture. Mum and I never had a whole house to ourselves.'

Gabriel joined in. 'When *my* mother was ill we had to sell everything we had of value to pay for her treatment and all cram into one room, but she was worth it.'

That made Maisie feel better, in a strange upside-down

way. Someone who'd never experienced poverty wouldn't understand how she felt about being prudent, but he did.

She was getting altogether too fond of Gabriel Harte. She wished – no, she'd better not wish for anything. It hurt too much when you didn't get what you wanted, and she'd suddenly realised that she'd never wanted anything so much as to spend the rest of her life with him.

Maisie was about to suggest going up to the bedrooms to check out every single item in the wardrobes and drawers in one room, so that she'd get a better idea of what the other similar rooms might contain, when she suddenly remembered the message in her teddy bear's waistcoat.

She was still holding the big bag, even though it wasn't the sort of thing you usually walked around with unless you were out shopping. Now, she set it down on the nearest small table and pulled Archibald out. She smiled at him involuntarily, he was such a cuddly little toy, then rolled him over and undid the safety pin to pull out the message. 'I found this last night sewn inside the bear's waistcoat.'

Biff took it from her and both men peered at the piece of paper.

'Do you know which book to look for?' Gabriel asked.

'I'm fairly certain it'll be *Winnie-the-Pooh* because this bear is like the illustrations in the book. I loved that story, even though I was too old for children's books, one librarian told me. I borrowed it several times, though, because I enjoyed looking at the pictures as well as following the story. It's got such charming illustrations.'

'I've seen several bookcases in the house. We could see if there is a copy of it anywhere, only, where do we start?' Gabriel asked. 'Do you remember what the cover looks like?'

She smiled reminiscently. 'Of course I do. It has a drawing on it of a little boy pulling a fat teddy bear out of what looks like a rabbit hole, helped by some rabbits. The cover is absolutely charming, too. No wonder the book is so popular.'

'How about we look first in the bookcases in the room behind the dining room?' Biff suggested. 'There were quite a few toys in that room, so perhaps the children played in there.'

'I wonder whose children they were?' Maisie murmured.

'Who knows? I want to ask this house a great many questions and I'm hoping its contents will offer us some answers,' Biff said.

'Perhaps there will be more messages. If there are, we're bound to find some of them as we sort through all the furniture and boxes.'

They divided up the bookcases and began checking the titles on books, working along the shelves, needing to pull some out to read the titles. No one found a book called *Winnie-the-Pooh*, though.

Then, just as Maisie was turning away in disappointment, about to suggest they look in another room, she saw a small pile of books on the windowsill, half-hidden by the edge of a curtain. She might as well check them, she thought, then cried out in delight as she found the book she was looking for near the bottom of the pile.

Her companions laughed at her excitement, admired the cover, and waited for her to check whether there was anything hidden inside the book.

She held it by the top and bottom of the spine, shook it, and two pieces of white paper fluttered out on to the windowsill. She picked up the nearest one, not realising what it was at first because it was only printed on one side and the writing was folded inwards. She gasped as she opened the paper up and suddenly realised what it was. 'This is a five-pound banknote! Oh, my goodness! I've never even touched one before. Customers don't use them when they're shopping for groceries. Well, most of our customers have accounts and rarely pay cash.'

Her mother hadn't dealt in five-pound notes either. Ida had always said she didn't trust white paper to be genuine money. Her savings had all been in green one-pound notes.

Gabriel picked up the other folded paper and handed it to Maisie. 'It's a handwritten note.'

It proved to be from Jane Chapman again, like the one Maisie had found in the teddy's waistcoat.

'What lovely handwriting!' Gabriel said. 'Read it aloud to us.'

She spoke slowly and clearly:

> *As you tidy up, you'll find more of these banknotes, not only in books. I hope the money helps you to settle in.*
>
> *Please use them to look after my house and turn it into a home again. I lived here myself and was very happy as a child.*
>
> *Jane Chapman*

Biff looked at it thoughtfully. 'She must have loved the house to go to all this trouble. But that still doesn't explain why there is so much furniture here and why she couldn't do all this openly and tell whoever inherited it why it's in such a state. There's enough furniture for three houses this size, if you ask me.'

Gabriel handed the handwritten note to Maisie.

She put it with the other one in the side pocket of her bag, then folded the five-pound note and put it in her purse. Afterwards she picked up the teddy again and sat him carefully inside the bag. 'Let's carry on. We need to find out more about what's here before we can plan how to deal with it all.'

Just then someone knocked on the front door.

'I'll answer it,' Biff said.

'No. Better it's me. I know more people in the town than either of you do.' Gabriel walked along the hall before they could stop him.

When he opened it, they all recognised the person standing there: Sergeant Deemer. His constable was slightly behind him and both of them were looking stiffly official, not wearing their usual smiles.

There was another man waiting at the end of the short garden path: Higgerson's man Dobbs. He watched what was happening with a sneering smile on his face.

'It's been reported that a group of people have broken into this house,' Deemer said. 'Could you please explain what you're doing here?'

Gabriel was puzzled by this question. 'Maisie owns this house now, as you know, Sergeant. You can't consider it a break-in for her to visit her own house. And I'm walking out with her, as you're also aware, so where else would I be but here, keeping her safe?'

Maisie came to join them, standing close to Gabriel, equally puzzled by this accusation.

Deemer lowered his voice. 'I have to do this by the book, given who the person is reporting the so-called break-in. The man has contacted the captain in charge of this area and *he* has ordered me to provide written proof of you owning the house, thus giving you the right to be here.'

He rolled his eyes to express his feelings, then added more loudly, 'Can you please supply me with written proof that you're the owner, Miss Lawson?'

Dobbs was grinning broadly now.

She frowned, trying to work out how best to do that. 'I think the best thing would be for Mr McLean, who is my lawyer in Rivenshaw, to verify it. He's dealing with this for Mr Neven, the lawyer in London who is in charge of executing the will. I believe you know both those gentlemen.'

'Yes, but I'm afraid I'll have to ask Mr McLean to confirm that before I can let you have free run of the house.'

She was starting to get angry. '*Let me?* What on earth do you mean by that? I *own* this house?'

Gabriel nudged her and said 'Shhh!' softly.

'The person reporting this said you might start stealing things if I didn't keep my eye on you.' He kept his back to the watcher at the gate and mouthed, 'Sorry.'

Biff moved forward to join them and also spoke in a low voice, 'I'd guess this is Higgerson showing you that he can cause a lot of trouble. I bet he's preparing the way for forcing you to sell the house to him, Maisie.'

'I presume Higgerson is the one who's reported this?' Gabriel said loudly.

'That's as may be. But you'll still have to prove you own it.' Deemer lowered his voice again and what he added was again for their ears only. 'Unfortunately, now that the captain is involved, I have to investigate the complaint and prove things to *his* satisfaction, and he doesn't know you or the people of the valley.'

'Why don't you send your constable to ask Mr McLean if he'd come and confirm that she's the owner while you stay and keep an eye on us dangerous criminals?' Biff said loudly. He grinned at the sergeant as he added in a whisper, 'I should think you're dying to have a look round the inside.'

Deemer kept his back to the street, but his eyes were twinkling now and his voice was almost a whisper. 'Well, I must admit to being curious. This house has been closed up for a good many years.' Loudly he added, 'I'd better stay and keep an eye on things while the constable fetches your lawyer, if you don't mind, Miss Lawson.'

'I don't mind at all. I respect the forces of the law.' She added quietly, amused by this double conversation, 'Have you ever been inside the house before?'

'No, never. Quiet, law-abiding folk, the Chapmans. Lived here for many years and never caused any trouble. Jane Chapman's fiancé was killed serving in the army in India, you see, and she didn't take up with anyone else after that. She looked after her parents as they grew older, minded her own business, and always seemed a bit sad to me.'

He beckoned to the constable, raising his voice again. 'Will you please go and fetch Mr McLean, the new lawyer? He lives in Gorton Street, the house next to the park. Tell him about the complaint we're answering and ask if he can come here to confirm that this lady is the new owner.'

'Yes, Sarge.' The young fellow strode off, deliberately bumping into the watcher at the gate and sending him stumbling to one side.

Dobbs looked from one policeman to the other, seeming undecided as to whether to follow the constable or stay where he was. He stayed.

Gabriel opened the door wider and said, 'Do come and wait inside out of the cold, Sergeant.'

'Thank you. It is a bit chilly today.'

As the door closed, they found they were all standing in the coloured reflections from the stained-glass windows on either side of the door.

'Isn't it pretty?' Maisie gestured with one hand that was turned red, then blue, then red again by the light as she moved it.

Biff peered through the other side window. 'Dobbs is still standing near the gate. Won't see much from there, will he? And there's a chill wind blowing.'

They showed the sergeant round the ground floor. He too was astonished at how much furniture had been crammed into each room.

'Where does it all come from?' Maisie wondered yet again.

Deemer stood thinking for a moment, then shared what he

knew. 'I expect it's what Miss Chapman inherited from her various relatives, though why she kept it all, I can't understand. If I remember correctly, there was a cousin who left her everything, and a godmother who did the same. They both died in the same year and by that time she was getting a bit frail herself. She wasn't what you'd call a healthy person.'

'I wish I'd met her.'

'She was well liked, did a lot of good in the town. There were a great many people at her funeral, poor folk paying their respects as well as those with money who'd known her socially.'

He moved across to stroke the surface of a small table. 'Mahogany. My favourite wood. Once you've dusted this and given it a good polish, it'll look beautiful.'

When they got back to the hall again after their tour of the ground floor, he said quietly, 'You'll need to be very careful with Higgerson, Miss Lawson. He's a nasty fellow and it's going around that he's got his eye on these three houses. He doesn't like to be bested and doesn't care what it takes, legal or illegal, to get it. I'll do everything I can to protect you, but I can't be with you day and night.'

He stood frowning for a moment or two, then turned to Biff. 'You were hired to protect her, weren't you? How long for?'

'A week or so, possibly longer, if it's needed.'

'Even during that time, you're only one man, and there's the house to protect as well. If you come with me after we've sorted this out, I can introduce you to a chap or two who would happily stand guard in this house for a few shillings a day each. Would that be all right with you, Miss Lawson?'

'If you think it necessary.'

'I do. Knowing Higgerson, you'll need to protect this house from now onwards, as well as yourself. And since Mr Neven is paying Mr Higgins here to protect you, I reckon our Irish friend,' he grinned as he said that, 'will be the best person to check the two watchmen out.'

He turned back to Biff. 'Do you think that London lawyer will pay from the estate to hire these men until further notice?'

'I'm sure he will when I tell him what's going on. I'll have to phone him.'

'You can do that from the police station.'

They both turned to Maisie and Gabriel who had been listening quietly, again standing very close together.

'We'll hire these men if you think it's necessary,' Gabriel said quietly.

There was a brief silence, then the sergeant chuckled suddenly.

The others looked at him, puzzled at this sudden change of mood.

'Higgerson got me sent here to annoy you. But actually, I think what we're arranging is going to help you, and there's no one nearby to eavesdrop on our plans. Eh, if he found out what I was doing, Higgerson would throw a fit.'

They all smiled.

15

There was a knock on the door and, when Gabriel again went to open it, he found his mother there with a basket over her arm.

He glanced past her at Dobbs, who was still standing near the gate with his hands in his pockets, shoulders hunched, looking chilled through. He wondered why the fellow was still hanging around, what else he expected to see, then his mother poked him in the ribs and he stepped aside to let her in, immediately locking the door again afterwards.

'I brought the food and—' She stopped to stare at Deemer. 'Why did you have to call the police in? Is something wrong?'

'We didn't call anyone in; Higgerson arranged the visit by making a complaint to an acquaintance in the police force,' her son told her.

'What's that horrible man up to now?'

By the time they'd explained there was another knock on the door, which turned out to be the constable returning with Mr McLean.

The sergeant came across to the door and took charge. 'Please don't say anything till you're inside, Mr McLean.'

Deemer stayed for a moment looking out at Dobbs, who was scowling at them as if he didn't like what he saw.

'That sod must be waiting around to keep an eye on things for Higgerson.' he muttered as he closed the door. He turned to the constable. 'You stand near the stained-glass window, lad, and keep watch. Make sure Dobbs doesn't creep down the garden path to eavesdrop outside one of the windows.'

'What do I do if he tries it?' The young policeman looked at him anxiously.

Deemer sighed, closed his eyes for a moment, then said in his usual quiet tone, 'You open the door and order him to leave the premises at once. The garden path is not a public thoroughfare.'

'Yes, sarge.'

The sergeant left him to it and turned to explain what was going on to Mr McLean.

The lawyer quickly grew angry. 'I've not been living in the valley for long and even so, I've already encountered other trouble caused by that Higgerson chap. Several times, in fact. Who does he think he is?'

'I reckon he's trying to take over as king of the valley,' Deemer said. 'I'll make sure he doesn't, though, by hell I will. I've a few years left yet before I retire. Anyway, Mr McLean, if you could come to the police station with me now and make a statement saying Miss Lawson has inherited this house, I can phone the captain and say it's done, then send it to him.'

'I'm happy to do that for you, Sergeant, but it's a ridiculous waste of all our time. Does your captain not know anything about the valley?'

'He's a foreigner. Comes from down south, somewhere near Bournemouth I think. Doesn't like the north. He's never said so, but you can tell.'

'I'm an outsider too.'

'You've fitted in well, though. We knew you would when Henry Lloyd chose you.'

'Thank you for the compliment.' He turned back to his client. 'I'll bring a similar written statement for you later as well, Miss Lawson, in case you need to show it to anyone else, though you shouldn't have to. My goodness, what is the world coming to when someone can waste police time like that?'

He looked up at the landing then back round the hall, where they were still standing. 'Can I please beg a quick look round the house by full daylight when I bring the statement here, Miss Lawson? I'd like to get a better idea of the contents.'

'I'll be happy to show you round, or let you wander on your own.'

'Thank you. Have you decided anything yet about moving in? It could make a beautiful home.'

'I wouldn't dare move in on my own.'

The sergeant looked thoughtful. 'It wouldn't be respectable for Miss Lawson to live here on her own, as well as not being safe.'

He turned to Gabriel and Maisie, who were standing close to one another. 'Since I know you two are courting, I'm not hesitating to tell you that the best thing you could do would be to get married quickly, then move in here together. After all, you won't have to save up for furniture or anything else. You should still keep a couple of guards living here with you for a while, though.'

While they were gaping in surprise at this, Mr McLean asked in a shocked tone, 'Is it really going to be that dangerous, Sergeant?'

'I fear it is. Higgerson can be both cunning and persistent. The fellow has no regard for other people, or for the law.'

'The valley is very different from where I was living in the south of England. Behind the times in some ways, Sergeant.'

'I suppose so. These hard years have left their mark on our Lancashire folk, and they've been suffering for a long time, since after the Great War ended. It's different for people living in the south, who've had it so much easier during the past few years. Sadly, Lancashire didn't even get as much in special

government grants to help local councils which were struggling as other areas did, Glasgow and Liverpool for example.'

McLean looked at him thoughtfully. 'And there's nowhere
worse than the Backshaw Moss part of the valley. I was horrified at the tumbledown houses and evident overcrowding.
The poverty and privations show all too clearly in the children's faces. That always upsets me. I've avoided that area
ever since.'

'We're doing what we can. Some charitable ladies are at
least making sure all the kids get a drink of milk every
morning at school. They started by giving out milk in the
village of Ellindale, setting it up in a room behind the pub,
Now it's being given out in all the elementary schools.
The ladies try to give the worst cases what food they can
scrounge as well, so we don't get children suffering from
rickets these days, at least.'

The lawyer made a gentle tutting sound, shaking his head
sadly. They'd all seen the sad sight of people with badly bent
legs who'd not been fed properly as children and as a conse-
quence had developed rickets. It was now known that milk
and sunlight could be a big help preventing it, thank goodness.

Deemer carried on, almost as if thinking aloud. 'Unfortunately, from what I've observed, and I'd be grateful if you don't
share this information with anyone, Higgerson is now flexing
his muscles again, so to speak. He's been lying low for a while,
following some previous trouble, but unless I'm very much
mistaken, he's getting ready to create more trouble. That man
doesn't need a god; he worships money – and himself.'

'How is it possible in the 1930s that he can get away
with it?'

'Bullies are born in every age and it's never possible to
control them all.' Deemer looked into the distance as he
continued. 'I'm gathering information on Higgerson, and one
day I'll have enough to pounce on him, but he has friends in

high places, and if he still wants to get hold of these houses, you'll have to be very careful indeed, Miss Lawson. He doesn't like to be bested.'

Gwynneth joined in the conversation, surprising them all. 'The sergeant is right about one thing. You two should get married straight away. In any case, I don't see any reason for you to wait, son. After all, you've got somewhere to live and you being with Maisie will help keep her safe till the good sergeant can do something about Higgerson.'

She waited a few moments, exchanging looks of agreement about this with the sergeant, then repeated gently, 'You're going to get married, so why not do it sooner, rather than later? How about it, Gabriel love?'

They were both stunned by this advice being so openly expressed, but when he saw his mother's determined expression, he knew at once that she wouldn't let the matter drop.

He looked down as he suddenly realised that he and Maisie were still holding hands. He didn't let go. It felt so right. Maybe they should get married quickly.

Eh, he'd never felt like this about a woman before.

Deemer took over again, changing the subject. 'Well, we'll leave you two to think about your future. There are a couple of pieces of information that I'll share with you all, but please keep them strictly to yourselves. The new Justice of the Peace, Mr Peters, has a name for being utterly honest and fair, so if you ever have to deal with him, you can trust him.'

'He's living with his sister, who is one of those helping the poor in our valley,' Gwynneth added.

Deemer studied the group and was silent for a while, chewing the left-hand corner of his lips as if trying to decide something. He also looked round the hall, as if studying the house as well as the people in it.

Instinctively everyone waited for him to speak. 'I feel sure

I can trust you all, so I'm going to tell you something else. But first I need you to swear you'll keep the information I'm about to share secret, for the sake of your country.'

Surprise showed on everyone's face due to the gravity of his expression and tone of voice, but all of them nodded and murmured a promise. They trusted him absolutely. Who wouldn't trust a man like Deemer?

He nodded as if sealing an agreement with them. 'Very well then. Certain things will be happening in our valley during the next few months and during the years that follow, if necessary. There are similar plans being made in secret across our whole country.'

Another pause, then, 'Some of us have been asked to help set up extra defences in our areas, in case there's another war, especially those of us who fought in the Great War and have proven ourselves patriotic.'

He let that sink in before continuing, 'I don't know whether you've noticed that there's a troublemaker come into power in Germany?'

'Hitler, you mean?' Gabriel said at once.

His companions all nodded to show their awareness of this situation. Well, it was mentioned often enough in the newspapers.

Deemer gave them a grim smile. 'Good. I see you're keeping watch on what's going on in Europe. That Hitler fellow has risen to power quickly, calls himself Führer now, which I gather means "leader", and he's re-arming Germany. Eh, the Allies shouldn't have allowed that, and so Mr Churchill has been telling them. So many lads gave their lives in the Great War, lads on both sides of the struggle. I blame the leaders for starting wars, not the people who fought in them.'

There were nods at this, and Gwynneth, who had lost beloved family members in the Great War said bitterly, 'Ordinary people just want to get on with their lives, whether they're Germans or British. And that can be hard enough, heaven knows.'

Her son patted her on the shoulder and found himself holding two women's hands now.

Deemer carried on explaining. 'Some leaders play games with their country's future and others don't do enough. Both are letting folk down. Fortunately there are chaps on our side who've learned hard lessons from last time, and who intend to do more this time to prepare. Just in case. There are important folk and not-so-important folk like me involved, and we're keeping an eye on the situation. I'll never forget that we were caught out with poor preparations when the Great War started.'

He smiled at their expressions. 'You're wondering why I'm going over this. Well, what it amounts to is that some of us don't intend for us to be caught out again. If the worst happens and we're invaded, as some think is a possibility, given Hitler is re-arming Germany, we'll be ready.'

When he paused again, he looked at Maisie in an assessing way. 'I think your house could be of use to our cause, lass. If there are people travelling from here to there secretly, in service of our country, they won't want to be seen in hotels. You could maybe give them shelter here for a night or two. Would you two be prepared to do that to help our nation?'

That made Maisie stare, then both she and Gabriel nodded vigorously, saying, 'Of course,' at the same time.

'I won't go into any more details at the moment because it's early stages yet, except to tell you that steps are being taken even here in Rivenshaw. I'm trusting you to say nothing about this to anyone, but it would be a help if you and Gabriel were married and living here. And of course, those of us working for our country will help keep you safer in return, lass, which is also important.'

He gave a sad smile. 'Thinking about your situation at a local level, I don't believe Miss Chapman realised that leaving her poorer relatives what some would see as a fortune, could set them up as targets for unscrupulous people. Probably to her, these seemed quite small houses. Trouble happened to the people next door when Bella inherited and now it's happening to you, Maisie lass.'

'We'll definitely think about getting married straight away,' Gabriel promised, putting his arm round Maisie's waist.

She put her arm round his waist as well. It felt even better than holding his hand.

Gwynneth let out a happy-sounding sigh and beamed at both her son and the young woman next to him. There was no doubt how much she wanted this.

'I have to get back to the police station now, and Mr McLean must come with me so that we can get his statement down to reassure my captain that you're within your rights, Miss Lawson,' Deemer said in a more normal tone. 'And Mr Higgins, if you'll come with me and Mr McLean, I'll send my constable out to fetch some chaps I know who'll help you keep watch on Maisie and the house, and who can be trusted absolutely.' He grinned and added with relish, 'They like Higgerson as much as I do.'

After the three men had left, no one said anything about what they'd been told, still trying to come to terms with it. Who'd have expected to be working for their country from a remote Pennine valley like Ellindale? What other mysterious preparations were being made?

Gabriel broke the tension. 'Let's give you a tour of the house, Mam.'

He and Maisie showed Gwynneth round the whole house, gradually relaxing and smiling as she oohed and aahed over its size and contents.

At the end of their tour she said, 'I can't believe you

two will be living here once you're wed. It could be such a beautiful house, a real palace of a place.'

'There will always be room for you as well here, Mrs Harte,' Maisie said impulsively, and got another of Gwynneth's sudden hugs for that, as well as a beaming smile from her son.

'It wouldn't stay beautiful if Higgerson got his hands on it,' Gabriel said. 'His properties seem to become run-down very quickly once they're crammed full of tenants.'

Gwynneth scowled at the mere thought of that man, and picked up her basket. 'Well, he's not going to get hold of this house, not with Sergeant Deemer on your side. I'll leave you two to chat now. Think about what I said. And what Sergeant Deemer has said about it helping our country as well.'

When they were alone Maisie looked at Gabriel, not knowing how to start, but surprised to feel quite sure of her own feelings. The time they'd spent together, especially the long walk across the tops, had shown how well they got on. But she needed to be sure of his feelings, too, hoped she hadn't mistaken that special warmth in his gaze.

'Shall we do it?' he asked. 'Shall we get married quickly?'

'I'm still worried that you're being pushed into it.'

'Maybe it's happening more quickly than we'd both have expected normally, but circumstances beyond our control have pushed us towards it, what with Higgerson, you inheriting the house, and what Sergeant Deemer has just told us.' He looked at her earnestly. 'Rest assured, Maisie love, that the more time I spend with you the more I like you, so I'm not at all reluctant. Is it too quick for you, though? If so, tell me now. I won't let them push you into something you don't want.'

And to her surprise she could speak as openly to him as he had to her. 'I'd be happy to marry you, Gabriel, really happy, and as soon as you like. I feel the same as you. I really enjoy it when we're together. I've never felt as comfortable with anyone in my whole life, not even my mother.'

'What a delightful compliment.'

He gave her another of his glowing smiles and she beamed back at him, feeling happy and even more sure this was right.

After a few more moments spent studying her face, he said, 'We'll do it, then. I don't know what the rules are for getting married quickly but we can find out tomorrow. I think you have to pay extra to do it without the usual month's notice.'

'I know a bit about it. A woman I worked with in Rochdale had to get married suddenly because her fiancé got the offer of a job in the Midlands in a car factory and he had to move there quickly to take it up. If I remember correctly, you have to give notice at the registry office, then wait a week.' She chuckled. 'I remember clearly that it costs three pounds, because she was absolutely furious about the extra charges being so high.'

'I can afford that, but I don't have much else saved because of buying my van recently. And – well, you're going to be quite a rich woman with this house belonging to you.' He felt he had to add, 'You know, you could find a husband who brings you better support than I'll ever be able to.'

'I'm twenty-six, almost twenty-seven, and I haven't ever met another man I'd consider marrying – and it's not for want of being asked out, especially when I was younger. I used to find them a bit boring, to tell you the truth.'

'I'm not surprised about you being asked. I'm just surprised and honoured that you'd consider marrying me.'

'I felt right with you straight away, and you're not at all boring. Why haven't you married?'

'Because of the difficulty of keeping a job – and also, I will confess, because I've never met anyone I'd want to spend the rest of my life with. I tried going steady a time or two, but I quickly got bored by the lasses, nice as they were. I'll tell you something else: I didn't believe that being attracted to someone could happen so quickly, wouldn't have believed anyone who said it had happened to them – till I met you. It still amazes me how well we get on, in the nicest possible way.'

'I feel the same.'

'Good.' He grinned at her, then suddenly picked her up and swung her round, making her squeak in shock then throw her head back and laugh. When he set her down, he kissed her as she'd never been kissed before.

She didn't hesitate to kiss him back. She hadn't known two people could want to kiss and touch like this. It felt . . . wonderful.

When they moved apart she had a sudden idea that might make him feel better about the money. 'Look, we have the five-pound note I found in the book. Let's use that to pay for the wedding. I think Miss Chapman would approve of it because moving in here will help us look after her house.'

He couldn't hide his relief at that suggestion. 'What a lovely idea! Yes, let's do that. Now, we need to work out how we arrange it.'

Soon afterwards Biff came back with two strong-looking men. 'These are Phil and Rob Becksley. Sergeant Deemer highly recommends them and they're happy to act as watchmen for you, Cousin Maisie. Mr Neven will be paying their wages at a daily rate, through me, from Miss Chapman's estate, till all the legal details are settled.'

'We're especially happy to help you against Higgerson, miss,' one said, moving his mouth as if he was about to spit at the mere mention of that name, then eyeing Maisie and their surroundings, and thinking better of doing it.

'Oh, good. I'm so pleased to meet you. I'm afraid I haven't got any food or even tea-making things here, but I'll be sure to have them available for you tomorrow. I think there is some coal in the cellar, so you can light a fire in the kitchen range to boil the kettle on. The gas won't be connected yet. I'd be grateful if you'd keep the fire burning because the house has a damp, unused feel to it.'

Biff was back to using his easy Irish voice, she noticed with a smile.

'Mr Neven gave me money for incidental expenses, so I can nip out and buy some tea, milk and sugar and maybe a sandwich from the shop in Birch End, Cousin Maisie. And if there's not much coal in the cellar, we'll get some more delivered.'

'Good idea.'

'I'll just show the lads round then go to the shop. We don't want to leave them without food for the night.'

'Thank you, Cousin Biff. I'd better be getting back to my lodgings now.'

'I feel we're leaving the house in good hands,' she said to Gabriel as they settled into his van.

'Strong hands too. There are few people in the valley who would mess with the Becksley brothers.'

When they got back to her lodgings, he said, 'Wait. Let me open your door.' He got out and took her by surprise, helping her out and keeping hold of her hand as he planted kisses on both her cheeks. 'That's for my own pleasure, but it'll also show anyone watching where we stand.'

'I like where we stand. Very much.' She returned his kisses by echoing his action and didn't even feel shy about doing it. In fact, she felt warm and happy as she went inside. She hadn't dared hope for him to *want* to marry her, but it had happened anyway.

Sometimes life could be kind to you, as well as harsh.

16

The following morning Maisie got up early, feeling excited. She didn't usually look forward to going to work, with such tedious tasks filling the whole day ahead. Today she was going to the shop at the usual time, but only to give in her notice. And the thought of doing that felt wonderful.

She decided not to mention her inheritance, however, as she joined the other lodgers for breakfast and then got ready to go out. She was unsure of how her future would unfurl and had decided to keep the details of her inheritance to herself for the time being as far as most people were concerned.

Biff had said he'd come with her to the shop to keep her safe, so she waited in the hall for him. She couldn't see anyone attacking her in broad daylight, but he was a pleasant enough companion, so she'd enjoy his company. No, he was a *cousin* for the time being and she must remember to call him that or people would think the worst of her. She wished she really did have a cousin or two, especially ones as nice as him.

Gabriel would go to his own work for the first part of the day. But he was going to ask Mr Tyler for time off so that they could go to the town hall and book their wedding. He felt sure they'd allow it because Mr Tyler was a good boss who looked after his workers, and he was sure Mrs Tyler would be on his side as well. She tended to the office side of things in the business, and was a really nice lady.

Besides, both Tylers loathed Higgerson, so he'd asked

Maisie's permission to tell them exactly what was going on. They'd understand because that man had played dirty tricks on them in the past to try to stop them doing well as builders.

As if anyone would believe tales of shonky building work by the Tylers, who were better by far at their trade than his company. What's more, they'd built up a sound reputation in the town over the decades, ever since Tyler's grandfather had started the business. Though when their only child had died a couple of years ago, just after he'd started working in the family business, things had slowed down for a while. You didn't easily get over such a big loss and Mr Tyler in particular had grieved deeply over losing his son so suddenly.

When Maisie and Biff got to the shop, she stood outside for a moment, not looking forward to actually confronting her employer. Then she squared her shoulders, told herself to get it done, and marched down the side alley to the staff entrance. The thought that this was the last time she'd have to come here made her feel braver.

Mr Midgely looked surprised when Maisie came across the shop towards him not wearing her overall and still in her outdoor things. 'You haven't changed into your working clothes, Miss Lawson.'

'No, because I've only come here this morning to give in my notice.'

He gaped for a moment, then said, 'You'll need to work out a week's notice.'

'I'm afraid I can't do that. I'm sorry to leave you in the lurch, but I have urgent family business to attend to and Jane is very capable of handling the bacon counter.'

'I wasn't aware that you had any family in Rivenshaw. What business is this?'

The cheek of the man! 'That's my concern. I'm only here to tell you that I shan't be able to continue working here.'

'Family matters shouldn't affect your work like this and

you'll regret it if you leave without proper notice because that will mean I shan't be able to give you a good reference.'

She'd guessed he'd say that. Everyone in the shop was listening by now, so she raised her voice and looked round challengingly as she spoke. 'I shan't need a reference because I'm getting married. And before anyone starts wondering, that's not because I'm in the family way and *have to* get wed, but because we want to get married.'

There was a shocked gasp from some when she said it so bluntly. She was enjoying being able to tell the truth and speak up for herself. She had often felt so frustrated at having to keep her real thoughts quiet since her mother's death.

The manager's voice sounded even sharper than usual. 'In that case, I'll ask you to clear out your locker and leave the premises immediately. And be sure to shop elsewhere for your groceries. I don't want you coming in here again because I don't believe you about not *having* to get married. We serve the better class of people here.'

She suddenly saw the ridiculous side of his petty attempts to punish her. She'd love to see his face when he found out about her inheritance, but wasn't going to gratify his curiosity by telling him any details today. 'I was already planning to shop elsewhere. You charge too much for your goods. I can buy the same things more cheaply at several other places, and just as good quality.'

He looked outraged but before he could say anything else, she swung round and went to clear out the few things she kept in her locker, knowing he wouldn't follow her into the women only area. He never poked his nose in there during working hours, seemed afraid of being alone with his female assistants.

She left the door open in case he insulted her in any way to the other staff while she was out of the shop, but there was dead silence there. It only took a couple of minutes to shove everything into the brown-paper carrier bag she'd brought with her.

When she went back into the shop, she slapped the locker key down on the counter in front of Midgely without saying a word and marched out of the shop's customer entrance, not the staff door, thus causing another gasp of shock.

As if that sort of thing mattered. What a silly snob he was, making such details important.

Biff was waiting outside grinning broadly. 'I couldn't resist listening to the conversation. He sounds a real Mr Nasty, but you certainly gave him what for.'

'He is thoroughly obnoxious. I shan't miss him at all, or the work, though some of the people I worked with were pleasant enough. You can't imagine how boring it was to spend my days slicing bacon, tearing up sheets of greaseproof paper, or arranging corned beef.'

'I think I have a good enough imagination to picture that.' He pulled out his pocket watch and glanced at it, showing her the time. 'Ready to go and see Mr Willcox?'

'Yes. He should be at work by now, don't you think?'

When they got to the furniture shop the man behind the counter looked at Biff. 'How may I help you, sir?'

He turned towards her. 'Sure an' it's my cousin who wishes to see someone.'

She took over. 'I'd like to speak to Mr Willcox, please.'

The man looked dubious and glanced quickly down at her left hand to check whether she was married. 'May I ask what it's about, miss? He's a very busy man.'

'My business is private, only for him to hear, but I'm sure he'll find it of interest.'

He frowned, but she stared at him unblinkingly while Biff gazed to one side, hiding a slight smile. Making an irritated sound, the man went off through a door behind the counter.

It was only a couple of minutes before the owner came through into the front of the shop with him.

'This is Mr Willcox,' he said.

The owner looked at them. 'Mr Higgins, isn't it? I rarely forget a face'

'Yes, but it's Miss Lawson who wishes to see you today. I'm a distant cousin of hers, just helping out till her fiancé can get away from work to join us.'

Neatly done to explain their presence together, Maisie thought, then took a deep breath and said, 'I'd rather explain what I want to see you about in private, if you don't mind, Mr Willcox.' She glanced meaningfully at another customer who was hovering nearby as she spoke, clearly trying to eavesdrop.

He followed her gaze and nodded. 'Very well. Come this way.'

When they were in his office with the door shut, she told the blunt truth again, starting by saying, 'I don't want word getting back to Mr Higgerson about this. He seems to have eyes and ears everywhere.'

She saw she'd gained his full attention with that.

'Please take a seat, Miss Lawson, Mr Higgins.'

When she explained her position, she saw Mr Willcox's eyes light up.

'I'd need to come and see the furniture and bric-a-brac before I could make any offers to purchase, but I'm always interested in acquiring new stock, especially if some of it is of as good quality as you say.'

'You wouldn't be free to come today, would you, Mr Willcox? Only, I've arranged to meet my fiancé there as soon as he can get away from work – Gabriel Harte. I think you know him. So we could show you round. There's a lot of surplus furniture involved.'

He looked surprised. 'Yes, of course I know him. I didn't

realise Gabriel was even courting. My congratulations to you both. Luckily I can make myself free today. Shall I meet you in Daisy Street in a few minutes?'

'That would be perfect. And – you will keep this to yourself, won't you?'

'Yes. Except for my wife. I always tell her what I'm doing.'

'How nice. I hope Gabriel and I will have that sort of relationship.'

When Biff stopped the car outside Number 21 there was no sign of Gabriel's van. Maisie was surprised at how disappointed she felt.

Biff seemed to read her mind. 'He'll be here soon, I'm sure.'

'Yes, of course.' She must learn to hide her feelings better, only she hadn't had such strong feelings for ages. She felt as if she were coming fully alive for the first time after years of trying not to draw attention to herself.

As they walked along the path the front door opened and Phil, the taller of their two guards, stood there looking grim.

'Did you have a quiet night?' Biff asked, his Irish accent in full play again.

'Not exactly. We decided to manage without lighting a lamp to keep our eyes used to seeing by moonlight. We just kept a torch handy – we found some in a kitchen cupboard, by the way. I hope you don't mind us using them. Rob nipped out to buy batteries with some of the money you left, Mr Higgins.'

'That's what it was for. Go on. What happened to make you look so annoyed?'

'Well, just after midnight someone tried to break in through the back. Good thing we'd shot the bolts as well as turning the key. We tried to catch him, but he got away. That's what's upsetting me. Sorry about that, miss.' He scowled at the memory.

'Did you recognise him?'

'No. There weren't any street lights working along the back. I went out to have a look this morning and I reckon they'd broken the one at the end of the rear alley by throwing stones at it. There were some lying on the ground around the base, together with pieces of broken glass.'

'Well, that's not your fault,' Biff said calmly.

Maisie decided to join in. She'd been automatically keeping quiet and listening to what the men were saying, but wasn't going to do that any longer. 'Well, I'm really pleased that you and Rob kept them out of my house, Phil. Thank you so much. You certainly earned your money last night.'

'I'm grateful for the work, miss, and I'll allus do my best. My brother feels the same. We're both happy that our kids will eat properly tonight. Um, you will pay us daily, won't you, Mr Higgins?'

'Yes. I can slip you a bob or two in advance now if you want to nip home and give it to your wife for today's meals, Phil.'

The man looked at him as if he'd been offered the moon. 'I wasn't pestering, but you understand how it is with kids. It hurts to see the little 'uns go hungry. The dole isn't nearly enough for growing lads.'

'Yes, I do understand because I went hungry myself in my younger days. We'll provide food for you and your brother while you're working here.'

'Thanks.' Phil beamed at him then turned back to Maisie. 'We only live a couple of streets away in Birch End, miss. Is it all right if I take the money to my wife now? I could take some money to Rob's wife while I'm at it. They live just across the street from us. That way you won't be left without extra help if you need it. I won't take long, I promise.'

'Go ahead.'

Biff took out some coins and gave them to him.

'I'll just tell Rob.' The man hurried through to the back,

then returned, followed by the other watchman, who was also beaming at them. 'Thanks for that, miss, sir. Kind of you.'

Maisie felt happy to be able to help someone who'd been down on their luck. Life could be hard.

She'd need to hire help in the house as well. It was far too big for one woman on her own to keep clean, and she knew how welcome any extra money would be to a woman whose family struggled to make ends meet.

Mr Willcox turned up soon after Phil had left, parking with one wheel on the pavement and not seeming to notice that mistake as he bounced out of the car, looking happily at Number 21.

'I heard that he's famous for being a bad driver,' Biff murmured with a grin, 'and now I've seen it for myself.'

Their visitor took his time to knock on the door, studying the front of the house, moving his spectacles off and on as if to improve his vision of various parts of it.

She opened the door, but he still continued looking, and in the end she grew tired of waiting and said loudly, 'Do come in, Mr Willcox.'

'What? Oh, yes. Could be a very nice house.' He stared, looking surprised at the careful way she locked the front door behind him.

'We've had people try to break in.'

'Already?'

'Yes. Ah, there you are, Biff. Would you like to join us?'

He nodded a greeting to Mr Willcox. 'Yes.'

'Let me start by showing you round the house quickly so that you can see how it's been left.'

Their visitor made no secret of his enjoyment at being one of the first to see the interior.

He was surprised at and then enthusiastic about the quality of some of the pieces of furniture. He warned her to be careful how she moved them because they seemed unmarked which would make them even more valuable.

She studied the clutter with a sigh. 'We'll have to move some of them out of the sitting room first so that we have room to sit in there in the evenings. Perhaps we could put them into the dining room, pile them up somehow. Oh, and one bedroom as well, of course.' She could feel herself blushing, but he didn't seem to notice.

'How about I store some of the furniture for you?'

'Would you do that?'

'Store some, sell some. No trouble at all. I can bring a couple of my men here tomorrow to move them. May I suggest you get rid of the bigger pieces that you don't like first, the ones you definitely aren't going to keep.'

'Good idea.'

'I can sell those to give you some money to modernise the place as well as making more room. I can store pieces you're not sure about till you've had time to see what you need. No charge for that since you'll be bringing me some good business.'

'That'd be very helpful. Thank you so much.'

'Make sure you only send men you can trust absolutely,' Biff put in. 'There was an attempt to break into this house last night. Probably sent by Higgerson. I gather you've had trouble with him too, Mr Willcox.'

Their companion's smile faded instantly. 'Yes. You don't need to worry about the men I'll be sending. I've learned to be extremely careful whom I employ. Mischief can happen to people on the town council simply for voting against Higgerson's wishes – as I found out when I got attacked once on my way to a council meeting. I take a strong chap to drive me there and back now.'

They were all silent for a moment or two, thinking of the trouble one arrogant man could cause in an isolated valley.

Mr Willcox turned round on the spot. 'All right then if we start removing some furniture for you tomorrow, Miss Lawson?'

'That'd be very helpful. And . . . I'd also appreciate your advice about what to sell, things that are too expensive for everyday use.'

'My pleasure.'

'Gabriel and I will need some money to have more modern amenities put in, so can you sell some pieces straight away?'

'I can sell one or two, but it's going to take some time to sort them all out and do it properly. I'll need to come back with my deputy to make a list.'

'We have to go to the registry office first thing tomorrow to book our wedding, but we should be able to get back from there by ten o'clock. Would that be all right?'

'Yes, of course. How about I tell you the value of some of the better pieces you don't like, Miss Lawson, then you can maybe choose a few to sell for a start. There are several pieces over twenty pounds in value each.'

'That much? Just for one piece of furniture? Oh, my goodness! I'll hardly dare touch any of them, let alone use them, till I know which are the most valuable.'

There was a knock at the front door. 'Excuse me.'

When she went to open it Rob moved to block her way. 'Let me answer it, miss.'

Biff nodded his approval of this.

Fortunately it was Gabriel arriving, but she could see Mr Willcox taking note of all their precautions. Despite his genial way of acting and talking, she felt sure he was as shrewd as they came when it concerned business – and safety. Well, people wouldn't be talking of making him the next mayor if he was a stupid man, would they?

With Mr Willcox's help, they settled on which items to sell first: a nest of tables with ornate carving on the legs and cross pieces, a small bookcase with glass doors, and a semicircular side table with beautiful inlays on the top. In addition she pointed out a large and very ugly sideboard and matching lumpy table with extra leaves to make it even bigger, which she would be glad to get out of her sight, plus three wardrobes from upstairs.

Mr Willcox assured her that they were the sort of items that would sell quickly.

When their visitor had left and Rob had gone back into the dining room, from which he could keep watch on the street, Biff said he wanted to take a look at all the locks on the various outer doors and tactfully left the two of them alone.

Gabriel said, 'Shall we?' and held out his arms.

She walked into them gladly. Each time they embraced she felt closer to him, more in love – and more sure he cared about her.

How could this have happened so quickly?

17

Higgerson glared at Dobbs. 'I told you to find out what she's got inside that house, damn you.'

'We tried to get in last night but they've stationed night watchmen there.'

'Who are these guards? Where do their families live? We might be able to persuade them to let us in on pain of being evicted from their homes.'

'Not a chance, I'm afraid, sir.'

'They're not tenants of mine, then?'

'No, sir. It's the Becksley brothers. And as you know, they live close to one another in Birch End, on Mallow Road, so if you arranged an attack on the home of one, the other would come to his help, and probably some of the neighbours too. I don't think you have any houses on that street.'

'Not yet. I shall one day, when I start providing for the better class of tenant. Hmm. There has to be a way to see inside that woman's house. I've been thinking about the other house of the trio as well, the one that's still standing empty. Maybe we should concentrate on that first? There must be some way I can buy it.'

Dobbs looked at him, hoping he'd managed to hide his surprise. Was Mr Higgerson starting to get a bit forgetful? He was a bit young for that, surely, but this wasn't the first time it had happened. Dobbs hoped he wasn't. There was a nice lot of money to be made by working for this man.

He reminded his master as tactfully as he could of the

situation. 'Unfortunately, the third house is another that's been left to someone in Miss Chapman's will and we don't know who it is, so we can't approach them to sell yet. If you remember, when we sent Foster to break in to see what it was like, he came back saying it was haunted, and we couldn't get him to try to get in again for love or money.'

'He's a liar, just being lazy. There are no such things as ghosts.'

Dobbs didn't even try to respond. He knew what he believed because he too had felt uneasy when he tried to find out what was in that particular house. He could have picked the lock quite easily, but even as he stood on the doorstep, something had made him shiver and turn away.

He felt a bit the same way, though not as bad, about a house on Clover Lane where Mr Higgerson was insisting on digging out an extra cellar room to rent. There was something – well, *strange* about the place. Gave him the shivers every time he went there.

He watched his employer thump one clenched fist down on the table. 'There has to be a way to get inside those two houses, Dobbs.'

'If there is, I haven't been able to find it, sir. They're well built, with such solid doors and window frames that smashing them would make a great deal of noise and bring neighbours running out to see what was going on. You know what they're like in Birch End, always keeping an eye on each other's houses. They should mind their own business.'

'Hmm. We might have another try to drive Cornish and his family away, then. I can always find another plumber, and that wife of his spoiled my plans when she inherited that house. I'll have to think of some way to do it. It's easy to get people to make a regular nuisance of themselves nearby. That usually pushes folk to move out. I'll get hold of that house of theirs one way or another.'

Dobbs waited patiently as his employer sat thinking aloud. He wouldn't be openly blamed by Higgerson, whatever happened, but might end up being attacked sneakily as a punishment if he displeased him.

Eventually Higgerson stirred and scowled at him. 'Until I've worked out a way round all that, you can go ahead with digging a side cellar under that tall house in the middle of Clover Lane. We can easily fit another family in there.'

Dobbs tried again to reason with him. 'I don't think that will be safe, sir. The men who did the extra cellar room at the rear said that the house's foundations aren't very strong.'

'Get it done, damn you! Stop holding back. You don't make money without an effort. We can prop up the walls with some old planks as needed.'

Dobbs knew by now when to give in. You could push his employer so far then he became, well, irrational was the best way of describing it. He kept his voice soft and calm. 'Very well, sir.'

When Dobbs had left, Higgerson sat scowling into the fire that was blazing in the hearth of the room he called 'my home office'. It was more used for getting away from his dolt of a wife, and his ungrateful son as well during the school holidays.

He should have married a more robust woman and got himself sons with more get up and go, instead of his two current softies. What if he got rid of Lallie? Was there still time to start and raise another family?

Probably not. He was too old. You couldn't turn the clock back however much money you earned. And anyway, you couldn't guarantee what another child would turn out like, or even if it'd be a boy. A girl would be no use to him. No, best to make sure Kit was properly trained to run a lucrative business. When he left school in July, Higgerson would take him in hand and start his real education, by hell, he would.

In the meantime, he would find a way to buy Number 21. A young woman from her background would be easily dazzled by money, surely, especially if he could get her away from that Harte fellow while he made the offer.

Upstairs Lallie sat in the small bedroom her husband didn't share with her and where she was sometimes allowed to sleep on her own. She prayed that he'd go out soon. She never felt safe when he was in the house, and from the way he was shouting at the servants, something had upset him.

She had to wait a full half hour past his usual departure time before he left and the minutes seemed to pass slowly. Only when her maid came to tell her he'd definitely gone out to his office did she relax a little. He probably wouldn't be home till late afternoon.

The two women stared at one another, their expressions communicating their relief at his departure. They didn't dare discuss it except in whispers in case any of the other servants overheard them, but they were united in trying to protect Lallie from her husband and to hide the bruises he sometimes gave her.

Pansy was grateful that she was too old to attract his attention and felt desperately sorry for the poor woman she served.

She'd seen what happened to an aunt of hers, who'd been married to a brute of a man and been killed by him, and was worried that Higgerson was getting worse and might do the same to his wife. She didn't dare leave his employment, though, or he might send one of his thugs after her. All the servants whispered that he'd had people killed before. And anyway, she had grown fond of her poor little mistress.

Eh, the world was a strange place. You never knew what would happen next, for good or bad. And being rich didn't save you from trouble, as she'd seen since she came to work here.

At least she had enough to eat, good clothes to wear, and a warm bed to sleep in. There were a lot of people in the valley who didn't have any of those comforts, some of them relatives of hers.

When Gabriel and Maisie left the town hall after officially registering their desire to marry as soon as the law allowed and booking a time the following week, they were both smiling.

Biff was waiting for them outside and was glad to see how happy they looked. He had no doubt that someone would alert Higgerson to the fact that they had booked a wedding, because you had to sign a public book that anyone could look at. Who knew what sort of trouble that nasty oik would cause in an attempt to prevent it.

He'd phoned Mr Neven yesterday and explained that Maisie would need protection for at least another week. The old lawyer had immediately approved his continuing on the job because he'd already done better than the previous man simply by finding her. They neither of them wanted anything to go wrong as they worked through the details of delivering the inheritance to Maisie.

'All sorted out?' Biff got out of the car to stretch and chat to them.

'Yes. The wedding is next Thursday at ten o'clock in the morning. Will you still be here?'

'Yes. Mr Neven wants me to stay on a bit longer and keep an eye on you, Maisie. I hope that's all right? Good. What's next on your list?'

'Sorting out the house. Mr Willcox is coming at ten o'clock tomorrow to take away the first load of unwanted furniture. We need to get a few rooms habitable before we move in, and clear out our bedroom drawers and wardrobe.'

'And if we can, we need to have a better plumbing system

installed, because we're going to move in straight after the wedding,' Gabriel added.

'Can you find a bedroom for me as well?'

They both looked puzzled.

'I thought you were only staying in the north for a week or so,' Maisie said.

'I suggested Mr Neven extend my time here, because Sergeant Deemer and I both feel there's trouble brewing. It'll be even harder to protect you and the house with people coming in and out to help you clear some of the rooms quickly, you see, so it'll be better if I can move in for a while.'

'We'd be happy to have your help and you can choose any bedroom you please, but you'll have to clear a bit of space for yourself.' Maisie flushed. 'Except for the one we're going to use, the biggest one at the front of the house.'

'I'll help you get the clothes out of it if you like. In fact, I'll help with anything I can. I prefer to keep busy.'

'Yes, please. We have such a long list of jobs to get done.' She sighed at the prospect. On the one hand, it was wonderful to own so many things, but there were too many crammed into this house and she felt overwhelmed by the prospect of dealing with it all.

Gabriel put his arm around her and gave her a quick hug. 'I took the liberty of asking Mr and Mrs Tyler to come and give us an estimate of what's needed, how much it'll cost, and how quickly they can do it. They'll be coming this afternoon.'

'What a good idea! It'll be good to have an inside lavatory.' Maisie stared at him. 'I never thought of that side of things. Oh, I'm so glad I've got you to help me and think how to do things, Gabriel. I'd never have managed on my own.'

'Mr Tyler says he can squeeze some of the urgent jobs in quickly by taking a few men temporarily away from working on the new row of houses opposite, and he can put a proper bathroom in at the same time as he does the ones across the street. He thinks he'll be able to connect the house to the electricity system as well as putting in a proper sewage connection before we get married.'

'How kind of him!'

'He set things up for future connections when he put electricity into the house next door and connected it to the town sewage system. He's good like that, looking ahead I mean. I'm learning a lot from him about how to approach jobs. The bathroom won't be finished, but I can sort it out, and the house will be ready enough for us to manage.'

'I'm not fussy. I didn't grow up in luxury, and my mother and I never had a bathroom just for ourselves.'

'I don't think any of us three did,' Biff said. 'The world's changed greatly, even in my lifetime.'

'I suppose things always do change,' she said. 'From what I've read, anyway.'

'Well, we can't stand here chatting all day, even though it is nice to get a bit of winter sun on our faces.' Biff looked up at the town hall clock. 'Let's drive back to the house and wait for Mr Willcox.'

When they got back to Daisy Street from the town hall, they saw someone going up the path to the middle house of the three.

The woman heard their car stop and turned round, hesitating as if unsure whether to speak to them.

'That's Mrs Cornish, another of the inheritors,' Gabriel said. 'You'll like her.'

Biff recognised her too. Well, he'd been hired to find her a few months ago, which was what had brought him to Rivenshaw the first time. He hadn't realised then that he was working for the cousin who wanted to take her inheritance away from her, because his employer had accepted the job, which the man said was to help him look after her, and assigned it to him. Biff had slipped away from the situation as soon as possible after he found out the truth and stopped working for that employer.

Gabriel pulled Maisie forward. 'Bella, I'd like you to meet my future wife, Maisie Lawson.'

Biff tipped his hat to the lady next door and moved forward. 'Mrs Cornish, how nice to see you again. We met briefly a few months ago. My name's Higgins and I'm currently employed by Mr Neven to help your new neighbours settle in. You've already met Gabriel, of course, but I don't think you've met his fiancée, who turns out to be a distant cousin of mine.'

She studied Biff, then nodded. 'Yes, I remember you. I didn't remember the Irish accent, though.'

'I mostly try to talk without it, because some people are prejudiced, but it slips in sometimes.'

She put her bag of shopping down on her doorstep and moved back to the pavement, smiling at Gabriel. 'I didn't realise you were courting. I'm pleased to meet you, Miss Lawson.'

Pity women didn't shake hands like men did, Biff thought. It made a better connection between people than just nodding.

'It was my mother who was the chosen heir,' Maisie said. 'Only she died a couple of years ago, so the house came to me. I didn't even know Miss Chapman.'

'I didn't know her either, but if you're connected to her, then you and I must be distant relatives of some sort, so please call me Bella.

'If your house is anything like ours was, it'll need modernising,' Bella added.

'It desperately needs it. And it's crammed full of furniture, so full you can hardly walk round it. Was yours like that?'

'No. Mine was crammed full of people renting rooms, but

I got rid of most of them. The agent employed to let rooms there had taken a few liberties, you see. We're still letting part of the upstairs, but to a nicer sort of person. And we had the whole house modernised. Bathrooms and electricity make life so much easier.'

'We're going to make improvements too.' It wasn't a very interesting conversation, Maisie thought. Who wanted to talk about bathrooms to someone who clearly was a friend of Gabriel's? But they were both making the effort to establish a connection. You didn't want to live in the next-door people's pocket, as the saying went, but it was good to know one another so that you could keep an eye on each other's home or help out in times of trouble, and if Gabriel was a friend of this woman, she must be all right.

Bella took a step back. 'Well, it's nice to meet you, but I'm sure you have a lot to do, and I'd like to put my shopping away. You must come round for a cup of tea sometime, Miss Lawson.'

'Maisie.'

'Maisie then.'

More nods, then Maisie went into the house with her two escorts. 'She seems like a pleasant woman.'

'She is,' Gabriel said. 'I got to know her late last year. She's married a widower and is helping him raise his children.'

'How blessedly normal that sounds,' Maisie said wistfully. 'I wish we could settle down into a peaceful life in my new home and not have to worry about what that horrible man will do next.'

Phil met them inside, telling them Rob was taking a nap and volunteering to help them move any furniture if they needed to look at something blocked by it before Mr Willcox arrived.

The poor man was so eager to please, clearly desperate for work, Maisie thought.

It suddenly occurred to Maisie that she'd need a nice dress to get married in. She currently had only the nondescript clothes she'd worn in an effort not to attract attention. She didn't intend to get married looking her worst!

That meant going to the shops. She smiled at the thought of Biff or Gabriel accompanying her to a ladies' dress shop, but the smile faded as she realised that she couldn't go out on her own at the moment, even to buy some new clothes. Well then, one or the other of them would have to wait outside the shop for her. She'd surely be safe inside it.

How long would this feeling of hovering danger continue? As a rich man, Higgerson knew important people like that police chief in charge of their area.

Could they really hold out against him if he was determined to buy her house? They had to. Somehow they'd come through this, whatever it took, she vowed.

18

In Hertfordshire that same week, Simeon Lawson was burying his wife. Minnie had been a good wife and mother, and he'd been fond of her, but she hadn't been the woman he'd wanted to marry. He'd not expected her to die so suddenly at forty-one, because she'd always seemed very healthy. Though he shouldn't have been surprised because the first woman he'd got engaged to had died at a mere twenty-one – and he'd never managed to forget her.

His older son hurled the flower they'd given him on to the coffin and scowled down at it. Simeon gazed sideways with a sigh. Joss looked and acted more like his maternal grandfather than his father. At nineteen, he was taller than Simeon already, bidding fair to become a physically strong man.

His younger son, Eric, was barely seventeen and not fully grown yet, but likely to be tall like his brother. He had been his mother's favourite and would miss her most of all. He was keeping his grief to himself, acting stoically throughout the ceremonies.

Simeon's gaze settled briefly on his twin sixteen-year-old daughters, clad in black and clutching one another. They looked so like their mother, pretty and home-loving. He watched them each throw a flower on their mother's coffin, tears rolling down their cheeks.

Who'd have expected a woman like Minnie to have twins, which didn't run in either family? But though his wife had carried them to term, the births had proved difficult and it had taken her a long time to recover. She'd never conceived another child after that, to his relief.

His older son was still scowling at the world, probably to hide the fact that he too was upset about his mother and fighting back tears. Men weren't supposed to weep, even at funerals. Why not? Joss would probably feel better for a good weep.

The lad would be a much better carpenter even than his grandfather, but Simeon was a better businessman and that had benefitted the whole family, who were more than comfortable financially these days thanks to his good management.

He shifted from one foot to the other and back again, wishing this fuss would end.

What had Ida's funeral been like? Had she even had a proper one? He'd told Minnie about her once, that she was a woman who'd died before he proposed and she'd simply bowed her head and accepted it. She'd been placid about most things, had only stood out against her father about who she would marry, because she had her heart set on a tall, good-looking husband to give her fine-looking children.

He watched his Lisle in-laws lead the way out of the churchyard, their grief for the loss of their only child clear for all to see.

Simeon and his children followed their grandparents. The mourners would be going to the Lisles' house because Mrs Lisle had begged him to let her do that last service for her daughter. He hadn't cared where the gathering was held. It wouldn't bring Minnie back, and he'd have to reorganise his life once this fuss was over.

'Those people aren't really mourners,' Joss said as they were driven back in the funeral company's limousine. 'They don't care about our mother.'

'They're polite enough to attend the funeral, and some of the women were truly her friends.'

Joss's only answer was another scowl.

Simeon sighed. Like his eldest son, he would be glad when all this fuss was over.

He had yet to tell them that he was taking a short holiday next week. He'd do that once they got home again. Their grandparents knew and had generously offered to move in and keep an eye on them.

No one would understand why he was going away, why he *needed* to go back to Rivenshaw and find the grave of the other woman he'd loved. But in the end they'd shrugged and accepted his decision, telling one another that grief took different forms, and if he wanted to visit the town where he'd been born, well, let him do so.

He'd made that decision during the last difficult month of watching poor Minnie.

Rivenshaw was very different from this cosy village he had lived in since his marriage, and he knew from his regular reading of the northern newspapers that life there had been very hard during the past few years, and that the north was behind the south in recovering from the Depression.

After he'd seen the death notice for Ida in the *Rivenshaw Gazette* all those years ago, he hadn't read the northern newspapers for several months. In the end, however, he'd come back to them, wanting to keep up with what was going on in the north.

He probably had cousins in Rivenshaw still and if so, it'd be nice to catch up with all the family news. He'd promised Minnie when they married that he'd leave his past behind and be a good husband. He'd kept his promise.

But now, he was going to keep the promise to himself because Minnie wasn't there to be upset by it. And it couldn't hurt anyone because the rest of the family wouldn't know what he was doing in Lancashire, would they?

He wanted to see where Ida was lying, needed to take

flowers to her. The death of someone you cared about did that to you, made you think hard about what you really wanted to do before your own life ended. He'd seen it in others, hadn't expected it to happen so abruptly to himself.

When Mr and Mrs Tyler came to look at the house with a view to making some improvements, to Maisie's surprise it was the lady who made the suggestions for how best to do that. She tried not to stare as Mr Tyler and Gabriel listened carefully, studied the area in question, and nodded approval of the suggestions.

Biff had left them to it for this and had gone to discuss something with Phil and Rob.

Mrs Tyler's suggestions seemed good to Maisie too, but all of them were agreed that first they'd have to clear out some of the furniture so that people could get in to do the necessary work, because even the kitchen cupboards were stuffed full of crockery and cooking utensils.

In the end it was decided, rather daringly, to have not only a bathroom on the first floor, but also an extra lavatory on the ground floor. Maisie was so amazed that they could even think this worth the extra expense that she simply left it to them, but had to admit to herself that this luxury would be very convenient.

The Tylers were more experienced in such matters because they'd lived in or worked on larger houses, whereas she hadn't even lived in a small house all on her own. In fact, most of the places she and her mother had lived in had only had a lavatory out in the backyard and a sink in their kitchen.

As they were leaving Mrs Tyler said, 'Take the rest of the week off work, Gabriel love. A wedding only happens once in a lifetime to most people, and you and Maisie have a lot to sort out here.'

He looked at Mr Tyler, who grinned and nodded. 'Do as

the lady tells you. But send us an invitation to the wedding. My wife loves weddings.'

Maisie shot a questioning glance at Gabriel as he said, 'We'd love to have you both join us. It's on Thursday of next week at the town hall, ten o'clock in the morning.'

'We'll be there,' Mrs Tyler said.

When Maisie and Gabriel were alone, he smiled at her. 'You seemed overwhelmed by what Mrs Tyler was suggesting.'

'I was. I was glad to have you to help decide.'

'You're sure you can afford it? I can give you a few pounds towards the improvements, but that's all I have.'

'I'll be selling the spare furniture to get the money, so it's the house that'll be paying for it, not us.'

'You're still happy about us getting married?'

'Definitely. It's the nicest thing that's ever happened to me.'

He gestured round them, seeming surprised. 'Nicer than inheriting all this?'

'Yes. People are more important than anything else. I've had so few of them in my life that having someone I know will be staying with me seems wonderful.'

'Well, I'll do everything I can to make sure we're happy together.'

Biff cleared his throat, which reminded them that they weren't alone.

'What time do you want us to pick you up tomorrow morning, Maisie?'

'Would seven o'clock be too soon? It'll be starting to get light by then. I still need to choose which pieces of furniture I definitely want to sell – and at some point I need to buy something nice to wear at the wedding.'

She was really sorry when it came time to return to her lodgings. How wonderful it would be to stay here in her own house and feel free to do as she pleased, not live by someone else's rules.

She knew she'd have to tell Mrs Tucker and the other lodgers about her inheritance and coming marriage, knew some would be envious.

The following morning Mr Willcox arrived and parked his car just as badly as before, this time with two wheels on the pavement. He got out without seeming to notice, and gave them a cheerful wave. He was followed by a big pantechnicon from which two men in overalls jumped down.

This brought some people from further along the street out to stand openly watching, and curtains twitched at the windows of other houses.

By that time Maisie had been up for hours because Gabriel had brought her to the house early to select the furniture she definitely didn't want to keep.

Mr Willcox beamed at her. 'We're ready to get rid of some of the stuff you're sure you won't want.'

'Good. Maybe then we'll have room to live here.'

It took most of the morning to remove the unwanted items, because other large pieces had to be moved to and fro to get the first lot of unappealing furniture out.

That afternoon Maisie decided to go and look for a wedding outfit, which would also serve as her Sunday churchgoing clothes afterwards. She decided to take Biff with her while Gabriel let the first of Mr Tyler's workmen into the back of the house, and their two watchmen caught up on some sleep.

Biff had bought himself a newspaper and didn't seem at all worried about waiting outside the dress shop, reading it.

She found an outfit very quickly, a two-piece suit in lighter than navy blue wool, with a fitted hip-length jacket and a slender skirt with two knee-high kick pleats front and back to make walking easier. With it she bought a blouse in a lighter blue material with a pale pattern of small flowers. She found a neat asymmetric hat, also in blue but with two pretty white flowers on the upper side of the brim. She felt delightfully elegant in this outfit – till she looked down at her shoes.

Biff accompanied her to a shoe shop, where she found some plain black court shoes with fairly low heels that fitted beautifully. They looked so much smarter than her worn workday shoes that she hated to take them off. Oh, she was being silly.

'I've never spent this much money on clothes in my whole life,' she confided in her companion as they waited at the bank to draw some more money out.

'Well, you've never got married before, and with a bit of luck you won't be doing it again, so you want it to be special.'

She smiled at him with tears welling in her eyes. 'I wish I did have cousins as patient and understanding as you.'

'I'm old enough to be your uncle.'

'Surely not? Well, I prefer to have you as a cousin. They come in all ages, after all.'

'Then that's what I'll be. Are you finished now?'

'I'm afraid not. I need to buy some other things at the haberdasher's, stockings and such.' You didn't talk about knickers to a man, however kind he was, but most of hers were darned and you didn't want a new husband to see you in darned knickers on your wedding night.

'Stop worrying, Maisie lass! I don't mind waiting. You do a lot of that in my job.'

After that Biff drove her back to her lodgings where she gave Mrs Tucker a rapid explanation and left the parcels on her bed, terrified that if she left them in the car, someone would break into it and steal them.

★

For the first time, the Daisy Street house felt like home and when she went inside, Gabriel yelled down the stairs, 'Come and see the bedroom now.' He must have heard the car stop outside the house.

The excess furniture had mostly been moved out and the main problem left was the extra bed and the pile of clothes covering both beds. The top garments looked old-fashioned but were of a very good quality.

'I could have some of these altered,' she decided as she studied them. 'For the time being, let's put them in one of the servants' rooms in the attic.'

She was exhausted but very happy by the time Biff dropped her at her lodgings. She hadn't wanted to leave the house, but it was dark now and felt as if there might be a frost that night.

She then had to face the other lodgers, who had somehow found out about her inheritance and wanted to know all about it. They were clearly dying to be invited to look round, but she wasn't going to do that.

She wasn't going to keep in touch with most of them, and she didn't want details about the interior of the house getting back to Higgerson.

Gabriel and Maisie worked hard for the rest of the week, trying to rearrange furniture but often finding it hard to decide which pieces they'd like to keep and use, and which they'd like to sell. Biff might be there mainly to protect her, but he proved to be a big help with the clearing out.

Mr Tyler's men had worked on the kitchen and set up the space and plumbing connections for the indoor lavatory downstairs. Either Biff or one of their watchmen had hovered nearby all the time the strangers were in the house, making sure no one else sneaked in.

Maisie had cleared out some of the kitchen cupboards,

when the men weren't around. She was astonished at how many pieces of equipment there were.

Biff moved into the bedroom that had space cleared for him that same night, and it felt safer to have him around.

Mr Tyler and his men worked late, performing miracles by giving them an indoor lavatory, a temporary connection to electricity, and even a few light bulbs dangling from wires so that the rooms could be lit. He promised to fit a gas geyser in the kitchen on the following Monday to provide them with hot water.

By Saturday evening they also had the living room set out nicely with the furniture they'd decided to use arranged round the fireplace. It was such a big room that though there were still too many pieces left, they were pushed back out of the way, leaving a sort of room within a room.

Gabriel drove her home on Saturday evening and lingered to remind her to be careful the following day when she went to church.

They had decided that he would still escort his mother to the little church in Birch End so that he could tell people about his coming marriage and show that it wasn't something he was ashamed of. His mother had suggested this because she didn't want it to look as if he was being forced to marry Maisie.

She would go to church with the fellow lodgers as usual, and Biff would sit at the rear, keeping an eye on her. He'd bring her up to the Hartes' home after church and they'd all have Sunday dinner together, with Maisie installed for the first time as Gabriel's fiancée.

'You're sure you'll be all right, Maisie love?' Gabriel asked.

'Of course I will. What do you think is going to happen to me at church, for goodness' sake? I've been going there every Sunday for two years, remember. I walk there and back with some of the other lodgers.'

'Yes. But you haven't had Higgerson wanting something from you before. Still, Biff will be following you and will be in the church to keep an eye on you.'

'Stop worrying.'

He smiled. 'All right, love.'

19

Maisie walked to church and followed other worshippers up the wide path that led to the large, stone church in Rivenshaw. She glanced back when she got to the main entrance and saw Biff drive slowly away to find a place to leave his vehicle.

She noticed a well-dressed gentleman with a rather large belly standing to one side of the church porch and felt indignant when she saw that his eyes were lingering on her breasts in a very rude way. It was Higgerson, she realised suddenly. She'd seen him around town, but usually only in the distance because he'd naturally never come into the shop and he didn't usually come to church, either.

'I didn't like the way that man looked at me,' she whispered to Nell, a fellow lodger who happened to be walking next to her.

'He does that to any pretty woman. He's a horrible man, isn't he? Just ignore him.'

Maisie paused briefly at the end of the aisle, wondering where to sit. She'd been thinking of sitting nearer the back with Biff, but he might be a while and it wouldn't look good to sit on her own. She'd better take her usual place midway up the row of pews with the other lodgers.

Higgerson hadn't come inside yet but would no doubt be joining the richer folk at the front, which at least meant he wouldn't be able to stare at her during the service.

She kept turning round to look for Biff, but by the time

he arrived there was no room left anywhere near her pew. He smiled at her across the rows of seated people and took a place at the rear. She felt better knowing he was nearby.

Today the service seemed to go on for even longer than usual. Well, it had never been more than a tedious necessity to attend this church. The elderly minister was a boring speaker at the best of times, using only trite subjects for his sermons.

Today Maisie didn't take in a single word of what he was saying, couldn't concentrate at all because she kept thinking about the house, marvelling at the mere thought of it being hers. She was absolutely longing to move into it, and at the same time a little nervous of doing so.

At last the service ended, but she and her fellow lodgers still had to wait their turn to leave because the rich people from the front rows always filed out first. She saw Higgerson glance sideways at her so tried to pretend she hadn't noticed him. But she had, of course she had. If the woman walking with her arm in his was his wife, the poor thing looked deeply unhappy.

Finally it was her turn to leave. Biff winked at her as she passed his pew, but he was trapped behind three other late-comers, and they would be the last of all to file out of the church. Maisie smiled back, trying not to be too obvious.

Before she could walk past the groups gathered to chat outside, the man who'd come to Daisy Street and stood at the gate blocked their way and touched his hat. 'Could I please have a word, Miss Lawson?'

She stopped out of politeness, and the other lodgers continued walking, but there was something about the man that made her feel nervous.

He spoke very quietly. 'Mr Higgerson would like a word with you.'

'What? Why would he want to talk to me? I've never even met him.'

'That's for him to tell you. Let me escort you to him.'

Before she could do anything, he had taken her hand and threaded it through his arm. When she tried to jerk away, he proved stronger than he looked, holding her arm in place quite easily with his other hand. 'Do you really want to make a fuss in front of everyone?'

She stopped dead and stared at him. Of course she didn't. She'd be the one who got gossiped about if she did.

'Don't worry. My employer isn't going to hurt you and I'll bring you back here safely afterwards.' He pulled her forward again, his fingers still digging into her arm.

She tried again to pull away but couldn't. 'I'd rather my cousin came with me. He'll be out of church in a minute. And you haven't told me your name.'

'Dobbs. I work for Mr Higgerson. Do try not to be stupid about this: my master wouldn't ask to speak to you in the churchyard if he meant to harm you, would he? It'd be only polite to see what he wants. And this has nothing to do with your cousin, whoever he may be.'

She saw Biff come out of church and knew he'd seen her and would follow her, so shot him a look that showed she wasn't happy and allowed Dobbs to start moving forward again. 'I hope this won't take too long. I have a lot to do today.'

'You'd be wise to stay for as long as Mr Higgerson wants. He's an important man in this town.' He tugged her to the right and she hung back till he jerked her forward again. 'This way, Miss Lawson. We need to go further round the church – unless you want everyone listening in on your business discussion?'

Business discussion? What did he mean by that? She went with him, walking as slowly as she could, feeling better when she caught a glimpse of Biff following them.

Higgerson was waiting at the rear of the church, half hidden by some large ornamental gravestones and monuments. There was no sign of his wife. Maisie would have felt better if another woman had been there.

Dobbs let go of her arm and stepped back, but only a little way, still blocking the path.

She hadn't liked the looks of Higgerson from a distance and it was worse close to him. She felt a creeping sense of unease because there was something so unhealthy about his puffy face and his pallid, pockmarked skin. It was as if he was a creature of the night come out into the sunlight by accident. You couldn't mistake the aura of power that surrounded him, though – or perhaps it was an aura of suppressed violence.

He didn't waste time on civilities. 'Did I hear correctly that you'd got yourself engaged to that Harte fellow?'

'Yes.'

'You could do much better for yourself than him. He doesn't have a good reputation in the valley.'

She raised her chin and scowled at him. 'I'm very happy to be engaged to Gabriel and I've heard nothing but good about him.'

'On your own head be it, then. You'll regret it.'

'I always prefer to make my own decisions. Now, I don't have a lot of time to spare, Mr Higgerson, so please tell me what you wanted to see me about, then I can get on with my day.'

He looked surprised at the crisp way she'd spoken to him, shot her a black scowl, then made a poor effort to change that into a smile. 'It's quite simple. I hear you've inherited a house and I wish to buy it from you. I'll pay three hundred pounds to take it off your hands as is. That's a lot of money and it'll set a woman like you up for life.'

He was trying to cheat her, must think her stupid to offer her so little! Houses like that one didn't sell for only £300, even without taking into account all the high quality furniture inside it.

Did he know about the contents? Probably not, because he hadn't mentioned them. Well, even Mr Tyler's workmen hadn't gone into the rest of the house, so not a lot of people knew what it was like.

She tried to speak calmly and politely. 'Thank you, but I don't wish to sell my house.'

He didn't trouble to hide his anger at her refusal and his right hand suddenly turned into a clenched fist and rose a little in the air. She moved instinctively back a step but didn't want to bump into Dobbs so had to stop. She wished now that she'd risked people talking about her and refused to come and speak to Higgerson.

'You'd be sensible to give my offer serious consideration, young woman. I'm sure it's more money than you've ever had in your life before. Houses like that cost a lot to maintain, you know. You've been sacked from your job and you weren't left any money with the house, so how are you going to live, let alone look after it?'

'That's my business. Thank you for your offer, but I shan't change my mind.' She became aware that Biff had come to stand openly at the corner of the church and relief ran through her like a tide. He must have been there all the time watching them, listening, as she'd hoped.

As she started to turn away, Higgerson signalled to Dobbs and pointed to Biff, making a pushing away gesture. His henchman stepped forward to bar the narrow path round the edge of the church and keep her and Biff apart.

Higgerson's voice was emphatic. 'You'll find that I usually get what I want in this town, missy, *whatever – it – takes.*'

She returned his stare, not knowing what to say to that obvious threat, so saying nothing. That was one of her mother's rules for difficult situations and it had proved a good one. She could hear Ida now, saying, 'If in doubt, say nowt.'

Higgerson seemed to expect her to reply and, when she didn't say a word but waited him out, he gave her a puzzled frown, then snapped, 'Good heavens, woman, you can have no attachment to the place. You only saw it for the first time last week and you aren't even from the valley. You'd be better taking the money, and afterwards my advice to you would be to go back to wherever you come from.' He paused, then added slowly, 'You might not be safe here in the valley.'

At these words, Biff moved forward to join her. As Dobbs blocked his path, he said, 'Get out of my way, you.'

Dobbs shot a glance at his master, then stepped aside.

Biff said, still quietly but somehow with a tone of confident authority, 'My cousin has given you her answer, Mr Higgerson, and our family is waiting for us. Maisie?'

'Stay out of this, whoever you are,' Higgerson snapped. He didn't wait to see his order obeyed but turned to Maisie and said, 'Three hundred and fifty pounds, and that's my final offer, Miss Lawson.'

'Thank you, but as I've already said, I have no desire what-soever to sell my house.'

'You'll definitely regret that.'

Biff was beside her now, offering his arm.

She took it and they moved away. As she clutched him tightly, she became aware that her hand was shaking. There had been something increasingly menacing about Higgerson and she'd begun to fear for her safety.

'Don't try to discuss this till we're on our own again,' Biff whispered.

She gave a slight nod, feeling safer when they got to the area where people were still lingering to chat. The meeting with Higgerson had left her feeling afraid of what such a man might do to get his way.

'Why did you go to speak to that man in the first place?' Biff asked. 'You should have stayed with your friends.'

'When that Dobbs person came up to me, they moved on, as if they were afraid of him. He'd taken tight hold of my arm before I knew it and I didn't like to make a fuss, which would have got me talked about. But I would have fought against him if I hadn't seen you come out of the church.'

She started to explain to him what Higgerson had demanded, but he suddenly said, 'Shh!'

She looked round and saw that the builder had followed them to the front of the church. He was still watching her and scowling, but at the same time he was speaking earnestly to Dobbs.

The latter was gazing at them scornfully and nodding from time to time.

'They're plotting something,' Biff said. 'And making sure we see them doing it.'

'I'll be even more careful about going out and about from now on.'

'How did he know about you and your inheritance?'

'I have no idea. But I did have to tell the other lodgers about the house, so it might have come from one of them.'

'I think we should mention Higgerson's offer to Sergeant Deemer tomorrow, or I can do it for you,' Biff said. 'It's important to let him know everything that happens because people who upset Higgerson have been known to vanish, and Deemer will be able to help keep you safe.'

'*Vanish!*'

'Yes. I've seen bad men in my job, but I reckon Higgerson is one of the worst I've ever encountered. He's got what I call the face of a killer, no emotion in his eyes whatsoever.'

'Except for anger if someone doesn't do what he wants.' She shivered.

'Yes. He might call himself a gentleman nowadays but he

doesn't act like one. He comes from outside the valley, and Deemer told me that no one has heard of his family. He's made a lot of money, and from what I've found out, has trodden on anyone who got in his way. How he married into one of the good families in town, no one can work out. He probably bribed his wife's family because her parents retired to the seaside. It still didn't make the better people invite him into their homes, though.'

'That poor woman looked dreadfully unhappy and nervous when he said something to her.'

'Who wouldn't be unhappy, living with him? People say he beats her.'

'That doesn't surprise me. It made me shudder just to be near him. And why did he think I'd accept such a low price for the house? It must be worth at least double that, without taking into account the contents.'

'Did he mention the contents at all?'

'No.'

'So he probably doesn't know what's inside the house. He's slipping!'

They were both quiet for a few moments, then Maisie said, 'I suppose he wants to turn my house into rooms to let. He could cram a lot of people into it.'

'He can buy other large houses though. He went after Bella's house too. He must really want those particular houses to have increased his offer,' Biff said thoughtfully. 'He doesn't often do that. I'm told that if he names a price for something you have to take it or suffer the consequences.'

'Well, he's not getting my house, however much he offers or however he tries to frighten me, which I admit he does.'

'We'll keep you safe, Maisie, whatever it takes.'

'His wife was with him in church, but no children. Does he have any?'

'They're grown up, at least the older son is. Felix Higgerson ran away from home a couple of years ago rather than work with his father. No one knows where he went, or if he's still alive even.'

'You've found out a lot about him for a newcomer to the valley.'

Biff smiled gently. 'That's my job. I'm rather good at gathering information. Now, why are we standing here chatting when we have dinner with the Hartes waiting for us?'

As they drove up the hill, she dared to ask about something that had been puzzling her. 'Biff is a strange first name. Is it short for something?'

'Yes, but I don't tell people my real name, not even you. Parents shouldn't inflict silly names on their children. I've not used mine since I left home as a young man.'

That made her smile, but his voice sounded so determined that she didn't pursue the matter, sitting quietly as he turned off the main road and drove through Birch End to where Gwynneth lived.

Biff didn't speak, either. He was more worried about Higgerson's interest in Maisie's house and consequent threats than he'd admitted.

He'd discuss the situation with Sergeant Deemer as soon as he got a chance. He didn't want anything bad happening to her. She was a decent lass and he too would have liked them to be genuinely related.

For the moment she was safe with him and the Harte family, but what would happen when he returned to London?

20

Simeon had planned to go north to Rivenshaw on his own immediately after his wife's funeral. The trouble was, his eldest son was proving so hard to deal with since his mother's death that Simeon couldn't, for shame, leave it to his wife's parents to handle the lad.

The Lisles were still very fragile, seemed sunk in grief over their daughter's death. They said they were willing to look after his younger son and the twins, and indeed, being with their three younger grandchildren seemed to give them comfort. But they admitted that they couldn't cope with Joss.

Simeon was finding it hard to cope with Joss, too. He was so full of grief and anger that you could hardly get a civil word from him. If Simeon went away, the lad's temper might get him into serious trouble. He was wondering whether to take Joss with him, but didn't want to do that, much preferring to make this sad journey on his own.

Jim Lisle had a word with him on the Monday, however. 'That lad needs some distraction. He's taking his mother's death hard – well, he was always her favourite. You'd better take him with you. He still listens to you but he pays no heed to what I say. Eh, it's a bad business.' He wiped a tear away openly.

'I'm upset by Minnie's death too, you know. And I need this journey into my past to put a few other things right in my mind, things I should have seen to years ago. But you have a point.' He couldn't hold back a sigh.

Jim patted his shoulder. 'Let's be frank about this. You were a kind, caring husband, which her mother and I appreciated, but if truth be told, you never loved Minnie deeply, so you're not as badly affected as we are.'

He held up one hand as Simeon would have protested. 'Nor did she love you deeply. She only ever wanted a husband to get children with and bring in the money to support them. She once told her mother he'd have to be good-looking so that they'd make pretty children together.'

Simeon was startled. 'She said that?'

'Yes. And you wanted a home and a family because you had none, we could see that. You fitted in well with our business, as well as with Minnie, so it was a fair bargain all round.'

'I'm glad you think so.'

On the Monday evening Joss proved his father's fears about what he might do were correct by getting drunk and ending up in a fight with a young chap who was usually a good friend of his. The police brought him home, told his father to pay for the breakages at the pub, and warned him about allowing Joss to get into trouble. They wouldn't be as lenient with the lad next time.

When Simeon looked at his son's grief-ravaged face, he had to face the fact that the lad needed to get away as much as he did. So be it. He took Joss aside. 'You can't go on like this, lad.'

'We can't all recover from losing Mum as quickly as you have,' his son threw at him.

'I haven't recovered. I don't think you ever recover completely from losing someone who's been such a big part of your life,' Simeon said as calmly as he could manage.

'You never loved her deeply! I've watched other people's parents and you two weren't loving. You were friendly, but you didn't even chat most of the time. And I could have been kinder to Mum, only now it's too late.' He sobbed and clapped one hand to his mouth as if to hold back more grief.

'Did it ever occur to you that your mother never loved me deeply either? Ask your granddad. She cared far more about her children than she could ever care about a husband – whoever he was.'

Joss frowned, stared down at his feet, knuckling away a tear. 'She was a wonderful mother and I miss her so much.'

'Of course you do. In her own quiet way she made us into a family, made this house into a home.'

'Then why are you running away when we still need to be a family?'

'I'm only going away for a week. I have to go back to where I grew up. I should have done that after I came back from the war. I need to see the people I grew up with – and visit the places I knew as a child.'

He waited for that to sink in, then forced himself to add, 'If you'd like to come with me, you can. But I warn you, I won't have you blaming me for things which happened in Rivenshaw before the war and long before I'd met your mother after I was demobbed.'

Joss frowned, sniffed back more tears, then said, 'All right. It'd be good to get away from . . . the memories.' Then he frowned. 'What things are you talking about? What happened?'

'I'll tell you when we get to Rivenshaw. Martha's agreed to take over the housekeeping. We'll have to ask her to pack for us. Damned if I'm any good at that sort of thing. Are you?'

'No. I've never had to do it. We never really went away from home, except for a week in Bournemouth every summer. Mum—' His voice wobbled. 'She loved it there, didn't she, walking along the seafront, going up and down in that lift thing on the cliff?'

'Yes.' It had seemed very tame to Simeon, brought up to go tramping across the Lancashire moors. And after a week, Minnie had always been ready to come home again.

'Will we be going to London, then? Or at least, will we see any of the famous bits from the train?'

Joss had mentioned wanting to see the capital before, so Simeon mentally revised his plans. 'We can go up to London on Tuesday, if you like, and have a quick look round a few of the sights, then go up to Lancashire on the Wednesday.'

His children definitely needed to see more of the world than their home town and Bournemouth. Minnie had wanted to keep them close. Simeon would prefer them to know a bit about the world and be able to stand squarely on their own feet, because you never knew what life would throw at you.

'That'll be smashing, Dad.'

It was good to hear Joss use that word again, which had been his favourite term of enthusiastic approval till his mother fell ill.

They travelled up to London, booking a room and leaving their luggage at a big hotel near the station. Simeon consulted the concierge who found them a cab to take them on a tour of the main sights during the afternoon.

This modest outing had Joss alternating between excitement and guilt at enjoying himself.

Simeon had seen London before when he'd been on leave during the war, and enjoyed his son's reactions more than the sight of the palaces and monuments.

From time to time he wondered how and when to tell his son about Ida. In some ways, the lad was still very young. Simeon had been much more aware of the complexities of life and people's relationships at that age than Joss was, not to mention having to depend on himself for getting enough to eat even before he left school.

If he'd had enough money, he'd have taken Ida with him to London when he moved away from Rivenshaw and then perhaps she wouldn't have died so young. He still felt guilty about that.

Or perhaps it'd have made no difference. The newspaper obituary hadn't said what she died of. People did drop dead occasionally because of some medical problem no one had known about. You read about it in the newspapers.

That was one of the things he wanted, no, *needed* to find out: what Ida had died of. He'd been so shocked to read of her death and know she'd already been buried without him being able to say a proper goodbye that he hadn't been able to think straight for a while.

It had taken him years to get over her and build a new life, then the Great War had intervened. The fighting and horrors of war drove everything else from his mind and all he'd wanted after it ended was to find himself a wife, start a family, and lead a quietly busy life.

They left London on the Wednesday morning, arriving in Rivenshaw mid-afternoon after changing in Manchester to a slower local train. By that time Joss was nearly bursting with suppressed energy.

They stood at the entrance to the station staring out at the big open square, and Simeon's son looked sideways at him, clearly wondering why they weren't moving on.

'Give me a minute or two to take it in, Joss. It's changed a lot, looks much busier. And of course, now there are cars parked in the square. There were hardly ever cars around when I was your age. I can't believe that about twenty-six years have passed since I left, or is it twenty-seven? I'm wishing now that we'd driven up here so that we'd have a car to get around in, but your granddad will need the family car for business calls.'

After a few moments Joss began fidgeting and sighing. 'It's not a big town, is it? Not pretty either. Our village is much nicer.'

'No, it's not pretty in that way, but it still feels like home to me. I was only twenty-one when I left. Eh, I really should have come back sooner. Well, we can't stand here all day.'

He signalled to the driver of the only taxi waiting outside the station and asked him if he knew a decent hotel where they could stay. The man nodded and deposited them at one that hadn't been there in the old days.

It wasn't a big hotel and there was only a double room available. He'd have much preferred a room to himself while he was here, but there you were: that's what came of travelling on an impulse.

He booked them a meal for that evening and whisked his son out for a brisk walk round the town centre in an attempt to get rid of the lad's suppressed energy and twitchiness.

'We'll go to the cemetery tomorrow,' he said as their meal ended.

'Are your parents buried there? Is that why we've come here? You still haven't told me why exactly.'

'I suppose they are buried there. I heard that they'd died a while ago. It wasn't like it is for you, mourning your mother, because they weren't very good parents. My father spent most of his evenings drinking with his friends, and my mother was a slapdash housewife who also drank a fair bit. I went hungry many a time as a lad.'

Joss goggled at him. 'You never said that before.'

'It's not something to be proud of, is it?'

'Why have you come back, then, if you don't care about them?'

'To make my peace with it all. And,' he took a deep breath and said it, 'to visit the grave of the woman I was, um, going to marry.' He'd never told anyone he'd already married Ida before he left, and hoped he wouldn't have to now. 'Only she died soon after I went away to London. I didn't even have enough money for her train fare, you see, was trying to make enough for her to join me. I've always regretted not waiting till I could take her with me, but a fellow was making life difficult for me here.'

Joss stiffened and scowled at him. 'You had another woman? What about Mum?'

'That all happened years before I met Minnie, and there was a war fought in between then and meeting your mother as well. There's no disrespect to her involved.'

'Oh. I see. You must have loved this northern woman a lot to want to visit her grave now.'

'I did.'

Perhaps he should tell Joss that he'd loved Ida enough to marry her? No, what did a two-week marriage matter now? He hadn't told his wife and her parents about it then, and there was no need to reveal it now.

Oh, they'd been so full of hope for the future when they got wed, he and Ida, and it had all ended with her death such a short time later. Eh, he'd wept himself to sleep a good few times that year.

It had been hard for a young man to cope with such grief on his own. It had taken him a while to pull himself together and get on with his life and he was just starting to do well in a little shop he'd bought into as a partner when he got called up into the army. The shop had been long gone when he came back from the war, though his elderly partner, who'd been looking after it, had been honest enough to pay the money it brought in to Simeon's bank account, thank goodness. Till he died in 1918, then there had been no more shop money.

'It's getting dark now, son. Let's go back to the hotel. I wonder if there's a cinema in Rivenshaw. If not, we're going to have a boring evening.'

There was a cinema and it was showing *The 39 Steps* which he'd taken his family to see last year. It was a really good film and had won awards for its director, a chap called Hitchcock, so they decided they'd enjoy seeing it again.

That kept Joss from asking too many awkward questions, thank goodness, and when they got back to the hotel, the lad fell asleep within a couple of minutes of getting into bed.

Simeon lay awake for a while, remembering Ida. He could still see her so clearly in his mind's eye. She'd had such a pretty face and lovely dark hair, had been much prettier than Minnie, prettier even than the heroine of the film.

He dreamed of Ida, of course he did, and woke a couple of times, feeling sad. He hoped Joss didn't guess how badly he'd slept, but luckily his son was more interested in eating his usual large breakfast than in chatting about a woman he'd never met.

21

On the Thursday morning Maisie woke before dawn and couldn't get back to sleep again. Her first thought was that she was getting married today and it instantly drove away the last of her drowsiness!

It was too early to get up, so she lay there marvelling at all that had happened to her in the past couple of weeks and thinking of the man she was going to marry. How could she have started to care about someone so quickly? How could she not when it was Gabriel, with his lovely smile and gentle ways?

Gradually the sky outside lightened and she went to peer out of the window hoping it'd stay fine. When she listened, she could hear a light wind blowing, but it wasn't raining and there were only a few stray clouds in the sky.

She got into bed again because it was cold, and lay counting her blessings. Most important was Gabriel. Dear Gabriel! She couldn't help smiling at the thought of his wonderful kisses. He had offered to marry her before they found out about her inheritance and hadn't even cared that she was bastard born. That mattered so much to her.

But she wasn't illegitimate, as she'd thought for most of her life. Knowing that Ida had been married made Maisie feel better about facing the world. It was very sad that her father had died so soon after the wedding, and in London all on his own, poor man. She didn't even know what he'd looked like, never would do now, she supposed.

The inheritance was another reason for happiness. She had never, ever, in her wildest dreams, expected to own so much. She was so looking forward to moving into her own home, her first real home, even if it was in a mess at the moment.

The other thing making her feel happy was that her life was going to be more interesting from now on. What's more – she caught her breath as she always did when she dared hope for what other young women usually took for granted – she might very well have children now and become part of a real family. She had never dared think that possible before. It had just been a dream.

For all the danger she was facing at the moment, it still felt as if she was living in a fairy story. She chuckled. Only this Cinderella had not only gone to the ball but had stayed there to marry her prince.

When Mrs Tucker's hard-working maid brought a cup of tea up to her room and said the landlady thought she deserved a treat today, that seemed to set the seal on her happiness. She could count on the fingers of one hand the number of times anyone had ever done such a nice thing for her.

She went down to breakfast dressed in her former working clothes, because she hadn't told the other lodgers she was getting married today, not wanting to face a barrage of questions. One of them had asked her last night why she was washing her hair midweek instead of at the weekend, but she'd pretended she'd got it dirty.

Mrs Tucker had winked at her from across the room at that question. She was the only one who knew the real reason.

Once the others had left for work Maisie went upstairs to change into her new wedding suit and pin her hair up in a low, loose bun, which would sit nicely under her new hat but wouldn't have been allowed at work. She stared at herself in the mirror and didn't think she was fooling herself that she was looking her best.

Mrs Tucker came up to see if she needed any help. She didn't, but it was a kindness that touched her.

'You look lovely,' the landlady said. 'I'll tell the others tonight that you've got married, as we agreed. I wish you well, Maisie. I'll miss you. My life would be a lot easier with more lodgers like you. Leave your trunk. I'll have it carried down to the hall later for your young man's brother to pick up.'

When she was ready, Maisie went to wait for Biff in the hall. He was driving her to the town hall because they'd decided to stick to the tradition that the groom mustn't see the bride on the wedding day till the ceremony itself.

Biff was on time and held out a flower to pin to her jacket. How lovely it looked! Another kindness on her special day.

Her happy mood came to an abrupt halt when they got to the town hall and Biff jammed on the brakes suddenly. She didn't need telling why, could see the jeering group of people standing in the car park there, blocking the way to the main doors of the town hall. As soon as they saw her in the car, they moved towards it and started throwing stones.

'Don't get out, and make sure your door is locked,' Biff said grimly. He drove to the far side, stopping as close to the entrance as he could, but the group followed the car and threw more stones.

Tears came into her eyes. 'What's going on? Why are they doing this?'

'I don't know. Don't try to get out yet. We don't want you getting hurt.'

'How am I going to get inside in time if they carry on doing that?'

'Someone in the town hall must have noticed what's going on and called the police. We'll wait for them.'

Another stone bounced off the roof of the car and she winced. 'Your car's going to be damaged.'

'It's only a tin box. It's you I want to keep safe.'

That same morning Simeon had found out from the land-lady that he had to go to the town hall to check where the grave was located in the cemetery. Surely Ida's family would have buried her there? He and his son got ready and set off just after half past nine to walk there.

When they got near the town hall, he stopped abruptly, because there seemed to be some sort of disturbance going on in the car park, with a group of people yelling and pelting a car with stones and rubbish.

'Don't go any closer,' he told his son.

An old man was watching this from the street and waving his walking stick angrily. 'Shame on them! Dirty rascals!'

Simeon went across to him. 'What's going on?'

'They're trying to stop that poor lass's wedding,' he said. 'Listen to what they're shouting.'

'Why would they do that?'

'I don't know. Maisie Lawson is as nice a young woman as you could ever meet, and decent in every way. She doesn't deserve this. I've chatted to her in the park a few times. And see that chap behind the big window next to the town hall door? That's the bridegroom, Gabriel Harte. Another decent person.'

Had he heard correctly? Had the old man really said the bride was called Lawson? Could she be a relative? 'Why are these people behaving like that, do you think?'

'I reckon that Higgerson chap must have paid them to do it. I don't know why he's trying to stop the wedding, but if he's set against them, they'll continue to meet trouble

one way or another unless they take the hint and leave town.
I've seen it happen to others over the years.'

Simeon jerked at this second shock. Higgerson! Was that
fellow still causing trouble? He'd expected the police to have
stopped him by now.

Before he could ask, his son chimed in. 'Did you say the
bride was called Lawson? That's our name. Could she be
a relative, Dad?'

'It's possible.'

As more stones hit the car, the door of the town hall
opened and three young men came out, clearly dressed in
their best for the wedding but looking grim and ready for
trouble.

'That's the bridegroom and his brothers. Eh, they'll get
their clothes ruined if they get into a fight,' the old man
said with a sigh. 'Shame on them folk for doing this, whatever they were paid.'

'Shouldn't we go and help them if she's called Lawson,
Dad?' Joss asked.

Simeon nodded grimly. 'Yes. I don't like to see a bride
treated like this anyway, whatever she's called. Try not to get
yourself hurt though. We just want to help get the bride inside
the town hall, not involve ourselves in someone else's battle.'

They hurried forward towards the three young men and
Simeon yelled, 'Need any help?'

The one pointed out as the bridegroom spun round. 'We'd
be grateful. My fiancée can't get out of the car till we've
stopped these people throwing stones.'

With five sturdy men ranged in a line and moving slowly
forward to block their way to the car, the group of troublemakers stopped throwing stones and hesitated, edging back
a little. There were more of them than the defenders, but
three were older women and the group of scruffy men didn't
seem to have an appetite for a more equal fight.

In the car Biff said suddenly, 'They've got help. Thank goodness. This would be a good time for you to get out and run into the town hall, Maisie. Slam your door shut if you can, but leave me to lock up the car. Just run for the main door fast as you can. We're not letting whoever's organised this stop your wedding. Go on! Get moving!'

She was out of the car in a flash, banging the door shut behind her and racing towards the town hall's main entrance.

One of the rioters saw her and yelled, 'That's her. Get her down!' He hurled a stone, but missed, and his next missile hit the arm of one of the young men dressed for the wedding. He quickly bent down to pick the stone up and hurl it back with a more accurate aim that had the attacker yelling in pain and clutching his forehead.

Just then a police car screeched into the car park and came to a halt.

The troublemakers hesitated as Sergeant Deemer and his constable got out, and the grey-haired doorman from the town hall came out belatedly to join the group of defenders.

As the police sergeant strode towards them looking furiously angry, the mob scattered and ran off, separating and rushing down different side streets.

Deemer stopped moving and stood watching them go, then pulled out his notebook and scribbled down some names. 'I know three of them and I'll be round their homes later to ask a few questions.'

Inside the foyer, Maisie was trying not to cry and Gwynneth had one arm round her shoulders, but at the same time was keeping watch on what was happening to her sons outside.

The young woman from behind the reception desk had come to hover nearby, keeping a wary eye on what was going on outside as well as checking on the bride.

'Is she going to faint?' she whispered to Gwynneth.

'No, I'm not!' Maisie mopped her eyes and blew her nose. 'I was just – upset. I'll be all right now. Well, I will as long as they don't hurt Gabriel.'

'What the hell was that about?' Deemer asked the bridegroom, preventing him from going inside straight away.

'They were trying to stop our wedding, shouting things like "Go home!" or "That bitch is not going inside" and worse.'

The sergeant sucked in his breath in shock.

'If these gentlemen hadn't come to our aid before you arrived, they might have hurt someone.' Gabriel turned to the two strangers. 'As it is, they've damaged Biff's car. I can't thank you enough for your help.'

'You can thank this old gentleman for us coming across.' Simeon gestured towards the old man who'd now hobbled across to join them. 'He told us the bride was a Lawson, and that's our name too.'

'I'll be damned!' Deemer studied him for a moment, frowning, then said suddenly, 'Lawson! What's brought you back after all these years?'

'I wanted to see the place where I grew up.'

'Hmm.' Deemer turned to the old man. 'Did you recognise any of the attackers, Barry?' He read out the names he'd scribbled down.

'Aye. They were there. An' I recognised a dead man come to life.' He gestured towards the older of the two strangers. 'I were told years ago that Simeon Lawson had died in London, but here he is, alive and well.'

Gabriel looked at him in shock at the sound of this name. Could it really be that Lawson?

'Who told you he'd died?' Deemer asked.

'Ida Fletcher. I found her in the park, crying her eyes

out. She showed me the entry in an obituary column from a London newspaper, sobbed against my shoulder for a long time that day, she did, poor lass.'

'It must have happened while I was working in another town. It'd have been some other Simeon Lawson who'd died, surely?' Deemer said.

'Nay, it said *Simeon Lawson from Rivenshaw, Lancashire* plain as anything in black and white. Someone had sent her the cutting, but there were no message with it, just the torn off bit of newspaper with its name and date at the top, saying as he'd died of pneumonia and been buried in some London cemetery or other.'

The world spun round Simeon and he clutched his son's arm, saying in a hoarse whisper, 'I was sent a cutting saying that Ida had died suddenly, also of pneumonia. That means we were both sent false information.'

Deemer gaped at him, but a man in a fancy morning suit came out of the town hall just then, stopping him from pursuing the matter.

'Which one of you is Mr Harte? Right. I'm the registrar and it's time for the wedding to start. Other people are waiting to get married, you know, so can you please hurry up. And I just hope you haven't brought any more trouble with you.'

He went inside again, pausing in the doorway to frown at them over his shoulder as if it was all their fault, and beckoning urgently.

'We'll be with you in a minute,' Deemer called, then looked at the stranger. 'Don't go away, Mr Lawson. I have a few questions to ask. But first we need to get these two young folk wed.'

The old man had been starting to edge away but stopped when the sergeant swung round and said, 'You'll need to stay too, Barry.'

'I had nothing to do with what was happening. I were just watching from a distance.'

'That means you're a witness, so I need you to stay.'

Barry looked as if he was going to protest, caught the sergeant's eye and shut his mouth again.

Gabriel turned to the stranger but decided not to ask him one vital question just yet. 'You'd be very welcome to join us for the wedding, especially if you're a Lawson as well. My fiancée thought she had no Lawson relatives left. I can't wait to see her face when I tell her your name.'

'Thank you. I'd like to join you and meet her. Was she the young lady who ran into the town hall?'

'Yes.'

Deemer wondered why the two of them were staring at one another as if they wanted to say something else. Then the stranger shook his head slightly and pulled his son towards the town hall.

'Well, let's get you wed, Gabriel lad,' the sergeant said. 'I'll come in with you in case the registrar tries to say you're too late. Or in case something else happens afterwards.'

Deemer began walking towards the entrance to the town hall, so everyone followed suit. He held the door open and saw them all inside, including Barry, before he joined them. He noted that two men he didn't recognise were still keeping watch on what was going on from the other side of the car park. He'd remember their faces now.

No doubt they'd tell Higgerson the couple had got wed. What would that sod do then?

Information about the dirty tricks played on Ida and Simeon many years ago was spinning round in his head, because he could guess who had done that. There was only one man in this town cruel enough. But now wasn't the time to pursue the matter. Now was the time for a very nice young couple to get themselves well and truly married.

He'd take the newly-weds and their guests out for a celebratory drink afterwards, just to show people in the town whose side he was on. That'd give him the chance to ask a few more questions.

22

I nside the town hall there seemed to be people peering out of every corridor or office as Gabriel walked across the reception area to put an arm round Maisie. 'Are you all right, love?'

'I am now. When you came outside I was terrified those people were going to hurt you.'

'I think they intended to, but as you must have seen, these kind strangers came to our aid. The troublemakers still outnumbered us, but they didn't seem eager to fight us when they weren't two to one, the cowards.'

He turned to the strangers. 'This is my fiancée, Maisie Lawson. You've just helped save our wedding, for which I'm extremely grateful.'

The older of the two strangers had already been looking as if something about Maisie's appearance had shocked him, but now he was gaping at her. Then he took a deep breath and said quietly, 'My name's Lawson too and this is my eldest son, Joss.'

'You're a Lawson?' Maisie stared at him in surprise. 'I didn't know there were any Lawsons nearby but—' She broke off, feeling as shocked as he looked. It couldn't be! Surely it couldn't?

She was about to ask what his first name was when the registrar interrupted, calling from the rear of the foyer, 'Come along, *please*, or I won't have time to marry you.'

'We'll have to go, love! We need to get it done before

anyone else tries to stop us.' Gabriel took her hand and looked at the two strangers and the old man. 'Please join us for our wedding. You've certainly earned a place. We can talk afterwards about how you may be related to Maisie, sir.'

Deemer turned to the constable. 'You stay here by the front entrance, lad. Keep an eye on the car park and ask everyone who wants to come inside what their business is. If they have no legitimate business, tell them I say to wait outside. We don't want any more interruptions to this wedding.'

The registrar was jigging about impatiently. 'Look! I'm sorry, Sergeant, but there are others waiting for me to marry them and more due to arrive any minute.'

Maisie gave up trying to sort out exactly who the stranger was. She could do it after the wedding ceremony. That was more important to her than anything else.

'We're coming,' Deemer told him, then clapped the old man on the shoulder. 'I'm glad you're joining us, Barry lad. I still want to ask you a few questions.' He ignored the fact that Barry looked anxious rather than pleased about this, and waved one hand in a shooing motion at Gabriel, Maisie and the others. He waited to go last of all, following the others across the foyer towards the rear of the building.

'Sorry to delay your wedding,' Gabriel said to the other couple sitting in the waiting area, presumably also about to get married. 'There was a bit of trouble in the car park.'

The man shrugged but neither he nor the woman with him looked best pleased.

Two burly men were sitting behind them and stood up with clenched fists and gloating looks on their faces when Maisie and Gabriel entered. They sat down again hastily as the sergeant came in, trying to hide their faces from him.

He stared at them, then took out his notebook. 'No need

to ask your names. I know exactly who you two are and I can guess why you're here.'

Gabriel, Maisie and their guests filed into the next room where the wedding itself would be celebrated and went to stand at the front at a gesture from the registrar.

Deemer stayed to stare at the two men in the waiting area, who exchanged glances and shakes of the head before standing up and moving towards the door. 'Don't let me see you again around town today!' he called after them, then went into the next room.

The brief ceremony began immediately Deemer closed the door and nodded to the registrar. The mood was at first tense, but the way the newly-weds looked at one another as they repeated their lines brightened up the atmosphere, as love always does.

In spite of the problems they might still be facing again outside, they were beaming at one another by the time the ceremony ended.

Deemer felt sentimental as he watched them kiss one another to seal the bargain.

'Did you book anywhere to go and celebrate afterwards?' he asked, once everyone had filed out into the waiting room, letting the next couple move into the inner room.

'We were going to my house. I've baked a cake,' Gwynneth said.

'Would you mind if we all went to the White Bull for a quick celebratory drink first, my treat?' Deemer said. 'It's a small place, but quiet, and it'll have just opened for the midday session. They'll let us use their back room at this time of day, so we can be private. We'll have a little chat there and see if we can work out why that attack was set up to stop you.'

He turned to Barry and the strangers. 'You two had better come with us, if you don't mind, Mr Lawson. You can talk to Maisie afterwards about how you're connected. Barry, I need you too, but I'll be buying you a drink, so cheer up.'

The older stranger nodded and murmured something to his son, but it took Barry a minute or two to nod, and he was still looking anxious.

'Come along then, *Mrs Harte*.' Gabriel took his new wife's hand. 'You can ride in style in the front seat of our van. Mam and Lucas will ride with Jericho. Pity his wife Frankie couldn't come too today, but she's not been well since she's expecting – and as it turned out, a woman in her condition is safer not being mixed up in this sort of trouble.'

Maisie kept hold of Gabriel's arm. She couldn't help looking round anxiously as they went out of the town hall and towards his van.

The two men who'd left the registry office so suddenly were now standing on the far side of the car park at the corner of a side street. They were talking to some other men, but when Deemer shouted, 'Hoy, you! Clear off!' they looked round in shock. They all hurried away up the street as he started striding across the car park towards them, radiating confident authority and followed by his tall constable.

Apart from them, the only people to be seen were a few women with shopping bags, hurrying along the nearby street and seeming completely unaware that there had been any problems at the town hall.

Deemer returned to the waiting group and ensured that the strangers and Barry squashed into the back of the police car, then set off, with the other three vehicles following him.

At the White Bull, a small but respectable pub just outside the town centre, Deemer had a quick word with the land-lady then led the way into the back room. The constable joined them, but sat close to the door, keeping an eye on the corridor that led into the main room at the front.

The landlady came in with a small pad and a pencil, saying, 'Congratulations!' to Gabriel and Maisie. When the sergeant asked everyone what they wanted to drink, she scribbled it down.

'I'm paying,' Deemer told her.

When she'd left, he said, 'Right, everyone. I think we should drink the newly-weds' health before we deal with some other, less pleasant matters.'

After the landlady had delivered the drinks, he stood up and raised his glass. 'May our young friends have a long and happy married life together.'

Once his good wishes had been echoed and the toast drunk, he set his glass of shandy down and signalled to his constable to get out his notebook, then turned to the strangers. 'Will you tell me what you saw today, sir?'

Simeon described what he'd seen, giving the exact number of people there, which clearly pleased the sergeant. His son did the same, but thought he'd noticed an older man peeping out of a shop doorway a little way up the side street nearest the troublemakers, watching what was going on.

'Would you recognise him again, lad?'

'Yes sir. I've got a good memory for faces.'

After he'd described him, the sergeant said thoughtfully, 'That sounds like Dobbs to me. You're an observant young fellow. Well done.'

Joss beamed at this compliment.

'Barry, I'll talk to you afterwards.'

Still looking rather anxious, the old man nodded to the sergeant and took another sip of his pint of beer.

Deemer turned back to the strangers. 'I've been wondering what made you get involved, Mr Lawson. Do you think you're a relative of Mrs Harte?'

'Before I answer that, Sergeant, can I ask her a few questions?' At the sergeant's nod, he turned to Maisie. 'Could you tell me who your mother was and when you were born, Mrs Harte? You look very like someone I once knew. In fact, you could almost be twins.'

'My mother was Ida Fletcher and I'm twenty-six.'

'Twenty-six!' He turned so white everyone stared at him anxiously.

His voice was hoarse. 'When did your mother die?'

'Four years ago.'

'Dear heaven! It was all false.' He covered his face with his hands and rocked about for a minute or two, looking like a man in utter anguish. His son patted him awkwardly on the back, looking bewildered.

After giving him a little time to recover, Deemer broke the silence by asking gently, 'What was false, Mr Lawson?'

'I was sent a cutting from the Rivenshaw newspaper, an obituary for Ida Fletcher. Nearly twenty-seven years ago that was, only two weeks after I arrived in London. I don't know how anyone found out my address there. When I thought Ida was dead, I was heartbroken.'

Maisie was shocked at what she was hearing, which seemed to confirm what she'd suspected about him. 'I found a cutting from a London newspaper among my mother's things, showing an obituary for a Simeon Lawson from Rivenshaw. And then – I found out only last week that she'd been married to him. Are you that Simeon?'

He shot an anguished look at his son, who was frowning in utter bewilderment now, then said in a low voice, 'Yes. How exactly did you find out?'

'My mother had hidden the marriage certificate in her sewing box in a secret drawer. I'd had the box ever since she died, but didn't know about the drawer till someone showed me how it worked recently.' She paused, opened her mouth as if to ask a question, then shut it again. But her eyes were devouring the stranger now.

'Can we – carry on this discussion later, privately?' he asked. His son tugged at his sleeve and he turned, saying gently, 'Joss, I will explain properly, I promise. But later, in private.'

The dark scowl returned to the lad's face as he stepped back.

Maisie reached for Gabriel's hand.

'Someone must have paid for those obituaries to be published,' Deemer said slowly. 'Someone who wanted to keep you apart perhaps.'

'Wanted to keep me away from Rivenshaw,' Simeon said grimly. 'Well, he succeeded. I'd had a few run-ins with a man called Higgerson, which was why, in the end, I went to look for a job in London. I was having trouble keeping jobs, thanks to him, and didn't want to spend my life trying to stop him harming me and mine. He had more money and power than me, even then. I'd already refused to work for him. I didn't intend to cheat and hurt folk.'

Barry joined in suddenly, 'I once heard Higgerson gloating about doing that to you when he was speaking to that Dobbs. Years ago that was, but I never forgot the cruelty of it. He said he'd make sure anyone else who was getting in his way left town. An' he did. A few folk left suddenly. It weren't only you he treated badly, Mr Lawson.'

'He'd not have done it or grown so rich if I'd been in charge in those days,' Deemer said. 'But he'd settled in as a property owner and married a young woman from a good family by the time I came back here to work. He made his money fast an' most of it was dirty money, I reckon.'

There was dead silence in the room now, then Barry spoke again, 'I knew he were doing bad things to make folk leave, but I were in no position to argue with a man like him, Sergeant. I were living with my old mum an' lookin' after her. Eh, she could hardly walk because of her rheumatiz, poor thing. There were only her an' me left, you see, an' I couldn't afford to get in that man's bad books. He'd have took it out on her to punish me. I seen him do that to others to make them toe his line, hurt their loved ones.'

'Gareth Higgerson,' the stranger said in tones of loathing. 'I shouldn't have run away to London, only I knew he'd go to any lengths to stop me, and I was selfish enough to want to marry and get on with my life. Well, I certainly paid dearly for it.'

Barry was looking at the sergeant, who was staring at him expectantly. 'Eh, don't make me get involved in this, Sarge,' he pleaded. 'I still dursn't go against a rich man like him. It's me as has the rheumatiz now an' can't hardly walk. An' I'm living in one of his houses, just a small room, but it's all I can afford.'

'Only you can tell us some of the details, Barry,' Deemer said quietly. 'We need your help if justice is to be done.'

'Didn't I just tell you I dursn't say any more? I've prob'ly said too much already. Higgerson will have me killed if I tell you the rest. I can't run away. I've nowhere else to go and no money, only my old age pension to live on. Please don't make me tell you anything else, Sergeant, an' don't tell other folk what I've already said.'

His distress and fear were so pitiful, Gabriel pulled Maisie to one side and said in a low voice, 'You and I have to help Deemer gather enough information to convict Higgerson or we'll never be able to live in peace and safety, any more than Mr Lawson would have done. Can we offer the old man a room in our house where he'll be safe till this is sorted out?'

As she hesitated, he added, 'I feel sure that if Higgerson isn't stopped, you and I won't be able to stay in the valley, either. Then he'll get your house.'

She stared at him, then at Barry, upset by his shaking hands and panic-stricken expression. She nodded and Gabriel sighed in relief. He hadn't been sure Maisie would agree to that, and he felt it was her house. But he had to help the sergeant, just had to. He didn't want to run away as Simeon Lawson had done, wouldn't run away, on principle.

Anyway, today had showed how far Higgerson was prepared to go to get that house.

Sometimes you had to fight evil and this was one of those times. Gabriel felt sure Higgerson wouldn't win against Deemer in the long run. The sergeant was not only a good man but a clever one. It was staying safe till that man was stopped once and for all that was going to be the difficulty.

He turned to the old man. 'If you came to stay with us, Barry, you'd be safe, because we've hired watchmen. You wouldn't be able to go out to the pub till this was all settled, but we'd feed you and look after you. That way, you can tell our good sergeant every single detail you know. I bet you've heard a lot just sitting in the pub.'

Deemer nodded thanks for this offer and looked at the old man expectantly, waiting for him to speak.

'You're sure of that?' Barry asked. 'I could have a room in your house for as long as I need it? I'll share my pension with you to pay for my keep.'

'Yes. We have plenty of spare rooms. We can go and get your possessions on our way back.'

'Then I'll say thank you an' do it. I hate that house I'm living in.'

The sergeant intervened. 'It'd be better if I went with him and got his things, then took him to the police station, pretending I'm arresting him. I'll bring him round to your house after dark and we'll try to keep his presence there secret. You're already providing beds for other folk if the troubles with Germany get worse, so it'll be good to try things out and see if certain steps I've already taken work.'

Both Lawsons were frowning at him, a bit puzzled by this, but though he gave them a quick glance, he didn't try to explain, just turned to the old man again. 'You have to be quite sure about this, Barry lad. There'll be no going back once you've moved out of your present room and spoken to me. Not till he's been dealt with, which might take as long as a year or two.'

The old man stared from one to the other, sighed and gave a couple of slow nods. 'Aye. I'll do it if I can be kept safe. It'll be a relief to get a few things off my conscience afore I die, things I've kept quiet about for too long. An' it'll be a relief to live in a clean house too. I can't abide mucky folk.'

Gabriel and Deemer exchanged satisfied glances.

'I'm thinking Higgerson has made a big mistake today, having you two attacked so openly,' the sergeant said quietly. 'The Greeks have a word for it: *hubris*. It means too much pride or self-confidence, leading to their downfall eventually.'

He saw Biff nodding and Maisie mouthing the word. They were a good, open-minded bunch of people, these. He'd not have many policing problems if everyone were like them.

He couldn't help noticing that Mr Lawson had gone back to staring almost hungrily at Maisie. Well, she looked very like her mother at the same age. After hearing about the trick with the obituaries, he could guess what it was all about and felt sorry for the lad who'd now discovered his father's secret and didn't seem yet to have realised how it'd affect him personally. But how to deal with that would be for them to sort out, not the police. He'd have enough on his plate with Higgerson.

Eh, people wrote books about strange things happening, but he'd seen a lot of strange and terrible things in real life that were far worse than those in books, and encountered behaviour that sickened him to the core. It seemed like you had to struggle constantly to hold back evil.

But he always consoled himself with the knowledge that there were good people around too, people like these. He'd spent his whole working life trying to protect and help such folk, had some small pride in what he'd achieved so far.

23

Deemer left the pub with Barry in the back of his car and drove him to his lodgings. Other people poked their heads out of nearby rooms as he helped the old man into the house and left the constable in the corridor outside.

He closed the door and helped Barry gather his belongings together, wrapping them up in the sweaty-smelling bedcovers for lack of anything else.

When they'd finished, he led the way out of the room, carrying one bundle, and telling the constable to bring the other two.

The man next door asked cheekily, 'Going somewhere, Barry?'

'I'm taking him away,' Deemer said. 'And he won't be coming back.'

'What's he done?'

'That's my business.' He turned to the old man and said in a deliberately rough tone, 'Come along, you!'

He had to wait for Barry to shuffle slowly out of the building and ease himself into the car. When he looked round, he saw the same man standing in the doorway, still watching them. The constable had to push past him with the other bundles.

As they settled in the car, Deemer said, 'Sorry to speak to you so roughly, but I wanted him to think I was arresting you.'

'Suits me, Sarge. That chap reports on the other tenants to Higgerson's rent agent. Nasty little sod, he is.'

At the police station Deemer took Barry and one of his bundles inside the building and left the constable to unload the others.

'I'll have to put you in a cell for the rest of the day, Barry, because we can't move you out till after dark, but you're not being arrested or anything. It's to keep you safe.'

'Higgerson seems able to get his bullies into anywhere,' the old man said gloomily. 'An' you've still got to get me to that young couple's house without anyone knowing, if I'm to have any chance of staying safe. How are you going to manage that? I'm worried that I'll be in danger.'

'I doubt Higgerson's men will get past my constable, and the back door to the cells is locked and bolted, so you'll be safe here. I have a new secret way of getting out of the station and into that house. I doubt even *he* knows about it.'

Barry looked faintly surprised. 'I just hope it stays secret, then, for all our sakes.'

'Trust me. In the meantime, you have a rest. I'll go home and get my dinner now. I'll bring you something to eat when I come back.'

The old man's face brightened.

'Do you want to read yesterday's newspaper to pass the time?'

Barry positively beamed at him. 'Yes, please. I pick up newspapers people have throwed away sometimes. I'm not a fast reader, but there's a lot in a paper to keep you interested, an' pictures sometimes too. I like to look at photos. Thanks, Sergeant.'

That old fellow didn't expect much from life, Deemer thought as he left him eagerly shaking out the newspaper and mouthing the headlines. He told the constable to look after the police station and ring the emergency bell if he needed help, then went across the backyard to his home for a midday meal.

He'd question Barry further this afternoon and get down as many details as the old man could remember. That might start him remembering other incidents.

Deemer also intended to go out for a little drive and call at the houses of those who'd been in the group throwing stones at Maisie. He doubted they'd be there, because they'd be expecting him, but he hoped his visit would make them reluctant to get into similar trouble for a while, and would certainly upset their families.

He had a quick word with the constable while he was at it, just to remind him that if Higgerson tried to blackmail him into giving him information about what went on here at the station by something like threatening his family, he was to report it at once If he was caught colluding with Higgerson, he'd lose his job instantly.

'I don't care what he threatens, you mustn't let him frighten you, lad. You're either on the side of law and order in this job or you're out on your ear. Eh, these hard times have driven some folk into breaking the law to survive, but the north is coming out of it all now, thank goodness, like the south mostly has.'

The young man stared at him, suddenly looking older and maybe a little wiser than when he'd first joined the police force. 'I'd not betray you or anyone else, Sarge. Apart from the fact that I loathe Higgerson an' what he does to decent folk, my dad would hit the roof if I gave in to bullying from anyone. He hates bullying an' says you must never give in to it. Any road, he's got friends who'd help keep him and the rest of the family safe – if they're threatened. Which I don't think they will be.'

'Good lad. You're turning into a fine policeman.' Deemer patted him on the shoulder and the young man straightened his back, clearly delighted by this rare compliment.

It was all beginning to mount up, Deemer thought.

Higgerson had made too many enemies. No one could control a whole valley full of people, and anyone who thought they could was out of touch with the realities of the modern world.

What's more, the new friends Deemer had made, who were as inspired by Mr Churchill's speeches as he was, were not only interested in using Maisie's house as a staging post, but would help him against such a predator if he needed it, he was sure. Well, they included Mr Peters, didn't they? No one would ever be able to buy off the valley's new JP. Deemer could recognise a scrupulously honest official when he met one.

Higgerson's latest target was that nice young woman and her inheritance, so he'd better let Peters know about it. The more people keeping an eye on her, the better.

Deemer had waited years to catch Higgerson, and he wasn't going to rush it on the last stretch and fail. He wanted his valley permanently clear of that villain and by hell, he was going to make it happen whatever it took.

When the sergeant had taken Barry away to collect his belongings, Maisie turned to Simeon Lawson. She was about to ask him the important question when he put one finger to his lips and whispered, 'Can we go somewhere to talk privately? It'd be very easy for someone to eavesdrop on us here, not just from the corridor, but from outside the window. I don't want this news getting back to anyone until I've had a chance to explain the situation to them.'

Joss stared at his father and frowned at Maisie, but didn't say anything.

'We'll take them to our new home, Gabriel,' she said. 'We can be completely private there.'

He gave her arm a little squeeze and a nod, as if to show he approved of this, but he was watching Lawson as if prepared to step in and protect her. It was wonderful not to be on her own.

She turned to Gwynneth and her other two sons. 'Thank you so much for coming to our wedding today. I'm sorry this wedding has been spoiled when you've baked a cake for us, but if what I think is true, meeting Mr Lawson is one of the most important things that has ever happened to me.'

They looked puzzled, but gave her and Gabriel hugs and left. She had never had so many hugs in her life.

Biff stayed behind. 'I need to be near you to help keep you safe, Maisie. I'm sure Higgerson hasn't finished playing dirty tricks.'

'He's right, love,' Gabriel said. 'Your safety is the most important thing and he needs to be involved.'

'Very well. Um, perhaps you can drive Mr Lawson and his son to Daisy Street, Biff, then I can speak to my husband privately on the way there?'

When Biff nodded, she looked at Gabriel and didn't quite manage to keep her voice steady as she said, 'Can we go now, love?'

In the van she couldn't hold her feelings back any longer. 'He must be my father, don't you think?'

'Yes. It's obvious if you know the rest of the story. Eh, to think of Higgerson playing a rotten trick like that on them – and getting away with it for all those years, too. Did you see how upset Lawson was? He must have loved your mother very much.'

'Yes, but why didn't he come back to Rivenshaw? I know he fought in the war, but that didn't break out till a few years after he found out she was dead – supposed to be dead. Surely, if he loved her so much, he would at least have come back to Rivenshaw to visit her grave?'

'Who knows why he didn't, Maisie love? Maybe he

couldn't face it. Maybe the war affected him, as it did many others. At least he's here now. Only her real grave isn't here in Rivenshaw, is it? Didn't you say she died in Rochdale? Presumably she was buried there? Are you going to tell him that?'

'Yes, of course. And I'll be very disappointed in him if he doesn't go to see her grave now.'

Gabriel started the van and set off. 'From what you've told me, even her relatives in Rivenshaw didn't know where she went after she left, and she was using a different name.'

'She used more than one name over the years, pretending she was married. After she died, I left Rochdale and changed my name officially to what I thought had been my father's name. Mum let it slip once when she'd had a few drinks and I could tell she'd loved that man more than any of the others. I never forgot it. It was the only clue I had to who I was.' Her voice wobbled on the last words.

Gabriel thought about this. 'Biff said even the other detective the London lawyer hired gave up the search for your mother, so Lawson might not have found her even if he'd tried. Luckily, when Biff came to hunt for her, he consulted Deemer, who was able to help him. I wonder how many bits of information our sergeant carries in his head.'

'He's like a walking encyclopaedia of the valley and the main families in it, isn't he?'

Gabriel waited and when she didn't say anything else but continued to frown into the distance, he said softly, 'There's something else to consider, too. Simeon must have got married before your mother died, so it wasn't legal. Joss and the other children are the ones who weren't born in wedlock, not you. That'll really upset her family and his other children.'

She looked at him in consternation. 'I hadn't thought that far. Oh dear, they'll find it hard if that gets out, because people can be so cruel about it. My mother made sure she called herself a widow, so that I had the name of someone people would think had fathered me. It's even written on my birth certificate, though how she managed that, I'll never know.'

'Well, you can be sure I don't care about that. It's you I fell in love with, and so quickly, as if we were meant for one another.'

'I feel like that, too. But I wish this hadn't come up on our wedding day. My thoughts are in a terrible tangle. I never expected to meet my father. I thought he was dead.'

'Well, if you want my opinion, he seems a nice chap – came to our rescue outside the town hall even before he realised who you must be.'

'Yes, he did.' Something eased in her a little at that thought.

'What a day! Look at all the things that have happened, apart from us getting married. It's definitely a day we'll remember for many reasons, good and bad.'

'Yes, and all I wanted was a quiet, happy day.'

'Well, they say "Man proposes, but God disposes" don't they? They're right.' He stopped the car.

'Oh! We're here.'

'Yes. Come on, love. Let's get ready for our visitors.'

They got out of the van and stood looking at their new home.

'Where do you think we should put Barry?' she wondered aloud.

'How about up in the attic? We haven't time to clear out another of the main bedrooms for him.'

She nodded. 'We'll take him up a good mattress, some bedding, and a few pieces of furniture, and make sure he's comfortable. It'll probably be safer for him to stay up there all the time than come downstairs. No one else need see him except Biff, Rob and Phil. Biff has sorted out a room for himself, so he'll be nearby at night in case there's trouble.'

'He'll be close to you as well till we get this trouble sorted out.' Gabriel gave her one of his special smiles. 'But not close enough to spoil our wedding night.'

She gave him a quick hug. 'I'm so glad we managed to get married.'

He brushed the hair back from her forehead and planted a soft, tender kiss on it, heedless of who saw them. 'Me, too. Very glad.' He gestured towards the house with one hand. 'This time it really does feel as if we've come home, doesn't it?'

'Yes. It's a lovely house – or it will be one day.'

Rob opened the front door before they got there, beaming at them. 'Congratulations, Mr and Mrs Harte!'

Gabriel smiled at him. 'Thank you for your good wishes.' He took Maisie by surprise, picking her up, ignoring her squeak of protest, and carrying her across the threshold.

'You fool.' But her voice was loving.

Rob was watching them with a grin. 'Did everything go off all right?'

'Actually, no.' Once they had the front door shut and locked, Gabriel explained quickly what had happened at the town hall.

Rob's face lost its smile. 'I'd like to strangle that Higgerson. He's caused more trouble and pain in the valley than anyone else. A cousin of mine had to leave because of him.'

'Well, for the moment your main job is to make sure Maisie is kept safe – and there will be another person staying here as well as our detective friend, an old man called Barry, who's going into hiding from Higgerson.'

He trusted both their watchmen enough to explain the details.

'I know old Barry slightly. He's well known all over

the town. He sits in the park on fine days, watching the world go by.'

Then there was a knock on the front door a couple of minutes later and Biff joined them, bringing the Lawsons.

24

Maisie and Gabriel asked Biff if he'd check that Rob and Phil were all right and choose a room in the attic for Barry while they took Simeon and Joss into the sitting room for a private chat.

He understood immediately what they wanted. 'I'll leave you in peace to sort things out with Mr Lawson. I hope it all turns out well for you.'

In the sitting room Simeon took the initiative, looking at her and saying, 'You've worked out that I'm your father, haven't you?'

'Yes. It seems obvious.'

'I didn't even know you existed, so it makes me feel as if I've been given a gift, that something of Ida and me has survived all the unhappiness I went through. I hope you're pleased about it, too. You chose my surname before we ever met. How did you find it?'

'I'd already guessed it, but I'll show you how I found out for certain.' She got her sewing box out of a small cupboard and took out the contents, handing him the marriage certificate, the newspaper cutting, and a rather battered photo of her mother as a young woman that she'd put in the drawer for safe keeping.

The photo brought tears to his eyes and he kept staring from her to the photo and back. 'You're so like her, I find it – well, unnerving to look at you, because it's as if she's suddenly come back to life. Though you have some of my family's features, like your hands, with the long, elegant fingers, and the red glints in your hair.'

Joss said nothing, but he was listening intently, with a sullen expression on his face as he stared from one to the other.

Simeon turned to him. 'Maisie is your half-sister and she's not at fault. She's as much a victim of that horrible man as I am.'

'But what about Mum? It isn't fair to her, you thinking about another woman so lovingly.' Something suddenly occurred to Joss and he gaped at his father, then threw words at him like daggers. 'You must still have been married to *her* when you married Mum! That means you weren't really married so—' He gulped, unable to continue.

'I didn't do it on purpose, son. At the time I thought Ida was dead and I was free to marry Minnie.'

'But you can't have loved Mum as you should, because you still look as if you care about that other woman, even after all these years.'

'You'll find that you can care for more than one person as you pass through this world, or else widows and widowers would never marry again.'

As Joss continued to look at him accusingly, he tried to explain, speaking to both his children now. 'I didn't go back to Rivenshaw because I never doubted that an obituary in a newspaper would be true. I was just recovering a little when the war began, which meant the army dictated what I did with my life for several more years. The fighting was – hard going and – very difficult to get over afterwards. I can't stop myself thinking about the horrors I saw, and sometimes I have nightmares about it all, even now, after all those years.'

He stared into space for a few seconds, then continued, 'When the war ended what I wanted desperately was a normal life and a family. I met your mother and it all seemed to fall into place, Joss, because she wanted that desperately too. She was ten years younger than me and she'd given up hope of finding a husband. So many young men of her own generation had been killed that many women never did find husbands. I really liked her quiet ways and appreciated her homemaking skills, so we got married and I think we made a good family life together.'

Joss shrugged his shoulders.

'I can't believe I've got a father *and* a brother,' Maisie said.

'*Half*-brother,' Joss snapped.

'You have another half-brother and twin half-sisters in Wiltshire, as well,' Simeon said.

She stared in surprise for a moment, then glanced at the brother who was now scowling down at his feet, avoiding looking at her. She couldn't help asking her father, 'Will they accept me as part of the family, though?'

'Once they get used to the idea, I'm sure they will. They're kind and decent young folk and they'll understand that what happened wasn't your fault – or your mother's. Joss, surely you can accept that?'

'What about you not being married to my mother?' the lad asked in a strangled voice. 'That makes us all bastards.'

'What does a word matter?'

'It'll matter to other people.'

There was silence and Maisie's heart ached for the lad.

Simeon spoke slowly, as if thinking aloud, 'Well, since Ida really is dead now and it won't hurt her, I wonder whether we three can keep quiet about the dates. What do you think, Maisie? Need anyone ever know that my second marriage wasn't lawful?'

He sent a pleading glance at her.

Her answer was more to her half-brother than her father. 'I see no need whatsoever to tell anyone and tarnish your mother's memory, Joss. Or my mother's memory, either. She lived with another man later on, even told everyone she'd married him. That wouldn't have been legal either.'

Gabriel laid one hand on her shoulder in unspoken support and she raised her hand briefly to touch it then he pulled it away.

Joss nodded slowly as he thought this through, so she went on, 'We can pretend my mother died during the war, so that your – I mean *our* father's second marriage wasn't against the law.'

He frowned then muttered, 'Yes. All right. We can do that. And well, um, thank you.'

Simeon chimed in. 'You shouldn't even tell your brother and sisters about this, Joss. It's far easier to keep secrets if you don't share them with too many people. Besides, it'd only hurt them to no purpose, as it's hurt you. I'm so very sorry about that.'

After another moment's thought, Joss nodded slightly.

Simeon gave him an approving glance then turned to take his daughter's hands, holding her at arm's length and studying her face as if memorising it. 'I'm also deeply sorry that I've missed all these years of your life, Maisie, but I can't be sorry about the children I had with Minnie. I love them all dearly.'

Joss flashed him another of those quick, assessing glances, blinking his eyes rapidly.

'Of course you love them,' she said at once. 'I loved my mother dearly too, though she wasn't perfect. She lived for the moment and I could understand that better after I found she'd been married to you so briefly.'

Biff knocked on the door just then and wheeled in a tea trolley with a large teapot on the top, milk and sugar next to it, with a mingled assortment of cups and a big plate of biscuits on the lower shelf.

Maisie welcomed the interruption, feeling they all needed

time to get used to their new relationships. She even wondered if Biff had been eavesdropping, it was such a good time to bring an end to a difficult conversation.

'I thought you might all fancy a cup of tea,' he said cheerfully.

'What a good idea!' She began sorting out the cups and saucers and setting them out on a small side table, then pouring the tea and letting Biff pass the cups to the others.

He sat down with a cup of his own when that was done, taking it for granted that he'd join them and murmuring in pleasure as he took a sip.

'When we've finished, I can nip to the village shop and buy some food for our evening meal, if you like, Cousin Maisie. And for tomorrow's breakfast as well, come to think of it. Though it'll have to be something like sandwiches and tinned soup for tea because I'm no cook.'

Maisie gave them all a rueful smile. 'I hadn't even thought about a meal. I couldn't think beyond getting married this morning. I'm not much of a cook either, I'm afraid, and I've no experience of keeping house for a family. So yes, please go shopping for us, Biff. Do you need some money?'

'No. Mr Neven's chief clerk gave me some for expenses.'

When they'd finished, Biff turned to Joss. 'Perhaps you'd like to come with me to the village shop, lad? We'll walk there and get a breath of fresh air. You can help me choose the food and carry it back. If you're anything like I was when I was your age, you'll be a hearty eater.'

'I do get a bit hungry sometimes, Mr Higgins. And yes, please. I'd love to stretch my legs.' He moved to join Biff near the door without even asking his father's permission, clearly eager to escape the tensions for a while.

As they were leaving, Gabriel whispered, 'Do you want me to leave you alone with your father, Maisie love?'

'No. You and I should face important things together now, don't you think?'

His smile was warm and he took her hand, patting it. 'It's how the rest of us Hartes do things, that's for sure. Welcome to the family!'

She gazed at him for a few seconds longer, surprised yet again at how comfortable she always felt, as if she could say anything to him.

They turned to Simeon, holding hands for a moment longer, then Maisie let go and indicated the trolley. 'I think there might be another few half-cups of tea in the pot, if you two don't mind a lukewarm drink. I'm having one anyway, because I'm still thirsty even if you aren't.'

They shared the tea that was left, then chatted more calmly, exchanging information about their lives. Simeon showed her a couple of photos of his family.

'You look a bit like your sisters, Maisie, and your hair is the same colour, dark with a reddish glint to it. It's an unusual shade. I'd guess it comes from my side of the family, because their mother's hair was a mousy brown. Ida's hair was dark, too, but a different shade to yours – and theirs. I wish we had coloured photos, then you'd see what I mean. They may colour them in by hand, but they can't put in the subtleties when they do that.'

She liked the idea of there being some sort of resemblance to him. She produced one of the last photos taken of her mother from her big handbag and he sucked in his breath, studying it avidly, even running one fingertip over the image of her mother's face. 'Ida didn't lose her looks as she grew older, did she?'

'No. She had a touch of grey at the temples and a few wrinkles round her eyes, but she was so lively, she always seemed younger to me than other women of her age.'

'She must have had to earn her own living. How did she do that?'

'She worked as a barmaid – in a respectable pub, mind. She was fun, and her customers loved her. Nothing made her sad for long. She always told me people have to carry on, whatever life throws at them.'

He smiled. 'I remember her saying that to me. She hadn't had an easy childhood, that's for sure. Eh, I wanted so much to give her a happier life.'

Maisie waited a moment for him to regain control of his emotions, then asked, 'Tell me about your other children.'

He smiled at the mere thought of them and took out a photo, seeming to be a truly caring father. They were a good-looking family.

She wished she'd had such a man in her life. It would have made things much easier, she was sure. But you couldn't go back and change the past. She would keep quiet about when her mother had really died, for the sake of Simeon's children.

If Simeon came back to see her again and people wondered, they'd just refuse to go into details about the past. She was determined to leave her mother in peace.

Biff and Joss returned from the shop with some food and Biff said he'd arranged for more to be delivered. 'I forgot how much would be needed when I suggested walking there. I decided we should feed our watchmen as well and that'll help their families, so I've bought quite a lot. They're part of keeping an eye on you, after all, so Mr Neven can pay for it.'

She hid a smile at that, knew he had a soft heart for people struggling to put enough food on the table. He must have had some difficult times himself.

The rest of the afternoon passed quickly after that, what with sorting out space in the larder for the food and helping Biff rearrange a bedroom for himself.

Having decided which one he wanted and checked that this was all right with Maisie, he got Gabriel's help to clear a space and move one of the three beds cluttering up his room to the attic, taking up the base as well as the mattress. There was plenty of storage space up there and Barry would be delighted with the new bed, he was sure. The poor old chap seemed to have been living in poverty for years.

While that was happening, Joss asked Maisie's permission to go off on his own to explore the house and examine its contents. 'I won't disturb things, but I think it'll be interesting. I don't like just standing around doing nothing.'

'Neither do I. You go ahead and explore. It's all in chaos still so you can't make it any worse.'

Maisie went looking for Joss after half an hour or so, to check he was all right. She came upon him in one of the children's bedrooms, sitting on the broad windowsill reading a book in the fading light. He looked up and closed it hastily as if he thought she'd object.

'What are you reading?'

He showed her: *The Story of Doctor Doolittle*.

'I know it's only a children's book, but it's very interesting,' he said.

'I love reading,' Maisie said.

'Do you? Didn't your mother mind?'

'No, of course not. She liked to read too, but mainly women's magazines. I'd rather have a long story.'

'We don't have any story books at home now, though we had a few when we were little. Mum thought they were a waste of time and said they just gathered dust, but I enjoy reading them, sometimes more than once. I had to sneak books home from the library and read in bed. Dad knew, but he didn't say anything.'

'You can keep that one if you like.'

He gaped at her. 'Really?'

'Yes, really. This house contains hundreds of books and that one doesn't interest me. If there are any others you'd like, show them to me. I shan't give you them if they're books I love or want to read, but I'm sure you can find plenty that won't appeal to me.'

'Oh. Well, um, thank you. That's very kind of you.' He began to fiddle with the book as if he didn't know what to say or do next.

'It's strange, isn't it?'

He looked at her, still wary. 'What is?'

'To meet someone who is a half-brother or sister, and you didn't even know they existed before.'

'Mmm. Very strange. I don't mean to be rude, but you don't *feel* like a sister.'

'Perhaps I will one day if I'm lucky. I envy you so much growing up with a brother and sisters. I used to long for a family when I was a child. There was only me and my mother most of the time. I miss her very much.'

Tears came into his eyes and he blinked them away hurriedly. 'I miss my mother too.'

She risked giving his hand a quick squeeze. 'I do understand how you feel about her dying, Joss. I lost my mother a few years ago and still think about her often. She died very suddenly of pneumonia.'

'Mum died of a growth. It took her two months to die. She was so brave when she was in a lot of pain.'

'You'll remember her with both love and admiration, then.'

'Yes. She was a good mother.'

Maisie waited a minute before changing the subject. 'Well, I'd better get on. We've still got to find a few pieces of furniture for Barry's bedroom. Not fancy stuff and not big pieces, either. The only places not crammed with who-knows-what are the three bedrooms in the attics, but they're not big rooms. There were only the bed frames left there and thin flock mattresses in dusty rolls, so Biff and Gabriel were going to find Barry something more comfortable to sleep on once they'd finished another little job. What other furniture do you think he'll need? He's going to be staying up there for a while.'

'A comfortable chair, then, and a chest of drawers. Oh, and a little table to eat at if he's got to stay hidden even for meals.'

'Yes, of course. Good thinking.'

'Maybe I can help you to find a few bits and pieces?'

'I'd be grateful if you would. We don't even know what's in the bedrooms on this floor apart from the one Gabriel and I are going to use, and the part of one Biff has cleared for himself. Gabriel and I have concentrated mostly on clearing the downstairs, the sitting room and part of the kitchen, because that's where we'll spend the most time.'

Joss stuffed the book into his jacket pocket, giving it an affectionate pat, then followed her out of the children's room. It was he who found a small chest of drawers and helped her empty it of old-fashioned children's clothes. He also found one or two other books for himself, beaming with delight when she said he could keep them.

When they rejoined the others, her father listened to Joss's tale of what they'd been doing, giving Maisie a smile and a wink when his son wasn't looking. So perhaps she had made a start at getting on well with them both. She hoped so.

Would she ever feel truly close to them, ever feel they were really her family? She'd do her best to bridge the great gap between their lives – oh, she would! – and she had some hope now that they would try too.

She was especially pleased at the thought that she and Joss might have taken a step or two closer after their little chat today. She didn't think she was fooling herself about that, hoped not. Poor lad. He was at such an awkward age, neither boy nor yet quite a man.

When it began to get dark, it was time for her father and Joss to return to their hotel for their evening meal, so Biff drove them back.

She and Gabriel agreed that it was too difficult to carry on searching the dark shadowy rooms lit only by a couple of old-fashioned oil lamps, because the temporary electric lights were only in the downstairs rooms and the main bedroom. Strangely, they hadn't found any more oil lamps, but there must surely be some.

Gabriel gave her one of his lovely smiles. 'This is our wedding night, Maisie love. We're entitled to sit down and spend a little quiet time relaxing together.'

He got the fire burning more brightly in the sitting room and they pulled the sofa a little closer to it. When Gabriel put his arm round her, it felt good to lean her head on his shoulder and she hoped Biff wouldn't hurry back.

'I'm longing to have proper electric light, aren't you, Maisie? It makes such a difference to long winter evenings to have bright, steady light instead of flickering shadows.'

'I agree.'

'Well, Tyler's men will be back at work here tomorrow so it'll only be a few days before we've got all the amenities. We'll have to be very watchful about who comes in and out of the house while they're working, though.'

She shuddered, hating this continuing sense of danger. 'A proper bathroom will be good, too. I hate having to go out with an escort to use the lavatory.' She grimaced at the thought then fell silent again, enjoying the warmth of the fire and staring into the flames, but most of all, enjoying the closeness to her brand-new husband.

She'd never met anyone she could sit with quietly like this.

It was a while before he spoke. 'Are you getting hungry? I know it isn't very romantic, but I'm afraid I'm ravenous.'

'I'm hungry too. Let's see what we can find to eat.' She got up, pulling him to his feet with her, not wanting to let go of his hand.

The rest of the food from the village shop had been delivered and was sitting on the kitchen table. It included some meat pies for their tea and a can of mushy peas, as well as tins of fruit and cream, so it was easy enough to get a simple meal ready. She hoped Gabriel wouldn't mind that she wasn't a very skilled cook. Perhaps his mother would teach her a few simple dishes.

His stomach rumbled as he spoke, and she laughed. 'You sound to be in desperate need of feeding and I'm rather hungry too. Let's make a start,'

Biff took longer than they'd expected to return. He came in carrying a big suitcase after they'd finished eating, and explained that he'd been chatting to his landlady as he collected the rest of his things from his lodgings.

'I'll just take my case up to my room.'

He was back almost immediately.

She gestured to the table and the covered plates and dishes on it. 'You must be hungry. There's food here and more bits and pieces in the pantry. Rob and Phil haven't eaten either.'

'I'll call them to eat with me, and you two can spend some more time on your own.'

'Thank you.' Gabriel took her hand and they went back to the sitting room where he put another few pieces of coal on the fire.

They discussed what sort of furniture they'd need in here, when they might be able to clear the room totally, then fell silent again and simply watched the flames.

After a while Maisie caught sight of the clock on the mantelpiece and realised it was nearly time for bed. She was starting to feel rather nervous about the coming wedding night and what it would involve.

'This has to have been the strangest wedding day ever,' she said and immediately felt annoyed with herself for sounding nervous.

'I'm still glad to be married to you, whatever it took.'

'Are you, Gabriel? Truly?'

'Of course I am.'

He picked up her hand and pressed a lingering kiss on it, which sent a rather nice little shiver running through her body.

He pulled her into his arms and dropped another of those delightful little kisses on her forehead. 'Am I mistaken or are you a little nervous about tonight?'

'I am a little, Gabriel. It's all right people telling you what to expect – my mother did that years ago – but the women I've heard talking about it seem to feel differently about what happens in bed. Some enjoy it, some don't, so how do you know what to expect?'

'You haven't – done it before, then?'

'No. I saw my mother treat it like a pleasant pastime and I wanted more than that if I ever found someone to marry. She said I read too many books and it wasn't like that in real life, but I think I was being sensible. Besides, I always worried about the money side of things as well. I didn't want to live in poverty and struggle to feed my children as I saw others doing.'

'That was important to me, too.'

'I'm older than most brides, too. Most women have a couple of children by my age.'

'You're not all that old, have just lived long enough to develop a bit of sense about life. I'm several years older than you, nearly thirty-three now. I hope you don't mind that.'

'Not at all.'

'It means I've had some experience with women, but not a lot because I felt a bit like you: I didn't want to end up having to marry someone simply because she was expecting a baby. I know you can take precautions to stop the babies, and I did, but they don't always work.'

After a brief pause, he added, 'And I've never, ever done it with love as I shall be doing tonight.'

'What a beautiful thing to say!'

'I mean it.'

There was a clatter from the kitchen and she jumped in shock. But the noise was followed by laughter and a man calling another person a 'clumsy clot', so she relaxed again. 'I keep expecting someone to try to break into the house,' she confessed.

'I very much hope they won't test our defences tonight. I want us to enjoy our wedding night without any interruptions. Remember, we'll have a wakeful watchman patrolling the house and another who can be woken up quickly sleeping on a mattress in the kitchen, not to mention Biff just along the landing.'

'And I doubt either of us would stand still and let someone cause trouble.'

'Well, I'd do my best to defend you – always – but I've never been much good at fighting. It's not a sane way to solve quarrels and I don't think I'm very good at it.'

'You saved me from Jeff Conway.'

He chuckled. 'Let's be honest about that, Maisie. I took him by surprise and we drove away before he could pull himself together.'

'Well, it worked, and you won, which is the main thing, surely?'

When they went up to their bedroom a short time later, she got undressed as quickly as she could, trying not to show too much of her body as she put on her nightie then climbed

nervously into bed. He quickly took his own clothes off and
lay down beside her, naked, which shocked her a little.

'Cuddle up to me,' he said softly. 'I'm not going to do
anything you don't like, I promise.'

He kissed her so beautifully it made her feel loved and as
if she wanted more of his touching and kissing. Soon she
forgot her fears and followed his lead into a pleasure that
took her by surprise.

Afterwards, they pulled the curtains back, using the moonlight to find their way around. They laughed as they found
the bedcovers in a tangle, since neither of them could work
out how that had happened.

By this time she was so tired she was having trouble staying
awake, and he patted her shoulder. 'Go to sleep now, love.
It's been a busy day. I'll get dressed again and go downstairs
to wait for our good sergeant to bring Barry here.'

'Oh dear! I'd completely forgotten about that. Are you sure?
Shouldn't I help?'

'I think I can find the way up to the attics to show Barry
where to sleep. Close your eyes. I'm going to switch the torch
on now.'

'Well, wake me if you need anything.' She couldn't hold
back a yawn, closed her eyes, and was asleep within seconds.

He stared down at the bed fondly. What a delightful woman
she was! His wife in every way now. He dressed quickly and
tiptoed out, glad to see there was an oil lamp burning low in
the hall. He waited for the sergeant, but didn't want to fall
asleep so every now and then he strolled round the ground
floor.

Deemer had said he'd be bringing Barry to the house
around midnight, though how they'd get inside without some
hidden watcher noticing, Gabriel had no idea. The sergeant
had mentioned coming via the cellar, but if there was a weak
spot there, Gabriel intended to make it more secure afterwards.

On that thought he took the lamp and stood it at the top of the cellar steps.

They were all certain there would be watchers outside the house still. Rob said there had been two men keeping an eye on it all day. Whoever it was hadn't tried to get inside or done any damage to the outside, so you couldn't stop them hanging around nearby, but it was annoying to know they were there.

25

Deemer took Barry out of the police station by the new secret entrance and let the car roll down a nearby slope. At first his constable walked behind them, keeping his eyes and ears open in case anyone was still out and about.

When Deemer stopped and Cliff got into the car, he reported no signs of anyone in this part of town. 'There's not likely to be, either. It's freezing cold.'

Fortunately the moon was nearly full so Deemer could drive safely without using his headlights. He went up the hill to Birch End by the back lanes where he'd played as a child. He didn't think any vehicle was following him, though he stopped to check that a couple of times, just in case, stopping the engine to listen for a minute or two each time, as well as watching out for other vehicles' headlights.

They saw and heard nothing.

To his amusement Barry seemed to have dozed off in the back of the car. Some people could sleep through anything.

When they got near their destination, he parked on some waste ground in the shadow of a building. Even if anyone passed by, he doubted they'd notice his car. He still sent Cliff out first to check that no one was watching this part of Birch End.

Only after the sharp-eyed young constable had reported no sign of anyone did they wake Barry and help him out of the car. Deemer offered the old man his arm and guided him into a yard round the corner, entered from a back alley. The gate hinges must have been well-oiled because it opened and shut silently.

Someone must have been watching out of the window for them because the back door opened as soon as Deemer and his companions had closed the gate behind them. All they could see was a shadowy figure inside, because the room was lit only by the moon.

The man beckoned to them without saying a word. Not until he'd closed the back door behind them, bolted it and drawn the curtains did he switch on a dim light, which turned out to be at the head of the cellar steps.

'This way, and last person please close the cellar door and bolt it.' He ran lightly down the steep, narrow steps, but they could only follow slowly because of Barry.

Once they were all standing in the cellar he opened a panel in the wall at the far end. It had looked as if it was just a series of shallow shelves containing a few oddments like dusters, but after he'd fiddled with something, one section of the shelves swung out like a door to reveal another flight of stairs leading down. He switched on a wall light at the top which lit their way.

These steps were much steeper, and Barry drew back, looking nervous.

'You don't have to worry,' Deemer whispered. 'We'll help you down. This leads into an old quarry which has been closed for centuries but had tunnels giving the workers short-cuts to the village. That means we can get across this part of the valley without being seen.'

Barry edged towards the top step and the sergeant continued to hold him steady and talk to keep him from worrying.

'The inner passages have stayed watertight, would you believe? They weren't stupid in the old days, whatever some idiots say about the past.'

'Eh, to think of the quarry standing there for all them

years with no one knowing about the passages,' the old man exclaimed.

'Keep your voices down,' their guide warned.

Deemer nodded but kept talking in a near whisper. 'Some folk must have known about it or we'd not be here now. Think on, though, the people who've opened all this up again are doing it for their country so you mustn't say a word to anyone about it.'

'Of course I won't. I'd never do owt to harm my country, never. Sorry I'm so slow. I'm a bit stiff these days.'

'Just take your time. There's no hurry.' Deemer continued to back down, steadying the old man, who was looking increasingly wobbly.

When they reached the bottom, their guide pulled forward a wheeled stretcher from a wider part of the corridor. 'Let's help him up on this. It's been put here in case anyone gets injured, but it'll help get you get through to your destination more quickly.'

Barry allowed himself to be helped up on it and lay down on the canvas with a murmur of relief.

As they set off, Deemer and his constable took one end of the stretcher each to guide it along. The way was now lit only by the man going in front of the group with a powerful torch, but the ground underfoot proved to be fairly smooth and they soon began to walk more confidently.

Deemer had been told that this underground route had been finished, but hadn't yet been along all of it. When they reached a flight of stone stairs leading upwards he slowed down instinctively, but their guide said, 'Not this exit, the next one.'

The sergeant wondered where these steps led and how many exits there were. That was another thing that had deliberately been left vague in his briefings.

The guide stopped. 'We're here.'

Deemer helped Barry sit up. 'Can you make it up some more steps?'

'I think so.'

Their guide went to the top and shone his torch down the steps to help them up, then opened another panel into a cellar. 'Here you are. Daisy Street.'

Gabriel must have heard them coming because he and Rob were waiting for them inside with a lamp set on a shelf.

He was holding a battered cricket bat as if ready to defend himself, and grinned as he waved it about. 'I wondered what that sound was, so I came prepared. I didn't realise there was a secret entrance that came out in here. I thought you'd be using the coal delivery shaft to get into the house, or else getting rid of the watchers for a few minutes.'

Deemer had his arm round the old man. 'Well, you can put your terrifying weapon down now and help me get Barry to bed. I think we'll have to carry him up to the attics. He's done well, but I reckon he's reached his limit now.'

As Gabriel dumped the bat to one side, Rob stepped forward. 'Let me carry him upstairs, Sarge. He can't weigh more nor a child.'

'Eh, you're a strong lad,' Barry muttered as he was lifted easily into Rob's arms.

'Aye. Comes in useful sometimes.'

Gabriel led them up to the attics and showed the old man the amenities arranged for him, including a chamber pot in the next room.

He stared round, seeming surprised. 'Eh, this place is far nicer than the room I've left an' I feel safer here already. I'm that grateful for your help, lads. I'll do my best to remember more things for you, Sergeant, and answer any questions you come up with, I promise.'

They left him with a small torch, but he switched it off

before the last person had left the room and it was clear that he'd soon be asleep again.

'They've done well to dig out those connecting passages without being caught,' Deemer said with satisfaction as they went back downstairs. 'I'll explore them properly when things quieten down a bit round here. We'll be all right in future if an escape route out of the valley is needed.' After a moment's thought, he added, 'Or a way to bring people in.'

'What would they have done about the secret passages if the new owner hadn't seemed absolutely trustworthy?' Gabriel wondered aloud.

'Locked up the secret entrance to your cellar and no one in the house would have been any the wiser about its existence,' Deemer said. 'I was the one who suggested they go ahead and make more than one set of passages in the first place. We weren't sure whether these houses on Daisy Street would ever be occupied because they'd been standing empty for about a decade, so we took a chance.'

He patted his host's shoulder. 'When Maisie inherited and you two got together, I soon felt certain you'd let us use the facility and be reliable hosts to travellers, if needed. She's a fine lass, that one.'

Gabriel smiled involuntarily at the thought of his new wife. 'I certainly think so. It makes you think, seeing the passages I mean. There must be other similar preparations being made in secret across the whole country. It won't only be happening round here.'

'There are definitely others. Mr Churchill believes in preparing for resistance to an enemy, in case of invasion, and he has considerable influence even though this government won't do anything about it. He's spoken on the radio and said his piece in various newspaper articles, telling the country it should prepare in advance in case it comes to out and out war. Some folk just won't believe it'll ever be necessary.'

He sighed and shook his head sadly. 'Fortunately, there are other patriotic people who experienced the chaos at the beginning of the Great War and therefore hold the same views as Churchill. And you'd be surprised at how many ladies are involved already, too. Well, we all found out during the last war how big a contribution ladies can make.'

He rolled his shoulders, looking tired. 'You're right in what you're thinking, lad. Folk who're trusted are being gently nudged into action all over the country. No one knows every-thing about what's going on. Safer that way if the worst happens.'

It was nearly half past one before Gabriel could get to bed, but he felt good about being trusted with this secret, as well as sad at the idea of another war. He hadn't been old enough to fight in the last one, thank goodness, but had spoken to chaps who had. And everyone had seen poor fellows who'd lost both legs pushing their way round the world on little trolleys because they couldn't afford fancy wheelchairs like rich folk could.

He prayed that it would never come to the madness of outright war again and that the tunnels and hiding places would never be needed. But if they were, and people round here had to act to defend their country, he and Maisie would do their bit, whatever it took. Shame on anyone who wasn't loyal to their king and country.

It was strange how sure he felt of her being in agreement about that, and about many other things. He'd been so lucky to meet her, and not because of her inheritance. He liked simply being with her, chatting, holding hands.

In fact, it felt as if they were meant to be together.

Maisie slept better than she had for several days and woke to find her husband lying next to her, smiling at her in the grey light of early dawn.

'Good morning, Mrs Harte.'

'Good morning to you, too, Mr Harte. Is it time to get up?'

'I've only been awake a minute or two myself and I can't hear anyone else stirring, so let's not get up yet. While you were snoring—'

'I do not snore!' She pretended to punch his arm.

He chuckled. 'That remains to be seen. But you're easy to tease.'

She suddenly remembered. 'What about Barry? Why didn't you wake me? Did he get here safely? I should have been helping him settle in.'

'No need. Deemer brought him to the house last night and Barry fell asleep as soon as we got him into bed. Did you know there's a secret tunnel leading into our cellar?'

'*What?* Heavens, I had no idea.'

'You'd never guess it's there, and Deemer said they weren't followed, so I doubt anyone could have seen Barry come in.'

'However did he know about the tunnel?'

'He knew there were some additional tunnels being made, but even he doesn't know all the details of the new system yet. It's been created by that group he's working with, the people we agreed to help.'

'Oh, that's all right then!'

'You don't mind helping out if we're needed, do you?'

'Of course not! Where exactly does the tunnel go? I'm dying to see it.'

'Apparently it leads into some passages that were part of an old quarry on the edge of the moors. It was abandoned over a hundred years ago and most people have forgotten it exists.'

She was frowning, trying to work it out. 'There was no sign of another door in the cellar.'

'It's behind a secret panel. I'll show you later how to operate it in case you ever need to get out without being seen.'

'How exciting! It's just like a *Boys' Own* adventure story, the goodies saving the world from the forces of evil – or at least foiling criminals who're trying to steal something. Mam always said that sort of thing was for boys, but I used to love reading the magazines when I could get hold of one.'

'I married a tomboy, eh?' He yawned. 'Mmm. I could just go back to sleep again, but I'd better not. It's going to be another busy day, I'm sure. Isn't Charlie Willcox coming to look at more furniture this morning?'

'Yes. And I'll be glad to get rid of some more pieces.' It was her turn to yawn. 'Just a few more minutes and we'll get up.'

However, they both fell asleep again and when she next woke it was fully light and Gabriel was shaking her.

'Come on, sleepy-head! It sounds as if the others have all got up before us, and someone's hammering at the door. But I'm sure they'll excuse us being tired.'

The thought of one of the reasons they'd think caused the tiredness made Maisie cheeks warm up, but she felt her face had gone back to normal by the time she joined the others in the kitchen. Well, she hoped it had.

Mr Tyler's men had started work as soon as it grew light and were already well into the day's jobs by the time Maisie and Gabriel went downstairs and had a quick visit to the lavatory.

That was embarrassing too because two men were just outside it, digging trenches and laying pipes to connect the house to the main sewage system.

Inside the house, two others were doing more work on installing the wiring inside all the rooms.

The electrics would take another two or three days, Mr Tyler said, and they'd worry about light fittings another time. The indoor plumbing and bathroom were well on the way and would continue rapidly as long as she didn't want a fancy bath ordering.

'Any bath will be wonderful,' she said feelingly. She'd had to use a tin bath and carry water to and from it to the sink for most of her life.

The newly-weds only had time to gulp down a cup of tea and gobble a piece of bread and jam each before the builder started them on a tour of the house, because he needed to ask where they wanted the electric points putting in each room, and whether they wanted the electricity to go up to the attic, which not everyone bothered about.

They exchanged worried glances. The only thing they were certain of was that they did want electricity in the attic. When he said they'd be better off with two plug sockets not one installed in each of the main rooms, they told him to go ahead and do that, but hadn't a clue where it would be best to put them.

It was soon apparent that Mr Tyler had a much better idea of exactly what would be needed and where to put it than they did.

After a while he grinned at them and suggested, 'How about I send for my wife and you leave it up to her to decide about the electrics, being as we are in a hurry to get it done? She's the best person I've ever met at working such things out, better than me and far better than you two, if you'll pardon my saying so. And she loves doing that sort of job.'

'Oh, yes. Please tell her we'd be extremely grateful for her help. I'm ignorant of such things because I've only ever lived in rented rooms in older houses where someone else had already chosen what to have,' Maisie confessed.

'You're not alone. I've seen quite a few people who're utterly bewildered when they're having electricity put in. Eh, I always think of my grandmother at times like this. She'd be astonished at how much more convenient modern houses are. But they'd be no cleaner than hers, mind. She was a demon for scrubbing and dusting.'

They left him to send for his wife and went to join Biff in the kitchen. By now they were both desperate for something more substantial to eat than their tiny breakfast snack.

'I'll take food up to Barry then stay around the kitchen area to keep an eye on who comes in and out of the house today, if it's all right with you,' Biff said. 'I told Mr Tyler about our worries and he assured me his men only need to use the back door, so we'll keep the front door locked. He's going to tell them to be particularly watchful here for strangers trying to sneak in, but I reckon when they're concentrating on what they're doing, they might not notice if someone slipped past them.'

'Do what you think best,' Maisie said with a shiver. There it was again, a reminder that she might be in danger.

Charlie Willcox arrived at ten o'clock as arranged to take away more furniture, by which time Maisie and Gabriel had eaten a boiled egg apiece and then had a quick look round the rest of the ground floor to pick out some more large pieces they didn't like the looks of, including a mahogany dining table with carved bulbous legs.

Maisie studied it and grimaced. 'Ugh. It looks like a monster that's squatting ready to pounce on anyone who goes too near.'

Charlie was amazed all over again at how much stuff had been crammed into the rooms, not just big pieces like the ones he'd already taken away, but smaller items and boxes of what might or might not turn out to be rubbish.

'Eh, I wish I had a house like this one to clear out every

week. It amazes me that no one really knows why it all got piled up in one house when there's obviously stuff from several houses here.'

'I shall be glad to see the back of the stuff you're taking away today,' Maisie said. 'Some of it's very ugly.'

'I must say I'd not like to live with that monster of a table myself,' he said. 'But don't you want to know what prices I expect to get before you let me have it?'

Gabriel shook his head. 'No need to tie yourself down to prices, Mr Willcox. We don't have a clue what things are worth. Just get us the most money you can. Everyone says you're honest.'

He beamed at them. 'I appreciate that compliment, I really do. I won't cheat you – or anyone. It saves a lot of worry, as well as hassles, being honest does. Which reminds me, I've already sold a couple of the pieces you gave me. Not my taste in furniture, but this customer is a big chap and I'd told him I'd look out for some larger than usual pieces, so I got in touch with him straight away about yours and he came at once. Isn't the telephone a marvellous invention?'

He paused for a moment to nod emphatically at that, then continued his tale. 'My client was delighted to find a sofa he could sit on comfortably and a dining table with what he called "decent sized chairs". Here's your money.' He slipped an envelope into Maisie's hand.

'Thank you. Oh, and if you find any envelopes containing messages from Miss Chapman among the things you take away, will you please return them to me?' she asked. 'They're not addressed to anyone specific just to the descendant who inherits.'

'Of course I will.'

It seemed rather rude to look at how much was in the envelope till after Charlie had left with his first load, and when she did open it, she gasped aloud and clutched her husband's arm. 'Gabriel, look! He got over twelve pounds for the two items he sold, and they were really horrible.'

'He'll have got more than that. Don't forget he's taken his percentage first.'

'Oh, yes, of course. What shall we do with the money?'

'Keep it somewhere safe till we need to pay Mr Tyler.' He looked a bit embarrassed as he added, 'I can't afford to pay him, that's for certain. I shan't be bringing in any wages this week, either, because it's more important for us to settle in here.'

'Money doesn't matter to me. You're helping keep me safe and making me feel happier than I have for a long time.'

'Truly?'

'Yes, truly.'

They spent a moment gazing blissfully at one another, then she had a thought. 'I'm assuming that you'll be doing a lot of the maintenance on the house when it's finished, though. That'll be an important contribution. And I do have some money saved from when I was on my own. I was always afraid I'd fall ill and need something to fall back on. It's in the savings bank.'

'You keep it there. That's your money.'

She shrugged. 'Unless we need it for the house.'

'We'll, I'll happily do most of the maintenance, I promise you, and that'll save us quite a bit.'

She was pleased to see that he looked cheered up by what she'd said, as she'd expected. She was getting to know him, and liking what she'd found.

'It doesn't worry you that I have so little to bring to our marriage, does it?'

'You've brought me the most important thing of all: yourself.'

He gave her a huge hug and spun her round for good

measure. 'Ah, what a lucky day it was when I met you. Now, where shall we keep our money?'

'How about in my mother's sewing box, in that secret drawer?'

'Good idea.'

They put it away, then she sighed. 'I keep wondering how my father is getting on today. It'll make him feel sad to see my mother's grave, I should think.'

'I'm sure he'll cope. And he's got Joss to cheer him up.'

'He said he'd come round tonight but he's worrying about his other children, feels guilty for leaving them so soon after the funeral. He may go to Wiltshire tomorrow. I do wish there were more time to get to know him. And Joss.'

'He'll come to visit you again, I'm sure, and bring his other children next time. And he said he'd write.'

She nodded and changed the subject. 'Let's start going through the clothing we took out of the furniture in our bedroom. It's all piled up in a corner and looks a right old mess. Charlie said to give him any that's half decent and he'll sell it in one of his pawnshops, even if it's old-fashioned in style.'

'Is there anything that man can't sell?'

'Not much, I should think. He says there was so much more material in the ladies' clothes from our grandmothers' days that today's women can often cut out the worn parts, make whole new dresses or skirts for themselves, and still have some material left over for children's clothes. They wore separate skirts and tops more often than dresses in the old days and sometimes, if the women don't care about fashion, they just need to shorten the skirts.'

'You seem to know a lot about the past.'

'I used to fill the evenings with reading. I don't know what I'd have done without the library. I like to learn things – anything, any time. Eh, let's get on with it and stop nattering.'

He couldn't help thinking she must have been one of the loneliest people he'd ever heard of, poor love. Well, he'd make sure she wasn't lonely any more. That was another thing he could give her, a share of his family.

A little later, as they were going through the last of the clothes from their bedroom, they found another of the handwritten notes from Jane Chapman in among some old-fashioned underwear. This too had a five-pound note enclosed.

Dear descendant,

If you're reading this note, you're doing a thorough job of clearing out the house. I could never face going through my mother's things and by the time I inherited my aunt's house and her clothes as well, I felt too weary to go through everything and simply left it in this house and sent my mother's things here as well.

I hoped I'd feel better and be able to tackle clearing it properly later but I never did, so I'm going to leave that job to you.

This money is to help with your living expenses. I expect by the time you've finished sorting everything out and selling the pieces you don't want, you'll have enough to do some renovations and put some money away for living on and for a rainy day as well. You'll certainly have earned it.

I hope you have a long and happy life.

Jane

'She sounds such a nice lady. I wish I'd met her.' Maisie stroked the signature, which was as near as she could get to her kind relative.

'Well, at least we have an idea of why stuff has just been piled up here now, but why didn't she simply pay to have it taken away?'

'Perhaps she loved some of the things she'd inherited too much to throw them out. She must have gone through some of it to have left these notes.'

'I suppose so.'

She looked up at the ceiling and said softly, 'Thank you, Miss Chapman.'

He echoed her words, thankful most of all for Maisie herself, though also for the house, of course. Who would not value such a gift? It made you feel rich, having a house of your own did, so few ordinary people managed it. It had definitely been beyond his most optimistic hopes.

But best of all was having Maisie to share her life with him.

Biff had taken on the task of taking a tray of food upstairs for Barry at meal times, and at midday he found the old man sitting near the dormer window in the small armchair they'd brought up for him. He was reading an old-fashioned magazine with the help of a magnifying glass. They'd found a pile of magazines and hoped they'd help him pass the time.

He smiled across at Biff. 'I've never had such a comfortable bed in all my life. The breakfast was grand, too, and now you're bringing my dinner up for me. I'm that grateful to you all.'

'You'll be helping out the sergeant, so you'll more than earn it.'

'I feel able to help him now I'm away from that Higgerson. My head feels clearer without all the worries that he'd throw me out of my room. He's such a horrible man.' He gestured towards the pile of magazines. 'And look at all these. I'm going to enjoy reading them, even if they are several years old. They're new to me, after all.'

'Do you want a newspaper as well today? There is one going spare downstairs from a couple of days ago.'

'Yes, please.'

But when Biff came up an hour later with a cup of tea and the recent newspaper, Barry was sleeping soundly in the armchair, snoring gently, and the magazine had fallen to the floor.

Smiling, Biff left the cup of tea, quite sure Barry would be happy to drink it, even if it was stone cold.

He went downstairs slowly, wondering how long it'd be before Higgerson struck again. There were bound to be more problems ahead, because a leopard doesn't change its spots, and that man was as nasty as any wild animal.

He'd write to Mr Neven later and try to make the situation clear to him, as well as the need for ongoing help to look after Maisie until Deemer's efforts to get rid of Higgerson paid off.

It'd be nice if there was a lull for a little while, though. Apart from anything else, Maisie and Gabriel were newly-weds and needed time together – deserved it, too. You never really knew someone properly till you'd lived with them for a while.

He would do his very best to help them.

26

Higgerson was furious that the men for whose services he'd paid good money had seen no sign of activity near Daisy Street during the night and no one had any idea where that old man had been taken after he disappeared from the police station.

He took out his temper on his wife, as usual.

For the first time ever, the worm turned and she fought back, throwing ornaments and anything that came to hand at him.

Trying to avoid the missiles, Higgerson tripped over some broken pieces, flailed wildly and fell. As he tried to get up, he found he'd hurt his ankle and couldn't bear to put any weight on it, let alone chase after her.

'Help me up!' he roared, astounded when she ran out of the room. He let out a howl of sheer rage that brought servants running.

By the time one of them phoned for the doctor and the gardener had been summoned to help his valet get him upstairs and on to his bed, his wife had vanished. He demanded her immediate presence, but no one could find her.

They didn't actually make a thorough search because they all felt sorry for the poor lady.

He lay back and glared at them. Lallie must be hiding somewhere in the house, he decided, so summoned her maid. A terrified housemaid, who was now wishing she hadn't come running to see what had happened, assured him that Pansy was in the kitchen and hadn't left it for the past hour.

He knew the maid couldn't have been involved in hiding his wife, but dammit, what did he pay her for? She should have been with her mistress.

When Pansy swore she didn't know where his wife was, he beckoned her closer.

Looking puzzled at this order, she moved forward, thinking he wanted her to pass him something. As soon as she was close enough, he slapped her across the face good and hard.

She screamed and leaped back, holding her cheek.

'That was to teach you that you *should* know where she is at all times! From now on, you are not to let your mistress out of your sight unless she's with me, or you'll be dismissed instantly. Once she crawls out of whatever hole she's hiding in, you are to bring her straight to me. You're bigger than she is so you'll have no trouble doing that. You can drag her here by the hair, if necessary.'

He flapped his hand at her. 'Go and look for my wife. Hmm.' He glanced at the clock. 'Just a minute. By the time the doctor's been to see me, I'll be ready for my lunch and afternoon nap. You can bring her to me after that.'

Pansy went back downstairs, fuming but trying not to show it. She told the housekeeper that he would kill the mistress if he went on like this and anyway, she had no idea where the poor thing was hiding.

'Your cheek's all red. Did he hit you as well?'

'Yes.'

The housekeeper was horrified. 'I'll not put up with it if he hits me. He's no gentleman, that one. What are you going to do, Pansy? Do you know where she is?'

'No, I don't. I was sitting here with you when she ran away from him, wasn't I, so how could I know where she is? We'll have to wait till she comes out of hiding.'

Pansy had a fair idea where to look, though, of course she did. When everything had settled down and she could get away without being noticed, she slipped up to the attic and said quietly, 'It's safe to come out now.'

Sure enough, her mistress was crouching out of sight in a narrow space behind one of the big trunks full of old clothes that were kept near the wall at the far side of the attic. She peered out from the shadows.

'It really is safe for a while, ma'am. He's with the doctor and then he's going to have his lunch and nap.'

Lallie crawled right out, her face streaked with tears and dust.

'Are you all right?'

'Badly bruised. I thought – I really did think he was going to kill me this time, Pansy.'

'You'll have to run away and leave him, or he will kill you.'

'How can I do that?'

'I'll help you get away and go with you. I'm leaving today myself, whatever you decide to do. He hit me as well and I won't put up with that from any employer.' She rubbed her cheek which still felt sore.

'I'd come with you, Pansy, I'd give anything to get away from him. Only, I've no money to pay for fares. You know he won't give me any of my own. And where could I go?'

'To your son, of course. Look, I'll pay our fares down to Wiltshire. I'm sure Felix will find you somewhere to hide, and me with you. That lad's very fond of you. And then I'll look after you – if you want me to stay, that is?'

Lallie gave her a big hug. 'Of course I do. I'd be lost without you.'

Pansy hugged her back, worried at how thin Lallie had become lately. 'Good. One thing you can do is take your jewellery with you, and if we need money, we can sell it. I know how to live very cheaply, so we'll be able to manage for a long time on what it brings, I'm sure.'

But Lallie still hesitated. 'Dare I run away? What will happen to my son?'

'Dare you stay?' She heard her mistress sob and added, 'He can always join us later if he finds he can't bear to be with his father any longer.'

'You're right, Pansy. I daren't stay. Gareth is getting worse all the time. You promise you'll stay with me?'

'Of course I will. I've already told you that.'

She waited, but Lallie didn't say anything, just sobbed again, so she said it bluntly, 'Stop that! There's no time to weep. I'm leaving as soon as I've packed, whether it's with you or on my own. The best thing to do is leave straight away, before he's had time to lock you in your room or find someone else to watch you. I'm definitely *not* staying.' She rubbed her cheek again, furiously angry that he should do that to her.

Lallie took a deep breath. 'I will do it. I'll leave. I'm covered in bruises from today.'

Pansy could see a few of them and Lallie's earlier screams of agony had reached clear down to the kitchen. 'I'll pack some clothes for each of us. I can hide yours in the laundry. No one will think anything of it if I take a bundle of your clothes down there because they know I wash your delicate things myself.'

'But we still have to get away from Rivenshaw.'

'We'll catch the first train that comes into the station, no matter where it's going.'

'Yes, of course. I wish I were clever like you.'

Pansy would have preferred a more intelligent mistress too, rather than this weak reed. But she simply couldn't leave the poor thing for him to beat like an old carpet. You got fond of people – decent ones, anyway – when you lived so intimately with them.

She spoke bracingly. 'Getting out of here will be quite easy if you do exactly as I say. We can sneak out while the other servants are eating their midday meal and make our way on foot to the station. We have to get out of the district as quickly as we can. That's more important than where the next train is going.'

'Won't someone see us leaving?'

'Not here at the house. The servants all relax after he's had his midday meal because he eats so much he always needs a long nap to sleep it off. Now, let's go back to your bedroom and see what to take.'

She went to look through the wardrobe, hurling a few of the simpler clothes on the bed, then going through the drawers equally rapidly and sorting out some underwear.

'They're my plainest clothes,' Lallie protested.

'You want to look more like a maid than a mistress as we travel, and maybe afterwards too. Put these on.'

'Oh, right. How clever.' Her mistress began putting on the clothes her maid had selected.

'When you're dressed, get all your jewellery together, every single piece, and wrap it in one of your scarves. Then stay here till I come to get you. I'll have to find a suitcase to put our clothes in.' She hesitated. 'You do trust me to look after you, don't you?'

'You're the only person I fully trust in this whole house, Pansy. One day I'll give you the reward you deserve for helping me. I promise.'

She was counting on that. 'Thank you, but at the moment, we have to get ready to leave, and do it as quickly as possible. No more crying. You'll attract attention if you have reddened eyes. Sort out underclothes and maybe a few handkerchiefs and any other small things you think of. And I mean small. You'll have to carry your own suitcase.'

★

The doctor came and bound up Higgerson's ankle, seizing the opportunity to warn him he was far too fat and would probably die of a seizure if he didn't lose some of his blubber.

When Higgerson told him not to be so damned impertinent, he shrugged. 'It's not impertinent to tell you the truth and it's my duty as a doctor to warn you of the dangers of getting so fat. It's your choice whether you take my advice or continue to put on weight and die sooner than you need.

'And if you wish to find yourself another doctor, do it. But he'll only tell you the same thing.'

After he'd left, Higgerson dismissed his manservant, a new fellow because he'd sacked the other idiot. He didn't quite trust this one, so sent for Dobbs, who would do anything he wanted and knew how to keep his mouth shut.

Dobbs was there within a few minutes and the maid who opened the back door, told him what had happened then took him up to the master's bedroom.

'Shut that door. Now, what have you found out about that old man?' Higgerson demanded as soon as Dobbs had closed the door. 'He can't have vanished into thin air, and we need to silence him.'

'One of the men you hired managed to get close enough to look through the police station windows during the early hours of the morning, sir. He shone his torch into both cells, but there was no one in either of them, and no one at the station keeping watch, either.'

'Dammit, they must have got the old fool away. But how did they manage to sneak him out of the police station without us noticing? We had watchers in front and to the rear.'

'Impossible to tell, sir. The men might have been taking a break at some stage and not wanted to confess to it.'

Dobbs waited a minute or two, then added, 'There's something else you need to know and take into account, sir. I've found out that the new JP has taken over all the judicial work from that stupid old fool, and you know what Peters is like from your friends in nearby towns: an interfering busybody. But he's got the law behind him, so I think it might be better if we tread carefully for a while, just until we find out what his weaknesses are.'

He didn't actually think Peters had any weaknesses, but this wasn't the time to say that, not with Higgerson so blindly angry.

'Hmm. We'll see. I have to rest my ankle anyway, so I shan't be able to be as active as usual.'

Active! Higgerson never did anything physical if he could help it these days, just waved one hand and told others what to do. No wonder he was getting so fat and puffy faced.

'Any more news about my older son, Dobbs?'

'Very little, sir. I got a letter from our watcher today. Apparently your son has moved and is working just outside Swindon now. He's well thought of by his new employer and is courting the man's daughter, which is how he came to get the job.'

'Maybe we can figure out some way to shake things up there, get Felix blamed for dishonesty or some such problem maybe. If I can get him dismissed, that'll also stop him courting. I intend to choose who he'll marry, and it'll be someone whose family will be of use to me, not a group of strangers in a southern town. Without a job and with his reputation destroyed, he'll be forced to come home and do as he's told. I'll work out a way to arrange that once I know more about how he's living.'

'Yes, sir.'

Higgerson continued, talking to himself more than to his companion. 'I shall make Felix regret disobeying me and going off on his own, if it's the last thing I do. And when my wife comes out of hiding, I'm going to give her a really thorough thrashing, then watch her crawl back to her bedroom. I'm not having *her* disobey me, let alone throw things at me. But I can't do that today. My ankle's too painful to stand up on.'

Dobbs held back a sigh at this vicious monologue. His employer was starting to act recklessly and seemed to think he could get away with anything. At this rate, he'd murder that poor lady and let alone she didn't deserve that, if he were caught, it'd put Dobbs out of a job.

More important, Dobbs was starting to worry about his own future. He didn't want to be sent to jail because of obeying his master's more unreasonable orders. It was starting to concern him what he was being asked to do at times. It was one thing to cheat poor folk out of a bit here and there. They had no way of getting back at his master. And Dobbs must be getting soft in his middle years, because he was starting to feel sorry for them.

What had got into Higgerson lately? To openly go against the law was stupid, whoever you were. And as for antagonising the better class of person in a small, isolated town, that was even more stupid, if you asked Dobbs. Rich people did have the power to strike back. There were some of the old guard in Rivenshaw who still refused to socialise with Higgerson.

He tried to distract his master. 'Maybe we'd better leave your son alone for the time being, just continue to have someone keep an eye on him. We should also keep an eye on your house in Backshaw Moss that's having its cellar extended. We don't want work like that done carelessly. First things first, I always say.'

'That cellar is something anyone can keep an eye on. No, I want *you* to go down to Wiltshire and find out exactly what Felix is up to: where he's living, whether he's really courting, how he spends the evenings – that sort of thing. The fellow who's supposed to be sending us information doesn't seem to have found out many details. Sack him while you're down there.'

Dobbs didn't say it, but the man in question had had to move from Chippenham to Swindon when Felix did, and sort out new lodgings and contacts, which all took time. Higgerson was so unreasonable about expecting changes to be made instantly.

Dobbs waited for the next order.

'Yes, it's definitely best if *you* go to Swindon. You'll need to spend a few days there to find out the situation, so I'll not expect you back till after the weekend. By that time my ankle should be a lot better if I rest it.'

No argument Dobbs put forward would change his employer's mind about him going to Swindon and in the end Higgerson yelled, 'Get on the next train, damn you, or I'll find someone else to do your job!'

Dobbs wasn't quite ready to stop working for him yet, because it was the best-paying job he'd ever had and gave him the chance to make a few nice side profits on his own behalf. He borrowed the railway timetable to check the times of trains, told the valet to let Higgerson know he had to leave immediately to catch the next train, and rushed home to pack. It'd be a close thing, but he could just make that train if he bustled. If it did nothing else, that would prevent Higgerson thinking up any more pointless tasks for him.

He not only felt dubious about this mission but was also worried about what Higgerson would get up to while he was away – very worried. No one else could nudge his employer away from ridiculous enterprises as well as Dobbs could. And even so, there were times when the fool dug in his heels and refused to act more prudently. Like now.

But if Higgerson got any more rash in what he did, Dobbs would definitely leave him and the town, both. He'd been saving his money carefully for years and it was nearly time to strike out for himself. He had it all planned: he was going to buy a small business somewhere in the Midlands and run it honestly. He was fed up of taking risks and worrying about the possible consequences.

He'd find himself a wife, a young widow would be best, one with a little money of her own, and he wouldn't mind if she had a child or two. And they'd live in peace. Peace was in very short supply when Higgerson was around.

Other men in Rivenshaw had left it too late to leave and he wasn't going to risk that, because there was Deemer to worry about as well as Higgerson, and he feared the police sergeant much more.

He wasn't quite sure about Peters. If he proved to be another interfering busybody, it would be another pressure on Dobbs to cut his losses short and leave. He wouldn't hesitate to do whatever was necessary to save himself. He felt no loyalty to Higgerson.

27

Simeon had been feeling guilty about leaving his family at such a crucial time, and went to see Maisie to explain in person why he was suddenly changing plans and going back home.

Remembering her anguish when she lost her own mother, Maisie told him to go and comfort his daughters.

'Maybe you can bring them here to visit us when they're past the worst.'

'You're very understanding.'

'I've got a very busy time happening in my own life.'

He took her by surprise, putting his arms round her and kissing her on first one cheek then the next.

Joss, who'd been standing nearby, smiled at her. 'Thank you for the books.'

'You're very welcome.'

Once again Biff drove them to the station because there was a train into Manchester at midday.

'They were in plenty of time,' he said when he came back.

'Yes.' She tried to smile at him and failed.

'If you don't mind my saying so, it's probably enough time together for a first encounter. You can think about each other and write, and then meet them when you're not so busy – and I hope you'll be able to do that without bringing them into danger from your enemy.'

She nodded. 'That hadn't even occurred to me. I'm not used to living in fear.'

'We'll find a way to deal with Higgerson once and for all.'

Pansy suddenly remembered an old Gladstone bag in the junk room off the laundry. It contained rags to be used for cleaning. That'd do for her mistress, then Pansy wouldn't have to risk being seen by the other servants carrying a second case down from the attic. She hurried back up to Lallie's bedroom.

There, she stuffed her mistress's clothes into a sheet and rolled it into a big bundle, explaining what she was doing and going downstairs to the laundry quite openly. She needn't have bothered to take care because *he* was having his nap, and the other servants were sitting enjoying a lazy cup of tea after their meal. She could hear them chatting.

After tipping the old rags from the bag into a corner, she pushed her mistress's things into it any old how and left it there. Since it wasn't one of the days for the laundry woman to come and do the wet work, it could stay there and no one would give it a second glance. Only, it wasn't going to stay there for more than half an hour at most if things went the way she'd planned.

She had a narrow escape a little later when she was going up the back stairs to pack her own things and bring down her bag. She heard someone start to come down from the attic and quickly pretended to be sorting through the aprons hanging in an alcove on the rear landing. These were donned by anyone doing dirty work.

The young maid didn't give her a second glance as she hurried past, eager for a break from work.

After Pansy had left her own bag in the laundry, she went back to her mistress's bedroom to collect Lallie. She took the jewellery that was piled up on the dressing table, wrapping it in a light scarf as Lallie should have done, and thrust it into the bottom of her own handbag.

'Now, follow me down the back stairs and do not make a single sound because if your husband catches us leaving, he'll definitely hurt us.'

'What about a coat?'

'There are some downstairs. Stop fussing around and hurry.'

Lallie's shiver was eloquent and her face was chalk white, but she moved more quickly after that.

Downstairs Pansy grabbed some of the old outdoor clothing used by the maids to run sudden errands on rainy days. 'Put these on quickly.'

Poor Lallie's hands were trembling as she did so and Pansy was itching to give her a good shake and tell her not to be such a coward.

She found a floppy beret that could be pulled down over the forehead, dragged it down as far as it would go on her companion, surprised at what a difference it made. Her own hat had a floppy brim that half hid her face. 'Now, you'll have to carry your own bag. And get a move on, for heaven's sake!'

Out in the street she linked her arm in Lallie's so that they could seem to be two friends going off on a visit, and they set off.

'We'd better call one another by first names while we're travelling. If I treat you as my mistress, people will think it very strange that we're travelling third class.'

'I shall be happy to do that – Pansy.'

'That's all right then – Lallie.'

They smiled at one another.

Luck was on their side, because the noticeboard said that one of the faster trains was about to come into the station.

This would take them into Manchester with only a couple of stops on the way.

'Couldn't be better,' said Pansy. She bought them third class tickets and, as soon as the train chugged slowly into the station, she found an empty compartment and gestured to Lallie to go first. She got in, closing the door before she shoved their luggage into the overhead net. 'I'm glad it's not a corridor train. Once we've set off no one will be able to even see us, let alone join us. At this time of day the train won't be crowded, either.'

She sat down, relief coursing through her. They were going to do it!

Further up, Simeon and his son were settling into a first class compartment on the same train.

'I'm not looking forward to another long journey,' Joss said, scowling.

'It's the price you pay for travelling.'

'I can see why Mother preferred to stay at home.'

Simeon shook open his newspaper and Joss pulled a book out of his pocket.

He'd buy his son books regularly from now on. His wife had made such a fuss if he wasted their money on them. That was because she had difficulty reading, but he'd never told anyone her secret.

He hid behind the newspaper all the way into Manchester, thinking about Maisie – and of course about Ida.

Just as the train was starting to creep slowly forward, a porter opened the door of the compartment and hurled a bag in, then a man leaped into the compartment after it and the door was slammed shut again.

As the train gathered speed, Pansy stared in horror as

Dobbs collapsed on to the seat opposite her, panting, eyes closed.

When he opened them, he stared at the two women in equal shock.

To Pansy's surprise it was her mistress who spoke first.

'If you do anything that lets my husband get hold of me again, he'll kill me. Look at what he did to me today!' She pulled her beret off and unwound the scarf from her neck, showing her badly bruised face. 'And there are other bruises on my body. Do you want to be involved in a murder?'

'You could hang, even for being only an accessory to murder,' Pansy added softly.

Dobbs opened his mouth as if to speak, then shut it and frowned at them. 'If he finds out I was on this train with you and didn't take you back to him, it's me he'll kill.'

To Pansy's surprise, Lallie answered threat with threat. 'If you betray us, I'll say you and I were running away together, that you've been secretly sweet-talking me.'

'And I'll confirm it.' Pansy's heart was thumping with fear and she'd bet Lallie's would be the same. Would their bluffs succeed?

Dobbs glared from one to the other. 'Oh, hell! I'll have to think about it. Where are you two going anyway? Will you be secure there?'

Pansy saw Lallie wilt and took over. 'We don't know where we're going yet. The main thing is, we have to be as far away from *him* as we can get. This was the first train after we ran away. We'll catch another from Manchester and probably end up somewhere in the south.'

Dobbs stared at them and suddenly snapped his fingers, giving them a calculating look. 'With your son in Swindon, perhaps?'

He watched them carefully as he said that, smiling as Mrs

Higgerson let out a squeak of dismay that showed he'd hit the target with his guess. 'Does Felix know you're coming?'

'What do you care?' Pansy said. 'Mind your own business and leave us to mind ours.'

'He doesn't know, does he?' Dobbs thumped his hand down hard on the seat beside him. He wished he hadn't caught this train and it was the worst possible luck that he'd scrambled into the same compartment as them. This was a complication he did not need, definitely not. But maybe he could turn it to his advantage. 'Why the hell didn't you plan this better?'

'We didn't plan it at all. He beat her badly today, as you can see. He was so furious I think he would have beaten her to death if he hadn't fallen over and hurt his ankle. He hit me too.' Pansy indicated the bruise on the side of her cheek, adding, 'For the first and last time. I won't work for anyone who treats me like that.'

Dobbs studied Mrs Higgerson again, shaking his head slightly at the extent of the bruising and trying to banish the feeling of pity.

'He's been acting strangely lately, as you of all people must know,' Pansy added.

Unfortunately she was right, Dobbs admitted to himself. Higgerson was acting more and more unreasonably. He seized the moment. 'Very well, then. If you give me some money, I'll forget I ever saw you.'

Both women let out mirthless laughs.

'If I had any money, do you think I'd be riding third class?' Mrs Higgerson asked. 'I had to borrow the fare from my maid.'

He felt aggrieved. You'd think a lady like her would have had *some* money tucked away.

'Can't you just forget you saw us?' Pansy pleaded.

'Shut up and let me think.'

He saw them exchange worried glances, but he didn't care about soothing them. He had to work out how best to deal with this for his own safety. Did he dare risk leaving them to continue their journey south from Manchester and not say a word about having seen them? Could he get away with that?

Maybe, maybe not. Higgerson would find out which train his damned fool of a wife had left Rivenshaw on. He'd soon realise it was the same train as his employee had caught. Could Dobbs be convincing about not having seen them?

Then he suddenly remembered glimpsing a couple of men he knew in the station as he ran to catch the train at the last minute. They'd been standing chatting and had turned to watch him in amusement. They'd probably just returned from Manchester. People were always popping in and out of the city these days, for the day, or even for a couple of hours. Those two would be able to bear witness that he'd been on his own and had been the last person to get on the train.

Had they seen Mrs Higgerson as well and recognised her?

Higgerson was very good at finding things out, had an amazing talent for putting a few details together and working out the whole picture. He wasn't as good as Deemer at that, but was still better than most people. It was partly how he'd made his fortune, that and brutal force.

He stared down at the floor for a few moments, feeling furious at being put in this position. What was best to do?

Suppose he never went back to Rivenshaw? He'd be safe then. He'd been planning to leave quite soon anyway.

No. He didn't want to leave yet, because that would mean abandoning most of his clothes and some possessions he valued. He would still have his bank account, and could get access to it from another branch, but why should he lose everything he owned and had worked so hard for?

'Damn you two for spoiling my plans,' he tossed at them suddenly.

'Damn you for spoiling ours,' Pansy threw back at him.

'Well, listen carefully. This is what we'll have to do . . .'

When their train arrived in Manchester, Dobbs got out quickly and strode away towards the ticket office.

As agreed, Pansy and Lallie waited till he was out of sight to leave their compartment, and then walked slowly along the platform.

'Let's hope there's a train heading south that doesn't leave for a while,' Pansy said. 'We shouldn't have agreed to wait.'

Once they'd walked onto the main concourse, Lallie stood with the luggage while Pansy went to buy them tickets to Swindon. To her relief there was no sign of Dobbs.

The maid came back, looking happier. 'There's a train in an hour, so we've time to get something to eat.'

'Um . . . if you don't mind spending the money, perhaps we could send a telegram to Felix first, to say we've run away and are coming to him for help.' Lallie flushed. 'I'm so sorry to keep asking you for money, but we should give him some warning, don't you think?'

Pansy stared at her in surprise. 'What a good idea! I should have thought of that. He could meet us at the station. Do you remember his new address?'

'Of course I do. I learned it by heart after the first time he wrote to me through you. It's one of the few things Gareth didn't find out about because I destroyed Felix's letters as soon as I'd read them.'

'Let's send a telegram straight away. I'm sure there'll be a post office somewhere on the station.'

'I think it's over there. See the sign?'

They both felt better after they'd sent a brief telegram and were able to have a quick cup of tea and a sandwich before they went to catch the train to London. Unfortunately they'd have to change again there for Swindon.

This time it was a corridor train and their compartment was full so they couldn't discuss their situation. They didn't see any sign of Dobbs, thank goodness, and they didn't mention his name.

At one point Lallie fell asleep with her head on her maid's shoulder and the bruises on her face showed up badly, but Pansy thought it was important for her mistress to get some rest, and what did it matter if the old lady opposite was shocked? They'd never see her again.

When they eventually arrived in Swindon, it was dark. As they got out, they looked round carefully, but there was no sign of Dobbs. Pansy wondered if he would try to follow them and whether he would in the end decide to tell Higgerson where they were.

But that was for another day. The most important thing at the moment was to find a taxi and go to the address Felix had given his mother. There were no taxis waiting at the stand, so they joined the short queue, shivering in the cold night air.

Then suddenly someone grabbed Lallie's arm and she squeaked in shock, about to call for help before she realised who it was.

'Felix! Oh, Felix, I've never been as glad to see anyone.'

He didn't answer because he was staring at her face. 'Did you have an accident, Mum?'

Even in the poor light from the station, her bruises must have shown. She hesitated, ashamed to admit what had happened, but Pansy stepped in.

'Your father's taken to beating her. We thought he'd kill her this time, but he tripped and twisted his ankle, so she got away – and that's why we came here. If you can't help us, he'll catch her and probably kill her next time.'

'Dear heaven, has the man run mad?'

'I think he has,' Pansy said. 'And getting worse all the time.'

'Well, I've got a car, so let's get you out of the cold.'

'Where can we go? Do you know of any cheap lodgings?'

'No need. I told my new employer and father-in-law-to-be about you and he said to take you to his house. We didn't know exactly why you were coming here, but it was obvious something was wrong. I'm sure once he sees your face, Mum, and we tell him what's been happening, he'll make sure you're kept safe. He's one of the kindest men I've ever met.'

'He'll house both of us?' Pansy asked.

'Of course. And now I know how you helped Mum to escape, I owe you a lot and I won't forget it.'

She couldn't help crying. She'd felt the responsibility of getting Lallie and herself away from Higgerson as a heavy load on her shoulders.

'S-sorry. It's just such a relief.'

It was Lallie's turn to put her arms round her maid and give her a hug.

Dobbs watched them from behind a pile of luggage on a big trolley. He'd heard what they said quite clearly in the still night air. So Felix's employer was getting involved, was he?

That might change what he did about all this. Rich people had far more power than he did. The most important thing from now on was to protect himself and to prepare for his intended future.

And after all, if he stuck to his story of not knowing Mrs Higgerson had been on the same train, no one from Rivenshaw could prove that he'd seen her and her maid.

He frowned. He was supposed to be watching Felix for Higgerson. He had to do something about that. But he didn't need to decide now. He'd be able to check what Higgerson's son was doing and who he was associating with during the next day or two.

Time enough to make a final decision when he had more information. It was best to consider every option before taking an important step, something Higgerson had never learned.

28

Lallie studied the house as the car drew up at the front. It was in a quiet avenue, large but not dramatically so. In fact it seemed to sit comfortably with its neighbours. She'd bet the gardens would be pretty in summer, they looked so neat now, even with the trees leafless and the earth bare.

Gardens had been her refuge and solace over the years. The plants here were still sleeping the winter away and she wished she could see them wake up.

Felix helped her and Pansy out of the car, picked up both bags and led the way up the short drive to the front door.

Lallie reached out to take hold of Pansy's hand, not sure what they'd be facing. Would a complete stranger really welcome them into his home and offer them protection as her son seemed to think?

And oh, how Felix had changed. For the better, definitely. He was so much a man now, not a boy, but he'd still hugged her.

A maid opened the door and a pretty young woman hurried out of a nearby room, followed by an older man. Lallie saw the exact moment the latter caught sight of her bruises and stared at her in shock. She felt so embarrassed.

He recovered more quickly than she did. 'Come in, my dear ladies. Welcome to our home.'

'This is my mother—' Felix began.

'Let's get inside properly before we begin the introductions.' The young woman didn't wait for a reply, but put an arm

round Lallie, gave her a lovely smile, and walked with her
into the nearby room. A blazing fire greeted them, and bright
electric lights made the whole room feel cheerful.

When the two visitors were seated, Felix started again.
'Mother, I'd like you to meet Edmund Tillett . . . and his
daughter, Eleanor, to whom I have the honour, the very great
honour, of being engaged.' He paused to exchange fond
smiles with his beloved before continuing. 'This is my dear
mother, who was christened Letitia but has always been known
as Lallie. And this is Pansy, my mother's maid but more a
friend than a servant.'

Lallie pulled herself together. 'Without Pansy to manage
our escape, I'd probably be dead by now. She is a true friend.'

Mr Tillett smiled at them both. 'I'm very pleased you came
to us.'

Felix took over, his voice as quiet as ever but his eyes bright
with tears. 'It's as I told you, Edmund: my mother and Pansy
need a safe place to stay. My father has hurt her badly, as
you can see, and I don't want him ever able to lay hands on
her again.'

'You won't find anywhere safer than here,' Mr Tillett said.
'But to make absolutely certain, I'll bring John Joe to stay
here for a while. He's an old friend of mine and keeps our
warehouses and offices secure. He'll stay in the house and
bring his dog. The two of them will guard you with their lives.
John Joe seems able to sniff out trouble before it strikes, says
he learned that where he grew up, and the dog will give
warning if anyone comes near the house during the night.'

Lallie had been looking round and spoke her thoughts aloud
without thinking. 'Is your wife not here?'

'My dear Mary passed away many years ago.'

'Oh dear, I'm so sorry. How clumsy of me.'

'There was no way you could know. There's just been me
and my lass for a long time, but now, not only do we have

your lad joining the family, but you and Pansy as well, if I may say so.'

'That's such a kind thing to say.' She'd never felt as warmly welcomed anywhere.

'I mean it.'

'Thank you.'

'Why don't you two sit here for a while and get yourselves warm? I'll ask my housekeeper to prepare rooms for you both.'

'Thank you. We are a bit chilled.'

'I'll deal with that, Father.' Eleanor left the room briefly, then came back and sat down next to Lallie, again taking her hand and patting it.

Mr Tillett stood up. 'I'll go and see to our safety now,' he said as he left.

'My father will be sending for John Joe,' Eleanor explained.

Lallie looked sideways and Eleanor smiled at her, which gave her the courage to ask something. 'I don't want to be awkward, but could Pansy share my bedroom, do you think? I'll sleep more easily with her nearby. So foolish of me, I know.'

'Not foolish at all. Perfectly understandable. I'll just go and tell the housekeeper.'

When the door had closed behind her, Felix said, 'Isn't she pretty? And she has such a kind heart. As does her father. I'm a lucky chap to have won her affection and his approval.'

'I'm happy for you, Son. Very happy indeed.' Lallie managed a smile, but oh, how she envied them that loving relationship!

Eleanor came back. 'Felix, Father thinks you'd better get your things from your lodgings and move in here for a while. We don't want anything happening to you, either. Wait till John Joe arrives and take him with you to collect your possessions.'

He nodded. 'Knowing my father and his bullying ways, I think it would be prudent, if you don't mind the inconvenience. He can treat people who upset him violently, whoever they are.' His eyes strayed to his mother's bruised face.

Whoever this John Joe was, they seemed to think very highly of him, Lallie decided. Could he really keep them safe? The warmth of the fire was wonderful but the feeling of safety was even better. She leaned back and smiled across at her son, who winked at her.

The housekeeper brought in cocoa and a rich fruit cake, and Lallie suddenly found that she was hungry.

'I've trained them to eat it the Lancashire way,' Felix said with a smile, cutting a slice of cheese to put on her cake, then doing the same for Pansy.

'It surprised us at first,' Eleanor said. 'Now, I much prefer it that way.'

They were trying to make her feel at home, Lallie realised – and they were succeeding. She was glad to see that Pansy ate two pieces of the delicious cake. She had trouble finishing one. It was a long time since she'd been truly hungry.

A few minutes later Mr Tillett came back, accompanied by a huge man with dark-coloured skin and a beautiful smile.

Lallie hoped she'd hidden her surprise at his appearance. She didn't want to offend anyone.

'This is John Joe, who saved my life when I was visiting America many years ago. He's been working for me ever since and you can trust him with your lives.'

When John Joe spoke, his voice was deep and somehow reassuring. 'I won't let anyone hit you again, Mrs Higgerson.'

She shuddered at the sound of her own name, because it was her husband's name. She had a sudden idea. 'Could I . . . Would you mind if I used my maiden name from now on? Fennell, it is.'

Felix nodded. 'I can understand that. I've been using it too, Mum.'

'Easy to remember, and I don't blame you,' Mr Tillett said.

'Thank you.' Lallie leaned back, feeling exhausted. The warmth was so soothing that she was starting to have trouble keeping her eyes open.

'Shall I take you up to your room now, Mrs Fennell?' Eleanor asked quietly. 'And you too, Pansy?'

'If it's not too much trouble.'

'No trouble at all.' She smiled across at the maid as if she really were a friend, and Pansy relaxed visibly.

What a lovely young woman Felix had chosen, Lallie thought.

She had never forgiven her family for forcing her to marry Gareth Higgerson after her father died. She'd feel so much better from now on using her own name.

Could she really have escaped from him?

When she'd shown the two visitors up to a comfortable modern room, with the luxury of its own basin and mirror in one corner, Eleanor went back to join her father and fiancé in the sitting room.

'I don't think either of them will be long getting to sleep. They're exhausted, poor dears.'

'I was shocked at the sight of my mother's face. I won't let *him* touch her again, whatever it takes,' Felix said.

'*We* won't let him hurt her,' Edmund corrected.

'Thank you for your kindness, sir.'

John Joe came to the door just then. 'I've got the car out. Shall we go and get your things, Felix?'

When they'd left, Edmund Tillett shook his head sadly. 'That poor woman has been beaten mentally as well as physically, Eleanor love. I've seen it before with bad husbands. The women become timid, afraid to do anything. What way is that to treat anyone? We'll have to look after her and build up her confidence.'

'If anyone can do it, you can, Father.'

He gave Eleanor a quick hug. 'I've been lucky, made money, but more importantly I got myself a delightful daughter and made good friends. Some people have been unlucky in what life's dished out to them, so if I can help them I do.'

'Felix had a bad time with his father as well.'

'Yes. But he turned out right in spite of that man. I like that lad very much. You've made a good choice of husband. He'll look after you.'

'I fell in love with him the first time I saw him smile. I had to encourage him a bit, though. He didn't think he was good enough for me.'

'He's just right for you, however you two got together. His not having much money isn't important to me, but the kindness and intelligence are. Those qualities must come from his mother's side, not his father's.' He added almost as an afterthought, 'How can a grown man beat a slip of a thing like Mrs Fennell? She'd be pretty if she weren't so thin and anxious.'

'We'll have to look after her, build up her health. I want my children to have a grandmother as well as a grandfather.'

'I've been wondering, and this settles it in my mind. Maybe we should bring the wedding forward? I won't force you, but what do you think, love? It'll mean a less fancy affair.'

'Yes, let's do that. I really don't want a fuss making, as I keep telling you. All I want is to be with Felix – and you.'

They sat quietly together, not needing to fill the silence with empty chitchat, till they heard the sound of a car drawing to a halt outside.

Felix returned with his possessions and Mr Tillett took John Joe away to consult him about keeping the house and its occupants safe. If that Higgerson chap's troublemaking servant was here in Swindon, he must have been sent to look for Felix, and he'd probably find his way to this house.

But he wouldn't find a way inside, not with John Joe keeping watch, Edmund was quite confident about that.

Upstairs Pansy watched Lallie sink down on the bed, too tired to do anything. There was a lovely fire burning in the grate. She got out their night things and was about to suggest getting ready for bed when there was a knock on the door.

A young maid stood there with two earthenware hot water bottles, complete with plush covers. Pansy took them from her, enjoying the warmth.

'The bathroom's at the end of the corridor, miss.' The girl pointed to the left.

'Thank you.'

'Do you need anything else?'

'No. We're both exhausted.'

'John Joe said to tell you that no one can possibly break into the house while he's here. He's such a clever man. There's nothing he can't mend or fix, and he'll do anything to help people. We're all very fond of him.'

'Please thank him for us.'

When she turned round, Pansy saw Lallie close her eyes as if about to fall asleep, so sent her to the bathroom then urged her into the main bed.

As she snuggled down afterwards in the truckle bed that had been set up for her, Pansy let out a long sigh of relief. 'We've done it,' she said softly. 'Escaped from *him*. And I trust these people, don't you, Mrs – um—?'

'Lallie from now on, remember. And yes, I trust them absolutely. I don't know why, I just do.'

'I've never seen Mr Felix look as robust and happy. He's a fine figure of a man now. And what a charming young woman he's got himself engaged to.'

'It's all . . . such a . . . relief.'

'Go to sleep now.' Pansy kept an eye on her mistress, glad to see her eyes stay closed and her breathing slow down by the light of the bedside lamp she'd insisted on leaving switched on.

Only then did Pansy allow herself to relax totally. They'd escaped, and someone else was keeping watch.

She didn't think Dobbs would get the better of John Joe and Mr Tillett. They were both such strong-looking men.

She yawned and let herself drift towards sleep. No more need to keep watch. She could give in to her own exhaustion.

Dobbs managed to hail a taxi and asked the driver to follow the car Mrs Higgerson had got into. He still wasn't sure what he was going to do about the two women, but it would be prudent to know where they were.

'Stop here! Back up a bit. I need to see what's going on, but I don't want them to see me,' he said when the car stopped outside a large modern house.

'What? I thought you were following them to their house.' The driver turned to glare at him. 'If I'd known you were sneaking around spying on Mr Tillett and his guests, I'd not have taken you as a fare. Very well-respected chap, our Mr Tillett is, does a lot of good for others.'

'I'm glad to hear it. I was following those two women, not Mr Tillett. A relative of theirs hired me. He was worried about their safety, you see, and asked me to check on them.'

'Hmm. Was he really? Well, you can tell him they'll be perfectly safe with Mr Tillett. And if he brings that chap of his in to keep watch over them, they'll be the safest people in Swindon, believe me.'

'What chap is that?'

'Never you mind. But he'll keep them safe, believe me. Now, do you want me to drive you anywhere else, somewhere that's *not* chasing other people, I mean? If not, I'll take my fare from you and get about my business.'

'Yes, I do need to go somewhere else – now I know they're safe. Could you recommend a hotel where I can get a room for a few nights? Not an expensive place, but clean and comfortable.'

'Yes.' The driver set off without waiting for his passenger to say anything else, and Dobbs didn't even manage to get the name of the street. But he had the name of the man who'd given them shelter. And would find out more about him easily enough, he was sure, if he was such a well-respected figure.

29

In spite of all the troubles and worries, Maisie had never been so happy or hopeful in her whole life. Gabriel was so easy to be with, and their quiet evenings together were a delight after the many years of being on her own while her mother worked in the pub, and then being on her own because she had no one else in the world to be with.

The bathroom was finished – well, finished enough to use – which was another relief. Gabriel still had to paint the walls and do what was needed to finish off the details, like tiling behind the washbasin and bath.

She could tell that doing those jobs made him feel as if he'd be able to contribute.

Having running hot water made her life a lot easier in many practical ways, not just in the kitchen. She took a great delight in her first bath, where she didn't need to lug a heavy tin bath into the house from where it hung in the yard and then heat water to fill it by the panful. And she beamed as she simply pulled the plug out to empty it, instead of scooping out the dirty water a panful at a time and then finally carting the bath itself outside to hang back up on the wall until next needed.

Then the permanent electrical wiring was finished and, after it had been inspected by the company, they got properly connected to the mains. Oh, the joy of clear light in every room at the click of a switch!

Even Barry was persuaded to take a bath with Biff's help,

something he didn't seem at all keen on till afterwards, when he admitted how much better he felt. He marvelled at the clean, if rather old-fashioned clothes available for him to change into.

He didn't realise how relieved the others were now that it was more pleasant to sit and chat to him, Biff thought with a smile.

Gabriel and Maisie also took advantage of the lull to clear out more of the larger furniture. Some of it they kept and stored in the spare attic rooms because it was of a beautiful quality. She didn't know why she did this, she just didn't want to sell it, so Gabriel simply smiled and got help carrying it upstairs.

It was going to take a long time to go through the many boxes of this and that which were piled everywhere: tea towels in one, enough to last for many years; ornaments in another, some beautiful, some horrible; crockery in several, more than they'd ever need; books, toys, clothes, blankets. You never knew what you would find underneath the top layer.

They gave a toy to each of the children next door, and a particularly nice china cabinet to Gabriel's mother. It felt wonderful to be able to do that and to see people's faces light up with pleasure.

They found two more envelopes containing messages from Miss Chapman to her unknown descendant in the few boxes they managed to find time to unpack. Once again, each had a five-pound note enclosed, which made them wonder how many more of those envelopes they would find in the other containers.

'We must check every single box before we give any of them to Mr Willcox,' Maisie said after she'd opened the message.

'Every single item,' her husband agreed fervently.

They were able to give Mr Tyler his first payment from the envelope money, to Gabriel's relief, and Maisie said she'd draw the rest of the money they needed out of her savings bank account later.

'I'm sorry we have to use your money,' he muttered.

'It's *our* money now, after all,' she said firmly.

But he shook his head. 'No, it's yours. You saved up for years and I hate to take it from you.'

She stopped arguing. It did no good. Their financial differences upset him whatever she said.

Most of her mother's money would still be there when they'd paid Mr Tyler, to fall back on if they needed it. That mattered so much to her.

Biff watched the newly-weds, seeing the way they were growing used to each other's ways. Privately, he thought the peaceful patch had happened mainly because they had Tyler's workmen still there and because Higgerson had hurt his ankle.

He felt as if he'd had a bit of a break too, with time to enjoy the occasional chat to Ryan Cornish from next door, who had put in the plumbing for their improvements. Ryan admitted one day that he was concerned his own wife might still be in danger from Higgerson's spite, but at least they had other people in the house, tenants they trusted. So it'd be harder for anyone to break in and attack her.

The men agreed to keep an eye on all three houses and their occupants, and to help each other if needed.

And everyone wondered who would inherit the final house. Since they hadn't known Miss Chapman, they didn't know any of her other relatives.

Biff kept an eye on Barry as well as Maisie. The old man was visibly benefiting from good food and comfortable lodgings. He was looking years younger, walking about upstairs.

He even expressed a desire to go outside and have a stroll up and down the street for a bit of fresh air.

'Not yet,' Biff told him. 'There are still people keeping watch on what goes on here. They might try to grab you.'

Barry shivered and stopped asking to go outside for a breath of fresh air.

Deemer called at the house a couple of times quite openly, but stayed outside, chatting to Gabriel or Maisie at the front door, where he could be seen by the watchers. That way, no one would think the old man was staying there and was the object of the visit.

The wily sergeant let them know each time that he'd be coming back for a visit that night via the tunnels to chat to Barry. This happened without any trouble, and he told them that he'd found out some more useful information. It was still hearsay, not proven, but it fitted more pieces into the total picture.

It was Deemer who told them that Dobbs had left town by train and had not yet come back.

'If he isn't around that will partly account for the reduction in nuisance activities, don't you think?' Gabriel commented.

'Probably. I'd be happy if he never came back,' Deemer said. 'Everyone knows that he's Higgerson's trouble organiser, and will arrange anything his master orders.'

He had a think and then said slowly, 'No, actually I don't think Dobbs would arrange a murder. He's too clever to risk being hanged and he's not quite nasty enough. I've seen him slipping pieces of bread to hungry little children when he thinks no one is looking.'

'Dobbs does that?'

'Yes. Surprised me, I can tell you. I'm quite certain, however, that Higgerson might kill someone one day if he hasn't already, whether by intent or by impulse, especially when he's in one of his furious rages.'

'How did you know Dobbs had gone out of town?' Gabriel asked.

'Someone told me he saw the fellow running to catch a train at the station and leaping into it at the last minute. My friend had a good old laugh at the way he fell into the compartment head first.'

'Rob's wife told him there's a rumour going round that Mrs Higgerson has left town as well, run away in fact,' Biff said. 'Is that true?'

'Well, she's not at home, so it could be, but the servants aren't saying anything about her. They're too frightened of losing their jobs – or worse. Her maid hasn't been seen for a while either, so presumably she's run away with her mistress.'

Deemer had another think, head on one side, and the others waited patiently to hear what else he could tell them.

'I'd guess she's gone to join her son. Higgerson didn't beat her when his lads were still living at home, well, not that anyone noticed, but since Felix has left, he's been taking out his anger on his wife and not caring whether the bruises show or not. I wonder what's going to happen when the younger son finishes school in the summer. I reckon Higgerson will try to make sure he can't escape as his older brother did.'

'And yet the man is still received socially by the better classes,' Gabriel said. 'That does surprise me.'

'He's only accepted by a few people, the ones who don't want to get on the wrong side of him. The more decent people won't have him in their homes at any price, and some of them have been targeted by vandals.'

'All this, in 1936,' Gabriel marvelled. 'It's like going back to the dark ages. I wonder what'll come of it all.'

Deemer scowled. 'What'll come of it is that I'll nab that nasty oik before I retire if it's the last thing I ever do, and put him behind bars where he can't harm anyone else. In the meantime, keep your wife safe, lad. He still seems to want these houses, and I'll wager he'd still be prepared to hurt Maisie to frighten her into doing as he wishes if he sees a chance – and Bella next door as well, for the same reasons.'

The workmen put in long hours, even at the weekend, but once they'd finished, the nuisances started again at Number 21. It came as a shock when bricks were lobbed through a front window during Saturday night.

The following night two of the tyres on Gabriel's van were slashed.

There would have been more damage to the vehicle, but their next-door neighbour was driving home late from sorting out a plumbing emergency at one of the posh houses in Birch End and Ryan saw what was going on. He screeched to a halt, honking his horn and yelling for help at the top of his voice.

Two youths leaped away from the car and ran off down the street.

Phil, who was on watch that night, came rushing outside to see what the matter was and when Ryan pointed, there were just enough street lamps to make out two fleeing lads disappearing round the corner at the far end of the street.

'No use going after them,' Phil said. 'Pity.'

Biff and Gabriel had heard the ruckus and joined them outside, while Maisie remained at the front door, wearing a coat over her night things.

Gabriel couldn't hold back a groan when he saw the damage to his van. 'Looks like the mischief is starting up again and getting more serious,' he said glumly. He'd saved long and hard to buy that van.

'We've nearly finished the rest of the plumbing. You'd be better keeping your van in the backyard like I do,' Ryan said.

'I'll definitely do that, but I'll need to find somewhere safe to keep it in the meantime. The electricians have dumped a pile of rubbish in the yard, but they said they'd clear it away tomorrow. Anyway, thanks for sounding the alarm, Ryan.'

'I only wish I'd returned earlier. You should ask Mr Tyler to make you a big double gate for the backyard, with barbed wire along the top, so you can leave your van locked up there at night.'

'Trouble is, he's a bit busy with the houses across the street at the moment.'

'He'll know someone else who can help you, I'm sure.'

The three men turned to stare across the road at the building work.

'You get an idea of what those houses will look like once they're finished when you see them in the moonlight, don't you?' Biff said.

'They're going to look really good. The council has set high new standards for anyone wanting to build new homes,' Ryan said approvingly. 'People will be queuing up to live in these.'

'Yes. Reg Kirby has been a very progressive mayor. He's done well by the town, and I'd vote for him again any time. I've overheard people saying Higgerson keeps trying in meetings to stop him wasting ratepayers' money like that, but Reg has a majority, thank goodness. We need a modern town not a collection of slums.'

Gabriel stared at his van again and sighed. He'd have to borrow money from Maisie's savings to pay to get the repairs done quickly, and wasn't sure how much the insurance company would pay out.

Ryan yawned suddenly and eased his shoulders. 'I'd better get some sleep or I'll be no good at doing anything tomorrow. Sorry about your van, lad.'

Phil went back to patrolling the house, and Biff vanished

into his own bedroom, leaving Maisie and Gabriel standing in the hall with the front door open.

She saw his expression as he glanced outside, and gave him a quick hug. 'I'm so sorry about your van, love.'

'I'll have to get new tyres put on it tomorrow.' He hesitated then added, 'I may have to borrow a little money from you to do that. Would that be all right?'

'Of course it would.'

'I won't bother to have the dents made good for the time being. That'll keep the cost down.'

'We can afford to do that,' she protested.

'I'm leaving them because I don't want to be without a vehicle even for a couple of extra days, especially now.' He took his overcoat down from the hall stand and put it on.

'What are you doing?'

'I'm putting on some warmer clothes. I'd better sleep in my van for the rest of the night in case they come back.' He looked at the hall stand as if searching for something, then shook his head and turned away without it.

She guessed what he'd been looking for. 'Wait a minute, love.' She felt underneath an old raincoat he'd worn to nip out to the van for something during a shower that morning. Yes, that was where she'd seen his scarf. She wrapped it round his neck, pulling him forward to kiss him on the tip of his nose. 'Be careful, you.'

He kissed her back, then lost his smile. 'Those lads are the ones who'd better be careful if they try to damage my van again.'

She watched him go outside, then went to find Phil and ask him to keep watch on the front of the house more than the rear for the rest of the night, explaining about Gabriel going out to stay in the van.

'My son would sleep in the van for a shilling a night,' he said at once. 'He's sixteen and a big lad for his age. Yes, and he's a light sleeper too, allus has been. They won't take him by surprise.'

'Done. Tell him to come tomorrow evening if the van's been repaired by then. If not, he can start whenever we get it back. I'll provide him with a nice warm blanket.'

'I'll send his younger brother as well. They can take it in turns to sleep.'

'Two shillings a night, then, and two blankets. Agreed?' She offered her hand and, after a brief hesitation, he shook it as he would have done a man's hand.

That reminded her that Gabriel would be better for a warm blanket too, and she went to find one from the pile they were collecting. She asked Phil to keep an eye on her, but took the blanket out herself.

Gabriel scolded her for coming out in the cold so lightly clad, but admitted that it was colder than he'd expected.

Hiring Phil's two sons made her thoughtful as she went upstairs to bed afterwards. It cost so little to hire people to do odd jobs. Times might have improved, but there were still a lot of people who couldn't find work, or not enough of it, and for whom every single farthing counted.

After this trouble settled down, she intended to see what she could do to help the poorest people in Backshaw Moss. She'd seen them walk past her house on their way to the slum area. Few of them wore warm clothes, however cold the day, and most were thin and gaunt for lack of proper food.

It especially upset her to see the women who were expecting, struggling to find clothing that covered their expanding bodies. She'd like to help them most of all.

She hoped to have children herself one day. Wouldn't that be wonderful?

Gabriel spent the rest of the night huddled down in the driving seat of the van, dozing lightly from time to time. He was delighted that Maisie had arranged for Phil's sons to take over this task as soon as the van had been repaired. He'd get big gates done as soon as possible, but in the meantime the lads would help. He needed his sleep so that he was fully alert to guard his wife and home. He was quite sure the troubles would soon start up again.

The following morning he phoned Todd Selby and went back into Rivenshaw with him when he towed the van away for repairs. He wanted to be there to make sure those lads hadn't done any hidden damage.

He hung around while Todd checked the van, then saw him go back to check one area again, frowning.

'Is everything all right? Those young devils might have, I don't know, tampered with the brakes or something equally bad. I want you to make absolutely certain it's safe to drive. Only, I don't want to be without it for longer than necessary in case of an emergency.'

Todd smiled briefly and Gabriel realised he'd already told him that. 'Sorry to keep repeating myself. I'm just so worried about her.'

'I don't blame you, not with Higgerson involved. Now, repairing the damage to the bodywork can wait, as you say, and they didn't do anything to the engine that I could find, thank goodness, but they did deliberately damage one of the wheels – must have been told how to do that without it showing at a casual glance. It's a good thing Ryan disturbed them or who knows what they might have done.'

'Oh, no!'

'I'm afraid I'll have to send for a new part from Manchester for that wheel. I can get it here by the end of the day if you'll agree to pay extra, and then I'll work on your van first of all tomorrow morning. It should be ready by midday, but I'm afraid there's no way of doing it more quickly than that. Maybe I can help you in the meantime, though. I've been offered a car to sell. If you can think of some way to keep it safe overnight, I'll make a phone call and see if I can arrange to lend it to you till your van is ready. No charge.'

'You'd do that?'

'I'd do a lot more than that to prevent *him* from hurting you and your wife – or anyone else. By hell, I would!'

'We were going to pay two of Rob's sons to sleep in the van at night till we can get the backyard cleared out and gates put up, to keep it off the road. We can do the same for your car tonight, let them sleep in it – and for as long as it takes.'

'I'll just phone Finn Carlisle then.'

He came back shortly afterwards. 'Finn says the car is yours for as long as you need it.'

Gabriel swallowed hard, greatly touched by this unexpected kindness, and his voice came out husky. 'Thank you. I'm very grateful. He's a nice chap, isn't he? Very quiet, but helps a lot of people.'

'He helps more folk than is generally known. I really admire him. You can go up to his place by the mid-morning bus and pick up the car. I'd drive you up there, but I need to finish another job so that I can give your van my full attention tomorrow. I'll phone Finn and tell him to expect you.'

When Gabriel had gone, Todd was very thoughtful. Higgerson again! Word was beginning to get round that he was getting worse – and anger at him was building steadily in town. It reminded Todd of what he had experienced during the Great War in places where unexploded bombs might go off any minute, an omnipresent worry hovering like a dark cloud.

Deemer thought Higgerson was getting even more over-confident about his powers than formerly, but he knew – well, they all did – that there would have to be incontrovertible proof of what the man had done before he could be arrested.

The sergeant had told those who were working closely with him to wait to pounce until he gave them the word. Keeping quiet was sometimes one of the hardest things of all to do, though.

30

In Swindon the taxi driver felt uneasy about the passenger who'd been watching Mr Tillett's guests. He worried about it all weekend. On the Monday morning he took the liberty of calling in at that gentleman's rooms and asking to see John Joe, because everyone knew that he was the one who dealt with such things on Mr Tillett's behalf.

To his surprise, it was Mr Tillett himself he was shown in to see.

'Sit down, please. John Joe's busy today. What do you want to see him for?'

'Someone was following those two women who came to your house on Friday night. I didn't realise what he was doing when I took the man on as a fare. I thought I should let you know about it.'

'You were quite right. You don't happen to know where the chap went afterwards, do you?'

'Oh yes. I took him to a hotel. And I overheard him giving them his name when I carried in his case.' He watched Mr Tillett write down the details and felt as if a load had been lifted from his shoulders.

'Good man! Thank you for coming to tell me. Much appreciated.' Edmund slipped a pound note into the driver's hand. 'We'll deal with this from now on.'

When the man had left, Edmund phoned John Joe at home and told him what the taxi driver had said. 'I think you'd better check this Dobbs chap out, don't you?'

'Definitely, sir.'

'I wonder if he followed them all the way to Swindon or was here for some other reason and just happened to catch sight of them.'

'I'll find out.'

'If you find he's come to watch them, or Felix – or both, tell him to leave Swindon. I'd rather this was all done quietly, so check things out first. If you think he should go back to Rivenshaw and leave poor Mrs Fennell alone, you can do whatever is necessary to persuade him to leave.'

'Very well, sir.'

John Joe went to see the two ladies and found out that they had met this chap on the train by sheer accident, and that they didn't trust him. When they told him the fellow worked for this Higgerson chap, doing his dirty work, he grew angry.

This definitely needed sorting out.

John Joe sent a man to keep watch on Dobbs and on the Tuesday afternoon he went to the hotel himself, chatting to the boot lad because such humble workers often saw more of what was going on than the person in charge.

'I need to speak to this Dobbs chap rather urgently.' John Joe fingered a half crown coin. 'Only I've never met him before so I don't know what he looks like.'

'I saw him sitting in the park earlier this afternoon while I was out on an errand. I can point him out to you if he's still there. It's not far.'

John Joe got permission from the owner of the hotel for the lad to come with him to identify Dobbs, and luckily the fellow was still sitting there, seemingly oblivious to the icy wind.

'You can leave me now. Thank you very much.'

'You're welcome, sir.' The lad caught the coin deftly.

John Joe stared at the motionless figure on the bench. That was a strange way to keep watch on someone who was nowhere near the park, nor likely to be. What was going on?

He strolled across the grass and sat down on the bench next to the Dobbs fellow, who looked at him in surprise. He was used to people staring because of the colour of his skin and always mentally classified them as those who accepted him and those who considered him an inferior being because of it. More fools they, as he'd proved many a time. He grinned at the thought.

To his surprise, this chap merely nodded a vague stranger's greeting, then went back to his thoughts. He didn't seem interested in John Joe one way or another.

'Mr Dobbs, isn't it?'

The man jumped in surprise. 'Yes. But I don't know you.'

'They call me John Joe. I work for Mr Tillett.'

Dobbs stiffened. 'Do you, now?'

'Mr Tillett doesn't want his guests being annoyed in any way – and that includes carrying information to her husband about where the lady is.' He smiled at the shock on the other man's face. 'I might be tempted to take a trip up to Lancashire if you tell him too much about her.'

'Actually, I was just trying to decide whether to let him know or not. I didn't come to Swindon to pursue her, by the way.'

'What did you come for?'

Dobbs hesitated.

'I can stay here for as long as necessary to get an answer, and I do believe I'm stronger than you if you're thinking of moving away from this bench before you've told me. I'm well known in this town, so they'll believe my version of what happened rather than yours.'

Dobbs studied his expression, then shrugged. 'Mr Higgerson wants to know what his son is doing, wants him to go back to work in the family business.'

'I believe Mr Felix is quite happy where he is.'

'Yes, and he's recently got engaged, I believe.'

'That's his business. But it certainly adds to his happiness with his life here. He won't want to leave, I promise you.'

Silence, then Dobbs shrugged. 'I shall tell Felix's father that he's settled in where he is, then.'

'You can do that quite soon. There's a train leaving for London at eight o'clock in the morning and I shall be at the station to see you off. I can easily find you if you try to stay in town. I'm sure Higgerson will accept any story you choose to tell him.'

'I see.'

'I've already assigned men to keep an eye on you until you leave.'

'You're very thorough.'

'Well, Mr Tillett is a good employer, so everyone always does their best for him.' He saw a faint smile on the other man's face and was surprised, wondering what had caused it.

'I'll be on the train.'

'Good.'

'And I won't say more than that I've seen the lady and she's well protected. I'll have to tell him something.'

'Yes, I suppose so. I'll see you tomorrow morning.'

Dobbs watched the man stand up and leave. He didn't know where a chap who looked like that came from, but he sounded American, spoke the way they did in films. Whatever, he could recognise a capable fellow when he met one.

Hmm. This was likely going to change things because

Higgerson would be furious and want to get back at the poor woman for daring to leave him.

Dobbs wasn't quite sure what he'd do. It might be time to leave Rivenshaw for good.

31

On the Sunday afternoon Bella at Number 23 was hit on the head by a stone as she was bringing in a tea towel that had been freshening up on the washing line in the backyard. She was knocked dizzy and fell to the ground.

A neighbour from further down the road was taking a shortcut along the back lane with her young son and saw a lad hurl a big stone at something, stare at her guiltily, and hesitate.

She didn't know what he'd been aiming at, but he had pulled another stone out of his pocket so must be trying to damage something. She immediately began screeching for help at the top of her very shrill voice and hurled her son's wooden toy at the youth before he could chuck the second stone.

He hesitated, glaring at her, so she snatched up a stone herself and flung that at him, yelling in triumph as she hit him. Only then did he drop his stone and run off.

She stared after him. What had he been intending to do?

By that time Phil had run out of the house next door to Bella's and come out of the back gate. They opened the gate and went to help Bella, who was still feeling dizzy but trying to stand up now.

Picking up the injured woman, he got her and the two passers-by quickly into the house and the helpful woman fetched water and a cloth to bathe the wound.

'I don't know what the world is coming to when lads throw big stones at decent people.'

That evening Phil's wife was attacked as she was walking home from the evening service at the small church in Birch End. Her loud shrieks for help and vigorous use of her handbag as a weapon saved her from serious harm, but her hat was knocked off and trampled. Her fury at the damage lent her extra strength to fight back.

Her fellow churchgoers came running to her aid, shouting loudly, and the attacker ran off through the back alleys.

What the hell was going on? Phil wondered.

At the same time, a couple of streets away Gwynneth Harte was shoved violently to the ground and her bag snatched as she too was walking home from church. Fortunately her youngest son Lucas was on his way to meet her and saw it happen.

He chased after the would-be thief and retrieved the bag after a short, sharp tussle. Then the attacker managed to land a painful knee in his lower belly and ran away along the street.

It took Lucas a few moments to catch his breath but he kept an eye on his mother, who was leaning against a nearby wall. 'Are you – all right, Mam?'

'More or less. I'm a bit shocked. Fancy such a thing happening in Birch End?'

'Didn't Gabriel warn you not to walk about on your own after dark? What were you thinking of?'

'I thought I'd be safe so close to the church, with other people nearby.'

'I don't think anyone who's upset Higgerson is safe at the moment. Did that chap hurt you?'

'Not much. My hat got the worst of it.'

'What does "not much" mean?'

'He twisted my arm as he was dragging at the bag handle.' She rubbed her shoulder.

When they got home, Lucas insisted on looking at that shoulder, saw the bruising on her arm and became even more angry.

A little later, when he was sure her employer was at home in the main part of the house, Lucas left his mother with the doors and windows securely locked in their living quarters and crept out the back way, clambering over garden walls so as not to be seen from the street.

He took great care to check that he wasn't being followed as he made his way to Daisy Street and went in by the back gate of his brother's house.

Rob was at the door before he'd even knocked, fist clenched ready to defend the house. 'Oh, it's you, Lucas. Come in.'

'Just so you know, our mother was attacked on the way home from church.'

Rob cursed under his breath. 'Damn them!'

Gabriel was as angry about this attack on their mother as Lucas was. Maisie, sitting listening to them, felt sick with worry because they'd just heard about Ryan's wife being attacked next door as well.

She had no doubt who'd organised this. Did Higgerson hate everyone who'd inherited a house in this row? What had he planned to do with them? There must be some reason for him to keep pursuing the new owners.

'Who will they go after next?' she wondered aloud.

'Not you,' Gabriel said grimly. 'You're not to leave this house unless someone is with you, not even to come out to the garden gate, and certainly not to go out to the washing line like Bella did.'

'No, I won't. I'm not stupid enough to need telling, either, not after these attacks.'

She looked at him challengingly and he nodded, accepting that. No one could ever call her stupid. She'd survived on her own for years.

'We're reporting this to the police straight away.'

'I agree.'

He went into the hall and picked up the telephone, but most unusually, Deemer was away from home, and his wife said he'd gone to a meeting out of town and wouldn't be back till late. She promised to let her husband know about the attack and tell him they'd be coming to see him to give him the details the following morning.

Deemer wasn't exactly 'out of town'. He'd set off to attend a rather special meeting, leaving before it was light that Sunday morning to avoid being seen. He told his wife the meeting was out of town to explain his early departure because he hadn't been allowed to tell even her what was going on.

Only patriotism would have made him lie to her, and he wondered if she suspected what was going on but knew she wouldn't do anything to spoil things for him. She was a fine woman, had always known how to keep quiet.

He got into the big Hillman when it pulled up behind his house and let Dennison Peters drive them.

They hadn't far to go, but Dennison stopped just off the main road once they were close to Birch End and switched off the car headlights, watching the valley road to make sure they weren't being followed.

'I just need another minute or so for my eyes to get used to the darkness properly, Gilbert, then we'll set off again without using our headlights. Keep your eyes open for other vehicles all the way there.'

No one else seemed to be out and about, so they set off again along a side road, meeting no one en route. They stopped at the entrance to the old abandoned quarry, where a man was on duty barring the way to all except those invited to the meeting. The minute he saw who was in the car, he pulled the wheelbarrow being used as a barrier out of the way and waved them through.

It was only just starting to get light, but they found several other cars already parked in the old quarry, all nicely out of sight of the main road.

Peters got out and studied the vehicles. 'Most of them are here.'

'Good. Shall I lead the way?'

'Yes, please, Gilbert. I've only been inside these tunnels once before. I'll memorise the route this time.'

They were each carrying a torch and used them to make their way safely along to a broader cavern where the meeting was to be held. Peters muttered to himself, memorising the turns.

An oil lamp was burning there and a gentle current of air was blowing in from somewhere else. They both knew all the people present, most of whom were perched on ledges at the sides, with the two people who seemed to be running the meeting sitting on big chunks of rock in the centre of the space.

'We're just waiting for another person, then we'll all be here,' one of the three women present said from her rock.

Shortly afterwards there was the sound of footsteps and a light could be seen in the tunnel growing brighter until Todd Selby appeared. He nodded to everyone and sat down next to Deemer on a ledge.

Unusually, it was a woman who conducted the meeting. She had a very confident air as if she'd done this many times before. 'Attention, everyone! Let's get started now we're all here.'

They all turned to face her, waiting politely.

'Unless anyone knows differently, I think all our planned

excavations have been completed and without attracting too much attention. Am I right, your lordship?'

'Yes. It's gone remarkably well. You should all make it your business to come here over the next few weeks and get fully acquainted with the layout. We are not providing any maps, and you are not to make any. Nor is anyone except me to keep a written list of our members.'

There were nods from everyone, since this was already common knowledge in the group.

'After today, we'll meet here every three months, on the first of the month, unless there's a crisis, in which case I'll simply send a date and time to everyone and see you here whenever.'

There were murmurs of 'Understood' and 'Agreed'.

Deemer leaned back against the rocky wall, watching his fellow conspirators and feeling proud to be one of the group. Every man and woman present today was there because they were certain that the troubles sweeping to and fro across parts of Europe were only the beginning of turbulent times. Sadly they all felt that war was the most likely outcome if Hitler continued to create mayhem for certain groups of people.

The sergeant agreed absolutely with the others that Britain had to be better prepared to fight this time than they had been last time, but it broke his heart to think of the innocent lads whose blood would be spilled if it came to another war.

However, you couldn't allow evil men to take over your country without fighting back every inch of the way, could you? It was as simple as that.

And this time, unlike the start of the Great War, there were people all across the country who intended to be prepared for the worst. Theirs was not the only group. If an invasion did occur this time, they would be ready to continue the struggle secretly, using modern techniques. He still shook his head in disbelief at the way they'd faced the early days of the last war with old-fashioned cavalry.

'Any questions?' the woman asked crisply.

An older, distinguished-looking gentleman raised one hand. 'It wouldn't hurt for us to know how things are generally in the town, Peters. Can we guarantee people's loyalty? It's the centre of our area, after all. You're living there; we're mostly scattered around the nearby countryside.'

Peters gestured towards Deemer. 'I've only just arrived in the valley. My colleague has a far better idea of the general state of affairs in Rivenshaw. No one knows as much about the valley as he does.'

They all looked towards Deemer, who said, 'There are a few people who'll bear watching if trouble does break out. They care more about money than being patriotic so may be weak points in future about supporting their country wholeheartedly. There is some trouble currently being caused by one man in particular, and he will need watching: a fellow called Higgerson.'

Someone muttered a curse at the sound of that name.

'And the town council?'

'Those we can trust absolutely won a slight majority last year, thank goodness. The ones opposing them – well, I can't say for certain how loyal they are. Some follow Higgerson's lead too closely to be trusted; others don't always do as he wishes. I'd never trust Higgerson to put his country's needs first, though. It's money he worships. I'm keeping an eye on him for all sorts of other reasons as well, but he's a slippery customer and utterly ruthless.'

'I'll inform others in nearby areas that he's the main one to be watched if it comes to outright war,' his lordship said. 'We intend to be always at the ready, so if you need our support in special circumstances, or you need extra money, let us know sooner rather than later because it has to be arranged unofficially for the present. We must hope and pray the worst will never happen, while staying prepared.'

'I'd prefer us to keep within the law.' Peters' quiet voice somehow commanded everyone's attention instantly.

'If there is a major problem, we may not be able to afford that luxury,' his lordship pointed out.

'In which case, if all other avenues have indeed been exhausted, the sergeant and I will do whatever is necessary, legal or not. Our country comes first, naturally.'

Deemer felt pleased at this quiet affirmation of intent. It was good to have such an important ally in town. He felt he'd been fighting the Higgerson problem on his own for too long. And so far he'd been unable to pin the man down.

On the way back Peters said, 'You'd better give me chapter and verse about this Higgerson and his activities. I don't know the fellow.'

'I have information I know to be correct about some of the things he's done, or at least arranged to have done, but I can't *prove* anything well enough to call the law down on him. *Not – yet.* I will have the necessary proof one day.'

'Tell me now, anyway. Correct me if I'm wrong, but I think it's getting you down a bit, isn't it, Sergeant?'

'I've certainly been feeling the need of support at a higher level – and not getting it from my immediate superior. I need more men. Even one more would make a big difference to policing our valley.'

'I'll look into that. I'm staying with my sister, as you know. Why don't you come round to her house tonight? I can offer you some rather nice sherry and you can give me a full private briefing about Higgerson. I might let her sit in on our little chat, if that's all right by you? She has useful connections round town and I'd trust her discretion and judgement absolutely.'

Deemer tried not to show too much pleasure at this invitation, but he felt it. He was extremely relieved to have found such a capable ally. Even with the best will in the world, there was only so much one man could do.

A full and frank discussion tonight would undoubtedly be useful. Peters was rising rapidly through the legal ranks and rightly so. He had a mind like a steel trap.

'You've done well,' the magistrate said that evening as their discussion ended. 'I like the way you think problems through, Deemer.'

Such a compliment from this man made the sergeant swell with further pride.

'You and I must share all and any new details that we find out from now on,' Peters added.

'You can be sure of that, sir.'

'Dennison when we're speaking privately, surely?'

'Certainly. Of course. And I'm Gilbert.'

'You can be sure of me sharing my gleanings with you, though I may send my sister to speak to your wife or to pass on a note some of the time, so that we're not seen meeting too often.' He nodded towards Veronica, who had sat quietly for most of the time.

She smiled at the sergeant. 'I'm already acquainted with your wife. We're on a charity committee together. I think you should give her a broad idea of what's going on, don't you agree, Dennison?'

'If you vouch for her, Veronica, of course.'

Deemer went home with the feeling of having had a burden lifted slightly. In addition, it was good to know that the knowledge he'd gained, tiny piece by tiny piece, would be safe with Mr Peters if anything happened to him. He didn't rule out anything where Higgerson was concerned and had already given his wife a note to that effect – just in case.

Was he being overly suspicious? No. Definitely not.

Would Higgerson arrange to have a representative of the law attacked? Yes. Definitely. That man would do anything he thought he could get away with.

Deemer would need to tell his wife to be careful of Higgerson from now on, and keep an eye on her safety.

He knew how Higgerson tried to subvert people by making them fear for their loved ones.

32

The morning following the attacks, Gabriel and his brother took their mother to the police station as soon as it opened, determined to report the attack on her officially.

Deemer looked at them, head on one side. 'My wife said you'd phoned. I'm glad you've come here to give me the details in person. I was attending a meeting outside the valley and didn't get back till late.'

He listened carefully to Gwynneth's tale of the attack, and Lucas's further explanation of how he'd intervened.

'Hmm. From what you and others say, it seems this is more than an isolated incident. Three attacks on one day is unusual, even for our troublemaker.'

Gwynneth looked at him in horror. 'How can that man get away with it? Has Dobbs come back? Is he the one organising these attacks?'

'No. That's what puzzles me. As far as I know, he hasn't returned yet.'

'Who else has been attacked?'

'Bella Cornish. Ryan contacted me even before the police station opened this morning to say his wife had been knocked dizzy yesterday by a stone someone threw at her in her own backyard, damn their cheek! She's lucky it didn't do more serious damage than a bruise and a headache.'

'Who was the third person attacked?'

'Phil Becksley's wife was attacked on her way home

from church. She screeched at the top of her voice and fought the attacker off till help came. She's a redoubtable woman.'

'What's the betting Higgerson was with other people at the time of all three incidents?' Gabriel said bitterly.

'I'd not take any bet on that. It's a certainty. But I'll still ask around, if only to make sure he knows I'm aware of his involvement.'

'He's got enough people afraid of him to keep walking roughshod through our lives, damn him!' Gabriel said.

'There are a few cracks opening in his walls.'

'Not quickly enough.'

When the sergeant made enquiries later that day, he wasn't surprised to find that Higgerson had indeed been elsewhere when the attacks took place. He'd attended church both morning and evening, something he didn't normally do more than once or twice a year.

He'd been limping and using a walking stick, apparently, and a dozen people could vouch for his presence at the times of the various attacks, and also for the difficulty he was having moving about. The latter problem, Deemer reckoned, was probably greatly exaggerated. And how had he got the injury, anyway?

When he asked if Mrs Higgerson had been at church, people shook their heads and tried to move away.

'Just a minute!' he said firmly each time. But further questioning about whether anyone had seen her lately had them even more reluctant to speak to him. Some avoided meeting his eyes and muttered 'Don't know', others didn't even attempt to answer.

After he'd turned a corner, one man caught up with him but insisted on speaking from behind some evergreen bushes. 'I saw Mrs Higgerson and her maid walking into the station on the Friday, both trying to hide their faces and *she* was wearing shabby clothes.'

'Oh? Did they get on a train?'

'I wasn't inside the station. I'd just left it on my way back from Manchester. But they'd not go there for any other reason than to catch a train, would they? Especially since they've not been seen since then.'

'What time was this?'

'Just before noon.'

'Thank you. Very helpful.'

There were footsteps approaching and the branches waved to and fro suddenly, so clearly the man had already left.

Deemer felt he'd had enough proof from several sources now that Mrs Higgerson had run away from Rivenshaw. He sincerely hoped her husband would never be able to force her to come back. He had often felt sorry for the poor, timid creature, who seemed afraid to open her mouth, whether her husband was with her or not.

When he got back to the police station he sat thinking hard. One thing he didn't understand was who had organised these latest attacks. He was fairly certain Dobbs hadn't come back to Rivenshaw yet, so who was doing the bullying and blackmailing for Higgerson in the meantime?

Had he found some other heartless rogue willing to play nasty tricks on vulnerable people? If so, who? He really must press for an additional policeman for his valley.

Dobbs arrived back in Rivenshaw on the Wednesday evening. He felt tired, so debated going straight to his lodgings, paying his landlady to make him something simple to eat, and then having an early night.

Unfortunately, Higgerson would want to see him as soon as possible and it'd be wiser to call in at his employer's house first and get the man's displeasure over with.

As usual he went through the back garden, leaving his case near the back gate. Since there was a light on in Higgerson's study, he tapped on the window. He yelled in shock when someone grabbed him and threw him to the ground, then the person cursed and stepped back out of the way of his boot.

He jerked quickly to his feet, expecting another attack, puzzled when it didn't happen.

'Sorry. Didn't realise it was you creeping around.'

Dobbs stared, not liking who he saw. Jem Stanley must have got out of jail early, and if Dobbs remembered correctly, he wasn't due out for another month. Jem didn't usually achieve an early release for good behaviour because he was a violent fellow. He must have been obeying the rules inside for once.

There would be no benefit from making a fuss and at least the other man had backed off when he recognised him, so Dobbs spoke mildly. 'You working for Higgerson now, Jem lad?' Well, he must be because there was no other reason he would be here at this time of the evening. But it never hurt to 'kid to be daft' as Dobbs' father used to say. 'What has he got you doing?'

Jem grinned smugly. 'You'd better ask himself about that.' He went and tapped on the window and it was opened a couple of minutes later by Higgerson.

'You have a visitor, sir.'

Higgerson looked beyond him. 'Ah. You're back, Dobbs. About time. I didn't expect it to take you this long. Better come inside, both of you.'

Dobbs waited till they were standing in front of the French doors and Higgerson had sat down. He was used to such rudeness, had never been offered a seat in this opulent room.

Jem was fidgeting, looking uncomfortable.

'Why didn't you bring my damned wife back with you, Dobbs? Surely you saw her on the train? Others saw her get on and asked me where she was going. Impertinence!'

'I didn't see her till we both got off the train in Swindon, actually, and unfortunately she had protection waiting for her there: your son Felix. I found out that he'd met her at the station and his employer has given her shelter.'

'Who the hell is this chap?'

'He's called Tillett and he's too important in the town for me to have challenged him openly.'

'He'd better not have touched her!'

'His daughter is living there, a highly respectable young lady, so it's not like that. I reckon we'd be better leaving her where she is for a while, to lull them into believing you've accepted her leaving you. Tillett's not only got money but a bodyguard looking after the household.'

'You don't usually back away from trouble. You surely knew I'd want her brought back straight away. You should have dealt with the bodyguard and got hold of her at once. What will people round here think of her being away for so long?'

Dobbs shouldn't have had to spell out the obvious but he did, slowly and clearly. 'I couldn't have managed it, sir. I was in a strange town, didn't have enough money to buy the help I'd have needed to abduct her, let alone a motor car to bring her all the way back to Rivenshaw. You can't take an unwilling person on the train, and I doubt she'd have come quietly.'

All he got was a glare, so he added some more information. 'I did investigate the situation carefully and believe me, there was no way to get near her. Her protectors know their business, and she never put her nose out of the house. It'd be better to let them believe you've let her go for the time being, then make plans to get hold of her later.'

'*I* will decide what to do! And since you've failed me, *you* won't be doing any deciding about anything for a while. If you want to continue working for me, you'll be answering to Stanley from now on. He's taken over as my chief assistant. You've been getting slack, need a few lessons in a more minor role before I'll trust you again.'

'I learned a lot in prison,' Jem said smugly. 'I was there this time with some very useful chaps.'

'I shall be glad to learn some new tricks from you, then,' Dobbs said calmly. He saw a flicker of surprise on the other man's face and had trouble not smiling. Jem Stanley had never quite been able to hide his feelings, but Dobbs could. Oh, yes.

Higgerson's treatment of him settled his dilemma about what to do next, though.

When he and Jem were dismissed, the other man grabbed hold of his arm once they got outside. 'I brought a friend with me from prison, a good friend. He'll be guarding my back. So don't try anything.'

'To tell you the truth, Jem, I shall be glad to step back for a bit. Higgerson's getting more and more careless. You'd better watch your own position or you might find yourself in prison again. Higgerson will toss anyone to the wolves to protect himself. And you don't need to worry about me troubling you. I never waste my time getting upset about things that can't be changed. Now, I'm exhausted after all my travelling. All I want is to get to bed.'

As he left, he enjoyed the memory of the anxious expression on Jem's face.

When Dobbs got to his lodgings, his landlady made him a simple meal. He ate quickly, telling her he was exhausted from all the travelling and would be glad to have a really early night, for once.

He could see the relief on her face. She was tired out, he could see. She usually was by this time of day, poor woman.

He began packing as soon as he'd locked his bedroom door, moving about quietly. He reckoned she'd be asleep within a quarter of an hour, if not sooner. She usually was, and her gentle snores would prove it.

He intended to be well away from Rivenshaw before Higgerson and Jem realised he'd gone. He looked at the piles of stuff, wondering how many of his possessions he could take with him. He didn't want to leave things behind, but there was a limit to what he could carry.

He'd deliberately found lodgings with a back entrance that wasn't overlooked and a landlady who slept soundly, and he reckoned she'd not hear him leave.

All he wanted from now on was a peaceful life. He just wished he had a car, then he'd be able to take everything with him and—

He froze for a few seconds then snapped his fingers, smiling suddenly as an idea came to him. He considered it, worked out how to put it into operation, and smiled even more broadly.

Bad at planning, was he? On the contrary, as he'd proved by staying out of Sergeant bloody Deemer's clutches all these years, he was very good at planning.

Oh, he was going to enjoy doing this, he really was. It was the perfect solution to his needs – and the perfect farewell gesture to a brute of a man who was getting more unreasonable all the time.

In Swindon John Joe had watched Dobbs get on the train. When it had gone, he strolled back to Mr Tillett's house. His employer hadn't gone to work yet, and listened to his report.

'So you don't expect any trickery?'

'No, sir. Actually, I don't think Dobbs' heart was in this job. From what he said as we chatted while waiting for the train to arrive, I reckon he's grown tired of working for Higgerson and has been considering making a change for a while.'

'He could have been saying that to fool you.'

'I don't fool easily. I'm sure he was telling the truth. How is Mrs Fennell this morning?'

'She looks pale and weary and so does the maid. But we'll make sure they get a good rest and we'll feed them up. My lass has already won their trust and she'll look after them.'

'Good.'

'Now, we're changing one of our plans a bit. Eleanor and Felix are getting married sooner than we originally decided and it'll be a much smaller affair.'

John Joe smiled. 'Those two suit one another, don't they, sir? They don't need a showy wedding to bring them close.'

'I agree. He wants you to act as his witness.'

'Me?'

'Yes, you.'

'Are you sure that's wise? Some people won't like dealing with me.'

'Some people can just mind their own business then.' He clapped John Joe on the shoulder. 'You became part of the family when you saved my life.'

'This is a step further. An honour. I shall look forward to it.'

Only in this house and with a very few others did John Joe feel totally accepted. He was sure the family would work their magic on Felix's mother too, as they had on him. She'd been too tired to care about anyone or anything last night.

Kindness and goodwill were infectious, he always thought when he saw how his employer affected those who dealt with him.

Eh, the poor lady was in a bad way. How long would it take for the bruises to fade?

And how long would it take to make her feel well inside herself?

If anyone could help her to recover fully, the Tilletts could.

33

D obbs didn't get undressed. He lay on top of the covers, with just a bedspread over him, waiting for midnight to strike on the church clock. He then took his possessions out of the house and left them near the backyard gate.

His landlady had been sleeping very soundly for well over an hour, making her usual little whiffling sounds that echoed along the landing from her room. She wouldn't stir now until the morning. She never did. And there would be few if any people out on the streets at this time of a cold winter's night.

He walked quietly through the streets, his breath clouding the air. He had to hide once as someone wove his drunken way home, but the man didn't notice him

The garage was at the rear of Higgerson's house, accessed through the back lane, and this was where Dobbs had to be most careful.

There was no one keeping watch, thank goodness, and he still had his keys, so he didn't even have to pick the lock to get inside. You'd have thought the idiots would have taken the spare keys from him, but Higgerson didn't seem to have remembered that he had them, and Jem never had been good about details, or he'd not have wound up in prison so often.

Dobbs opened the doors of the garage and undid the handbrake. It was hard work pushing the car out of the garage, but he managed it, putting the handbrake back on while he locked the garage door again. Then he tossed the door key down the nearest drain. It was sheer pleasure to do that.

Now came the hardest part. He had to push the car till he got it to the top of the slight slope. He took the handbrake off again and put his shoulder to the boot, but the car only rocked forward a little. He thought he wasn't going to manage it, but a surge of anger at Higgerson and determination not to be beaten gave him just enough strength to get the car moving upwards.

At the top of the slope he ran round to the driver's door and jumped into the vehicle, which had begun to roll slowly down the gentle slope. He cursed as he banged his head, then let the car continue to freewheel down the hill, steering carefully, ready to haul on the handbrake if necessary.

To his utter relief he got to the bottom without incident. There the ground levelled out at the back of the park, so the car gradually slowed to a halt. Only then did he switch on the engine and drive back up the slope to the rear of his lodgings. It amused him to think that if anyone saw him, they'd assume he was doing a job for Higgerson and stay out of his way.

He left the engine running and worked quickly to load his belongings into the vehicle before setting off again, heading south.

Once he got out of the town, exhilaration surged through him. He'd done it! He began to sing at the top of his voice as he drove along the country roads.

He knew a chap in Manchester who would pay him good money for this car and sell him a cheaper but legitimate vehicle in return. That'd leave him with a little more money in his pocket as well as all his possessions.

Oh, Higgerson was going to be furious!

Dobbs would be in Manchester well before daylight, but his friend wouldn't mind being woken up if there was a fat profit to be made. He was going to buy a neat little van to use in whatever business he chose to pursue once he settled somewhere. His friend would know where to get one legally.

After that, Dobbs intended to head south, possibly as far as Devon, and find a little country town where he could become an honest citizen for the rest of his life. He nearly choked with laughter at that thought.

He'd already chosen his new name: John Smith, the most common name he knew.

He might even look for a wife, preferably a widow who brought something to the marriage.

He began singing again. He'd been told he had a pleasant voice. Perhaps he'd join a church choir. That thought made him burst out laughing again.

Higgerson scowled at the sight of the breakfast table, set for one person. He didn't like eating on his own. Having an audience was one of the reasons for keeping a tame little wife.

Nonetheless he made a hearty meal. He enjoyed his food and the cook knew exactly what to serve him. You couldn't beat starting the day with a nice thick slice of ham, a couple of eggs and sausages, accompanied by rolls fresh from the baker's, followed by toast and strawberry jam.

He sat on at the table for a while, wondering whether to go out today. No, he'd pretended to be more incapacitated than he was, so he'd better stay at home.

It wasn't till mid-afternoon that he got so fed up, he sent the gardener's lad off to summon Jem Stanley to drive him out across the moors. The scenery out there was pretty and wild, not cluttered with stupid people. He always thought best when being driven round.

He had to get his damned wife back. How best to do that was the main thing he needed to work out. It was clearly going to be a bit tricky, from what Dobbs had said about the fellow she was staying with, but there had to be a way to do it. There always was, whatever it took.

He saw Jem come through the garden and watched him tap on the window.

'Come in!'

He stared at the man. Not nearly as presentable as Dobbs. He wondered if he'd been somewhat hasty in giving him the main job. Anyway, that was for sorting out another time.

'Get the car out. I want to go for a drive.'

'Yes, sir. If you'll just give me a key . . .'

It was only then that he realised Dobbs had the spare key. 'I'll have to give you mine. You can get the spare one back from Dobbs later.'

He tossed the keys to Jem, who caught them and strode out to the garage.

He was back only a couple of minutes later. 'The car isn't there, sir.'

Higgerson stared at him, open-mouthed. 'It must be there! I've not had it out since you took me to church last Sunday.'

'It definitely isn't there now, sir.'

He had to go and see for himself before he could believe it, then limp back to the house and phone Deemer. He reported the theft and demanded that the sergeant come and investigate at once. There had been no sign of the garage doors being forced, so he could guess who'd done it: Dobbs.

'Sorry, sir. I'm in the middle of another job and can't come straight away. And there are no lives at risk in your case, so the other problem has priority. I'll be there once I've finished.'

Before he could say anything the sergeant had put the phone down.

Higgerson stared at the handset, shocked at this treatment,

then slammed it down. He'd add this poor service to the list of faults Deemer had committed. One day he'd pay the fellow back for being such a nuisance. Oh, yes.

Deemer set the phone gently down, grinned, and took another sip of tea. He hoped someone had not only stolen the car but taken it far away so it couldn't be retrieved. That would make his day.

Who could it be? Would Dobbs really steal his employer's car? Well, if what Higgerson said was correct, it'd have been easy to do. Deemer had heard that Dobbs had returned to Rivenshaw by train yesterday evening.

Had the fellow gone straight round to see his employer? He must have done. Higgerson always demanded to be kept abreast of every detail of jobs people were doing for him. What had happened between them to make Dobbs take the car?

There was another cup of tea in the pot, so the sergeant poured it, taking care not to get tea leaves in his cup, something he hated. He put in some sugar and milk, stirred it slowly and sipped it with pleasure.

Why? He shook his head, unable to think why Dobbs would have taken his employer's car, as Higgerson claimed. Had the two had a falling out? Dobbs must have done a runner in the car.

He hoped Dobbs would never come back. It would be good to know that one villain had left the valley. Where could he have gone, though? Anywhere in England, that's where. And knowing the man's cunning, Deemer doubted there would be any use chasing around looking for him. He'd probably got rid of the car by now. That's what Deemer would have done.

But he rather thought he'd call in at Dobbs' lodgings before he went to see Higgerson. If all Dobbs' belongings had gone, the man would definitely have left for good. Heaven help whoever had to deal with his tricky behaviour from now on. They were welcome to him.

Deemer stopped and frowned. Who would take his place in Higgerson's little empire of evil? Or had someone already done that?

Wasn't there some Chinese curse that said, 'May you live in interesting times'?

If Higgerson didn't choose his next lieutenant very carefully, he might have taken another step towards retribution. And Deemer would see that his descent proved *interesting* in more ways than one.

Or was that just wishful thinking? After all, Higgerson had survived and prospered for years now.

Ah, who knew for certain what was going on? He'd better share this information with Peters as well as reporting to his inspector about the car theft.

Deemer didn't set off for Higgerson's house until two hours later, during which time the man had phoned the police station twice demanding attention. For the umpteenth time the sergeant blessed his luck in finding such a clever wife, who could pretend ignorance and put the phone down with dignity on ill-mannered people.

Before he left, he went across to kiss her on the cheek. 'You are a treasure, my dear.'

She didn't have to ask why he'd said that. 'I enjoyed putting the phone down on *him*. I'm at your service any time you need that doing, my dear.'

Deemer collected his constable from the police station, put up a sign saying 'Back soon', and drove across town, stopping outside an ostentatious dwelling which had once been an elegant Georgian residence but had now been embellished with flashy shutters, rather crude ornamental statues, and who knew what else? He would take his constable inside with him as a witness.

As they strolled to the front door, it banged open and the Higgersons' housekeeper appeared, looking flustered and glancing uneasily over her shoulder. 'This way, Sergeant. He, um, wants you to hurry.'

Deemer strolled slowly into the room at the back of the house.

'About time.' Higgerson scowled at him.

When he wasn't asked to sit, the sergeant turned as if to leave.

'Hoy! Where the hell are you going?'

'You clearly don't need my services if you can't even offer me a seat.'

The two men locked gazes, one with fury simmering in every line of his fleshy face and body, the other with a calm half-smile on his neat features.

'Sit down, if you must. You, wait outside!' He pointed to the constable.

Cliff looked at Deemer, who stood up again. 'My constable is here to take notes. I prefer to have a witness to this conversation and you should want that as well. Two people can sometimes come up with better solutions than one.'

'Oh, let him stay, then. Now, I want you to—'

Deemer took over. 'Before we decide on any action, please tell me exactly what has happened, when you found out about the car and so on.'

He listened to the recital, feeling gleeful that the theft hadn't been discovered till far too late to hope to find the car, then asking to be shown the garage.

Higgerson hesitated, which made Deemer wonder what he kept in it that needed to be kept secret, but he said nothing, just waited politely then followed the owner outside, beckoning to Cliff to join them.

His host led them into the garage, not limping badly now. There a man was pacing up and down near it, a man who was instantly recognisable.

Deemer smiled. 'Out of jail, are you, Jem? How long will it be before you go back in this time, I wonder?'

'I've turned over a new leaf,' Jem said. 'Honest employment for me from now on.'

'I shall be interested to see how long that lasts.' Deemer paced up and down the garage and went out into the laneway behind. No sign of breaking and entering. Whoever had taken the car must have had keys to both the garage and the vehicle.

'After what you said earlier, I took the liberty of calling at Dobbs' lodgings on my way here,' Deemer said. 'The landlady said he'd already left when she got up this morning. He'd left her a week's lodging money in lieu of notice and taken all his things with him. She can't even tell us exactly when he went because she heard nothing.'

He waited.

'Well, you'll need to go after him,' Higgerson said at once.

'If you can tell me where he was heading, I shall be happy to do that.' Which was the truth, but he doubted anyone would know where Dobbs had gone, and he wasn't wasting his time rushing here, there and everywhere.

'How the hell should I know where he went?'

'Precisely. How should anyone know that, sir? I'll put the word out that your car is missing, of course, but that's the best I can do. If you hear anything, do let me know and I'll be happy to help you further.'

Higgerson gaped at him. 'And that's all you're going to do?'

'That's all anyone *can* do . . . sir.'

Deemer walked back through the house, followed by a broadly smiling constable, who opened the front door without waiting for the maid and drove them back to the police station, grinning all the way.

Deemer had made Higgerson angry, hoped it would nudge him into doing something rash.

At the very least, he'd enjoyed the encounter hugely.

Back at the station, he prepared a statement about the missing car, then got on with his other work.

Higgerson added the sergeant's unwillingness to do anything to his tally of dissatisfactions. He was done with shilly-shallying, was going to take matters into his own hands.

The following morning he contacted someone he knew who was higher up in police echelons than Deemer and demanded they replace him with a sergeant who would provide a better service.

However, his friend said hastily that he didn't have the power to force Deemer to do more, because what could anyone do in such circumstances? And you didn't replace sergeants on someone's whim.

Higgerson wasn't in a position to make a fuss. He didn't want to offend this man, who had done him several small but useful favours over the years.

He put the phone down and sat very still, anger rising even higher in him.

Jem was waiting outside and when Higgerson beckoned him in, he asked what he could do to help.

'You can clear off until this evening. I need to do some thinking and planning.'

At some stage the housekeeper peeped in to ask if her master was ready for his luncheon and he yelled, 'Get out! And don't come back until I send for you.'

He was not going to be treated like this by a stupid policeman who was too old to do the job properly. Deemer had to go. He'd put that on his list, too.

And he was not going to let those two women who'd in-herited houses which should by rights be his get away with it, either. He'd offered to buy them, hadn't he? Well, if they hadn't the sense to sell to him, he'd find another way to get hold of the houses. Both women had husbands who doted on them, the fools. That was often the best way to deal with a situation: attack someone's nearest and dearest.

And finally, once he'd dealt with the situation close at hand, he'd deal with his wife in such a way that she would never, ever defy him again. She had promised in church to obey him, and was his to do with as he pleased.

34

An uneasy peace seemed to hover over the whole valley for the next few days. Higgerson wasn't seen much and was rather quiet and unsteady on his feet when he did go out. He'd acquired a brand new car, not from Todd Selby in Rivenshaw but from someone in Manchester. Jem Stanley was driving him round in it, not Dobbs.

No one knew where Dobbs or Mrs Higgerson had gone, and there was a lot of whispered speculation about it all.

Gabriel saw him limping along in the town centre and stopped to scowl across the street. Whether the man was ill or not, he didn't trust him to stop playing tricks.

He took great care to ensure that neither Maisie nor his mother went anywhere on their own, enlisting Lucas's help to ensure that their mother in particular understood the seriousness of the situation this time.

Phil told them that his wife had enlisted the help of some women friends and would also go nowhere unaccompanied from now on. He grinned and added, 'She has a spanner in that handbag of hers and is quite prepared to clock someone with it, if necessary. Actually, I think she's hoping for the opportunity to do that. She's still hopping mad that someone dared attack her and ruin her best hat.'

Maisie said she liked the idea of that. She remembered seeing a set of spanners in one of the rooms and chose one small enough to hold comfortably yet large enough to act as a weapon. She put it in her bag, wrapped in a silk scarf.

While Gabriel didn't want to leave her, he couldn't refuse to do a quick job for Tyler, who was still his employer, after all, and had been so good to them about fitting in the renovations to their house. The job was on the northern edge of town, not far away. It would only take him away for a couple of hours.

While he was away Maisie went shopping, making a quick trip to the village store, because no one could manage without food. She was accompanied by Rob and would be taking the main route to the shop in Birch End and back again, so felt perfectly safe.

Higgerson struck again with unprecedented speed and using greater numbers of men – and only one person was targeted.

When time passed and neither Maisie nor Rob returned from the shop, Phil began to worry and was glad when Gabriel returned home sooner than expected.

When Phil told him they'd not come back, he set off to follow the same route. He was horrified when a lad came running up to him. 'We've found Rob Becksley lying unconscious at the back of my grandma's house. He's got blood all over his head.'

Gabriel did not, however, follow the lad immediately and that probably saved his life. Instead he beckoned two chaps he knew who were standing on a street corner, as men often did when out of work, and offered them money to walk a little behind him, just in case this was a trick.

When two men leaped out on him as soon as he turned a corner, he yelled for help and the two men he'd hired came running. They managed to capture one of the assailants, though only after a fierce struggle. The lad who'd spoken to Gabriel had vanished the minute the fighting started.

They left the man securely bound in a shed belonging to a friend of Gabriel's.

There was no sign of Maisie on the route she'd have taken home, so he phoned Deemer from the village shop and explained the situation.

'Do not go out on your own again, whatever anyone tells you, Gabriel,' the sergeant ordered. 'This sounds to have been carefully planned and I reckon they'll be after you as well. I'll drive up to Birch End straight away.'

But he didn't set off until he'd phoned Mr Peters to let him know what had happened.

'I'll put the word out among our group of friends that Maisie has been captured and Gabriel attacked,' the magistrate said. 'Watch yourself, Gilbert. They'd be very happy to put you out of operation.'

'Oh, I'll be extremely careful, believe me.'

He put the phone down and went out to join Cliff, who switched on the car engine the minute he saw him and set off as soon as the sergeant got in.

However, on the way through Rivenshaw, the sergeant said suddenly, 'Turn next left. I want to call on someone at Number Fifteen.'

It wasn't the first time he'd been glad they'd continued appointing special constables even after the Great War had ended the desperate need for them. When you were short of manpower, specials could be a godsend.

'Wait for me.' He got out of the car and hammered on the door. 'Gabriel Harte's wife Maisie is missing. We think Higgerson has got her. Can you call out any specials who're free and ask them to start searching for her? Try any place where Higgerson's thugs hang about.'

The man nodded. He'd been looking sleepy when he answered the door but he was wide awake now.

Gilbert got back into the car. No one hated Higgerson like Steve Rustom, because though no one had been able to prove it, it must have been him who'd ravished Steve's daughter, and when the poor lass found herself expecting a child, she'd slit her wrists and died, rather than face the shame of it.

'Drive up to Daisy Street as fast as you can, Cliff lad.'

Maisie moved her head, which gave her a stabbing pain, and suddenly realised that her wrists were tied together in front of her, so she didn't fully open her eyes. What had happened? Where was she? It was very dimly lit. Was it a cellar?

'She moved. Maybe she's coming to. Shall I hit her again?' someone asked.

She kept perfectly still, hoping they'd think her still unconscious.

'No, you fool. *He* wants to speak to her an' if you hit her too hard, she might not be able to answer his questions. If she wakes up an' tries to shout for help, we can allus gag her.'

'Shall we have a go at her while we're waiting? I've not had a woman for days.'

'Better not. *He* said not to touch her an' if you want to go against him, you can, but I'm not going to risk it.'

Silence, then a loud and regretful sigh.

Maisie kept still and tried to breathe slowly and evenly. What sort of horrible people were these, to talk of using women like that or hitting them?

She heard a woman's voice in the distance, then a little scream as if she'd been hurt. It was followed by the sound of a slap and a louder scream of pain, after which the woman yelled, 'I won't say nothing. Don't hurt me, Ollie. Ouch.'

Maisie opened her eyes the tiniest bit and tried to peep out, seeing a youngish, rough-looking man with his head turned towards the door. Her handbag was lying on the floor nearby. The purse had been pulled out and lay open next to it. She could see that her money had gone from it, but that was the least of her worries.

Her captor turned back to stare at her and she hoped he hadn't noticed that she'd been peeping.

Someone else clumped back into the room and the man near her turned away again to speak to him. She could do nothing against two of them, could only hope someone would find her before they took her to Higgerson, because the '*he*' they were talking about could only be him.

She could guess what he wanted from her and there was no way she'd willingly sign anything giving him her house.

But what if he found some way to hurt her husband? What would she do then?

Gabriel was frantic with worry about Maisie by the time he saw the police car pull up outside. He was about to run out to speak to Deemer when someone knocked on the back door.

'Go and answer it, Phil, but be careful.'

Deemer opened the car door and called, 'Any news of where they might be?'

'No. Not a word.'

A woman walking past stared at them but didn't stop.

'We need to organise a search party,' Deemer said. 'I called in at Steve Rustom's on the way and asked him to get some specials to start looking for her.'

There was a yell from the back of the house and Gabriel jerked round. 'Phil was answering the door.' He ran into the house followed by Deemer.

They found Phil bleeding from one arm but with the back door closed again.

'What happened?'

'Two men. Said you were to do as you were told or your wife would suffer for it. They sliced at me with a knife, saying that was a reminder of what they could do to her, but I managed to step back, so it's only a shallow cut.'

As Gabriel took him into the kitchen to wash it, he stopped. 'Is that Barry calling out upstairs?'

Phil pushed him away 'I can wash this myself. Go and see what Barry wants. He sounds desperate to see you.'

Gabriel ran up the stairs two at a time and found Barry had come down to the bottom of the attic stairs. 'What's the matter?'

'I were looking out of the window an' saw 'em. Came up to the back door, they did, bold as brass. Some of Higgerson's bullies. They beat me up once, them two did.'

'Who are they?'

'Vic and Ollie. Don't know their second names. They live in Backshaw Moss, far end of Clover Street. What did they want?'

'Maisie has gone missing. They brought a message that I'm to do as I'm told.'

'Don't believe a word they say. Go an' rescue her.'

'Do you have any idea where they might have taken her?'

'Old shed behind the reservoir,' Barry said without hesitation. 'They hurt people in the cellar there to punish them for upsetting Higgerson. No one can hear them, you see. Everyone thinks it's a ruin.'

'Thanks, lad. You go back up and sit down again.'

'Never mind me. Take care how you go, lad.'

Gabriel raced down the stairs and told Deemer what Barry had said.

'It's worth a try.'

As he was speaking, Mr Tyler came across the street. 'By your faces something's wrong. Can I help?'

Deemer explained. 'You can keep an eye on the house for us. We're going to see if there is a hiding place near the reservoir as Barry told us.'

'There is an old hut behind it, but it's in ruins. I never noticed a cellar, though.'

'We'll go and check it,' Deemer said. 'Barry seemed very certain.'

Deemer and his constable drove towards the reservoir, stopping to one side, out of sight of the hut.

Gabriel drove up to join them a minute later. 'How do we get round to the hut without being noticed?'

Cliff, who was tall enough to see over a nearby drystone wall suddenly darted to one side and grabbed a woman who'd been creeping along on the other side of it, bent double.

She stared at him in shock, then grabbed his arm. 'You've got to save her.'

'Who?'

'Gabriel Harte's wife.'

'Ah. Come and tell the sergeant about it.'

'I daren't. If anyone sees me talking to him, Ollie will kill me.'

'If you don't talk to him, I'll be the one to give you a drubbing,' he said fiercely, and dragged her across to the sergeant.

'Only you can tell us where exactly they are, lass.'

'And if my wife is hurt in any way . . .' Gabriel added.

She took one look at the three men's grim expressions and said hastily. 'They've got her in the hut.'

'It's derelict, roof full of holes. I've peeped in it a couple of times, just to check no one was using it,' the sergeant said.

'There's a cellar. Trapdoor's in a corner. You'd never notice it unless you knew. That's where they've taken her. Let me go now, please.'

'I'll let you go, but you're to go to the house behind the police station and stay there with my wife.'

'But Ollie will—'

'He won't be able to hurt you if we can catch him. They'll lock him away for years. Go the back way down the valley, along the edge of the moors to that lane near my house. It'll take you a while to walk down into Rivenshaw, but you'll be safe there.'

She stared at him, then sagged. 'I hope you do catch him, Sergeant. Otherwise he'll kill me.'

'No he won't. Whatever happens we'll get you away from him.' He hated men who beat their wives.

Another long stare, then she nodded. 'It's my only chance. I hope you mean it about helping me escape.'

'I do, lass.'

When she'd gone, the three men crept along towards the ruined hut by the way she'd come, bending low so that they were hidden by the wall.

'There's someone coming,' Vic called suddenly. 'I can hear stones rattling.'

'It'll be my Lil going home.'

'No. It's someone coming towards us. Let me get down that ladder and then we'll pull the trapdoor shut. No one knows about the cellar. As long as we keep that woman quiet, they'll not find anything.'

They scrambled down the ladder, moving Maisie out of their way with their feet, paying no regard to whether or not they bumped her against something. All their attention was on getting the trapdoor in place quickly.

She risked opening her eyes and saw that she was closer to her bag, so stretched out her bound hands and managed to fumble the spanner out, still covered in the scarf. Pressing it into a fold of her skirt, she lay there in an uncomfortable position. If she got even the slightest chance she'd somehow manage to hit one of them or scream for help.

'Blow out that candle, you fool!' one of the men whispered. 'If she tries to make a sound, put your hand over her mouth.'

And then they waited.

It wasn't pitch dark, she found. Moonlight was coming in from one or two holes in the cellar ceiling.

Let it be someone come to rescue her, she prayed.

Deemer led the way into the hut, shining his torch to and fro. He put one finger to his lips and mouthed, 'Stand still.'

No one spoke, but they looked round, and then, because he knew roughly what to look out for, Cliff saw the faint outline of a trapdoor in one corner. He pointed to it but said loudly. 'No one here, Sarge. It's like I said, just a ruin.'

However he crept over to the corner and Gabriel followed.

Deemer pointed to each of them in turn and then gestured downwards with a jab of the finger. The two younger men nodded and got into place on either side of the filthy wooden square.

Deemer waited till they were ready, then pointed downwards and whispered, 'Go!' Cliff lifted the trapdoor, banging it back, glancing quickly down and then jumping into the hole, landing nearly on top of one man. Gabriel climbed down more carefully.

The other man had grabbed Maisie, however, and yelled, 'I'll hurt her if you don't move back. I've got a knife.'

They both hesitated, seeing the knife in his hand.

Maisie took everyone by surprise, jabbing the spanner upwards with her bound hands and managing to knock the knife to one side. That was enough to allow Cliff to grab the hand that held the knife and thump it against the wall, sending the weapon clattering across the stone floor.

The other man kicked Gabriel out of the way and scrabbled for the ladder but though he managed to get up the bottom few rungs, Deemer was waiting for him with a truncheon and brought it down on his shoulder as hard as he could.

He fell to the bottom, moaning and writhing about in pain.

By then Cliff had the other man pinned to the wall and had pulled out his handcuffs.

Gabriel moved to stand between Maisie and the man who'd tried to escape, but it was clear that he was in too much pain to do any more fighting.

'Here!' Deemer threw his pair of handcuffs down to Gabriel, who locked them on the groaning man before he had time to realise what was happening.

Only then did Gabriel pull Maisie into his arms. 'Are you all right? Did they hurt you?'

'They knocked me unconscious at first so I pretended to be worse than I was.'

He smothered her face in kisses.

'Look, you fool, will you please get this rope off my hands before you do any more kissing.'

'Sorry. I'll need to find a knife.'

'There's one on the floor over here.' Cliff picked it up and cut the rope. 'Are you all right, Mrs Harte?'

'I will be now, thank you, Constable.'

Gabriel pulled her into his arms and hugged her convulsively. 'Thank goodness. Thank goodness.'

'You can hug him all you like later, lass. Just come up the ladder first,' Deemer called.

Just then there was the sound of a car stopping nearby and footsteps tramping towards the hut.

Deemer peered out. 'It's Rustom and the specials. Good. They can take these two to the police station. I want to get you home, lass. Are you sure you're all right?'

'I will be.'

But she was shivering with shock now and glad of Gabriel's arm round her shoulders.

No one got much sleep for the rest of that night. Deemer and Cliff had great satisfaction locking up their two kidnappers, but try as he might, Deemer couldn't get them to say who had told them to do this.

'We wanted to earn some money,' they said. 'A stranger offered us the job.'

It had happened like this before, the sergeant thought in frustration. For the bigger jobs, Higgerson primed the men with what to say and presumably paid them and their families to keep quiet, even if they were sent to jail.

This time Higgerson had sent Jem for the doctor, who had been at his house at the time Maisie was kidnapped. And after the doctor left, Jem had stayed to help his employer get around. He swore blind he hadn't gone out after the doctor left, let alone arranged anything.

The poor beaten woman turned up, exhausted from her long walk, and Mrs Deemer tended her injuries and promised to find her a job elsewhere.

She joined her husband, who was looking grim.

'Am I ever going to catch that devil out?' he asked.

'Yes, you will. I'm sure of it. Not this time, but he's getting careless.'

'Not careless enough. But you're right. He's slipping towards danger.'

'And you've got friends in high places with your new project, Gilbert love. That's one avenue of support that's being denied to him most of the time now. Things are changing.'

'I suppose you're right. But who is he going to hurt next?'

'Not his wife. Lallie got away. That's another good sign. And if Higgerson runs true to form, he'll not do anything for a while after such a failure.'

'I'll make sure he's carefully watched from now on if I have to pay for it from my own pocket.'

'Get your special group of people to help you make a plan. It'll be to everyone's advantage to stop that man.'

Deemer looked at his wife. 'You're right.' He grabbed her

and danced her round the room. 'I was getting too fed up about it. But what with Peters now based in the valley and my friends with an interest in keeping things here on a level . . . Yes, I don't have to do it all by myself from now on. We'll close in on him, deal with him together. I bet he doesn't last more than a few months at most, less if we're lucky.'

He hugged her again. 'Eh, you've lifted my spirits, love. I was getting bogged down in my disappointment, didn't see that we really have taken another step forward.'

35

A few days later, Maisie said suddenly over breakfast, 'Deemer was right about Higgerson lying low for a while. There have been no other nasty incidents. We all need cheering up, so let's take this opportunity to have a party.'

'A party?' Gabriel gaped at her. 'Why?'

'Well, you and I never had a proper wedding celebration, and the renovations are finished now, and . . . um, well, it's my birthday next week.'

She flushed as she added, 'I don't normally bother to celebrate it at all, but I'll be twenty-seven, and I've never had a birthday party because I've never had anyone to invite to one. I feel I've got a family now, so let's just have a little party, with your family and Bella and her husband from next door perhaps. It'd cheer us all up, I'm sure.'

'Didn't your mother do anything to make your birthdays special?'

'No. For a while we didn't have any spare money and when times were better, she said she didn't believe in birthday parties. They only cost money that could be better spent on other things, and once you were grown up, they just showed how old you were getting. She hated growing older, would have kept her age a secret if it hadn't been for having a grown-up daughter.'

He nodded, thinking how sad and quiet his wife must have felt on that special day in other years. What a lonely life she had led! 'I like the idea of a party. My mother would love to help us arrange it, I'm sure.'

Maisie beamed at him. 'We've got enough space cleared in the house now. I can tidy the living room up a bit more. I'm no good at cooking, as you've found out.'

He grinned. 'You've learned to do a couple of meals now, thanks to my mother.'

She grimaced. 'They still don't taste as nice as your mother's versions do. But we can buy a few bits and pieces from the village shop for the party. It needn't cost too much.'

'Usually, no one can afford the expense of a party, so everyone brings a plate of whatever they can afford. Let's get my mother to arrange the food. She's done it many times before and can work wonders cheaply.'

'Would she mind?'

'Not at all. She'd be delighted.' Especially when she found out Maisie had never had a birthday party before.

'Oh, I shall so look forward to it.'

'You invite the Cornishes next door, and I'll ask my family.'

He smiled as he left his mother's home later. He was going to surprise Maisie, make it a very special day for her. He'd already written the letter to her father and would slip it in the postbox on the way home.

That wouldn't stop them being watchful about Higgerson, of course, but a birthday party for Maisie would raise all their spirits.

On her actual birthday, Maisie got a message, passed on by the owner of the village shop. Vi, the manager of Charlie Willcox's second-hand clothes shop had phoned to say there was a rather nice dress come in which her employer thought would just suit Mrs Harte. Would she like Vi to set it aside?

Gabriel looked at her. 'Why don't I drive you into town this afternoon to look at that dress? It'd make a lovely birthday present for you.'

'You've already bought me a present.'

'A box of chocolates. That's not nearly special enough for a wonderful wife like you.'

'Oh. Well, all right. I'll enjoy a little drive out.'

'And do your hair loose. I like it most of all that way.'

'It's not practical.'

'You don't have to be practical on your birthday. You have to look your best. That's in the birthday rule book.'

'Oh, all right, if you say so!'

He swept her off in the van before she could change her mind. She didn't realise it, but he'd asked Charlie to keep an eye open for a pretty dress or suit for her.

The minute they were out of sight, Bella sent word to Gwynneth that the coast was clear. Barry let the two women into the house and they made a start by putting up decorations, chains made from pieces of coloured paper stuck together at the ends to make loops. Bella's step-children had had great fun making them. They also set the table in the unused dining room.

There they found a bag of small treats hidden under the table that Gabriel had smuggled in from the shop.

'Imagine never having had a birthday party, and she's twenty-seven this time,' Gwynneth said. 'That mother of hers must have been so selfish.'

In Rivenshaw Maisie tried on the dress and couldn't resist it. 'This is the prettiest dress I've ever had. And it's really good material. It'll last me for years.'

'Happy birthday, darling. Why don't you keep it on?'

She opened her mouth to say no, then changed her mind. Why not?

As they walked out of the shop, someone stared at Maisie in shock.

'What's wrong? Have I got a smut on my face?' she asked when the woman had moved out of earshot.

'She's surprised to see how lovely you can look,' Gabriel said.

'You're just biased.'

'I truly have never seen you look so pretty.'

She went bright pink, but stopped trying to push her hair back, and even let him take her out for a fancy afternoon tea at the café in the hotel.

'I feel spoiled,' she said as they walked back to the car.

'Well, you deserve it. And it is your birthday.'

She gave him a long, serious look. 'No present will ever be as good as meeting you. That's the best thing that has ever happened to me.'

It was his turn to go a bit pink.

When they got back to Daisy Street darkness was falling. Several cars were parked along the road, but there was no sign of anyone moving about.

'I wonder where the people from those cars went?' she murmured, then couldn't resist stroking the beautiful material of the dress she was wearing.

Inside the house there was silence, and Gabriel quickly hung up their coats before holding out his arm. 'Walk with me, Mrs Harte.'

As they entered the living room, someone switched on the lights and a roomful of people called 'Happy birthday, Maisie!'

She stood gaping because the room was full, with not only

their neighbours and all the Hartes, but the Tylers and Sergeant Deemer and his wife, even Barry from upstairs.

And her father, together with Joss. Had they really come all this way to see her?

Tears came into Maisie's eyes and she looked at Gabriel, saying in a choked voice, 'Did you arrange this?'

'Me and Mum, plus everyone brought a plate of food, as we've learned to do during the hard times.'

'Oh, Gabriel, it's wonderful.'

'Can I have my first ever birthday kiss from you?' Simeon held out his arms.

She let her father kiss and hug her, then turned to Joss, who held out his hand and kept his distance as he muttered, 'Happy birthday.'

'They're staying here tonight, so you can have a natter later,' Gabriel whispered.

'Thank you.'

She turned back to their smiling guests. 'Thank you so much, everyone!'

Gwynneth came forward, taking charge as she usually did at family gatherings. 'You'd better open your presents, Maisie.' She gestured to a table.

'*Presents!*'

'Of course.'

They were only small things, but they meant so much to Maisie, who kept having to pause to wipe her eyes.

It was clear that these were happy tears, so people exchanged smiles, delighted that the young woman they'd all grown so fond of was happy. Even during their hardest times, anyone who could tried to make some small happiness on a person's birthday, especially when that person was a child.

When they led Maisie into the dining room and she saw the table full of food, she was speechless, but recovered enough to eat with them, chat to them one by one, tease Joss about his hearty appetite, and most of all, go back to Gabriel to stand clutching his arm and beaming round.

As a surprise, Mrs Tyler played the piano for a sing-song, and all the old favourites were performed, songs that had helped carry soldiers through the war, old folk songs, and of course 'Happy birthday'.

Then, it was time for a final glass of lemonade, beer or cider, and the women began to clear up, refusing to allow Maisie to help, after which the guests began to take their leave.

When they were alone again, Maisie and Gabriel chatted for a while to her father and half-brother, then went up to bed.

'It was wonderful,' she said dreamily. 'You and your family are so kind.'

'Your family too. Your father came a long way to be with you.'

She gave him a misty-eyed smile. 'Yes, he did, didn't he? I shall never forget tonight.'

'Good. I don't think our troubles will have stopped, but we'll get through them. There are enough good people working together to defeat evil.'

He stood up and pulled her to her feet. 'Now, you're nearly asleep. Get into bed.'

'I'm tired but very happy, and I want to fall asleep in your arms.'

'Your wish shall be granted, Mrs Harte.'

And if both of them fell asleep almost immediately, they did it cuddling one another, which was something Maisie had already grown addicted to.

Endnote

Secret defences before and during World War II

This thread in the story was inspired by my ongoing reading about the era in which the Backshaw Moss series is set. If you're interested in the topic, you can read more about it in:

History in Hiding by Stewart Ross (Robert Hale, London, 1991), final chapter in particular

Churchill's Underground Army by John Warwicker (Frontline Books, London, 2008), especially Chapter 18

We all know about Bletchley Park these days, but I'm quite sure we don't know all the secrets involved in the past and ongoing defence of Britain or any other country.

Great-Grandpa Lord

Great-Grandma Lord

My father, aged 10 in c.1930

CONTACT ANNA

Anna is always delighted to hear from readers and can be contacted via the Internet.

Anna has her own web page, with details of her books, some behind-the-scenes information that is available nowhere else and the first chapters of her books to try out, as well as a picture gallery.

Anna can be contacted by email at anna@annajacobs.com

You can also find Anna on Facebook at www.facebook.com/AnnaJacobsBooks

If you'd like to receive an email newsletter about Anna and her books every month or two, you are cordially invited to join her announcements list. Just email her and ask to be added to the list, or follow the link from her web page.

www.annajacobs.com

——— This book was created by ———
Hodder & Stoughton

Founded in 1868 by two young men who saw that the rise in literacy would break cultural barriers, the Hodder story is one of visionary publishing and globe-trotting talent-spotting, campaigning journalism and popular understanding, men of influence and pioneering women.

For over 150 years, we have been publishing household names and undiscovered gems, and today we continue to give our readers books that sweep you away or leave you looking at the world with new eyes.

Follow us on our adventures in books . . .
𝕏 @HodderBooks   f /HodderBooks   ◎ @HodderBooks

HODDER &
STOUGHTON